THE DOCT...
A PRI...

BY
LEANNE BANKS

WITHDRAWN

All the characters in this book have no existence outside the imagination of the author, and have no relation whatsoever to anyone bearing the same name or names. They are not even distantly inspired by any individual known or unknown to the author, and all the incidents are pure invention.

All Rights Reserved including the right of reproduction in whole or in part in any form. This edition is published by arrangement with Harlequin Enterprises II B.V./S.à.r.l. The text of this publication or any part thereof may not be reproduced or transmitted in any form or by any means, electronic or mechanical, including photocopying, recording, storage in an information retrieval system, or otherwise, without the written permission of the publisher.

This book is sold subject to the condition that it shall not, by way of trade or otherwise, be lent, resold, hired out or otherwise circulated without the prior consent of the publisher in any form of binding or cover other than that in which it is published and without a similar condition including this condition being imposed on the subsequent purchaser.

® and ™ are trademarks owned and used by the trademark owner and/or its licensee. Trademarks marked with ® are registered with the United Kingdom Patent Office and/or the Office for Harmonisation in the Internal Market and in other countries.

First published in Great Britain 2012
by Mills & Boon, an imprint of Harlequin (UK) Limited,
Eton House, 18-24 Paradise Road, Richmond, Surrey TW9 1SR

© Leanne Banks 2011

ISBN: 978 0 263 89416 5

23-0312

Harlequin (UK) policy is to use papers that are natural, renewable and recyclable products and made from wood grown in sustainable forests. The logging and manufacturing processes conform to the legal environmental regulations of the country of origin.

Printed and bound in Spain
by Blackprint CPI, Barcelona

Leanne Banks is a *New York Times* and *USA TODAY* bestselling author who is surprised every time she realises how many books she has written. Leanne loves chocolate, the beach and new adventures. To name a few, Leanne has ridden on an elephant, stood on an ostrich egg (no, it didn't break), gone parasailing and indoor skydiving. Leanne loves writing romance because she believes in the power and magic of love. She lives in Virginia with her family and four-and-a-half-pound Pomeranian named Bijou. Visit her website at www.leannebanks.com.

This book is dedicated to all those underestimated women with tender hearts and big fears who hide it all with a big smile. Thank you for being so much more than we give you credit for.

Prologue

Ryder McCall raced the double baby stroller into the elevator just as the doors started to close. The twin boys cackled with glee at the wild ride as he pressed the button for the eighth floor. He'd already rescheduled the appointment with his attorney three times and he would have done it again if he'd known the nanny was going to bail on him. Again.

In the back of his mind, he counted his pulse. His heart rate was higher now than when he'd run a half marathon last year. His life was far different now, he thought as he glanced at the boys and caught a swishing movement behind him. Stepping to the side, he saw a woman dressed in a pink cocktail gown that skimmed over her creamy shoulders and her curvy body. The dress ended just above her knees, revealing a tempting glimpse of her legs and high-heeled sandals. The medical expert in him knew the negative impact of high heels on the human body, but the man in him was trying to remember the last time he'd been out with a woman. He was having a tough time remembering.

The woman smiled at him and gestured toward the twins. "They're adorable. I bet they keep you busy."

He nodded. "More than you could—"

The elevator suddenly jolted and dropped several feet, then stopped.

Ryder glanced at the boys at the same time he heard the woman's intake of breath. "Everyone okay?"

The twins just looked at them with wide eyes.

"Are we stuck?" the woman asked, her brow furrowed with worry.

"Let me see," he said and pushed the button for another floor. The elevator didn't move. He pushed the button to open the doors and nothing happened. He pushed the alarm button and a piercing sound filled the elevator.

The woman covered her ears. "Oh, my—"

A voice came on an intercom. "This is building security. Do you have a problem?"

"We're stuck," Ryder yelled over the terrible pulsating alarm. He heard a sob from one of the boys. A half beat later, the other started, louder.

"So sorry, sir. We'll come and fix it soon."

"Soon," he echoed as the twins began to cry in earnest. "When is soon?"

"As soon as possible," the woman on the intercom said and there was a clicking noise. The alarm shut off, but the boys were in high gear.

"Oh, the poor things. They must be frightened," the woman in the elevator said. She paused a moment, then shrugged. "Here, I'll hold one of them."

Ryder shot a skeptical glance at her. "They haven't had their baths and they're very messy eaters." Tyler was wearing a gross combination of yellow and orange on his blue shirt while Travis clearly had not enjoyed his strained peas. Green smudges decorated the light blue shirt that matched his brother's.

The woman made a tsking sound. "Well, we have to do something. We can't let them keep screaming." She set her purse on the floor and held out her hands. "Go ahead, give one of them to me," she insisted in a voice that sounded as if she were accustomed to having her orders followed.

As a medical doctor and acting chief adviser for the residents at Texas Medical Center, he, too, was accustomed to having his orders followed. This time, though, he decided to allow the woman to take Tyler because the baby was clearly beyond upset. As soon as he set the boy in her arms, she bobbed as if she'd handled a crying baby before. Ryder hauled Travis out of his stroller seat and also bobbed.

The woman made soothing sounds and Tyler gradually quieted between hiccups. As usual, Travis took a little longer. He was the louder boy of the two.

"That's better," she said. "Who am I holding?"

"Tyler," Ryder said. "This is Travis. I'm Ryder Mc-Call. Thank you for your help."

"You're quite welcome," she said in a voice that seemed to combine several accents, none of which originated from Texas. "I'm Bridget," she said and fanned herself with the shawl draped over her arm. "Whew, it's getting warm already."

"And it's only going to get hotter until they fix the elevator. Are you feeling faint?" he asked, aware that plenty of people would grow light-headed in this situation.

She shook her head. "No."

"I'd offer you some water, but I was in a hurry when I left the house, so all I've got are bottles for the boys."

"Well, at least you have that," she said and glanced at her watch. "I hope we're not stuck for long. Perhaps I should call my friends." She bent toward the floor and shook her head. "I'm sorry, Tyler. I'm going to have to put you down for a moment," she murmured and carefully placed the tot in his stroller seat. She picked up her phone and punched some numbers, then frowned.

"Let me guess," Ryder said. "No service."

She nodded.

"Figures. The steel doors can sustain most catastrophes known to man, so they're bound to make it difficult to get a cell connection."

She bit her lip and winced. "Oh, I wonder if someone will call my security."

"They're on their way," he said, wondering if she hadn't understood the conversation he'd had with the woman earlier. Maybe she hadn't heard correctly, he thought, between the alarm bleeping and the boys screaming. "At least, they better be on their way. I hope the boys don't—"

"Need a diaper change?" she asked, nodding in understanding. "Time for the—"

"Nanny," he said in complete agreement. "I just wish I could find one who would stay around longer than two weeks."

"That sounds difficult. Are you working with an agency?"

He nodded. "Part of the problem is I work long hours."

"Hmm, and your wife?"

"I don't have a wife," he said.

Her eyes widened. "Oh, that must make it very difficult."

Ryder sighed. "I'm actually the boys' godfather. My brother and his wife were killed in an automobile accident one month ago."

Bridget gasped. "That's terrible. Those poor boys, and you, oh my goodness. Do you have any help at all?"

"Not unless I hire them," he muttered. "Do you have any children?"

She shook her head quickly, the same way he would have before he'd learned he would be raising the boys. "Two baby nieces," she said.

"That's how you knew to bob up and down with Tyler," he said.

"Yes," Bridget said and glanced at her watch again, growing uneasy. She'd agreed to the charity appearance she would be attending as a favor to her sister's long-time friend, and her security was only a three-button code away if she should need them. If her sister's friend became uneasy, however, she might call Valentina.

Valentina might call security to check on her and…
She shuddered at the public scene that would cause.
Bridget was here in Dallas to do the job her brother had
asked of her and as soon as she was done, she was off
to Italy.

It was so warm that she was getting past the glow
stage. Right now, she probably looked like she'd just finished a spinning class, although she did those as rarely
as possible. Getting sweaty wouldn't matter that much
to her if she weren't being photographed. During the last
year and a half, however, it had been drilled into her that
her appearance in front of the camera was a reflection
of her country. It was her duty to look immaculate and
to avoid scandal at all cost.

Bridget had slipped a few times on both counts. She
might be a princess, but she wasn't perfect. Nor was
she particularly patient. She could tell that Ryder, the
other adult in the elevator, wasn't patient either. He was
glancing upward as if he were assessing the structure
of the lift.

"You're not thinking of climbing out, are you?" she
couldn't resist asking.

"If no one shows up, I may have to," he said.

"And what were you planning to do with the babies?"
she demanded, panicked at the prospect of being left
alone with the twins. Now that she thought of it, Ryder's
presence had made her feel much more reassured.

He shot her a level look. "The purpose of getting out
would be to ensure safety for all of us."

He looked like a no-nonsense kind of man, strong,
perhaps intolerant of anyone weaker than himself.

Which would include her. Okay, she was making assumptions. But what else could she bloody do? She was stuck in an elevator with the man. She couldn't deny the appeal of his strong jaw and lean but muscular body. She also couldn't deny her admiration that he had taken on his brother's orphaned twins.

An instant parent of twin boys? The mere thought made her sweat even more. Bridget would have forced herself to accept her responsibility in such a situation, but hopefully with sufficient support. Multiple children, multiple nannies.

She sighed, glancing at the emergency button. "We've heard nothing. Do you think we should call again?"

"It will make the boys cry again," he said, clearly torn.

"I'll take Tyler," she said and picked up the baby. He flashed her a smile that gave her a burst of pleasure despite their situation. "You're a little flirt, aren't you?" she said and tickled his chin.

Ryder stabbed the button and the shrieking alarm started. Tyler's smile immediately fell and his eyes filled with fear. He began to scream. His brother began to wail.

Seconds later, the alarm stopped and a voice came on the intercom, but Bridget couldn't make out the conversation with Ryder as she tried to comfort Tyler. The only thing she knew was that Ryder had spoken in a firm, commanding voice that rivaled that of her brother's, and anyone in their right mind had better obey.

The intercom voice went away, but the babies still cried. Bridget and Tyler bobbed. "What did they say?"

"They said they would take care of us in five minutes," he yelled over the cries of the boys.

"How did you do that?"

"I told them I was climbing out in three," he said.

"Effective. I wonder if I should try that sometime," she mused. "Is there anything else we can do to settle them down?" she asked loudly, still shielding Tyler's closest ear with her hand.

A long-suffering expression crossed his face. "Just one thing," he said. "Row, row, row your boat, gently down the stream."

Bridget stared in amazement at this man who reminded her of a modern-day warrior singing a children's song and something inside her shifted. The sensation made her feel light-headed. Alarm shot through her. Or perhaps, it was the heat. Pushing the odd feeling and any self-consciousness aside, she sang along.

Six minutes later, the elevator doors opened with a swarm of firemen, paramedics and Bridget's security guard standing outside.

"Your Highness," her security guard said, extending his hand to her.

"Just a second," she said, putting Tyler into his stroller seat.

"Your Highness?" Ryder echoed, studying her with a curious gaze. "Why didn't you—"

"It—it causes a fuss," she said. "Will you be okay? Will the children be okay?"

"We're fine," he said, and she felt foolish for questioning such a capable man.

"Well, thank you," she said and extended her hand

to his, noting that his hands were smooth, but large and strong. She felt an odd little spark and immediately pulled back. "And good luck."

"Your Highness, a medical professional is waiting to examine you," her security said as she stepped off the lift.

"I don't need a medical professional," she murmured. "I need a cosmetic miracle."

Chapter One

Sitting at the kitchen table of her brother-in-law's ranch, Bridget watched Zach Logan hug her sister Valentina as if he were leaving for a yearlong journey. Instead, she knew he would be gone for only a couple of nights. Bridget resisted the urge to roll her eyes. Zach and Valentina just seemed so gooey in love.

"Call me if you need anything," he told her, then swung his young daughter, Katiana, up into his arms. "Are you going to be good for your mommy?"

Katiana solemnly nodded.

"Give me a kiss," he said.

The toddler kissed his cheek and wrapped her little arms around his neck.

Despite her earlier reaction, the scene tugged at Bridget's heart. She knew Zach and Tina had gone through some tough times before they'd gotten married.

Zach shot Bridget a firm glance that instinctively

made her sit up straighter. He was that kind of man, confident with a strong will. Although she was happy Tina had found happiness with him, Bridget knew she would want a totally different kind of man. Charming, average intelligence, playful and most likely Italian.

"You," he said, pointing his finger at Bridget. "Stay out of elevators."

She laughed. "I can only promise that for a few days. When I go back to Dallas, I'm sure I'll have to face more elevators if I'm going to complete Stefan's latest job for me. If I have anything to do with it, I'm going to take care of it as quickly as possible."

Tina shot her a sideways glance. "Are you saying you're already tired of us?"

Bridget shook her head and walked to give her sister a hug. "Of course I'm not tired of you. But you know I've had a dream of having a long-delayed gap year in Italy and studying art for years now. I want to make that dream come true while I'm still young."

Tina made a scoffing sound, but still returned the hug. "You're far from losing your youth, but I agree you deserve a break. You've taken on the bulk of public appearances since I left Chantaine and moved here. I don't understand why you didn't take a break before coming here. I'm sure Stefan would have let you."

Stefan, their brother, the crown prince, could be the most demanding person on the planet, but what Tina said was true. He not only would have allowed Bridget a break, he had also encouraged it. "I want a year. A whole year. And he believes Chantaine needs more doctors. I agree. Especially after what happened to Eve—"

Her voice broke, taking her by surprise. She'd thought she'd gotten her feelings under control.

Tina patted her back with sympathy. "You still feel guilty about that. I know Eve wishes you didn't."

Bridget took a careful breath, reining in her emotions. "She saved my life when the crowd was going to stampede me. Pushed me aside and threw herself in front of me. I'm just so glad she survived it and recovered. I don't know what I would do if she hadn't…" Her throat closed up again.

"Well, she survived and you did, too. That's what's important," Zach said and pulled Bridget into a brotherly hug. "And now that you're in my territory, I want you to think twice before getting on elevators."

Tina laughed. "So protective," she said. "It's a wonder he doesn't find some kind of testing device for you to use so you won't get stuck again."

Zach rubbed his chin thoughtfully. "Not a bad idea. Maybe—"

"Forget it," Bridget said, the knot in her chest easing at the love she felt from both her sister and her brother-in-law. "I'll be fine. Think about it. How many people do you know who have gotten stuck in elevators? Especially more than once?"

"You were a good soldier," Tina said in approval. "And you still showed up for your appearance at Keely's charity event."

"She probably wasn't expecting me in my sad state with droopy hair and a dress with baby-food stain on it."

"Oh, she said they loved you. Found you charming.

Were delighted by your story about the elevator. Most important, the donations increased after your arrival."

"Well, I guess baby-food stains are good for something, then. I'll leave you two lovebirds to finish your goodbyes in private. Safe travels, Zach."

"You bet," he said.

Bridget scooped up her cup of hot tea and walked upstairs to the guest room where she was staying. Her sister had redecorated the room in soothing shades of green and blue. The ranch should have given Bridget a sense of serenity. After all, she was miles from Stefan and his to-do list for her. She was away from Chantaine where she was recognized and haunted by the paparazzi whenever she left the palace. But Bridget never seemed to be able to escape the restlessness inside her. That was why she'd decided to skip a short vacation and take care of this significant task Stefan had asked of her. After that, she could take her trip to Italy and find her peace again.

No one had ever accused Bridget of being deep. She voiced her distress and upset to her family at will, but presented the rest of the world with a cheery effervescent face. It was her job.

Some of the conditions she'd witnessed during the past year and a half, the sights and sounds of children sick in the hospital, Chantaine's citizens struggling with poverty, cut her to the quick and it had been difficult to keep her winsome attitude intact. It irritated her how much she now had to struggle to maintain a superficial air. Life had been so much easier when she hadn't faced others in need. Life had been easier when someone hadn't been willing to sacrifice her life for the sake of Bridget's safety.

Even though Eve had indeed survived and thrived since the accident, something inside Bridget had changed. And she wasn't sure she liked it. Eve and Stefan had fallen in love and married. Eve cared for Stefan's out-of-wedlock daughter as if she were her own. On the face of it, everything was wonderful.

Deep down, though, Bridget wondered if her life was really worth saving. What had she done that made her worthy of such an act?

She squeezed her eyes shut and swore under her breath. "Stop asking that question," she whispered harshly to herself.

Steeling herself against the ugly swarm of emotions, Bridget set her cup of tea on the table. She would complete the task Stefan asked of her. Then maybe she would have settled the score inside her, the score she couldn't quite explain even to herself. Afterward she would go to Italy and hopefully she would find the joy and lightness she'd lost.

After three days of being unable to meet with the head of residents at Texas Medical Center of Dallas, Bridget seethed with impatience. Dr. Gordon Walters was never available, and all her calls to his office went unanswered. Thank goodness for connections. Apparently Tina's friend Keely knew a doctor at University Hospital and there just happened to be a meet and greet for interns, doctors and important donors at a hotel near the hospital on Tuesday night.

Bridget checked into the hotel and her security took the room next to hers. One advantage of being at Zach's ranch meant security was superfluous. Not so in Dallas. She dressed carefully because she needed to impress and to be taken seriously. A black dress with heels. She resisted the urge to paint her lips red. The old Bridget wouldn't have batted an eye.

Frowning into the bathroom mirror in her suite, she wondered what that meant. Well, hell, if Madonna could wear red lipstick and be taken seriously, why couldn't she? She smoothed her fingers over her head and tucked one side of her hair behind her left ear. She'd colored her hair darker lately. It fit her mood.

She frowned again into the mirror. Maybe she would dye it blond when she moved to Italy.

She punched the code for her security on her cell phone. Raoul picked up immediately. "Yes, Your Highness."

"I'm ready. Please stay in the background," she said.

"Yes, ma'am. But I shall join you on the elevator."

A couple moments later, she rode said elevator to the floor which held the meeting rooms and ballrooms. A host stood outside the ballroom which housed the cocktail party she would attend. "Name?" he asked as she approached him.

She blinked, unaccustomed to being screened. Doors opened at the mention of her title. Not in Texas, she supposed. "Bridget Devereaux and escort," she said, because Raoul was beside her.

The man flipped through several pages and checked off her name. "Welcome," he said. "Please go in."

"The nerve of the man," Raoul said as they entered the ballroom full of people. "To question a member of the royal family," he fumed as he surveyed the room.

Bridget smiled. "Novel experience," she said. "I'm looking for Dr. Gordon Walters. If you see him, by all means, please do tell me."

Thirty minutes later, Bridget was ready to pull out her hair. Every time she mentioned Dr. Walters's name, people clammed up. She couldn't squeeze even a bit of information about the man from anyone.

Frustrated, she accepted a glass of wine and decided to take another tack.

Dr. Ryder McCall checked his watch for the hundredth time in ten minutes. How much longer did he need to stay? The latest nanny he'd hired had seemed okay when he'd left tonight, but after his previous experiences, he couldn't be sure. He caught a glimpse of the back of a woman with dark brown wavy hair and paused. Something about her looked familiar.

The dress was classic and on a woman with a different body, it would have evoked images of that actress. What was her name? Audrey something. But this woman had curves which evoked entirely different thoughts. The sight of the woman's round derriere reminded Ryder of the fact that he hadn't been with a woman in a while. Too long, he thought and adjusted his tie.

Curious, he moved so that he could catch a side view of her. Oh yeah, he thought, his gaze sliding over her feminine form from her calves to her thighs to the thrust of her breasts. He could easily imagine her minus the dress. His body responded. Then he glanced upward to her face and recognition slammed into him.

The woman speaking so animatedly to one of his

top residents, Timothy Bing, was the same woman he'd met in the elevator the other night. Princess whatever. Bridget, he recalled. And of course, his top resident was utterly enthralled. Why wouldn't he be? The poor resident was sleep-deprived, food-deprived and sex-deprived.

Ryder was suffering from the same deprivation albeit for different reasons. He wondered why she was here tonight. Might as well cure his curiosity, he thought, if he couldn't cure his other deprivations. He walked toward the two of them.

Timothy only had eyes for Her Highness. Ryder cleared his throat. Both Timothy and the woman turned to look at him.

Timothy stiffened as if he were a marine and he'd just glimpsed a superior. Ryder almost wondered if he would salute. "Dr. McCall," he said.

Bridget looked at him curiously. "Doctor?" she echoed. "I didn't know you were a doctor."

"We didn't have much time to discuss our occupations. Your Highness," he added.

Out of the corner of his vision, he saw Timothy's eyes bulge in surprise. "Highness," he said. "Are you a queen or something? I thought you said you were a representative of Chantaine."

Bridget shot Ryder a glare, then smiled sweetly at Timothy. "I am a representative of Chantaine. A royal representative, and I hope you'll consider the proposal I gave you about serving in Chantaine for a couple of years in exchange for a scholarship and all your living expenses."

Ryder stared at the woman in horrified silence. She

was trying to seduce away one of his prized residents. Timothy was brilliant. His next step should be to one of the top neurological hospitals in the States.

Ryder laughed. "Not in a million years," he said.

Bridget furrowed her brow. "Why not? It's a generous offer. Dr. Bing would benefit, as would Chantaine."

"Because Dr. Bing is not going to make a gigantic misstep in his career by taking off for an island retreat when he could be one of the top neurological surgeons in America."

Bridget's furrow turned to a frown. "I find it insulting that you consider a temporary move to Chantaine a misstep. Our citizens suffer from neurological illnesses, too. Is it not the goal of a doctor to heal? Why should there be a prejudice against us just because we reside in a beautiful place? Does that mean we shouldn't have treatment?"

"I wasn't suggesting that your country doesn't deserve medical care. It's my job, however, to advise Dr. Bing to make the best decisions in advancing his career and knowledge."

Princess Bridget crossed her arms over her chest and looked down her nose at him. "I thought that was Dr. Gordon Walters's job, although the man is nowhere to be found."

Timothy made a choking sound. "Excuse me," he said. "I need to…" He walked quickly away without finishing his sentence.

"Well, now you've done it," she said. "I was having a perfectly lovely conversation with Dr. Bing and you ruined it."

"Me?"

"Yes, you. The whole tenor of our conversation changed when you appeared. Dr. Bing was actually open to considering my offer to come to Chantaine."

"Dr. Bing wanted to get into your pants," Ryder said and immediately regretted his blunt statement.

Bridget shot him a shocked glance. "You're the most insulting man I've ever met."

"You clearly haven't met many residents," he said wearily. "I apologize if I offended you, but Timothy Bing doesn't belong in Chantley or wherever you said you're from."

"Chantaine," she said between gritted teeth. "I will accept your apology if you can direct me to Dr. Gordon Walters. He is the man I must meet."

Ryder sighed. "I'm afraid I'm going to have to disappoint you. Dr. Gordon Walters is not here tonight. He hasn't been working in the position as chief resident adviser for some time. It's not likely he'll return."

She cocked her head to one side and frowned further. "Then who will take his place?"

"No one will take his place. Dr. Walters is rightfully loved and respected. I am serving as his temporary successor."

Realization crossed her face. "How wonderful," she said, when she clearly found the news anything but.

Bloody hell, Bridget thought, clenching her fingers together. Now she'd put herself in a mess. She took a deep breath and tried to calm herself. Yes, she and Dr. McCall had engaged in a spirited discussion, but surely he would come around once he heard more about Chantaine and the program she was offering.

"Well, I'm glad I've finally found the person who is currently in charge. Our first meeting in the elevator showed that you and I are both responsible, reasonable adults. I'm sure we'll be able to come to an understanding on this matter," she said, imbuing her words with every bit of positive energy she could muster.

Dr. McCall shot her a skeptical glance. "I'll agree with your first point, but I can't promise anything on the second. It's good to see you again, Your Highness." His gaze gave her a quick sweep from head to toe and back again. "Nice dress. Good evening," he said and turned to leave.

It took Bridget an extra second to recover from the understated compliment that inexplicably flustered before she went after him. "Wait, please," she said.

Dr. McCall stopped and turned, looking at her with a raised eyebrow. "Yes?"

"I really do need to discuss Chantaine's medical needs with you. I'm hoping we can come to some sort of agreement."

"I already told you I couldn't recommend that Timothy Bing spend two years in your country," he said.

"But you have other students," she said. "I'm sure you have students interested in many different areas of medical care. Coming to Chantaine would enable the physicians to get hands-on experience. Plus there's the matter of the financial assistance we would offer."

"I'm sorry, Your High—"

"Oh, please," she said, unable to contain her impatience. "Call me Bridget. We've sung together in an elevator, for bloody sake."

His lips twitched slightly. "True. Bridget, I'm not

sure I can help you. Again, my number-one priority is guiding my students to make the best career decisions."

Her heart sank. "Well, the least you can do is give me an opportunity to discuss Chantaine's needs and what we have to offer."

He sighed and shrugged his shoulders in a discouraging way, then pulled a card from his pocket. "Okay. Here's my card. My schedule is very busy, but call my assistant and she'll work you in."

Work her in. Bridget clenched her teeth slightly at the words, but forced a smile. "Thank you. You won't regret it."

"Hmm," he said in a noncommittal tone and walked away.

She barely resisted the urge to stick out her tongue at him.

Raoul appeared by her side. "Are you all right, Your Highness? You look upset."

"I do?" she asked, composing herself into what she hoped look like a serene expression. She was finding it more and more difficult to pull off instant serenity these days. "I'm fine," she said. "I've just encountered a slight obstacle to completing my assignment for Chantaine."

She watched Ryder McCall's broad shoulders and tall form as he wove through the crowd. Slight obstacle was putting it mildly, but she'd learned that a positive attitude could get a woman through a lot of tricky spots. "I need to know everything about Dr. Ryder McCall by morning, if not before," she muttered and glanced around the room. It was amazing what one could learn about a person in a social situation such as this. She might as well make the best of it.

* * *

Ryder walked into his house braced for chaos. His home life had become one big state of chaos bigger than the state of Texas since he'd inherited his brother's boys. Instead of pandemonium, his home was dark and quiet, except for the sound of a baseball game. Ryder spotted his longtime pal Marshall lounging on the leather couch with a box of half-eaten pizza on the coffee table and a beer in his hand.

"Your sitter called me," Marshall said, not rising. "As your official backup. She said one of her kids got sick, so she couldn't stay. Just curious, where am I on that backup list?"

Pretty far down, Ryder thought, but didn't admit it. There were two middle-aged neighbors, an aunt on the other side of town and his admin assistant before Marshall. Ryder suspected he'd called in favors too often if everyone had refused but Marshall. "Thanks for coming. How are the boys?"

Marshall cracked a wily grin. "Great. Gave them a few Cheerios, wore them out and tossed them into bed."

"Bath?" he asked.

"The sitter took care of that before I got here. That Travis is a pistol. Didn't want to go to sleep, so I gave him my best Garth Brooks."

Ryder gave a tired smile. "Must have worked. I'll give a quick check and be right back."

"Cold one's waiting," Marshall said.

Ryder trusted Marshall to a degree, but he didn't think leaving the kids with his buddy from high school on a regular basis was a good idea. He wouldn't put it past Marshall to slip the boys a sip from his beer if he was desperate enough. When pressured, Marshall could get a little too creative, like the time he hot-wired the car of one of the school's top wrestlers because his own car had died.

Marshall owned a chain of auto-mechanic shops across Texas. He wore his hair in a ponytail and tattoos were stamped over his arms and back. He hadn't attended college, but he'd made a success of himself. Most people couldn't understand their friendship because they appeared to be total opposites, but a mutual appreciation for baseball, some shared holiday dinners which had always included hotdogs and hamburgers and the fact that they both tried to show up during the hard times had made them like family.

With his brother Cory gone, Marshall was the closest thing to family Ryder had. His gut twisted at the thought, but he shoved the feeling aside and gently opened the door to the nursery. He'd learned to walk with stealthlike quiet during the last month. The possibility of waking the boys made him break into a cold sweat.

Moving toward the closest crib, he glanced inside and even in the dark, he knew that this was Tyler, and he was in Travis's bed. Travis was in Tyler's bed. He wasn't going to complain. They were both lying on their backs in la-la land. Which was exactly where he would like to be.

Instead, he walked on quiet footsteps out of the room and gently closed the door behind him. Returning to the den, he saw Marshall still sprawled on his sofa with the same beer in his hand.

"They're asleep," Ryder said and sank into a leather chair next to the sofa. He raked his hand through his hair.

"I coulda told you that," Marshall said. "I made sure they would sleep well tonight."

He shot a quick glance at Marshall. "You didn't give them any booze, did you?"

Marshall looked offended. "Booze to babies? What kind of nut job do you think I am?"

"Well, you aren't around kids very much," Ryder said.

"Maybe not now, but I was an in-demand babysitter in junior high school. Some things you don't forget. And just in case you're worried, this is my second beer. I wouldn't go on a bender when I was taking care of your kids."

Chagrined, Ryder rubbed his chin. "You got me. Sorry, bud. Being in charge of two kids is making me a little crazy."

"A little?" Marshall said and shook his head. "You've turned into the nut job. You know what your problem is, you're no fun anymore. Those babies sense it and it gets them all uptight, too. It's like a virus. You spread it to the babysitters and it makes them crazy, so they quit. You need to get laid and go to a ball game."

"Thanks for the advice," Ryder said. "I'll take your advice in a decade or so."

"Lord help us if you wait that long," Marshall said. "Maybe I could set you up with somebody. Take the edge off."

Ryder slid him a sideways glance. "I'll pass. You and

I may root for the Texas Rangers, but we don't share the same taste in women."

"Your loss," Marshall said, sitting upright. "I know some women who could wear you out and make you sleep like a baby."

"I've learned babies don't always sleep that well."

"It's your aura," Marshall said. "That's what Jenny, my ex, would say. Your aura is poisoning your environment."

"A dependable nanny is what I need," Ryder said.

"Well, if you can get a sitter, I've got tickets to the Rangers game on Thursday. Take care, buddy," he said, rising from the couch and patting Ryder on the shoulder. "Keep the faith, bud. And move me up on that backup list. I'm more dependable than your Aunt Joanie. I bet she's always busy."

Ryder smiled despite himself. "You got it. Thanks. If I can find a sitter, I'll go to that game with you."

"I'll believe it when I see it. 'Night," Marshall said and loped out of the house.

Ryder sank farther into his chair, kicked off his shoes and propped his shoes onto the coffee table. He considered reaching for that beer, but drinking anything would require too much energy. Hearing the roar of the crowd and the occasional crack of the bat hitting the ball from the game on his flat-screen TV with surround system, he closed his eyes.

Making sure the twins were safe, taking care of his patients and covering for Dr. Walters were the most important things in his life, but he knew he needed help, especially with the twins. He'd never dreamed how difficult it would be to find dependable caretakers for the boys. His head began to pound. He could feel his blood pressure rising. Pinching the bridge of his nose, for one moment, he deliberately chose *not* to think about the next nanny he would need to hire and the deteriorating mental health of his mentor, Dr. Walters.

Ryder thought back to his high school days when he'd been catcher and Marshall had pitched. They'd won the state championship senior year. That weekend had been full of celebration. He remembered a cheerleader who had paid attention to him for the first time. She'd given him a night full of memories. Blonde, curvy and wiggly, she'd kept him busy. He hadn't lasted long the first time, but he'd done better the second and the third.

His lips tilted upward at the memory. He remembered the thrill of winning. There had never been a happier moment in his life. He sighed, and the visual of a different woman filled his mind. She had dark shoulder-length hair with a wicked red mouth and cool blue eyes. She wore a black dress that handled her curves the same way a man would. She would be a seductive combination of soft and firm with full breasts and inviting hips. She would kiss him into insanity and make him want more. He would slide his hands into her feminine wetness and make her gasp, then make her gasp again when he thrust inside her….

Ryder blinked. He was brick-hard and his heart was racing as if he were having sex. He swore out loud.

He couldn't believe himself. Maybe Marshall was right. Maybe he just really needed to get laid. His only problem was that the woman in his daydream had been

Problem Princess Bridget Devereaux. Yep, Marshall was right. Ryder was a nut job.

Bridget read Dr. Ryder McCall's dossier for the hundredth time in three days. He hadn't had the easiest upbringing in the world. His father had died when he was eight years old. His mother had died two years ago.

Ryder had played baseball in high school and won an academic scholarship. He'd graduated first in his college class, then first in his medical-school class.

His older brother, Cory, had played football and earned a college scholarship. Unfortunately, he was injured, so he dropped out, took a job as a department-store manager and married his high-school sweetheart. They'd waited to have children. Six months after the birth of twin boys, they'd attended an anniversary dinner but never made it home. A tractor trailer jackknifed in front of them on the freeway. They both died before they arrived at the emergency room.

An unbelievable tragedy. Even though Bridget had lost both her parents within years of each other, she had never been close to them. Ryder had clearly been close to his brother. Now, a man who had previously been unswervingly focused on his studies and career, was alone with those precious motherless babies.

Her heart broke every time she read his story. This was one of those times she wished she had a magic wand that would solve all of Ryder's problems and heal his pain. But she didn't. As much as she wished it were true, Bridget was all too certain of her humanity.

In the midst of all of this, she still had a job to do. She needed to bring doctors to Chantaine, and Dr. McCall's assistant hedged every time Bridget attempted to make an appointment. She would give the assistant two more tries, then Bridget would face Ryder in his own territory. If he thought an assistant would keep her at bay, he had no concept of her will. Surprise, surprise, especially to herself. She may have portrayed an airy, charming personality, but underneath it all, she was growing a backbone.

Chapter Two

Ryder left the hospital and picked up the boys after the latest sitter unexpectedly informed him that her child had a medical appointment she could not skip. He had an important meeting with several members of the hospital board this afternoon which *he* could not skip. He hated to press his admin assistant into baby service again, but it couldn't be helped.

After wrestling the boys in and out of car seats and the twin stroller, he felt like he'd run a 10K race as he pushed the stroller into his office suite. Instantly noting that his admin assistant was absent from her desk, he felt his stomach twist with dread. She'd left her desk tidy and organized as usual. She'd also left a note on his desk. He snatched it up and read it.

Miss Bridget Devereaux called 3x this a.m. I can't put her off forever. Gone to my anniversary

celebration as discussed. Thank you for letting
me off.

—Maryann

Ryder swore out loud then remembered the boys were
in the room with him. "Don't ever say that word," he
told them. "Bad word."

He recalled Maryann asking for the afternoon off—it
had to have been a week or so ago. He'd been busy when
she asked and hadn't given it a second thought. Now,
he had to juggle his boys and an important meeting. He
shook his head. Women managed children and careers
all the time. Why was it so difficult for him? He was a
healthy, intelligent man. He'd run marathons, worked
more than twenty-four hours straight, brought a man
back to life in the E.R., but taking care of these boys
made him feel like a train wreck.

Ryder sat down at his desk and flipped through his
contact list on his computer for someone he could call to
watch the boys during his meeting. He sent a few emails
and made three calls. All he got were voice mails.

"Well, hello, Phantom Man," a feminine voice called
from the doorway.

Ryder swallowed an oath. Just what he needed right
now. He didn't even need to look to know it was *Princess Persistent*. But he did and couldn't deny that she
was a sight for sore eyes. Wearing another black dress,
although this one looked a slight bit more like business
wear, she smiled at him with that wicked red mouth that
reminded him of what he hadn't had in a long time.

Dismissing the thought, he lifted his hand. "I have
no time to talk. Important meeting in less than—" He

glanced at the clock. "Thirty minutes. Got to find some-one one to watch the boys."

"Not having any luck?" she asked.

"No."

"You sound desperate," she said, sympathy lacking in her tone.

"Not desperate," he said. "Pressed."

"Oh, well as soon as you give me a time for our meeting, I'll get out of your way."

"I already told you I don't have time," he said in a voice that no one in their right mind would question.

She shrugged. "All I want is for you to pull up your calendar and ink me in," she said. "You already agreed."

"Not—"

She crossed her arms over her chest. "You have your job. I have mine."

Travis arched against the stroller restraints as if he wanted out. The baby wore an expression of displea-sure, which would soon turn to defiance and fury, which would also include unpleasant sound effects. Ryder loos-ened the strap and pulled him into his arms.

Tyler looked up expectantly and began the same arch-ing action against the stroller. Ryder withheld an oath.

"Want some help?" Bridget asked.

"Yes," he said. "If you could hold Tyler, I have one more person I can—" He stopped as he watched her settle the baby on her hip. An idea sprang to mind. "Can you keep them for an hour or so?"

Her eyes widened in alarm. "An hour?" she echoed. "Or so?"

"Just for this meeting," he said. "I'll leave as soon as possible."

She shot him a considering look. "In exchange for an opportunity to discuss Chantaine's medical proposition with you, and you having an *open mind*."

"I agree to the first half. The second is going to be tough."

"How tough would it be to take your twins to your important meeting?" she challenged.

The woman was playing dirty. "Okay," he said. "As long as you understand, my first priority is my residents' professional success."

"Done," she said. "Did you bring a blanket and some food?"

"Whatever the sitter keeps in the diaper bag," he said, relief flowing through him like a cool stream of water. "Thank you," he said, setting Travis in the stroller seat. "I'll see you after the meeting," he said and closed the office door behind him.

Bridget stared at the babies and they stared at her. Travis began to wiggle and make a frown face.

"Now, don't you start," she said, pointing her finger at him. "You haven't even given me a chance." She set Tyler in the other stroller seat and dove into the diaper bag and struck gold. "A blanket," she said. "You're going to love this," she said and spread it on the floor. Afterward, she set Travis on the blanket, followed by Tyler.

The boys looked at her expectantly.

"What?" she asked. "You're free from the bondage of the stroller. Enjoy yourselves." She narrowed her eyes. "Just don't start crawling or anything. Okay? Let's see what else is in the bag."

Unfortunately, not much. She used up the small

container of Cheerios within the first fifteen minutes and fifteen minutes after that, both boys had lost interest in the small set of blocks. She pulled out a musical toy and helped them work that over for several minutes.

Peekaboo killed a few more minutes, but then Bridget started to feel a little panicky. She needed more snacks and toys if she was going to keep the little darlings entertained. Grabbing some blank paper from Ryder's desk, she gave each boy a sheet.

Travis immediately put it in his mouth.

"Let's try something else," she said and crumpled the paper.

He smiled as if he liked the idea. Great, she thought. More paper. She crumpled a few sheets into a ball and tossed it at them. They loved that. They threw paper all over the room.

After a few more minutes, Travis began to fuss, stuffing his fist in his mouth.

"Hungry?" It would help so much if they could tell her what they needed. Luckily two bottles were also stuffed in the bag. She pulled out one and began to feed Travis. Tyler's face crumpled and he began to cry.

"Great, great," she muttered and awkwardly situated both boys on her lap as she fed them both their bottles.

They drained them in no time. Travis burped on her dress.

Bridget grimaced. A second later, Tyler gave her the same favor.

At least they weren't crying, she thought, but then she sniffed, noticing an unpleasant odor. A quick check revealed Travis had left a deposit in his diaper.

* * *

Ryder opened the door to his office prepared for screaming, crying, accusations from Bridget. Instead the boys were sprawled across her lap while she sang a medical magazine to the tune of *Frère Jacques*. He had to admit it was pretty inventive. His office looked like a disaster zone with papers strewn everywhere and he smelled the familiar, distinct scent of dirty diapers. He must have wrinkled his nose.

She did the same. "I didn't think it would be considerate to toss the diapers into the hallway, so they're in the trash can. I bundled them up as best as I could."

The boys looked safe and content. That was what was important. "It looks like you had a good time."

"Not bad," she said with a smile. "Considering my resources. You're really not set up for babies here."

"I can't agree more," he said and snatched up a few wads of paper. "What were you doing?"

"Playing ball with paper. It worked until Travis was determined to eat it." She gingerly lifted one of the boys in Ryder's direction. "So, when do we have our discussion?"

He tucked Tyler into the stroller and followed with Travis. Ryder was tempted to name a time next year but knew that wouldn't be fair. Better to get it over with. "Tonight, at my house," he said. "Do you like Chinese?"

"I prefer Italian or Mediterranean," she said, frowning as she rose to her feet. "At your house?"

"It's the one and only time I can guarantee for the foreseeable future."

She sighed. "It's not what I hoped for. How am I going to have your undivided attention?"

"Maybe we'll get lucky and they'll go to sleep," he said.

Four hours later, Bridget could barely remember what she'd said or eaten for dinner. The boys had taken a nap in the car on the way home and woken up cranky. She suspected they hadn't gotten enough of an afternoon nap. Although she resented the fact that she wasn't getting Ryder's undivided attention during their discussion, she couldn't really blame him. In fact, despite the fact that he was clearly a strong man, she could tell that caring for the twins was wearing on him. He loved them and would protect them with his life, but the man needed consistent help.

It was close to eleven before the twins truly settled down.

"I'd offer you a ride to wherever you're staying, but I can't pull the boys out of bed again," he said, after he had made the trip up and down the stairs five times.

His eyes filled with weariness, he raked a hand through his hair. Her heart tugged at his quandary. The urge to help, to fix, was overwhelming. "My security is always close by. He can collect me. It's no problem."

"I keep forgetting you're a princess," he said.

"Maybe it's the baby formula on my dress," she said drily.

"Maybe," he said, meeting her gaze. The moment swelled between them.

Bridget felt her chest grow tight and took a breath to alleviate the sensation.

"I'm sure you're tired. You could stay here if you want," he offered. "I have a guest room and bath."

Bridget blinked. She *was* tired, but staying here? "I don't have a change of clothes."

He shrugged. "I can give you a shirt to sleep in."

The prospect of sleeping in Ryder's shirt was wickedly seductive. Plus, she *was* tired. "I'd like to get your nanny situation in order for you."

"That would be a dream come true," he said. "Everything I've done so far hasn't worked."

"There may be a fee for an agency," she said. "I'm not sure how it works here. I'll have to ask my sister."

"I took the first and second suggestions that were given to me and they didn't pan out. It's imperative that I have excellent care for the boys. "

"I can see that," she said. "But do you also realize that you will have to make some adjustments as time goes on? Later, there will be sports and school activities where parents are expected to attend." Bridget remembered that neither of her parents had attended her school activities. Occasionally a nanny had shown up, but never her parents. "Have you figured out how you'll address that?"

He frowned thoughtfully. "I haven't figured out much. I haven't had custody very long. It's still a shock to all of us. I know the boys miss their mother and father, but they can't express it. I hate the loss for them. And I'm not sure I'm such a great choice as a parent. I've been totally dedicated to my career since I entered med school. Add to that how I've been filling in for Dr. Walters and it's tough. I don't want to let down my residents or the twins."

Bridget studied Ryder for a long moment. "Are you

sure you want to step in as their father? There are other options. There are people who would love to welcome the boys into their—"

"The boys are mine," he said, his jaw locking in resolution. "It may take me some time, but I'll figure it out. The boys are important to me. I held them minutes after they were born. I would do anything for them. We've just all been thrown a loop. We're all dealing with the loss of my brother and sister-in-law. I will be there for them. I will be."

She nodded slowly. "Okay. I'll try to help you with your nanny situation."

He paused and the electricity and emotion that flowed between them snapped and crackled. "Thank you."

She nodded. "It's late. I may need to borrow one of your shirts and I should talk to my security."

"No problem," he said, but the way he looked at her made her feel as if he'd much prefer she share his bed instead of taking the guest bed alone.

Bridget took a quick shower and brushed her teeth with the toothbrush Ryder supplied. Pushing her hands through the sleeves of the shirt he left in the guest bedroom for her, she drank in the fresh scent of the shirt. She climbed into bed, wondering what had possessed her to get involved in Ryder's situation and she remembered all the things she couldn't control or influence. Maybe, just maybe she could wave a magic wand in this one and help just a little.

It seemed only seconds after she fell asleep that she heard a knock at the door. She awakened, confused and disoriented. "Hello?"

"Bridget," a male voice said from the other side of the door. "It's me, Ryder."

The door opened a crack. "I just wanted you to know I'm leaving."

Her brain moved slowly. She was not at the hotel. She was at Ryder's townhome. "Um."

"The boys are still asleep."

She paused. "The boys?" She blinked. "Oh, the boys."

He came to the side of her bed. "Are you okay?"

"What time is it?"

"Five a.m."

"Is this when you usually leave for work?"

"Pretty much," he said.

"Okay," she said and tried to make her brain work. "What time do they usually get up?"

"Six or seven," he said. "I can try and call someone if—"

"No, I can do it," she said. "Just leave my door open so I can hear them."

"Are you sure?"

"Yes. Check in at lunchtime," she said.

"I can do that," he said and paused. "Did anyone ever tell you how beautiful you are when you're half-asleep?"

Unconsciously, her mouth lifted in a half smile. "I can't recall such a compliment."

"Nice to know I'm the first," he said, bending toward her and pressing his mouth against hers. Before she could say a word, he left.

Bridget wondered if she'd dreamed the kiss.

She fell back asleep for what must have been 30 seconds and she heard the sound of a baby's cry. It awakened her like cold water on her face. She sat upright, climbed out of bed and walked to the boys' room. She swung open the door to find Travis and Tyler sitting in their cribs and wailing.

"Hi, darlings," she said and went to Travis. "Good morning. It's a wonderful day to be a baby, isn't it?" She saw a twisty thing on the side of the crib and cranked it around. The mobile turned and music played. "Well, look at that," she said and touched the mobile.

Travis gave a few more sobs, but as soon as he looked upward, he quieted as the mobile turned.

Bridget felt a sliver of relief. "Good boy," she said and went to Tyler's bed and cranked up the mobile. Tyler looked upward and gave up his halfhearted cry, staring at the mobile.

Diaper change, she thought and took care of Travis. Then she took care of Tyler and hoisted both boys on her hips and went downstairs. She fed them, changed them again and propped them on a blanket in the den while she called her sister's friend for a reference for the best nanny agency in Dallas. Three hours later, she interviewed four nannies in between feeding the twins and changing more diapers and putting them down for a nap. When they fussed at nap time, she played a CD more repetitious than her brother's top-adviser's speech on a royal's duty. She'd heard that lecture too many times to count. The huge advantage to the babies' CD was that it included singing. Bridget wondered if she might have been more receptive to the lecture if the adviser had sung it.

The second prospective nanny was her favorite. She received letters of reference on her cell phone within an hour and sent a generous offer that was immediately accepted. After she checked on the boys, she ordered a nanny/babycam. Next in line, she would hire a relief nanny, but right now she needed a little relief of her own.

Bridget sank onto the couch and wondered when her day had felt so full. Even at this moment, she needed to use the bathroom, but she didn't have the energy to go. She glanced at herself, in her crumpled dress from yesterday with baby formula, baby food and liquid baby burp. That didn't include the drool.

Crazy, but the drool was sweet to her. How sick was that? But she knew the twins had drooled when they'd relaxed and trusted her.

She laughed quietly, a little hysterically. Anyone in their right mind would ask why she was working so hard to find a nanny for a doctor with two baby boys. Maybe a shrink could explain it, but these days, Bridget had a hard time turning down a cause of the heart. And Ryder and the boys had struck her straight in the heart with a deadly aim. She hoped, now, that she would feel some sort of relief.

Leaning back against the sofa with her bladder a little too full, she closed her eyes. Heaven help her, this baby stuff was exhausting.

Ryder left the office early, determined not to leave Bridget totally in the lurch with the boys. Stepping inside the front door, he found Bridget, mussed in the most alluring way, asleep on his couch.

She blinked, then her eyes widened. "Oh, excuse me. Just a second," she said, then raced down the hallway.

He listened carefully, automatically these days. A CD played over the baby monitor, but there were no other sounds. A double check never hurt, he thought, and strode upstairs to listen outside the nursery door.

Nothing. He opened the doorknob in slow motion and pushed the door open. Carefully stepping inside, he peeked into the cribs. Both boys were totally zoned out. He almost wondered if they were snoring but refused to check.

Backing out of the room, he returned downstairs to the den. Bridget was sipping from a glass of water.

"Are they still asleep?" she asked.

He nodded.

She grimaced. "I hate to say this. You have no idea how much I hate to say this, but we need to wake them or they'll be up all night. And I'm not staying tonight."

"Yeah," he said, but he was in no rush.

"I hired a nanny. She can start Monday. I've also ordered a baby/nannycam for your peace of mind. The next step is hiring a relief nanny because the twins are especially demanding at this age. Well, maybe they will be demanding at every age, but we have to deal with the present and the immediate future."

Ryder stared at her in disbelief. "How did you do that?"

She smiled. "I'm a fairy princess. I waved my magic wand," she said. "Actually I got into the best nanny agency in Dallas, used my title, interviewed four highly qualified women in between changing diapers, selected one applicant, received references, blah, blah, blah and it's done." She lifted her shoulders. "And now I'm done."

"I'm sure you are. In any other circumstance, I would invite you out to dinner for the evening."

"Lovely thought," she said. "But I feel extremely grungy. The opposite of glamorous. I'm going to my sister's ranch for the weekend. You can call me next week about all the doctors you want to send to Chantaine."

His lips twitched. "You don't really think I'm going to sell out one of my residents for this, do you?"

"Sell out is such a harsh term," she said with a scowl. "I believe it's more accurate that you're giving them an opportunity for hands-on experience in a beautiful environment with a compensation that allows them to concentrate on treatment rather than their debt."

He lifted an eyebrow. "Pretty good."

She shrugged. "It's the truth. My security is waiting to drive me to my sister's house. Can you take it from here?"

"Yes, I can. Do I have your number?" he asked. "For that dinner I promised."

She looked at him for a long, sexy moment that made him want to find a way to make her stay. "Some would say I'm more trouble than I'm worth," she said.

"They haven't seen you with twins," he said.

She smiled slightly and went to the kitchen. Out of curiosity, he followed and watched her scratch a number across the calendar tacked on the fridge. "Good enough?" she asked.

"Good enough," he said.

"Don't wait too long to call me, cowboy doctor," she said and walked toward the front door.

"I won't," he said, his gaze fixed on the sight of her amazing backside. "G'night, gorgeous."

She tossed a smile over her shoulder. "Same to you."

Bridget felt Valentina search her face. "Twin boys? Dr. Ryder? What does any of this have to do with you?"

It was Saturday morning. Noon, actually, as she sipped her tea and entered the world of the waking. "I didn't mean to get involved, but I didn't have a choice. I mean, the boys were orphaned. Ryder is grieving at the same time he's trying to take care of the babies. Trying to take on someone else's job because he's medically unable."

Tina stared at her in disbelief. "Are you sure you're okay? Maybe you need more rest."

Bridget laughed. "I'm sure I'll take another nap, but the story won't change tomorrow. It was something I had to do." She paused. "You understand that, don't you? When you have to fix it if you can?"

Tina's face softened and she covered Bridget's hand with hers. "Oh, sweetie, I'm so sorry," she said, shaking her head.

"For what?"

"The Devereaux fixing gene has kicked in," she said. "It's a gift and a plague."

"What do you mean?"

"I mean, you finally understand what it means to be a Devereaux Royal," she said, her expression solemn. "If you see a need, you try to fill it. If you see a pain, you try to heal it. It's your purpose. It's our purpose."

"So, I'm going to be doing stuff like this the rest of my life?" Bridget asked, appalled.

Tina nodded and Katiana banged on the tray of her high chair, clearly wanting more food.

"Oh, I hope not." Bridget didn't want to feel that much. She didn't want to get that emotionally involved. Surely, she could get this out of her system once and for all with Ryder and the babies and then get back to her true self in Italy.

Bridget sighed. "What I really want to do is wrap up

this doctor thing as soon as possible. I'm concerned it may not happen as quickly as I like."

"Why not?" Tina asked as she gave Katiana slices of peaches.

"I don't understand it all, but the way Ryder talks about it, going to Chantaine would be death for a physician's career. Sounds a bit overdramatic to me, but I need to get further information. In the meantime, Stefan has asked me to make some more official appearances, so I'll be traveling and spending more time in Dallas."

Tina frowned. "I don't like that," she said. "I thought you were going to spend most of your time here with me."

"I'll still be coming to the ranch as often as possible, but you know how Stefan is. He likes to maximize our efforts."

"How well I remember," Tina said with a groan. She dampened a clean cloth and wiped off Katiana's face and hands.

Katiana shook her adorable head and lifted her hands. "Up," she said.

"Of course, Your Highness," Tina said and gave her daughter a kiss as she lifted her from the chair.

Katiana immediately pointed at the floor. "Down."

"Please," Tina said.

Katiana paused.

"Please," Tina repeated. "Can you say that?"

"Psss," the toddler said.

"Close enough," Tina said with a laugh.

Bridget stared at her sister in jeans and a T-shirt and sometimes had to shake her head at the sight of her. "I'm just not used to seeing you quite so domesticated."

"I've been living here for more than two years now."

"Do you mind it? The work?" she asked. "At the palace, you could have had several nannies at your beck and call."

"I have Hildie the housekeeper, who may as well be Katiana's grandmother, and Zach. I like the simplicity of this life. Before I met Zach, I always felt like I was juggling a dozen priorities. Now between him and Katiana, the choice is easy."

"Must be nice," Bridget muttered as Hildie, Zach's longtime housekeeper, strode through the door carrying a bag of groceries.

"Well, hello, all Your Highlinesses. We've got a roomful of royalty today. Miss Tina, did you offer your sister some of that strawberry bread? Looks like you're having a late breakfast. Although that should come as no surprise considering when she got here last night," Hildie said, lifting her eyebrow.

Bridget wasn't quite certain how to take the stern-looking gray-haired woman. Tina insisted the woman had a heart of gold, but she seemed to rule the house with an iron hand. "Good morning, Miss—"

"Call me Hildie, and it's afternoon. Do you feel like some pancakes or a turkey sandwich? You looked pretty rough when you got in last night," Hildie said as she began to put away groceries.

"She was taking care of twin babies," Tina said, clearly still amazed.

Hildie's jaw dropped. "Twin babies," she said. "You?"

Bridget grimaced. "I know it's totally improbable. Hopefully I won't be put in that type of situation again."

"She was helping a doctor who had become a

guardian to his brother's two babies because the brother and sister-in-law were killed in an accident."

Hildie shook her head, her brow furrowing in deep sympathy. "That's terrible, just terrible. You did the right thing," she said to Bridget. "Let me fix you a pie. I'll fix you any kind you want."

Surprised, Bridget felt a rush of discomfort mixed with pleasure. "Oh, I don't need a pie. You're delightful to suggest it, but—"

"I insist," Hildie said.

Tina lifted her shoulders helplessly. "You're going to get a pie whether you like it or not. You may as well pick what you like, and I guarantee it will be the best pie you've eaten."

"Well, if you must, I would like the most decadent chocolate pie you can bake."

Hildie cackled with laughter. "Chocolate. You can tell the two of you are sisters. And you may try to hide it, but you have that fix-it compulsion just like your sister."

"I don't have that compulsion," Bridget insisted. "It's temporary. Like a virus. As soon as I take my long break in Italy, I'll be cured."

Hildie laughed again and shot her a look of sympathy. "Don't worry, Your Highliness. It may take a while, but you'll figure it out."

Bridget frowned because it seemed that Hildie knew something she didn't. Hmm. The prospect didn't please her, but the chocolate would help.

Chapter Three

Three nights later, Ryder met Bridget at an exclusive Mediterranean restaurant in Dallas. He remembered she'd said she preferred Mediterranean and Italian food. With the Dallas skyline outside the window beside them, he couldn't look anywhere but at her. Her blue eyes sparkled with a combination of sensuality and warmth. Her black dress—yet another one—dipped into a V that cupped her beautiful breasts and her lips were, again, red.

"Thank you for joining me," he said after they'd placed their order.

"Thank you for inviting me. Who's watching the twins?" she asked.

"A neighbor and her daughter. I'm paying double. Amazing how easy it was for them to commit when I said that," he said.

She laughed. "They're adorable but exhausting. How was the new nanny?"

"Scary efficient. This was her first day and she's already whipping all of us into shape," he said, amazed at how good he felt just to be with Bridget.

"Good. Next step is to get a backup," she said and took a sip of wine. "In the meantime, about Chantaine's medical program…"

He stifled a groan. "Do we have to discuss business?"

"Briefly," she said and lifted an eyebrow. "Remember that we held our discussion while the twins were screaming *after* I had cared for them during your meeting and—"

"Okay, okay," he said. "Do you want me to be blunt?"

"I would love it," she said, leaning forward and propping her chin on her hands.

"The truth is, there's no true professional advantage for the residents to go to Chantaine after they graduate. There's no extra education, association with an expert, or certification."

"So money is not enough," she said.

"No," he said.

"Hmm." She tilted her head. "So the whole game would change if Chantaine could offer exposure to a noted expert in a particular field?"

He nodded.

She took another sip of her wine. "Thank you."

He could tell her brain was already racing. "You're plotting and planning," he said.

She smiled, her sexy red lips lifting upward, sending a sensual heat through his veins. "Yes, I am. I'll figure something out. It's the Devereaux way."

"I did an internet search on you," he admitted. "You've *mostly* stayed out of trouble. How did you manage that?"

"I'm flattered. Of course, I did research on you right after the cocktail party. How did I stay out of trouble?" she asked. "It's all relative. My sisters did me a huge favor. I wouldn't wish it on her, but Ericka went to rehab, and then after that, Tina got pregnant. What a scandal. So my little tumbles—"

"Like the time you got smashed at the nightclub in Chantaine and made a scene—"

"That was Stefan's fault. Eve was with me and he couldn't stand the fact that she wasn't with him." She waved her hand. "But I won't fault him too much. He'd just discovered he had a baby from an earlier affair and was trying to work out his relationship with Eve."

"I remember reading an article about some sort of incident. A gang. She was hurt."

He stopped when he saw her gaze darken with emotion.

"She saved my life and nearly lost her own," Bridget said quietly as she ran her finger around the top of her glass. "It all happened so fast. I wish I had responded differently. She was hurt. She almost died." She lifted her glass and took a quick sip. "It was wrong. Her life shouldn't have been put in jeopardy for my sake."

He was shocked at the stark guilt he saw on her face. "These things happen. Decisions are made in microseconds. She's a Texas girl. She acted on instinct."

She bit her lip. "Maybe I need to learn some of those Texas-girl instincts," she muttered.

"Your instincts are pretty damn good. You took care of the twins when we were in a jam," he said.

"That's different," she said.

"Not as far as I can see. I won't lie to you. I can't make any promises about sending doctors to Chantaine. On the other hand, I've thought about having you in my bed way too much. I wish I could say it's just because you've got a killer body and I've done without, but the truth is, there's something else about you that gets me going."

Her lips parted in startled disbelief. "I—" She broke off and shook her head. "I don't know what to say."

"You don't have to say anything. I just wanted you to know," he said.

She met his gaze and he could tell she was undecided. He saw want and hesitation, and he understood it, but he was driven to find a way to get her to meet him halfway.

After a delicious dinner, Ryder drove Bridget to her hotel and insisted on walking her to her room. "You know security is watching me," she said as they stood outside her door.

"Do you want to step inside your room?"

An illicit thrill raced through her. Her guard would report to Stefan and he would fuss. She would dodge his calls the same way she had after spending the night at Ryder's house. What a hassle. "For just a moment," she said and slid her key card into the lock.

Ryder pushed open the door. Seconds later, she felt her back against the door and his mouth on hers.

"Do you know what your red mouth does to me?"

he muttered and plundered her lips. He slid his tongue into her mouth, tasting her, taking her.

Her heart slammed against her ribs. She couldn't resist the urge to lift her fingers to his hair and scalp.

He groaned in approval and rocked his hips against hers.

Bridget gasped, her breath locking somewhere between her lungs and throat. Somehow, someway, she craved his warmth and strength. His passion and need struck her at her core.

"I want you," he said. "You want me. Let me stay for a while."

A terrible wicked temptation rolled through her. If he stayed, he would fill her and take her away from her uncertainty and emptiness. She knew he could take care of her, if only for a little while.

He French-kissed her, sending her around the world at least a couple of times.

"You want me to stay?" he asked, sliding his mouth down over her ear.

She inhaled, grasping for sanity. Closing her eyes, she tried to concentrate. "Yesandno," she said, running the words together. She dipped her head so that her forehead rested against his chin. "This is a little fast."

He gave a heavy, unsatisfied sigh. "Yeah, it is. But it's strong."

She nodded. "Sorry," she whispered.

"It's okay," he said cradling the back of her head. "It wouldn't work out anyway."

"Why is that?" she asked, leaning back to look at him.

"I'm a doctor. You're a princess," he said.

"So?" she asked.

"The two don't mix," he said. "And never will. Sweet dreams, Your Highness."

He left and Bridget stared at the door, frowning. *Why couldn't they mix?* Not that she *wanted* them to mix. And the *sweet dreams* thing really grated on her. That was what Eve had often said. It had seemed so sweet when she'd said it. Not so with Ryder. Bridget snarled. He was gone. Good riddance.

Ryder heard a knocking sound and shook his head as he glanced up during the meeting he was in to discuss the performance of the residents.

Dr. Wayne Hutt, Ryder's nemesis, knocked on the table again. "Dr. McCall?" he said. "Anyone home?"

"Pardon me," Ryder said in a crisp voice. "I was studying my notes."

"Apology accepted," Hutt said. "Drs. Robinson and Graham are having attendance issues."

"Dr. Robinson is concerned about the welfare of his family in rural Virginia and Dr. Graham's wife has just gotten pregnant," Ryder said. "They just need a little time to refocus. It won't be a problem."

"How can you be sure?" Hutt challenged.

Ryder fought his antipathy for his associate. "I'm sure," he said. "Just as Dr. Gordon Walters would be sure," he said, pulling rank because everyone knew Dr. Walters trusted Ryder over anyone else.

Hutt gave an odd combination of a frown and grimace.

Dr. James Williams, chief of everything, nodded.

"We'll give these two interns two weeks to make adjustments. Dr. McCall, you'll speak to them?"

"Yes, sir."

Seven minutes later, the meeting ended, thank God. He returned to his office and sent emails to Drs. Robinson and Graham to set up appointments. He answered another fifty emails and stood to make late rounds with his patients.

A knock sounded outside his door and Dr. Hutt walked inside. "Hey, Ryder. Late night. I'm surprised you can do this with the twins."

Ryder resisted the urge to grind his teeth. "I've hired a new nanny and am getting new backup. Thanks for your concern. I need to do late rounds."

"Just a minute," Hutt said. "How's Dr. Walters doing? No one's talking."

"He's working through his recovery. These things take time," Ryder hedged.

"That's pretty vague," Hutt said.

"You know I can't discuss the confidential status of patients," he said.

"But Walters isn't really your patient," Hutt continued.

"He's my mentor and friend, the closest thing I've had to a father since my own father died when I was a kid. I'm not discussing his condition," Ryder said.

"It must not be good," Hutt said. "You know if the twins are too much for you, I'll be glad to step in and help."

Ryder just bet Hutt would like to step in and *help*. What Hutt really wanted was a promotion. What Hutt really wanted was to snatch Walters's position away from Ryder. Although Ryder hated that Walters couldn't fulfill his duties any longer.

"Thanks for the offer," he said.

"Seriously, Ryder. I have a wife and a child. The wife is the critical element. She makes it easy for me to do my job. When you don't have a wife…"

"I have a good new nanny," he said.

"It's not the same as a wife," Hutt counseled.

"Hmm. See you. Good night," he said and headed out the door. What Hutt didn't understand was that Ryder had never had any intention of getting married and having children. He'd observed his parents' disastrous marriage, his father's death and his mother's subsequent descent into alcoholism and death.

After that, Ryder had resolved that he wanted to heal people. Bag the personal relationships, with the exception of his brother and his family. His family became his patients, and after he completed his residency, his family included the new residents. And always Dr. Walters. He would never take a wife. His mind wandered to a visual of Bridget the last time he'd seen her, her eyes catlike with sensuality, her mouth soft and sensual, taking him into her. His mouth into her. When he really wanted to give her a lot more.

Ryder swore under his breath. This was all libido. He'd taken care of this issue before with other women doctors as career-driven as he was. No-ties sex provided a release that allowed him to do his job. Maintaining his focus on his profession and the twins was the most important thing. Bridget was just a distraction.

Bridget wandered around the medical association meeting and was bummed that Ryder wasn't there. He was probably taking care of the twins. She felt a deep tug of sympathy and quickly tried to brush it aside. Ryder didn't want her sympathy. They would never work. Remember? She covered her irritation with a smile as she nodded at someone else she didn't know.

Halfway through the evening, the shrimp bowl was refilled and Bridget put a few on her plate.

"I always wait for the refill at these things," a distinguished older man said to her.

She nodded in agreement. "I agree. Fresh is better. Bridget Devereaux," she said, extending her free hand.

"Dr. James Williams, University Hospital," he said shaking her hand. "Are you a pharmaceutical sales rep?"

She opened her mouth and it took a moment to speak. She smiled. "Not exactly. I'm representing the country of Chantaine. Very small country in the Mediterranean. We're trying to recruit more doctors. We're offering complimentary living expenses and paying special scholarships in addition to salary for a two-year stay."

Dr. Williams lifted his white eyebrows. "Really? I'll have to speak to my physician in charge of residents about that. Perhaps a couple of them could benefit from that."

"I would appreciate that very much. I'm sure you're a very busy man. Would you mind if I touch base with you in a week or so?"

"Not at all," he said. "Some of our residents have money challenges. Don't we all in this economy?"

"So true," she said. "Are you the speaker tonight?"

He shook his head. "No, I'm lucky. Eat and leave."

She laughed. "Don't rub it in," she said.

He laughed in return. "Tell me your name again. I don't want to forget."

"Bridget Devereaux," she said, deliberately leaving out her title. "I represent Chantaine. I'm honored to meet you."

"My pleasure to meet you, Miss Devereaux," he said, and ate his shrimp cocktail.

Bridget worked the room the rest of the night and arranged a visit to the pediatric wing at Texas Medical Center to make a public service announcement for public health. She also met several doctors who wanted to pursue a more personal relationship, but she demurred at the same time that she gave them her card which contained a number for her assistant.

By the time the evening was done, her feet were also done. Her mind wandered to Ryder and the babies, but she tried to push her thoughts aside. With a glass of white wine in her hand, she kicked off her high heels and watched television in her suite at the hotel.

She closed her eyes. Soon enough she would be in Italy with a gorgeous Italian man keeping her company. She smiled at the image, but soon another image flashed in its place. Ryder, sans shirt, stood before her and dragged her into his arms and began to make love to her. He was so hot that smoke rose between them, but the sensation of his skin against hers made her dizzy. His kiss made her knees weak. He made her want in a way she never had....

She felt herself sinking into the couch, her body warm and pliable. And alone.

Bridget blinked and sat up against the couch. This was just wrong. He'd already said they wouldn't work because of who he was, because of who she was. A part of her rebelled against the notion one moment. The next, she didn't. She didn't have room for this drama in her life. She had goals. She had Italy in her future.

Bridget washed her face and brushed her teeth, determined to put Ryder from her mind. As she fell asleep, though, she dreamed of Ryder and the boys.

A few days later, Ryder followed up on a surgery patient midday. The young man had been admitted to the E.R. with appendicitis. Ryder had operated and needed to give his stamp of approval for the teen to be discharged. He was stopped because there was filming in the pediatric unit.

Slightly irritated, he checked his text messages on his cell and answered a few.

"She's a princess making a video," one nurse said to another.

He snapped his head up at the comment. "Princess?" he repeated.

"Yes," the nurse said. "But she's very nice. Not at all snooty. I got her coffee and she was very grateful. More than a lot of doctors."

"She wasn't trying to save lives," Ryder said.

The nurse shrugged. "Anyone can say please and thank you, and she did."

Minutes later, Bridget appeared, lighting up the room with her smile. The chief of Pediatrics accompanied her, clearly dazzled.

"Thank you," she said. "Thank you so much from Chantaine and me. You have been wonderful."

"Isn't she wonderful? Now *that* is a princess," the nurse said.

Ryder wanted to make a wry, cynical response, but he was too busy staring at Bridget. And the damned pediatric chief. She seemed to glow. He remembered how she'd felt in his arms, how that wicked red mouth had felt against his. He remembered how she'd made him smile. Not many people had managed to do that during the last few months.

She squeezed the pediatrics chief's arm, then glanced around the room and waved. Her gaze locked with his and he felt a surge of need all the way down to his feet. It was sexual, but more, and confused the hell out of him. She gave a quick little wave and returned her attention to the pediatric chief.

Ryder felt an inexplicable surge of jealousy. *Where the hell had that come from?* Pushing it aside, he continued to his patient's room for the final exam. Less than five minutes later, he headed down the hallway toward his office. Rounding a corner, he nearly plowed into Bridget and Dr. Ware, the pediatrics chief, who was chatting her up. His body language said he wanted to eat her with a spoon. His hand placed on the wall above her head, he leaned toward her. Ryder fought the crazy urge to push him away, but turned his head instead.

"Ryder. Dr. McCall," Bridget said.

He slowed his steps and turned around and nodded in her direction.

"How are you? The twins? The new nanny?" she asked, her gaze searching his.

Ware stepped beside her. "Whoa, she knows a lot about you, McCall. How did that happen?"

Ryder shrugged. "Just lucky, I guess. I'm good. The twins are good and the new nanny is fantastic. I could say I owe you my life, but I'd be afraid you'd take it."

She shot him a look of mock offense. "You know better than that. Besides, it's not your life that I want," she said with a laugh.

Ware looked from one of them to the other, clearly curious. "What *does* she want? And why in the world wouldn't you give it to her?"

"She wants my residents," he said, meeting her gaze.

"After they've completed your program," she insisted. "Plus, I only want to *borrow* them for a couple of years, and they'll be well compensated."

"You could throw her one or—" Dr. Ware's pager sounded. "Please excuse me. I need to go. You have my card, Your Highness. Give me a call. Anytime," he said with a hopeful smile and rushed away.

Bridget sighed and turned to Ryder. "Are you going to do the civilized thing and ask me to join you for lunch?"

"If I haven't been civilized before, why should I start now?" Ryder retorted because Bridget made him feel anything but civilized.

"I suppose because you owe me your life," she said with a glint in her eyes.

He gave a muffled chuckle. "Okay, come along. I better warn you that lunch won't last longer than fifteen minutes."

"Ah, so you're into quickies. What a shame," she said and began to walk.

"I didn't say that," he said, but resisted the urge to pull at his collar which suddenly felt too tight.

"I can't say I'm surprised. All evidence points in that direction."

"How did we get on this subject?" he asked.

"You said you wouldn't last more than fifteen minutes," she said, meeting his gaze with eyes so wide and guileless that he wondered how she did it.

"I said *lunch* won't last—" He broke when he saw her smile. "Okay, you got me on that one. I hope you don't mind cafeteria food."

"Not at all," she said as they walked into the cafeteria.

He noticed several people stared in their direction, but she seemed to ignore it. They each chose a couple dishes and he paid for both, then guided her to a less-occupied table at the back of the room. "How did your video go today?"

"Hopefully, well. I interviewed Dr. Ware about preventative health for children. I also need to do one for adults. But enough about that. How are the twins?" she asked, clearly eager for information.

"I think the new nanny is making a big difference for them. This is the most calm I've seen them since I took custody of them," he said. "The nanny also suggested that I do some extra activities with them, but I haven't worked that into the schedule yet."

"What kind of activities?" she asked, and took a bite of her chicken.

"Swimming," he said then lowered his voice. *"Baby yoga."*

"Oh. Do you take yoga?" she asked and sipped her hot tea.

"Never in my life," he said. "The nanny seems to

think this would increase bonding between the three of us."

"That makes you uncomfortable," she said.

He shrugged. "I hadn't planned on having kids. I guess I'm still adjusting, too."

"You've been through a lot. Perhaps you should see a therapist," she said.

"We're doing okay now," he said defensively.

"I don't suggest it as an insult. The palace is always giving us head checks especially since my sister Ericka had her substance-abuse problem. I'm surprised it's not required in this situation."

"A social worker has visited a few times to check on things. She actually suggested the same thing," he said reluctantly. "She said I need to make sure I'm having fun with the boys instead of it being all work."

"There you go," she said. "I think it's a splendid idea. You just seem incredibly overburdened and miserable."

"Thank you for that diagnosis, Your Highness," he said drily and dug into his dry salmon filet. "Funny, a friend of mine said something similar recently."

"We all have to protect against burnout. I would say you're more in danger of it than most."

"Is there such a thing as princess burnout?" he asked.

"Definitely. That's what happened to my sister Valentina. She carried the load too long."

"And what are you doing to prevent burnout?"

"I have an extended break planned in my future. In the meantime, I try to make sure I get enough rest and solitude whenever possible. As soon as I wrap up the doctor assignment, I'll get a break. I'm hoping you'll toss me one or two of your residents as Dr. Ware suggested to get the ball rolling."

"It's going to be more difficult than that," he said.

"I don't see why it needs to be. It's not as if I'm seriously asking for your top neurosurgeons. We would love a general practitioner or family doctor. In fact, we would prefer it."

"You and the rest of the world. We actually have a shortage of family physicians, too."

"Again, I'm only asking to *borrow* them."

"What do you think of Dr. Ware?" he asked, changing the subject again.

"He's lovely. Unlike you, he's totally enchanted with my position and title."

"Part of my charm. Part of the reason you find me irresistible."

"You flatter yourself," she said.

"Do I?" he challenged. "You've missed me."

"Of course I haven't. You already said nothing would work between us. Of course, that was after you tried to shag me against the hotel door. I mean, you obviously have the attention span of a fruit fly when it comes to women and—"

He closed his hand over hers. "Will you shut up for a minute?"

Surprisingly, she did.

"I dream about you whenever I get the rare opportunity to sleep. I've dialed your number and hung up too many times to count. You can't want to get involved with me right now."

"It's not for you to tell me what I can and can't want. Lord knows, everyone else does that. Don't you start."

"Okay," he said wearily.

"So what are you going to do about it?" she challenged.

If he said what he *wanted* to do, he could be arrested. "I think I'll show instead of tell," he said and watched with satisfaction as her throat and face bloomed with color. He wondered if her blush extended to the rest of her body. It would be fun to find out.

Chapter Four

Two days later, Bridget's cell phone rang and her heart went pitter-patter at the number on the caller ID. "Hello," she said in a cool voice.

"Hello to you, Your Highness. How are you?" Ryder asked.

"I'm actually getting ready to make an appearance for a children's art program in Dallas," she said, smiling at the people who were waiting for her.

"Okay, I'll make this quick. Are you free tonight?"

She rolled her eyes. The man clearly had no idea how many demands were placed on her once people got word she was in the area. "I'm not often free but can sometimes make adjustments. What did you have in mind?"

"Swimming," he said.

"Excuse me?" she said.

"Swimming with the twins and pizza," he said.

"The pizza had better be fabulous. Ciao," she said and disconnected the call, but she felt a crazy surge of happiness zing through her as she followed the museum representatives inside the room where the children and press awaited.

Bridget gave a brief speech about the importance of art at all levels of society and dipped her hands and feet in purple paint. She stepped on a white sheet of paper, then pressed her handprints above and finished with her autograph.

The crowd applauded and she was technically done, but she stayed longer to talk to the children as they painted and worked on various projects. Their warmth and responsiveness made her feel less jaded, somehow less weary. Who would have thought it possible?

After extensive rearrangements of her schedule, Bridget put on her swimsuit and had second thoughts. What had possessed her to agree to join Ryder for a swim class when she was in a nearly naked state? She didn't have a perfectly slim body. In fact, if honest, she was curvy with pouches. Her bum was definitely larger than her top.

Her stomach clenched. Oh, bloody hell, she might as well be thirteen years old again. Forget it, she told herself. It wasn't as if anything could happen. She and Ryder would have two six-month-old chaperones.

Within forty-five minutes, she and Ryder stood in a pool with Tyler and Travis. Tyler stuck to her like glue, his eyes wide and fearful. "It's okay," she coaxed, bobbing gently in the water.

Ryder held Travis, who was screaming bloody murder.

"Are we having fun yet?" he asked, holding his god-son securely.

"Should we sing?" she asked, trying not to be distracted by Ryder's broad shoulders and well-muscled arms and chest. For bloody's sake, when did the man have time to work out?

"They would throw us out," he said. "You look good in water."

She felt a rush of pleasure. "Thank you. Is Travis turning purple?"

"I think it's called rage," he said.

"Would you like to switch off for a moment?"

"Are you sure?" he asked doubtfully.

She nodded. "Let me give him a go," she said.

Tyler protested briefly at the exchange, then attached himself to Ryder. Travis continued to scream, so she lowered her mouth to his ear and began to quietly sing a lullaby from her childhood. Travis cried, but the sound grew less intense. She kept singing and he made sad little yelps, then finally quieted.

"Aren't you the magic one?" Ryder said.

"Luck," she said and cooed at the baby, swirling him around in the water. "Doesn't this feel good?" she murmured.

By the end of class, they'd switched off again and Travis was cackling and shrieking with joy as he splashed and kicked and Ryder whirled him around in the water.

As soon as they stepped from the pool, they wrapped the boys in snuggly towels. Ryder rubbed Travis's arms. She did the same with Tyler and he smiled at her. Her heart swelled at his sweetness. "You are such a good boy. Isn't he?" she said to Ryder.

"You bet," Ryder said and pressed his mouth against Tyler's chubby cheek, making a buzzing sound. Tyler chortled with joy.

"That sound is magic," she said.

Ryder nodded as he continued to rub Travis. "Yeah, it is." His glance raked her from head to toe and he shook his head. "You look pretty damn good."

Bridget felt a warmth spread from her belly to her chest and face, down her legs, all the way to her toes. "It's just been a long time for you," she said and turned away to put some clothes on Tyler.

A second later, she felt Ryder's bare chest against her back. An immediate visceral response rocked through her and she was torn between jumping out of her skin and melting. "Yeah, it has," he said. "But that shouldn't make you so damn different from every other woman I've met."

Her stomach dipped. "Stop flattering me," she said. "Get your baby dressed. You don't want him chilled."

After pizza and a raucous bath time, Ryder and Bridget rocked the babies and put them to bed. Ryder would have preferred to usher Bridget into his bed and reacquaint himself with the curves he'd glimpsed in the pool, but he would have to bide his time. Hopefully not too long, he told himself as his gaze strayed to the way her hips moved in her cotton skirt. He'd thought he was so smart getting her out of most of her clothes by inviting her to the baby swimming class. Now he would live with those images all night long.

"Wine?" he asked, lifting a bottle from the kitchen before he joined her in the den.

She had sunk onto the sofa and leaned her head back against it, unintentionally giving him yet another seductive photo for his mental collection. One silky leg crossed over the other while the skirt hugged her hips. The V-neck of her black shirt gave him just a glimpse of creamy cleavage. For once, her lips were bare, but that didn't stop him from wanting to kiss her.

Her eyes opened to slight slits shrouded with the dark fan of her eyelashes. "One glass," she said. "I think everyone will sleep well tonight."

Speak for yourself, he thought wryly and poured her wine. He allowed himself one glass because he wasn't on call.

"It's amazing how much they can scream, isn't it?" she said as he sat beside her.

"They save up energy lying around all the time. It's not like they can play football or baseball yet."

"Have you thought about which sport you'll want them to pursue?" she asked.

"Whatever keeps them busy and tired. If they're busy and tired, they won't be as likely to get into trouble," he said.

"So that's the secret," she said with a slow smile. "Did that work for you?"

"Most of the time. I learned at a young age that I wanted a different life than the life my parents had."

"Hmm, at least you knew your parents," she said.

"Can't say knowing my father was one of my strong points."

"Well, you know what they say, if you can't be a good example, be a terrible warning."

He chuckled slightly and relaxed next to her. "I don't want to be the same kind of father he was. Drunk. Neglectful. Bordering on abusive."

"You couldn't be those things," she said.

"Why not? You've heard the saying, an apple doesn't fall too far from the tree."

"You've already fallen a long way from that so-called tree," she said. "Plus, you may be fighting some of your feelings, but you love those boys." She lifted her hand to his jaw. "You have a good heart. I liked that about you from the first time I met you."

"And I thought it was my singing voice," he said and lowered his mouth to hers, reveling in the anticipation he felt inside and saw in her eyes.

She tasted like a delicious combination of red wine, tiramisu and something forbidden that he wasn't going to resist. Ryder was certain he could resist her if he wanted. If there was one thing Ryder possessed, it was self-discipline. The quality had been necessary to get him through med school, residency and even more so now in his position at the hospital and with the twins.

For now, though, Ryder had decided he didn't want to resist Bridget. With her lush breasts pressing against his chest, discipline was the last thing on his mind. She was so voluptuously female from her deceptively airy attitude to her curvy body. He slid one of his hands through her hair as she wiggled against him.

A groan of pleasure and want rose from his throat as she deepened the kiss, drawing his tongue into her mouth. The move echoed what he wanted to be doing with the rest of his body and hers. He wrapped his hands around her waist. He slid one down to her hips and the other upward to just under her breast.

He was so hard that he almost couldn't breathe. She was so soft, so feminine, so hot. With every beat of his heart, he craved her. He wanted to consume her, to slide inside her....

Ryder slid his hand to her breast, cupping its fullness. Her nipple peaked against his palm. The fire inside him rising, he tugged a few buttons of her blouse loose and slipped his hand under her bra, touching her bare skin, which made him want to touch every inch of her. He couldn't remember wanting to inhale a woman before.

The next natural step would be to remove her clothes and his and after that, caress her with his hands and mouth. After that, he wanted to slide inside her.... She would be so hot, so wet....

All he wanted was to be as close to her as humanly possible.

From some peripheral area of his brain, he heard a knock and then another. Her body and soul called to him. He took her mouth in another deep kiss.

Another knock sounded, this time louder, but Ryder was determined to ignore it.

Suddenly his front door opened and Marshall burst into the room.

"Whoa," Marshall said. "Sorry to interrupt."

Ryder felt Bridget pull back and hastily arrange her shirt. "Who——" she said in a breathless voice.

"My best friend from high school, Marshall," Ryder said. "He has a key," he continued in a dark voice.

Marshall lifted his hands. "Hey, I called and you

didn't answer. I started getting worried. You almost always answer at night. We've had a beer three times during the last week." His friend stared at Bridget and gave a low whistle. "And who do we have here?"

Irritated, Ryder scowled. "Show a little respect. Prin—" He stopped when Bridget pinched his arm. Staring at her in disbelief, he could see that she didn't want him to reveal her title. "Bridget Devereaux, this is Marshall Bailey."

His friend moved forward and extended his hand. Bridget stood and accepted the courtesy.

"Nice to meet you, Bridget," Marshall said. "It's a relief to see Ryder with a woman."

Embarrassment slammed through Ryder and he also stood. "Marshall," he said in a warning tone.

"I didn't mean that the way it sounded. The poor guy hasn't had much company except me and the twins." Marshall cleared his throat. "How did you two meet anyway?"

"Okay, enough, Mr. Busybody. As you can see, I'm fine, so you can leave."

"Oh no, that's not necessary," Bridget said and glanced at her watch. "I really should be leaving. I have an early flight tomorrow."

"Where?" Ryder asked.

"Chicago. They have a teaching hospital. I'll be meeting with the hospital chief to present the proposal for Chantaine's medical exchange."

"Oh," he said, surprised at the gut punch of disappointment he felt when he should feel relieved. "I guess this means you've given up on our residents."

"No, but you haven't been at all receptive. My brother

Stefan has instructed me to explore other possibilities. Your program was our first choice due to the quality of your residents and also the fact that you have so many family doctors and prevention specialists. But because you're unwilling to help…"

"For Pete's sake, Ryder, help the woman out," Marshall said and moved forward. "Is there anything I can do?"

Marshall was really getting on Ryder's nerves. "Not unless you have a medical degree and are licensed to practice," Ryder said.

"I believe my driver is here. Thank you for an action-packed evening," she said with a smile full of sexy amusement.

Ryder would have preferred a different kind of action. "I'll walk you to the car," he said, then shot a quick glance at Marshall. "I'll be back in a minute."

Ryder escorted Bridget to the limo waiting at the curb. A man stood ready to open the door for her. Ryder was disappointed as hell that she was headed out of town. Stupid. "So how long will you be gone?" he asked.

She lifted a dark eyebrow and her lips tilted in a teasing grin. "Are you going to miss me, Dr. McCall?"

His gut twisted. "That would be crazy. The only thing I've been missing for the last month is sleep," he lied.

"Oh, well, maybe you'll get lucky and get some extra sleep while I'm gone. Ta-ta," she said and turned toward the limo.

He caught her wrist and drew her back against him. The man at the car door took a step toward them, but she waved her hand. "Not necessary, Raoul."

"You must enjoy tormenting me," he said.

"Me?" she said, her blue eyes wide with innocence. "How could I possibly have the ability to torment you?"

"I don't know, but you sure as hell do," he muttered and kissed her, which only served to make him hotter. He turned her own words on her. "So, Your Highness, what are you going to do about it?"

She gave a sharp intake of breath and her eyes darkened as if her mind were working the same way as his. She bit her lip. "I can call you when I return from Chicago."

"Do that," he said.

Ryder returned to his house to find Marshall lounging on the sofa and drinking a glass of red wine. "This isn't bad," he said.

"Glad you like it. In the future, give me a call before you drop in. Okay?"

Marshall looked injured. "I did call you. You just didn't answer." He shook his head and gave a low whistle. "And now I understand why. That's one hot babe, and she reeks money. A limo came to pick her up? You sure know how to pick 'em. How did you meet her?"

"In an elevator," Ryder said, not wanting to give away too many details. As much as he liked his old friend, Ryder knew Marshall could gossip worse than an old lady.

"Really?" Marshall said, dumbfounded. "An elevator. Was it just you and her? Did you do anything— adventurous?"

"Not the way you're thinking," Ryder said in a dry tone, although if it had been just him and Bridget in that elevator without the twins, his mind would have gone in the same direction.

"Well, I'm glad you're finally getting some action," Marshall said.

Ryder swore. "I'd say you pretty much nixed that tonight. Between you and the twins, who needs birth control?"

Marshall chuckled. "Sorry, bud, better luck next time. I thought I'd see if Suzanne was hanging around tonight. She stays late for you sometimes."

Realization struck Ryder. "You didn't come by to see me. You came to see my nanny. I'm telling you now. Keep your hands off my nanny. She's not your type."

"Who says?"

"I say."

"Why isn't she my type? She's pretty. She's nice," he said.

"She's six years older than you are," Ryder said.

"So? She doesn't look it. She's got a fresh look about her and she's sweet. Got a real nice laugh," Marshall said.

"I'm not liking what I'm hearing," Ryder said, stepping between Marshall and the television. "So far, Suzanne is the perfect nanny. I don't want you messing with her. The boys and I need her."

"She's an adult. She can decide if she wants me to mess with her," he said with a shrug.

"Marshall," he said in a dead-serious voice. "She's not like your dime-a-dozen girls running fast and loose. She's not used to a guy like you who'll get her in the sack and leave her like yesterday's garbage."

Marshall winced. "No need to insult me. I've had a few long-term relationships."

"Name them," Ryder challenged.

"Well, there was that redhead, Wendy. She and I saw each other for at least a couple of years."

"She lived out of town, didn't she?" Ryder asked. "How many other women were you seeing at the same time?"

Marshall scowled. "Okay, what about Sharona? We lived together."

"For how long?"

"Seven weeks, but—"

"Enough said. Keep your paws off Suzanne."

Marshall slugged down the rest of the wine and stood. "You know, I'm not a rotten guy."

"Never said you were."

"I just haven't ever found the right girl," Marshall said.

"As long as you and I understand that Suzanne is not the right girl for you, everything will be fine."

Three days later, Bridget returned from her trip to Chicago. She hadn't snagged any doctors, but she'd persuaded one of the specialists she'd met to visit Chantaine and offer lectures and demonstrations. She was getting closer to her goal. She could feel it. Even though what she really wanted to do tonight was soak in a tub and watch television, she was committed to attend a charity event for Alzheimer's with the governor's son, who was actually quite a bit older than she was. Part of the job, she told herself as she got ready. She thought about calling Ryder, but every time she thought about him, she felt a jumpiness in her stomach. Bridget wasn't sure how far she wanted to go with him because she knew she would be leaving Dallas as soon as she accomplished her mission.

There was something about the combination of his strength and passion that did things to her. It was exciting. And perplexing.

Preferring to have her own chauffeur, Bridget met Robert Goodwin, the governor's son, in the lobby of her hotel. He was a distinguished-looking man in his mid-forties who reminded her of one of her uncles. She decided that was how she would treat him.

Her bodyguard Raoul, who occasionally played double duty in making introductions, stepped forward. "Your Highness, Robert Goodwin."

She nodded and extended her hand. "Lovely to meet you, Mr. Goodwin. Thank you for escorting me to an event that will raise awareness for such an important cause."

"My pleasure, Your Highness," he said, surprising her when he brought her hand to his mouth. "Please call me Robert. May I say that you look breathtaking?"

"Thank you very much, Robert. Shall we go?"

By the time they arrived at the historical hall, Bridget concluded that Mr. Goodwin's intentions were not at all uncle-like and she prepared herself for a sticky evening. Cameras flashed as they exited the limo and Mr. Goodwin appeared to want to linger for every possible photo as he bragged about her title to the reporters.

"Everyone is excited to have a real princess at the event tonight. People paid big bucks to sit at our table."

"I'm delighted I could help the cause." Sometimes it amazed her that a single spermatozoa had determined her status. And that spermatozoa had originated from a cheating jerk of a man who had never gotten her first name right. Her father.

"Would you join me in a dance?" Robert said, his gaze dipping to her cleavage.

"Thank you, but I need to powder my nose," she said. "Can you tell me where the ladies' room is?"

Robert blinked. "I believe it's down the hall to the left."

"Excuse me," she said and headed for the restroom, fully aware that Raoul was watching. She wondered if she could plead illness. After stalling for several moments, she left and slowly walked toward her table. Halfway there, Ryder stepped in front of her.

"Busy as ever," he said.

Her heart raced at the sight of him. "So true. I arrived back in town this afternoon and had to turn right around to get ready for this event."

"With the governor's son," Ryder said, clearly displeased.

"He could be my uncle," she said.

"Bet that's not what he's thinking," Ryder countered.

She grimaced and shrugged. "It's not the first time I've had to manage unwelcome interest, and if my appearance generates additional income for this good cause..."

"True," he said, his eyes holding a misery that grabbed at her.

"What brings you here?"

"Dr. Walters. He has had an impact on hundreds of doctors, but now he can't recognize himself in the mirror."

"I'm so sorry," she said, her heart hurting at the

expression on his face. "Seeing you, hearing you, makes me glad I came. I'm ashamed to confess that I was tempted to cancel because I was so tired after returning from Chicago."

His gaze held hers for a long emotional moment. "I'm glad you didn't give in to your weariness this time."

"Even though I have to face Mr. Anything-but-Good Robert Goodwin," she said.

"Give me a sign and I'll have your back," he said.

She took a deep breath. "That's good to know. I can usually handle things. This isn't the first time."

His gaze swept over her from head to toe and back again. "That's no surprise."

Her stomach dipped and she cleared her throat. "I should get back to my table. I'm told people paid to sit with me. I'm sure it has nothing to do with my title."

His lips twitched. "Not if they really knew you," he said.

"You flatter me," she said.

"Not because you're a princess," he said.

"Call me tomorrow."

"I will," he said.

Bridget returned to her table and tried to be her most charming self and at the same time not encouraging Robert Goodwin. It was challenging, but she was determined.

After the meal had been served, he turned to her. "I'm determined to dance with you."

"I'm not that good of a dancer," she assured him.

He laughed, his gaze dipping over her cleavage again. "I'm a good leader," he said and rose, extending his hand to her. "Let me surprise you."

Or not, she thought wishing with all her heart that he wouldn't surprise her. She didn't want to embarrass the man. She lifted her lips in a careful smile. "One dance," she said and stood.

They danced to a waltz, but he somehow managed to rub against her. She tried to back away, but he wrapped his hands around her waist like a vise, drawing him against her. Suddenly, she saw Ryder behind Robert Goodwin, his hand on his shoulder. Robert appeared surprised.

"Can I cut in?" Ryder asked.

Robert frowned. "I'm not—"

"Yes," Bridget said. "It's only proper."

Robert reluctantly released her and Ryder swept her into his arms.

"Thank goodness," she murmured.

He wrapped his arms around her and it felt entirely different than it had with Robert. She stared into his eyes and felt a shockwave roll through her. "When did you learn to dance?"

"A generous woman taught me during medical school," he said, drawing her closer, yet not too close.

Bridget felt a spike of envy but forced it aside. "She did an excellent job."

He chuckled. "It was all preparation," he said. "Everything we do is preparation for what waits for us in the future."

"I would have to be quite arrogant to think your preparation was for me," she said, feeling light-headed.

"You look beautiful tonight," he said, clearly changing the subject. "I hate having to share you with anyone else."

Her stomach dipped. "It's part of who I was born to be. Duty calls," she said.

"But what does Bridget want?" he challenged. "Meet me in the foyer in fifteen minutes."

"How?" she asked.

"You'll figure it out," he said.

Chapter Five

She would figure it out, Bridget thought as she surreptitiously glanced at the diamond-encrusted watch
that had belonged to her grandmother. Two minutes to
go and she was supposed to be introduced to the crowd
within the next moment.

"As we continue to introduce our honored guests,
we'd like to present Her Highness, Princess Bridget
Devereaux of the country of Chantaine."

Bridget stood and smiled and waved to the applaud-
ing crowd. She hadn't known she was a table head, but
it wasn't unusual for event organizers to put her in the
spotlight given the chance. Because of her title, she was
a source of curiosity and interest.

Spotting Ryder leaning against the back wall as he
pointed to his watch, she quickly squeezed her hand
together and flashed her five fingers, indicating she
needed more time. Then she sank into her seat.

Robert leaned toward her. "I was cheated out of my dance. We need to hit the floor again."

"I wish I could, but my ankle is hurting," she said.

Robert scowled. "Maybe because of the man who cut in on our dance."

She lifted her shoulders. "Perhaps it's the long day catching up with me."

"You're too generous. We could try a slow dance," he said in a low voice.

"Oh no, I couldn't hurt your feet that way," she said. "But I would like to freshen up. Please excuse me," she said and rose, wondering why she was going to such extremes to meet Ryder when she was supposed to be concentrating on making an appearance.

Her heart was slamming against her rib cage as she tried to take a sideways route through the tables along the perimeter of the room. With every step, part of her chanted *This is crazy—this is crazy.* But she kept on walking, so she must indeed be crazy. She stepped into the foyer and glanced around the area.

Something snagged her hand. She glanced over her shoulder and spotted Ryder as he pulled her with him down a hallway. "Where are we—"

"Trust me," he said and pulled her toward the first door they came upon. It was an empty dark room with a stack of chairs pushed against a wall.

"What are we doing?" she asked, breathlessly clinging to him.

"Hell if I know," he said, sliding his hands through her hair and tilting her head toward his. "I feel like a car with no brakes headed straight for you."

"So, we're both crazy," she said.

"Looks that way," he said and lowered his mouth to hers.

Her knees turned to water and she clung to him. His strength made her feel alive despite how tired she felt from her long day of travel. Shocked at his effect on her, she loved the sensation of his hard chest against her breasts. She wanted to feel his naked skin against hers. She growled, unable to get close enough.

He swore under his breath as his hands roamed over her waist and up to the sides of her breasts. "I can't get enough of you," he muttered and took her mouth in a deep kiss again.

She felt dizzy with a want and need she denied on a regular basis. It was as if she was suffering from a more delicious version of altitude sickness. His mouth against hers made her hotter with every stroke of his tongue. More than anything, she wanted to feel him against her.

"Ryder," she whispered, tugging at his tie and dropping her mouth to his neck.

He gave a groan of arousal. "Come home with me. Now," he said, squeezing her derriere with one hand and clasping her breast with the other.

Too tempted for words, she felt the tug and pull of duty and courtesy over her own needs. Bloody hell, why couldn't she just this once be selfish, irresponsible and rude? A sound of complete frustration bubbled from her throat. Because she just couldn't. She was in the States on official business from Chantaine and she'd been assigned to represent a cause important to her and her people.

"I can't," she finally managed. "It would just be

wrong and rude and it's not just about me. I'm sorry," she whispered.

"I don't know what it is about you, but you make me want to be more reckless than I've ever been in my life. More reckless than flying down Deadman's Hill on my bicycle with no hands when I was ten."

Bridget felt the same way, but she was holding on by the barest thread of self-restraint. Suddenly the door whooshed open and closed, sending her heart into her throat. Her head cleared enough to realize this situation could provide the press with an opportunity to paint her family in a bad light.

She held her breath, waiting for a voice, but none sounded.

"It's okay," he said as if he understood without her saying a word. "Whoever opened the door must have glanced inside and not spotted us. I'll leave first, then you wait a minute or two before you leave. I'll warn you if it looks like there's a crowd waiting for you."

She paused, then nodded slowly.

Ryder gave her shoulders a reassuring squeeze and kissed her quickly, then walked toward the door. Bridget stood frozen to the floor for several breaths and gave herself a quick shake. She moved to the door and listened, but the door was too thick. She couldn't hear anything. Counting to a hundred, she cracked open the door and peeked outside. No crowd. No photogs. Relief coursed through her and she stepped outside.

"Your Highness, I was worried about you," Robert said from behind her.

Her stomach muscles tightened and she quickly turned. "Robert, how kind of you."

"What were you doing in there?" he asked.

"My sense of direction is dismal," she said. "I went right when I should have turned left. Thank you for coming to my rescue. Now I can return to our table."

He slid his hand behind her waist and she automatically stiffened, but he seemed to ignore her response. "We can leave, if you like. I could take you to my condo…."

"Again, you're being kind, but we're here for an important cause."

"Afterward—"

"It's been a full day for me flying from Chicago. I appreciate your understanding that I'll be desperate to finally retire," she said. One of her advisers had instructed her that one should speak to another person as if they possessed good qualities…even if they didn't.

"Another time, then," Robert said, clearly disappointed.

Bridget gave a noncommittal smile, careful not to offer any false hope.

When Bridget didn't hear from Ryder for three days, she began to get peeved. Actually, she was peeved after day one. He'd behaved like he was starving for her and couldn't wait another moment, then didn't call. She considered calling him at least a dozen times, but her busy schedule aided her in her restraint.

On Tuesday, however, she was scheduled to meet with a preventative adult health specialist in preparation for a video she would be filming with the doctor as a public service announcement for Chantaine.

Afterward, she meandered down the hall past his

office. She noticed Ryder wasn't there, but his assistant was. Bridget gave in to temptation and stepped into the office. "Hello. I was wondering if Dr. McCall is in today."

The assistant sighed. "Dr. McCall is making rounds and seeing interns, but he may need to leave early for family reasons. May I take a message?"

"Not necessary," she demurred, but wondered what those family reasons were. "Are the twins okay?" she couldn't help asking.

The assistant nodded. "I think so. It's the nanny—" The phone rang. "Excuse me."

The nanny! The nanny she'd selected for Ryder and the boys had been as perfect as humanly possible. Perhaps more perfect. What could have possibly happened? Resisting the urge to grill the assistant about her, she forced herself to walk away. Her fingers itched to call him, but she didn't. It would be rude to interrupt his appointments with patients or the residents.

Bothered, bothered, bothered, she stalked through the hallway. The pediatric department head saw her and stopped in front of her, smiling. "Your Highness, what a pleasure to see you."

"Thank you, Doctor. How are you?" she said more than asked.

"Great. Would you like to get together for dinner?" he asked.

"I would, but I must confess my immediate schedule is quite demanding. Perhaps some other time," she said.

"I'll keep asking," he said and gave her a charming smile that didn't move her one iota.

Brooding, she walked down the hall and out of the hospital to the limo that awaited her. A text would be less intrusive, she decided, and sent a message. Two minutes later, she received a response. *Nanny had emergency appendectomy. Juggling with backup.*

WHY DIDN'T YOU CALL ME? she texted in return.

Her phone rang one moment later and she answered. "Hello."

"It's been crazy. I've even had to ask Marshall for help."

"Why didn't you ask me?" she demanded.

"You told me your schedule was picking up. I figured you wouldn't have time," he said.

True, she thought, but she was still bothered. "You still should have called me."

"You're a busy princess. What could you have done?" he asked.

Good question. She closed her eyes. "I could have rearranged my schedule so I could help you."

Silence followed. "You would do that?"

She bit her lip. "Yes."

"I didn't think of that."

"Clearly," she said.

He chuckled. "In that case, can you come over tomorrow afternoon? My part-time nanny needs a break."

"I'll confirm by five o'clock tonight," she said. "I have to make a few calls."

"Impressive," he said. "I bet your reschedules are going to be disappointed. Too bad," he said without a trace of sympathy.

She laughed. "I'll call you later," she said and they hung up and her heart felt ten times lighter.

The following afternoon, Bridget relieved the backup nanny while the twins were sleeping. From previous experience, she knew her moments of silence were numbered. She used the time to prepare bottles and snacks for the boys.

Sure enough, the first cry sounded. She raced upstairs and opened the door. Travis was sitting up in his crib wearing a frowny face.

"Hello, sweet boy," she whispered.

He paused mid-wail and stared at her wide-eyed.

"Hi," she whispered and smiled.

Travis smiled and lifted his fingers to his mouth.

Bridget changed his diaper. Seconds later, Tyler awakened and began to babble. Tyler was the happier baby. He was a bit more fearful, but when he woke up, he didn't start crying immediately.

Bridget wound Travis's mobile and turned her attention to Tyler. She took each baby downstairs ready to put them in their high chairs. Snacks, bottles, books, Baby Einstein and finally Ryder arrived carrying a bottle of wine.

"How's everybody?" he asked, his gaze skimming over her and the boys, then back to her. "Did they wear you out?"

"Not too much yet," she said. "It helps to have a plan."

He nodded. "With alternatives. I ordered Italian, not pizza. It should be delivered soon."

"Thank you," she said.

"I'm hoping to lure you into staying the night," he said.

"Ha, ha," she said. "The trouble with luring me after an afternoon with the twins is that I'll be comatose by nine o'clock at the latest. I talked to your part-time sitter and she told me Suzanne will be out for a few more days. Is that true?"

He nodded. "She had laparoscopic surgery, so her recovery should be much easier than if she'd had an open appendectomy."

"Then I think the next step is to get a list of your backup sitters and inform them of the situation and make a schedule for the children's care. So if you don't mind giving me your names and contact information, I can try to get it straight tomorrow."

He blinked at her in amazement. "You're deceptively incredible," he said. "You give this impression of being lighthearted and maybe a little superficial. Then you turn around and volunteer to take care of my boys, recruit doctors for your country and make countless appearances."

"Oooh, I like that. Deceptively incredible," she said, a bit embarrassed by his flattery. "Many of us are underestimated. It can be a hindrance and a benefit. I try to find the benefit."

Ryder leaned toward her, studying her face. "Have you always been underestimated?"

She considered his question for a moment, then nodded. "I think so. I'm number four out of six and female, so I think I got lost in the mix. I'm not sure my father ever really knew my name, and my mother was beginning to realize that her marriage to my father was not going to be a fairy tale."

"Why not?"

"You must swear to never repeat this," she said.

"I swear, although I'm not sure anyone I know would be interested," he said.

"True enough," she said. "My father was a total philanderer. Heaven knows, my mother tried. I mean, six children? She was a true soldier, though, and gave him two sons. Bless her."

"So what do you want for yourself?" he asked. "You don't want the kind of marriage your parents had."

"Who would?" she said and took a deep breath. "I haven't thought a lot about it. Whenever Stefan has brought up the idea of my marrying someone, I just start laughing and don't stop. Infuriates the blazes out of him," she said, and smiled.

"You didn't answer my question," he said.

His eyes felt as if they bored a hole through her brain, and Bridget realized one of the reasons she was drawn to Ryder was because she couldn't fool him. It was both a source of frustration and relief.

"I'm still figuring it out. For a long time, I've enjoyed the notion of being the eccentric princess who lives in Italy most of the year and always has an Italian boyfriend as her escort."

"Italian boyfriend," he echoed, clearly not pleased.

"You have to agree, it's the antithesis of my current life."

"And I suspect this life wouldn't include children," he continued with a frown.

Feeling defensive, she bit her lip. "Admit it. The life

you'd planned didn't include children…at least for a long while, did it?"

He hesitated.

"Be honest. I was," she said.

"No," he finally admitted. "But not because I was in Italy with an Italian girlfriend."

"No, you were planning to do something more important. A career in medicine. Perfectly noble and worthy, but it would be hard to make a child a priority when you have the kind of passion you do for your career. A child would be…inconvenient."

He took a deep breath. "We choose our careers for many reasons. I wanted to feel like I had the power to help, to cure, to make a difference. It was more important for me to feel as if I were accomplishing those goals than building a family life." He shrugged. "My family life sucked."

"There you go," she said in complete agreement. "My family life sucked, too. In fact, I wanted to get so far away from it that I wanted to move to a different country."

He chuckled. "So how is it that Princess Bridget is changing diapers and taking care of my twins?"

Bridget resisted the urge to squirm. "I won't lie. I once thought children were a lot of trouble and not for me, but then I got a couple of adorable nieces. I still thought I wouldn't want to deal with them for more than a couple hours at most with the nanny at hand to change diapers, of course." She bit her lip. "But it's just so different when they're looking at you with those big eyes, helpless and needing you…. And it would just feel so terribly wrong not to take care of them."

"And how do I fit into it?" he asked, dipping his head toward her.

"You are just an annoying distraction," she said in a mockingly dismissive whisper.

"Well, at least I'm distracting," he said and lowered his mouth to hers.

Bridget felt herself melt into the leather upholstery. She inhaled his masculine scent and went dizzy with want. He was the one thing she'd never had but always wanted and couldn't get enough of. How could that be? She'd been exposed to everything and every kind of person, hadn't she?

But Ryder was different.

She drew his tongue deeper into her mouth and slid her arms around his neck. Unable to stop herself, she wiggled against him and moaned. He groaned in approval, which jacked her up even more.

From some corner of her mind, she heard a sound.

"Eh."

Pushing it aside, she continued to kiss Ryder.

"Eh."

Bridget frowned, wondering….

"Wahhhhhhh."

She reluctantly tore her mouth from Ryder's. "The babies," she murmured breathlessly, glancing down at Travis as he tuned up. The baby had fallen on his side and he couldn't get back up.

"Yeah, I know," Ryder said. "I'm starting to understand the concept of unrequited l—"

"Longing," she finished for him because she couldn't deal with Ryder saying the four-letter L word. It wasn't possible.

"Bet there's a dirty diaper involved," Ryder muttered as he tilted Travis upright.

"Could be," she said and couldn't bring herself to offer to change it. She covered her laugh by clearing her throat. "I wouldn't want to deprive you of your fatherly duty."

He gave her a slow, sexy grin. "I'll just bet you wouldn't."

"It's an important bonding activity," she said, trying to remain serious, but a giggle escaped.

"Can't hold it against you too much," he said. "You've been here all afternoon."

Bridget rose to try to collect herself. Her emotions were all over the place. Walking to the downstairs powder room, she closed the door behind her and splashed water against her cheeks and throat. Sanity, she desperately needed sanity.

The doorbell rang and she returned as Ryder tossed the diaper into the trash before he answered the door. He paid the delivery man and turned around, and Bridget felt her heart dip once, twice, three times.... Adrenaline rushed through her, and she tried to remember a charming, gorgeous Italian man who had affected her this way. When had any man affected her this way?

Oh, heavens, she needed to get away from him. She felt like that superhero. What was his name? Superman. And Ryder was that substance guaranteed to weaken him. What was it? Started with a K...

"Smells good. Hope you like lasagna," Ryder said.

"I can't stay," she said.

"What?" he asked, his brow furrowing.

"I can't stay. I have work to do," she said.

"What work?" he asked.

"Rescheduling my meetings and appearances. I also need to take care of the childcare arrangements for the twins."

He walked slowly toward her, his gaze holding hers. She felt her stomach tumble with each of his steps. "You're not leaving because you have work to do, are you?"

She lifted her chin. "I'm a royal. I always have work to do."

He cupped her chin with his hand. "But the reason you're leaving is not because of work, is it?"

Her breath hitched in her throat.

"You're a chicken, aren't you?" he said. "Princess Cluck Cluck."

"That was rude," she said.

"Cluck, cluck," he said and pressed his mouth against hers.

After making the schedule for the twins' care, Bridget paid her sister an overdue visit. Valentina had threatened to personally drag her away from Dallas if Bridget didn't come to the ranch. Her sister burst down the steps to the porch as Bridget's limo pulled into the drive.

"Thank goodness you're finally here," Tina said.

Bridget laughed as she embraced her sister. "You act like I've been gone for years."

"I thought you would be spending far more time here, but you've been appearing at events, traveling to Chicago. And what's this about you helping that physician with his twin babies? Haven't you helped him enough?"

"It's complicated," Bridget said. "He's had some childcare issues. I think they're mostly resolved now."

"Well, good. I think you've helped him quite enough. Now you can spend some time with me," Tina said as she led Bridget into the house. "I have wonderful plans for us. Two aestheticians are coming to the ranch tomorrow to give massages and facials then we spend the afternoon at the lake."

"Lake?" Bridget echoed. All she'd seen was dry land.

"It's wonderful," Tina reassured her. "The summer heat and humidity can get unbearable here. We have a pond with a swing, but we're going to the lake because Zach got a new boat. Zach and one of his friends will be joining us tomorrow afternoon. Then we'll have baby back ribs for dinner."

Bridget's antennae went up at the mention of Zach's friend. "You're not trying to set me up, are you?"

"Of course not. I just thought you'd enjoy some no-pressure male companionship. Troy is just a nice guy. He also happens to be good-looking and eligible. And if you two should hit it off, then you could live close to me and—" Tina paused and a guilty expression crossed her face. "Okay, it's a little bit of a setup. But not too much," she said quickly. "Troy and Zach are business associates, so we'll have to drag them away from talk about the economy."

Bridget's mind automatically turned to Ryder. There was no reason for her to feel even vaguely committed to him. Her stomach tightened. What did that mean? she wondered. "I'm not really looking right now," Bridget said.

"I know," Tina said. "As soon as you take care of the

doctor project, you're off to Italy and part of that will include flirtations with any Italian man who grabs your fancy. But if someone here grabs your fancy…"

"Tina," Bridget said in a warning voice.

"I hear you," Tina said. "Let's focus on your amazing niece."

"Sounds good to me. I've missed the little sweetheart," Bridget said as they walked into the kitchen.

"Missed her, but not me!" Tina said.

Bridget laughed. "I adore you. Why are you giving me such a hard time?"

Tina lifted her hand to Bridget's face and looked deep into her gaze. "I don't know. I worry about you. I wonder what's going on inside you. You smile, you laugh, but there's a darkness in your eyes."

Bridget's heart dipped at her sister's sensitivity, then she deadpanned. "Maybe it's my new eyeliner."

Tina rolled her eyes. "You're insufferable. I always said that about Stefan, but you're the same, just in a different way."

"I believe I've just been insulted," Bridget said.

"You'll get over it. Hildie made margaritas for us and she always makes doubles."

Chapter Six

Bridget's morning massage coupled with one of Hildie's margaritas had turned her bones to butter. By the time she joined Tina, Zach and Troy on the boat, she was so relaxed that she could have gone to sleep for a good two hours. For politeness' sake, she tried to stay awake, although she kept her dark sunglasses firmly in place to hide her drooping eyelids.

Troy Palmer was a lovely Texas gentleman, a bit bulkier than Ryder. Of course Ryder was so busy he rarely took time to eat. A server offered shrimp and lobster while they lounged on the boat.

"Nice ride," Troy said to Zach.

Zach smiled as Tina leaned against his chest. "My wife thought I was crazy. She said I would be too busy."

"Time will tell," Tina said. "But if this makes you take a few more breaks, then I'm happy."

"You're not neglecting my sister, are you?" Bridget asked as she sipped a bottle of icy cold water.

Zach lifted a dark eyebrow. "There's a fine line between being the companion and keeper of a princess."

"I believe that's what you Americans call baloney. You work because you must. It's the kind of man you are. I love you for it," Tina said. "But I also love the time we have together."

Zach's face softened. "I love you, too, sweetheart."

Bridget cleared her throat. "We're delighted that you love each other," Bridget said. "But I'm going to have to dive overboard if we don't change the subject."

Tina giggled. "As you wish. Troy, tell us about your latest trip to Italy."

"Italy?" Bridget echoed.

"I thought that might perk you up," Tina said.

Troy shrugged his shoulders. "I go three or four times a year. Business, but I usually try to work in a trip to Florence."

"Oh, Florence," Bridget said longingly. "One of my favorite places in the world."

Troy nodded. "Yeah, I also like to slip down to Capri every now and then…"

Bridget's cell phone vibrated in the pocket of her cover-up draped over the side of her chair. She tried to ignore it, but wondered if Ryder was calling her. Dividing her attention between Troy's discussion about Italy and thoughts of Ryder, she nodded even though she wasn't hanging onto his every word. Her phone vibrated again and she was finding it difficult to concentrate.

She grabbed her cover-up and stood. "Please excuse me. I need to powder my nose."

"To the right and downstairs," Zach said. "And it's small," he warned.

"No problem," she said cheerfully and walked around the corner. She lifted her phone to listen to her messages. As she listened, her heart sank. Tomorrow's sitter was canceling. She was calling Bridget because Ryder was in surgery and unreachable.

Pacing at the other end of the boat, she tried the other backup sitters and came up empty. Reluctantly, she called Marshall who answered immediately.

"Marshall," he said. "'Sup?"

"Hello, Marshall," she said. "This is Bridget Devereaux."

"The princess," he said. Ryder had told her that Marshall had performed a web search and learned who she was. "Princess calling me. That's cool."

"Yes," she said, moving toward the other end of the boat. "There's some difficulty with sitting arrangements for Ryder's boys tomorrow morning. I was hoping you could help me with a solution."

"Tomorrow morning," he said. "Whoa, that's a busy day for me."

"Yes, I'm so sorry. I would normally try to fill in, but I'm out of town at the moment," she said.

"I might have a friend—"

"No," she said. "As you know, Ryder is very particular about his backup sitters. He won't leave the twins with just anyone."

"True," Marshall said. "Although I'm last on the list." Silence followed.

"I'm last on the list, aren't I?" Marshall asked.

"Well, you're an entrepreneur," she managed. "Ryder

knows you're a busy man with many demands on your time."

"Yeah," Marshall said. "How much time does he need?"

"Five hours," she said, wincing as she said it.

Marshall whistled. "That's gonna be tough."

"Let me see what I can do," she said. "I'll make some more calls."

"If you can have someone cover things in the early morning, I could probably come in around ten."

"Thank you so much. I'll do my very best," she said.

"Bridget," Tina said from behind her.

"Bloody hell," she muttered.

Marshall chuckled.

"To whom are you speaking?" Tina demanded.

"A friend," Bridget said. "Forgive me, Marshall. My sister is after me."

"Good luck. Keep me posted," he said.

"Yes, I will," she said and clicked off the phone. She turned to face her sister with a smile. "I'm just working out the timing of an appearance."

"Which appearance is that?" Tina asked.

"In Dallas," Bridget said. "I must say I do love Zach's new toy. I think it will be a fabulous way for the two of you to relax."

"Exactly which appearance in Dallas?" Tina said, studying her with narrowed eyes.

"Stop being so nosy," Bridget said.

Tina narrowed her eyes further. "This is about that doctor with the twins, isn't it?"

"His sitter for tomorrow has cancelled so we have to find another."

"We?"

Bridget sighed. "If you met him, you'd understand. He performs surgery, advises residents and he's an instant father."

"Perhaps he should take some time off to be with his new children," Tina muttered.

"It's not that easy. His mentor has Alzheimer's and he's trying to fill his position unofficially."

Tina studied her. "You're not falling for him, are you?"

Bridget gave a hearty laugh at the same time she fought the terror in her soul. "Of course not. You know I prefer Italian men."

Tina paused, then nodded. "True, and although you love your nieces, you've always said you couldn't imagine having children before you were thirty."

"Exactly," she said, though she felt a strange twinge.

"Hmm," Tina said, still studying her. "Is this doctor good-looking?"

Bridget shrugged. Yes, Ryder was very good-looking, but that wasn't why she found him so compelling. Giving herself a mental eye roll, she knew Tina wouldn't understand. "He's fine," she said. "But he's not Italian."

Tina giggled and put her arm around Bridget. "Now that's our Bridget. That's the kind of answer I would expect from you. Come back and relax with us."

Bridget smiled, but part of her felt uncomfortable. She knew what Tina was saying, that Bridget wasn't a particularly deep person. The truth was she'd never wanted to be deep. If she thought too deeply, she suspected she could become depressed. After all, she'd been a fairly average child, not at all spectacular. She hadn't flunked out in school, but she hadn't excelled at anything either. Except at being cheerful. Or pretending to be cheerful.

"I'll be there in just a moment. I need to make a few calls first."

"Very well, but don't take too long. Troy may not be Italian, but he's very good-looking and spends a fair amount of time in Italy."

"Excellent point," Bridget said, although she felt not the faintest flicker of interest in the man. "I'll be there shortly."

Several moments later, Bridget used all her charm to get the part-time sitter to fill in for the morning. Relieved, she called Marshall to inform him of the change.

"Hey, did you hear from Ryder?" he asked before she could get a word in edgewise.

"No. Should I have?" she asked, confused. "I thought he was in surgery."

"He's apparently out. He just called to tell me Dr. Walters passed away this morning," Marshall said.

Bridget's heart sank. "Oh no."

"Yeah. He's taking it hard. He hadn't seen Dr. Walters in a while and he'd been planning to try to visit him later this week." Marshall sighed. "Dr. Walters was the closest thing to a father Ryder had."

Bridget felt so helpless. "Is there something I can do?"

"Not really," Marshall said. "The twins will keep him busy tonight and that's for the best. The next few days are gonna be tough, though."

She saw her sister walking toward her and felt conflicted. "Thank you for telling me."

"No problem. Thanks for taking care of the childcare for tomorrow morning. Bye for now."

"Goodbye," she said, but he had already disconnected.

"You look upset," Tina said.

"I am."

After 9:30 p.m., Ryder prowled his den with a heavy heart. His mentor was gone. Although Dr. Walters had been mentally gone for a while now, the finality of the man's physical death hit Ryder harder than he'd expected. Maybe it was because he'd lost his brother so recently, too.

Ryder felt completely and totally alone. Sure, he had the twins and his profession, but two of the most important people in the world to him were gone and never coming back. He wondered what it meant that aside from his longtime friend Marshall, he had no other meaningful relationships. Was he such a workaholic that he'd totally isolated himself?

A knock sounded on his door, surprising him. Probably Marshall, he thought and opened the door. To Bridget. His heart turned over.

"Hi," she said, her gaze searching his. She bit her lip. "I know it's late and I don't want to impose—"

He snagged her arm and pulled her inside. "How did you know?"

"Marshall," she said, then shot him a chiding glance. "I would have preferred to hear it from you."

"I thought about it," he said, raking his hand through his hair. "But you've done enough helping with the babies."

"I thought perhaps that you and I were about more

than the babies, but maybe I was wrong," she said, looking away.

His heart slamming against his rib cage, he cupped her chin and swiveled it toward him. "You were right. You know you were."

"Is it just sex? Are you just totally deprived?" she asked in an earnest voice.

He swallowed a chuckle. "I wish."

Her eyes darkened with emotion and she stepped closer. She moved against him and slid her arms upward around the back of his neck. She pulled his face toward hers and he couldn't remember feeling this alive. Ever.

His lips brushed hers and he tried to hold on to his self-control, but it was tough. She slid her moist lips from side to side and he couldn't stand it any longer. He devoured her with his mouth, tasting her, taking her. Seconds later, he realized he might not ever get enough, but damn, he would give it his best shot.

He slid his fingers through her hair and slid his tongue deeper into her mouth. She suckled it and wriggled against him. Her response made him so hard that he wasn't sure he could stand it. His body was on full tilt in the arousal zone.

He took a quick breath and forced himself to draw back. "I'm not sure I can pull back after this," he said, sliding his hands down over her waist and hips. "If you're going to say no, do it now."

Silence hung between them for heart-stopping seconds.

He sucked in another breath. "Bridget—"

"Yes," she whispered. "Yes."

Everything in front of him turned black and white

at the same time. He drew her against him and ran his hands up to her breasts and her hair, then back down again. He wanted to touch every inch of her.

She felt like oxygen to him, like life after he'd been in a tomb. He couldn't get enough of her. He savored the taste and feel of her. Tugging at her blouse, he pushed it aside and slid his hands over her shoulders and lower to the tops of her breasts.

She gave a soft gasp that twisted his gut.

"Okay?" he asked, dipping his thumbs over her nipples.

She gasped again. "Yesssss."

He unfastened her bra and filled his hands with her breasts.

Ryder groaned. Bridget moaned.

"So sexy," he muttered.

She pulled at his shirt and seconds later, her breasts brushed his chest. Ryder groaned again.

The fire inside him exploded and he pushed aside the rest of her clothes and his. He tasted her breasts and slid his mouth lower to her belly and lower still, drawing more gasps and moans from her delicious mouth. Then he thought about contraception. Swearing under his breath, he pulled back for a second. "Give me a few seconds," he said. "You'll thank me later."

He raced upstairs to grab condoms and returned downstairs.

"What?" she asked.

"Trust me," he said and took her mouth again. He slid his hand between her legs and found her wet and wanting.

Unable to hold back one moment longer, he pushed

her legs apart and sank inside her. Bridget clung to him as he pumped inside her. She arched against him, drawing him deep.

He tried to hold out, but she felt so good. Plunging inside her one last time, he felt his climax roar through him. Alive, he felt more alive than he'd felt for as long as he could remember…. "Bridget," he muttered.

Her breath mingled with his and he could sense that she hadn't gone over the top. He was determined to take her there. Sliding his hand between them, he found her sweet spot and began to stroke.

Her breath hitched. The sound was gratifying and arousing. A couple moments later, she stiffened beneath him. He began to thrust again and she came in fits and starts, sending him over the edge.

He couldn't believe his response to her. Twice in such a short time? He wasn't an eighteen-year-old. "Come to bed with me."

"Yes," she said. "If I can make my legs move enough to walk upstairs."

He chuckled and knew the sound was rough. Everything about him felt sated, yet aroused and rough. "I'll help."

"Thank goodness," she said.

He helped her to her feet, but when they arrived at the bottom of the steps, he swept her into his arms and carried her up the stairs.

"Oh, help," she said. "I hope I don't give you a hernia."

"If you do, it'll be worth it," he said.

She swatted at him. "You're supposed to say I'm as light as a feather even though I may weigh half a ton."

"You took the words out of my mouth. You're light as a feather," he said.

She met his gaze and her eyes lit with a glow that both warmed and frightened him. "Excellent response," she said and took his mouth in a sensual kiss that made him dizzy.

"Whoa," he said and stumbled the rest of the way to his room. He set her on the mattress and followed her down. "You smell amazing," he said inhaling her scent. "You taste incredible," he said and dragged his tongue over her throat. "I want to be inside you all night long."

Her breath hitched again and she swung her legs around his hips. Sliding her fingers into his hair, she pulled his mouth to hers. "Do your best," she whispered and he thrust inside her.

Later that night, Bridget awakened, finding herself curled around Ryder. She was clinging to him. Her body said she wanted all of him, as much as he could give, as much as she could receive. But it wasn't just her body that craved him; some part deep inside her felt as if she belonged exactly where she was.

Her breath abandoned her. How was she supposed to manage this, this physical, yet highly emotional relationship with a man like Ryder? It wasn't even a man like Ryder. It was Ryder himself.

Ryder slid his thigh between hers, sending her sensual awareness of him into high mode. "You're awake," he said, sliding his arms around her. "You weren't planning on going anywhere, were you?"

"No. Just thinking."

"I'll put a stop to that," he said and distracted her again with his lovemaking. Afterward, she fell asleep.

The sound of a baby crying awakened her minutes later.... *Had it really been hours?* she wondered as she glanced at the alarm clock. Looking beside her, she saw that Ryder had already left the bed. The second baby started crying and she rose from the bed and pulled on one of Ryder's shirts. Thank goodness it covered her nearly to her knees because she'd left her own clothes downstairs.

She met Ryder in the hallway as he carried a baby in each arm. "Sorry our good-morning song woke you," he said with a wry, sleepy grin. His hair was sleep-mussed and a whisker shadow darkened his chin. Shirtless, he wore a pair of pajama pants that dipped below his belly button. She couldn't remember when he'd looked more sexy.

Reining in her thoughts, she extended her hands to take one of the twins. "I can help."

Tyler immediately fell toward her and she caught him in her arms.

"He made that decision pretty quickly. Can't fault his judgment," he said with a chuckle. "I already changed their diapers."

"Really?" she said, astonished.

"Don't look so surprised," he said as he led the way down the stairs. "My baby-care skills are improving."

"Congratulations," she said and put Tyler into one of the high chairs while Ryder slid Travis into the other high chair. She immediately put a few Cheerios on the trays while she prepared the bottles.

Ryder prepared the oatmeal. "You're getting faster at this baby stuff, too."

"I watched Suzanne one morning and took notes. She's so efficient."

"I'll be glad when she can come back," he said.

"Oh, speaking of that," she said. "The part-time sitter should be here any—"

A knock sounded at the door and Bridget felt a sliver of panic as she glanced at her bare legs and thought of her clothing strewn across the den. "Oh, bloody—Stefan will have my head. I'll be back in a couple moments," she said and grabbed her clothes and scrambled upstairs to get dressed. She glanced in the mirror and tried to tame her hair before she returned to the stairs.

Ryder met her halfway with an inscrutable expression in his eyes. "Embarrassed to be caught with an American doctor?"

"Not embarrassed so much as I wouldn't want my brother Stefan to find out. He really prefers we maintain a squeaky-clean image. And unfortunately we never know when someone may leak something to the press. That can turn into a huge mess."

"So you keep all your lovers hidden?" he asked.

"There haven't been that many," she said. "Do you really want paparazzi standing outside your door assaulting you with questions about me?"

"Good point," he said. "I'm going up to my study for a while. Dr. Walters's wife has asked me to write a eulogy for his memorial service."

Bridget's heart twisted at the grief Ryder was clearly trying to conceal. "I'm so sorry. Are you sure I can't do anything for you?"

His lips twitched. "You did a damn good job distracting me last night."

She felt her cheeks heat. "I was thinking of a cup of tea."

He shook his head. "I drink coffee. Breakfast would be nice, though."

She blinked. "Food. You want me to prepare food?" she echoed, at a loss. She'd taken one cooking class in her younger years and couldn't remember anything from it except how to put out a fire on a stove top.

He chuckled. "Sorry. I forgot your position, Your Highness."

She immediately felt challenged by his tone. "Well, it's not as if I can't prepare a meal. I just don't do it on a regular basis."

"When was the last time?" he asked.

She lifted her chin. "I prepared lunch for the twins just last week."

He laughed again, this time louder. "Bottles and jars of fruits and vegetables."

"They seemed to like it," she said. "Okay, what would you like for breakfast?"

"I'm guessing eggs Benedict would be too much to ask," he said.

She glowered at him.

"Okay. I'll go easy. Scrambled eggs, toast and coffee."

"I'll be right back with it," she said, muttering to herself as she continued down the rest of the stairs. This was ridiculous. Why should she care if Ryder considered her unskilled in the kitchen? He obviously respected her other talents such as organizing his childcare.

After a brief consultation with the sitter, however,

Bridget burned everything, even the coffee. She cleaned up her mess and started over, this time cooking everything on low. It seemed to take forever, but she finally got the job done and took the tray to Ryder's upstairs study.

He opened the door, wearing a distracted expression. "Thanks," he said, took the tray and closed the door.

She frowned, but took a breath. He was performing a difficult task. He needed understanding and patience.

Bridget went to his bedroom and arranged for a cleaning service. In her opinion, the house needed regular servicing. The sitters shouldn't be expected to clean in addition to keeping the twins. The twins were already a handful. An hour later, the cleaners arrived and she decided to take more coffee to Ryder.

She knocked on his door with the cup outstretched.

"Thanks," he said, still distracted as he accepted the cup. He closed the door again. She hesitated to interrupt, but thought it best to remove the dirty dishes, so she knocked again.

He opened the door, his eyebrows furrowed. "What?" he asked, almost in a curt voice.

"I thought I would take your dishes from breakfast," she said.

"Breakfast?" he said, his brow furrowing more.

"Yes, the eggs and toast you requested," she said.

"Oh," he said and went into his office. Seconds later, he returned with his uneaten eggs and toast.

"You didn't touch them," she said.

"Yeah, sorry. I'm really hung up over this eulogy."

Her frustration spiked. "I fixed these eggs and you didn't take a bite."

"I apologize. Really," he said, his face grief-stricken. In another instance, she would have screamed. But she knew Ryder was suffering.

"Fine," she managed in a tight voice. "What would you like for lunch?"

"Oh, anything. A ham sandwich. Thanks, *B*," he said and closed his door again. *B?* She'd never been called *B* in her life.

She helped the sitter with the boys, then took another trip to Ryder's study with a ham sandwich.

"Thanks," he said and accepted the sandwich.

"Are you okay?" she asked before he could close the door in her face.

He shook his head. "I'm not there yet." He leaned forward and pressed a quick kiss against her mouth.

After that brief meeting, Bridget left because she sensed Ryder needed his space and she was determined to respect it.

Ryder finally finished writing the eulogy. He had no idea what time it was until he glanced at the clock. 4:30 p.m. Whoa. Later than he intended. Good thing he'd cancelled all his appointments and that this wasn't a surgery day. Stretching his neck, he glanced around the room and noticed the sad-looking ham sandwich on the table on the other side of the room.

His heart swelled at the thought of Bridget bringing him food, reaching out to him. Taking the plate, he walked downstairs expecting to see the fresh, sexy face of Bridget Devereaux.

Instead he was greeted by Marshall.

"Hey, dude," he said. "How's it going?"

"Okay," he said. "The twins?"

"Down for a nap," Marshall said.

"Bridget?"

Marshall lifted a brow and smoothed back his hair with his hand. "She was here?"

"Yeah. She fixed me breakfast and a sandwich for lunch," Ryder said, frowning.

"Breakfast," Marshall repeated.

Reluctant to reveal details about his relationship with Bridget, he shrugged. "She showed up early. You should know. You told her about Dr. Walters. I was working on his eulogy."

Marshall winced. "Sorry, bro. I'm guessing she left a while ago. The sitter didn't say anything about her."

Ryder's gut tightened. "Okay, I guess she had other things to do."

"Well, she *is* a princess," Marshall said.

"Yeah," Ryder said.

"You're starting to fall for her, aren't you?" Marshall asked.

"Hell no."

Chapter Seven

"Dr. Walters was more than a brilliant doctor. He was a father figure to many of us who'd never known a father. He was an advocate at the same time that he demanded the best of every resident who crossed his path. He was the best man I've ever known," Ryder said and glanced at the large group who had gathered to remember Dr. Walters.

His gaze skimmed the crowd and stumbled over a classy young woman wearing a black hat and black dress. *Bridget.* Her presence gave him a potent shot of strength.

He continued with the rest of his eulogy, then made his way toward Bridget. The seat beside her was empty. Her eyes widened as he stepped in from the aisle.

"Thanks," he whispered, sitting down and clasping her hand between them.

"There was no other choice than to be here for you," she whispered.

His heart swelled at her words and he squeezed her hand, trying to remember the last time someone had been there for him like this. No expectation, just support and some kind of emotion close to love. Yet it couldn't be love, he told himself.

Her hand, however, sure felt great inside his.

A couple hours later, Ryder and Bridget joined Mrs. Walters for an afternoon meal. Dr. Walters's widow seemed to have aged a decade within the last year.

"You were his favorite," she said to Ryder, her eyes full of pain as she smiled. "He wasn't supposed to have a favorite, but he did."

Ryder's heart squeezed tight. "He was the father I never had. He challenged me and empathized with me. He made me want to be my best."

Mrs. Walters nodded. "He was an inspiring man."

"I'm lucky that he was my mentor," Ryder said.

Mrs. Walters nodded and frowned. "He was a wonderful, wonderful man. But we never had children. Our family life was always dependent on his schedule." She paused. "If there was one thing he might have changed before he…went away…" She swallowed over her grief. "I think he may have spent more time with his family. Me. His brothers and sister. Until he began to fade, he didn't realize how important relationships were." She closed her eyes for a moment, then shrugged. "I'm rambling." She patted Ryder's hand. "Never forget that you are more than that hospital. Never," she said.

Shaken by her fervent expression, he took a quick breath. "I won't," he said.

Within a half hour, he escorted Bridget to his car. "Come back to my house," he said.

She paused a half beat, then nodded. "Yes."

Moments later, they walked into his house. The sitter sat on the couch reading a book. "Hi," she said. "Everything go okay? The twins are sleeping and they've been no trouble."

"Good to hear it," he said. "I'm gonna change my clothes. Will you be here for a while?"

The sitter nodded. "I'm scheduled to be here till six. Then I have a class."

"Thanks," he said and turned to Bridget. "There's a place I want to take you."

"If it involves hiking or swimming, I'll need to change clothes," she warned him.

"You'll be okay."

Seven minutes later, he pulled in front of a waterfall fountain. Man-made but spectacular.

"It's beautiful," she said as they walked close to the fall and lifted her face to the spray. "Have you been here often?"

"Yes," he said, squeezing her hand.

"I can see why," she concluded and closed her eyes. "Whenever I have a few minutes near water, it reminds me of Chantaine. For all my complaining about being chained there the last year, I can't deny the effect water has on me. Makes me wonder if I have a gill somewhere. What about you?" she asked. "You've been landlocked most of your life, haven't you?"

"Yes, but I find that spending some time near water,

and I mean more than a shower or swimming pool, balances me out. Especially if something is bothering me."

"It's natural that Dr. Walters's passing would upset you," she said.

"It's more than that," he said. "Now that he is really gone, his position with the residents will need to be filled."

"You want it very much, don't you?" she asked.

Ryder felt torn in two completely opposing directions. "I feel a huge responsibility. The other doctor who would want the job comes off as callous. He doesn't care about helping residents with problems. His first instinct would be to cut them from the program. Dr. Walters probed deeper before making that kind of decision and he made himself available to residents for conference. The goal at our hospital is to approach the physician as a complete person so that he or she, in turn, treats the patient as a complete person."

"The doctors in your program are very fortunate to receive that kind of benefit, but based on what Dr. Walters's wife said, it must be difficult for the adviser to strike the balance as a complete person." She sighed. "In a different way, serving our country as royals can be an all-consuming proposition. Makes you wonder if there's such a thing as balance outside of a yoga class."

Her yoga reference made him smile. "How is it you can make me feel better on such a dark day?"

"One of my many delightful skills." She glanced again at the fountain. "Have you ever wanted to jump in one of these and get completely wet?"

"Yes," he said. "Where I was raised we had a small

fountain in the town in front of a bank. When I was a little boy, I jumped in it and stomped around. Got a paddling that kept me from sitting down for a week."

"Was it worth it?" she asked.

"Before and during, yes. Afterward no."

"I almost took the plunge once in Italy, but I knew I would be arrested and there would be a big fuss."

"So you restrained yourself," he said.

She frowned. "Yes, but one day. Maybe soon after I'm able to bring back some doctors to Chantaine and I take my long vacation in Italy..."

"Is that why you're in such a rush to import doctors?"

"Trust me, I've earned this break. Even Stefan agrees, but he and I both know Chantaine needs doctors. After my sister-in-law was injured so horribly while saving my life, it became even more clear. I still—"

The darkness in his eyes surprised him. "You don't still hold yourself responsible, do you?"

She paused a half beat too long. "Of course not. The gang stampeded her. Even security was taken by surprise," she said as if by rote.

"But you still feel responsible," he said.

"She wouldn't have been there if I hadn't begged her to join me," she said. "For someone to put her life on the line for me, and it wasn't as if she had taken an oath to protect me. She just did it because of who she is."

"And because of who you are," he said.

"Now that's a stretch," she said. "I spend a lot of time at charity events and school and business openings. It's not as if I'm in a research laboratory finding cures for dreadful diseases."

"No, but you're helping raise money for those

research scientists, and someone needs to do it. Don't underestimate your importance. You inspire people to give more than they usually would."

"Perhaps," she said, but clearly wasn't convinced. "Now I just need to find a way to inspire doctors to come to Chantaine. At least I've already got one specialist willing to hold seminars," she said, then shook her head. "But today isn't about me or Chantaine. It's about you, Ryder. How else can I help you with your grief?" she asked in a solemn tone.

His mind raced in a totally different direction down a path filled with hot kisses and hot bodies pressed against each other. He couldn't help but remember the sight of her naked body in his bed. He couldn't help but want her again.

Her eyes widened as if she could read his mind. "You're not serious," she said. "Men. Sex is the solution for everything."

"There are worse ways to deal with grief," he said.

"True, but with the sitter at your house, it would be difficult to indulge that particular solution," she said.

"You're right," he said. "I should get back to the hospital. I canceled my schedule for the rest of the day, but making up for a lost day is hell."

"Absolutely not," she said, then bit her lip. "I suppose we could go to my suite."

His gut twisted at the prospect of holding her again. He didn't understand his draw to Bridget. All he knew was that his life had seemed full of darkness and when he was with her, he felt lighter. With his demanding schedule, he felt as if he needed to snatch whatever stolen moments he could with her. "That's an invitation I can't imagine turning down," he said, sliding his fingers over a silky strand of her hair.

Her breath hitched and he found the response gratifying and reassuring. He was damn glad to know he wasn't the only one feeling this crazy attraction.

After an afternoon spent drowning his devils in Bridget's bed, a cell-phone alarm sounded.

"Time to go," Bridget said, then rubbed her mouth against his cheek and pulled away.

He caught her just before she rose from the bed. "What's the rush?"

"It's five-thirty. The sitter will be leaving at six," she said with a soft smile and pulled on a robe.

"Damn, it's that late?" He glanced at the alarm clock beside the bed to confirm her announcement and shook his head. He raked his hand through his hair. "Hey, come back to the house with me. We can get something delivered."

"I'm sorry, I can't. I have a previous commitment this evening. I'm attending a forum to promote the prevention of gang violence. As I'm sure you can imagine, this is a cause near and dear to my heart. The Dallas district attorney will escort me," she said.

Ryder's gut gave a vicious twist. He'd heard the current D.A. was quite the lady's man. "I'm guessing Corbin made those arrangements," he said, unable to keep his disapproval from his tone.

"I believe he did. I'm only using a part-time assistant while I'm in Texas, but the arrangements went through her. She left me a dossier on him, but I've been too busy to scan it."

"I can tell you what you need to know," he said rising from the bed. "Aiden Corbin was elected two years ago and is a hound dog when it comes to women."

"What exactly is a hound dog?" she asked.

Ryder scowled. "It's a man who will do just about anything to get women into his bed."

"Is that so?" she said and shot a sideways glance at him. "It seems to me I've met several *hound dogs* here in Dallas."

"Hey, I'm no hound dog. I'm a hardworking doctor trying to take care of my brother's twin babies."

"It's really hard for me to buy your defense with you standing naked in front of me," she said, her glance falling over him in a hot wave that made it hard for him to resist pulling her right back into bed.

"I'm not used to being with a woman who has to fight off my competitors with a stick," he said.

She blinked. "Competitors," she echoed. "That would suggest I view these men on the same level as you, which I don't."

"What level is that?"

She paused then frowned. "Different. Besides, I don't have to beat the men off with a stick. And you must remember their primary attraction to me is due to my title and perhaps the erroneous view that I'm loaded."

"You underestimate your appeal."

"Hmm," she said. "Minus my title, I'm extremely average."

"You're wrong," he retorted. "You're beautiful and talented. You're…magic," he said, surprising himself with his words. Even though they were all true, they weren't the kinds of things he would usually say.

Bridget paused. Her eyes shimmering with emotion, she threw herself against him and wrapped her arms around him. "That's the nicest thing anyone has ever said to me. I'm not sure I agree, but it's quite wonderful that you would actually think those things about me. Thank you, Ryder. I will cherish your words forever," she said, then pulled away.

Something about her thank-you reminded him that his relationship with Bridget was temporary. That was fine with him. Lord knew, with everything on his plate, he didn't have time for a real relationship with a woman. For that matter, he'd never taken time to have a *real* relationship with a woman. He'd always been too busy with his career. So this relationship was no different, he told himself, but something about that didn't settle right with him.

That night, after he'd tucked the twins into their cribs and watched the rest of the ball game, he half glanced at the local news. Just as he was about to switch the channel, a video of Bridget and the D.A. appeared.

"Her Royal Highness, Bridget Devereaux of Chantaine, accompanied Dallas's district attorney, Aiden Corbin, to a special discussion at the Dallas Forum tonight. Reporter Charles Pine reports."

"Your Highness, welcome to Dallas. I'm curious, how can a small, idyllic island like Chantaine have a gang problem?"

"My country is quite idyllic, and we're quite fortunate that we have only occasionally had problems with gangs. Still, there have been incidents, and we are always exploring ways to prevent such problems in the future. Mr. Corbin has generously offered to present his experiences and knowledge by visiting our country in the future."

"Sounds like a rough gig, Mr. Corbin," the reporter joked.

Corbin gave a wide smile that looked lecherous to Ryder. "The princess is being very generous with her public and charitable appearances while she visits our city. The least I can do is to share my expertise in return."

Ryder bet the D.A. wanted to share more than his expertise. His stomach burned from the pizza he'd eaten earlier. His cell phone rang and he saw the caller ID belonged to Marshall.

Ryder answered the call, but Marshall started talking before he could open his mouth.

"Hey, what's your babe doing with our slimeball D.A.?"

"It's just business," he said, grinding his teeth at the same time.

"Business with the horn dog of the century?" Marshall asked. "If she was my woman, I wouldn't let her anywhere near Corbin."

Ryder bit his tongue. He'd had the same strange primitive reaction, but he had to contain himself.

"Whoa," Marshall said after the short silence. "You didn't say anything. Does that mean she's fair game? Because I gotta tell you that's one sweet piece of—"

"Don't even think about it," Ryder said. "With a sharp knife, I could disembowel you in less than sixty seconds."

Marshall gave a dirty chuckle. "Gotcha. I was just

kidding. I'm focused on someone else. I could tell something was cooking between the two of you. The way you
act about her. The way she acts about you."

"What do you mean the way she acts about me?"

"Well, she's busted her royal ass trying to make sure
your boys have got good care," Marshall said. "Speaking
of good care, I took a bucket of chicken to your nanny
the other day. Seemed the charitable thing to do."

"You took food to Suzanne?" Ryder said. "I told you
to leave her alone."

"It was just chicken. She's been recovering, for God's
sake. Give the poor girl a break," Marshall said.

Ryder narrowed his eyes. "You don't deliver chicken
unless you're hoping for something for yourself."

"I'm insulted," Marshall said. "I can be a nice guy.
Listen, I don't have time for this. I'll just tell you that
you might want to keep an eye on your little princess
because Aiden Corbin is known for poaching. G'night,
Mr. M.D."

Ryder opened his mouth to reply, but he knew Marshall had clicked off the call. Marshall had always called
him Mr. M.D. when he thought Ryder was getting too
big for his britches. Trouble was, what Marshall had said
about Corbin was right. The other trouble was Ryder
had no real claim on Bridget, so the only thing left for
him to do was stew. No way, he told himself. There was
no good reason to stew over a temporary woman. He'd
never done it before, and he wasn't going to start now.

Bridget left two messages on Ryder's cell during the
next two days, but he hadn't answered. She worried that
something may have happened. What if there'd been

a problem with the nanny? Had his workload tripled as a result of Dr. Walters's death? She already knew he'd been reluctant to touch base with her when things weren't going well, so she decided to make a quick trip to his office at the hospital.

He was in a meeting with a resident, but just as she started to leave a message with his assistant, the resident exited his office.

"I'll let him know you're here," his assistant said.

Another moment later, Ryder opened his door. "Come in," he said.

Wondering at his abrupt tone, she entered his office and watched as he closed the door behind her. "I was concerned when I didn't hear back from you. Is everything okay with you and the twins?"

"No problem," he said. "Suzanne returned to work and the boys seem to be fine."

She frowned at how remote he seemed. "Are you sure you're okay? You seem—"

"Busy," he said in a firm voice.

"Well, I didn't mean to bother you," she said.

"I have another two or three minutes," he said.

Her jaw dropped of its own volition. "Excuse me?"

"I said I have another two or three minutes. Then I need to go to a meeting."

"Why are you acting this way?" she demanded.

"What way?"

"As if we're strangers," she said. "As if we've never shared a bed."

His eyes suddenly darkened with turmoil. "We don't have a committed relationship."

Bridget's heart twisted. She felt as if he'd slapped her. "Does that mean you have to act rude and uncaring?"

He paused. "No, but we both know this isn't a long-term relationship. You have your reasons. I have mine. There's no need to pretend anything different."

If she felt he'd slapped her before, she now felt he'd stabbed her. "I wasn't pretending. I was just caring," she said. "Clearly a mistake," she said and turned toward the door.

He grabbed her arm just before she reached the doorknob.

She turned, feeling more confused than she could remember in her life. "Why are you acting this way?"

"Our relationship isn't normal," he said.

"Well, you're not normal and neither am I, so why should it be?"

"I have no right to comment on what men you spend time with," he said

Realization swept over her. "Oh, for bloody sakes, is this about the D.A.?"

"Saw you on the news," he said. "He was trying hard."

"And got nowhere," she said. "Do you really think I would hop into bed with him after I'd just been with you? Do you really think I would hop into bed with anyone? You must think I'm the most promiscuous woman ever born."

"You get a lot of offers," he said and she could see he was torn. He was accustomed to being in control and now he wasn't.

"I get offers because I'm a princess, not because I'm me," she said.

"Not—"

She shook her head. "Okay, we'll have to agree to disagree. Again. The point is I haven't engaged in a meaningless affair, well, ever," she said. "It's just not my nature. And my affair, I'm not sure I like that word. My relationship with you isn't meaningless. I don't exactly know what it means because you and I seem to be headed in different directions. But I'm incredibly drawn to you. I can't explain it and I don't particularly like it. It's bloody well inconvenient, but damn it, you're important to me."

He stared at her for a long moment, then gave a short, humorless laugh. "Ditto."

"What does that mean?"

"Exactly what you said. I'm willing to ride this horse to the end of this race if you are."

Bridget had to digest his words. She wasn't accustomed to such references.

"I mean we'll take it till the end and then kiss each other good-bye," he said.

The word good-bye bothered her, but she didn't feel as if she had any other choice.

"Deal?" he asked, extending his hand.

She slowly placed her hand in his. "Deal."

He pulled her against him. "Come over tonight," he said.

Her heart slammed against her rib cage. "I'd like to, but I have a previous engagement."

"Damn," he said. "Just tell me it's not with Aiden Corbin."

She shook her head. "It's with the head of Pediatrics."

Ryder swore. "That's better?"

"You told me if I bring medical experts to Chantaine to do temporary training, then I'll have a better chance of attracting doctors."

"Why can't you choose old, married experts?" he grumbled.

She smiled. "Introduce me."

He lowered his head and gave her a long kiss that made her head spin.

When he pulled back, they were both breathing hard. "What about tomorrow night?"

"I have an engagement," she said. "But I'll rearrange it."

"Okay. Tomorrow night is another water class for the twins. I'll order takeout for us." He gave her a quick firm kiss. "You'd have more fun with me than the Pediatrics department head tonight."

Ryder arrived home a few minutes late that night to find Marshall's truck parked in front of his house. He opened his front door to find Marshall bouncing Tyler on his knee while Suzanne was changing Travis's diaper.

Tyler squealed. Marshall grinned. "Looks like somebody's glad to see you," he said and immediately handed the baby to Ryder.

Ryder's heart lifted at the baby's obvious joy and he kissed him on his soft cheek. Travis also gave an ear-splitting shriek.

Suzanne glanced up at him. "I've already fed them, but they're a little worked up. That may be due to Marshall," she said with a faintly accusing expression.

"Hey, I was just entertaining them until you got

home," Marshall said and picked up Travis. "I thought I'd try to give Suzanne a break from the heavy lifting."

Uh-huh, Ryder thought. "It's okay. I'm glad they're in a good mood. Can you give me a quick minute to talk to Marshall?"

"Of course," Suzanne said. "There's no rush. And if you want to change clothes, I can wait for that, too."

"Thanks," he said and gave a sharp jerk of his head to go outside to Marshall.

Ryder carried Tyler in his arms and Marshall carried Travis. "What the hell do you think you're doing?" Ryder demanded.

"Hey, I'm just helping out your nanny. You don't want another one to quit because of these wild boys, do you?"

"Suzanne had no intention of quitting. She's just recovering from her appendectomy," Ryder said.

"All the more reason for me to stop by and help her. These boys are getting bigger every day."

"She doesn't need your help."

"Says who?" Marshall challenged.

"Says me," Ryder retorted. "You just want to get into her pants."

Marshall shot him a quelling glare that would have worked with any other man.

Not Ryder. "Stay away from my nanny."

"You're just edgy because you're not getting any," Marshall said.

"That's none of your damn business," Ryder said.

"It is if it makes you act like a jerk," Marshall said, then sucked in a quick breath. "Listen, I like Suzanne. I think she likes me. I wanna give this a try."

"She's not your kind of woman," Ryder said.

"Well, maybe I've been going after the wrong kind of woman."

Ryder groaned. "If you wreck my nanny, I'll kill you."

"Give me a chance," Marshall said. "She is."

Ryder swore under his breath. "Okay, but if you mess up her mind..."

"Yeah, yeah, yeah," Marshall said. "When are you supposed to see your princess again? For the sake of all of us, I hope it's soon."

Filled with misgivings, Ryder watched his nanny drive off in Marshall's wake to a restaurant. Maybe he was just jealous, a voice inside him said, and he brushed it aside. The boys were rowdy and demanding and absorbed every ounce of his energy by the time they fell asleep.

When he awakened the following morning to the sound of Travis screaming at the top of his lungs, he could have sworn it was the middle of the night. Instead, it was 6:30 a.m.

Stumbling into the twins' bedroom, he picked up the baby and held him against him. "Hey, bud, what's up? You're okay."

Travis's cry melted to a whimper, and Ryder sensed the baby was missing his real father and mother. The thought twisted his gut. Poor kid would never know his real dad and mom. He was stuck with Ryder, and Ryder knew he would never be the father his brother would have been.

Chapter Eight

Later that morning, Ryder joined the chief of staff with Dr. Hutt in a meeting to discuss the future of the adviser program.

"There's been some debate over how we should continue this program in the future now that Dr. Walters is no longer with us," the chief of staff said.

"It's one of the things about our program that makes it distinctive and appealing to residents," Ryder said. "I can't imagine changing it."

"I agree that the program should continue," the chief said. "But Dr. Walters was one of a kind and we may need to make changes."

"Not if those changes will negatively impact the residents," Ryder countered.

"The residents needed to be toughened," Hutt said. "They've chosen the medical profession. It's a demanding field, so they need to be ready to take on their jobs.

Long hours and dedication to excelling in their fields are critical."

"They also need to deal with their patients as individuals. We enforce that teaching by treating them as individuals," Ryder said, feeling his back get up, ready for a fight.

"You're too soft on them," Hutt said.

"You treat them like a machine because that's how you treat your patients," Ryder said.

"Gentlemen," the chief of staff intervened. "There's no need for insults."

Ryder resisted the urge to glare at him and took a quick breath. "Forgive me," he said. "But Dr. Walters was very important to me. It would be an insult to him if I didn't present his point of view in this discussion."

"And you think I'm not," Hutt said. "Dr. Walters was my adviser, too. I worshipped the ground he walked on. What he taught me was the importance of discipline."

Ryder couldn't disagree. Discipline was critical to a doctor's success. "I've never disagreed with the importance of discipline, but Dr. Walters also emphasized to me to remember the human element."

"You're both right," the chief said. "And you've both clearly demonstrated your superior ability as medical doctors. The difficulty is that Dr. Walters spent an unbelievable amount of time counseling residents at the same time he managed his patient load. There was rarely a time he wasn't here at the hospital. Neither of you can make that kind of time commitment."

"I have a very understanding wife."

"I have a perfect nanny."

"Therefore," the chief of staff said. "I am going to assign both of you as intern advisers."

That sounded like a horrible idea to Ryder. "I can't imagine that Dr. Walters would approve."

"Unfortunately, Dr. Walters isn't here to give his advice. I agree that the advisership is one of the unique features of our program, but I can't in good conscience assign the total advisership to you, Dr. McCall, given your new family obligations."

"The two of you will have to work together or I will find new advisers," the chief continued. "The three of us will meet in two weeks."

Ryder led the way out the door, barely resisting the urge to slam it shut behind him. "This is a joke," he muttered.

"Hey, I don't want to work with you either. Just because you were Gordon's favorite doesn't mean the rest of us didn't see how great he was. And don't try to deny it. How did you get the financial relief you needed when your mother was dying?" he challenged.

Ryder's fingers itched to punch Hutt in his face. "He pointed me in the direction of several teaching opportunities. One of them worked out. It was that or wait tables. How did *you* get through med school?"

"You know how I got through. My parents paid for me. I started partying a little too much once I graduated and he told me I had to toe the line or go somewhere else. Rode my butt every time I walked into the hospital. I learned the hard way the importance of discipline."

"I did, too. I just learned it about ten years earlier than you did because I had to," he said and turned away.

Hutt caught his arm. "Just curious, what would it

take for you to give up the advisership and let me take it over?"

"A miracle," Ryder said.

"Too vague. I can't shoot for that," he said.

His colleague's response took him by surprise. "You gotta understand the guys who don't have parents who can pay their way. You gotta understand the guys who don't get into school because their daddy knows somebody. I'm not sure you can get there. Ever."

"You're an ass," Hutt said.

"So are you," Ryder said.

"Maybe that's why the chief is making us work together."

"Unless he's hoping we'll kill each other," Ryder muttered and went to his office.

That night, although Ryder physically did everything the teachers instructed them to do with the babies, Bridget could tell his mind was somewhere else. She tried not to focus on it as she watched Tyler put his face in the water and blow bubbles.

"Good boy," she said, praising the baby. "Good for you. Such a brave, brilliant boy."

Travis must have taken a competitive cue because he plunged his face in the water and lifted it, choking. Frightened, he began to cry.

"Oh no, that water went down the wrong way," she said, passing Tyler to Ryder and holding out her hands for Travis. "Poor thing. No need to go diving," she gently chastised him. "Watch," she said and lowered her mouth to the water and blew bubbles.

Ryder followed her lead and blew bubbles, making a sound with his deeper voice.

Travis quickly dried up and stared.

"Do it again," she said.

Ryder repeated and Travis let out a belly laugh.

Bridget couldn't resist laughing, too. "What a brilliant sound," she said. "Do it again."

Ryder dipped his head and shot her a dark, mocking look. "Yes, Your Majesty." He blew bubbles and this time, both Travis and Tyler laughed.

"Well done," she said. "Just a couple more times."

"Want to give it another go?" she asked Travis. "We can do it together." She lowered her mouth to the water to blow bubbles. "Come on."

Holding him securely, she dipped his chin in the water. He made a motorboat sound with his lips. Slowly, she lowered his mouth and he made the same sound. Just before he breathed in water, she pulled up his chin, and again he let out a belly laugh.

"Good boy," she said. "Brilliant."

"You never say that to me," Ryder muttered.

"Perhaps you need to try harder," she retorted.

He groaned and she felt his gaze sweep over her body with a flash of instant need before he hid it. 'You could drive a man insane, Your Majesty," he said.

"Your Majesty is incorrect. If you're going to address me correctly, you should say Your Highness. Or if you want to irritate me, you could use the term my brother-in-law's housekeeper uses. Your Highliness."

"I like that," he said. "Has a nice ring to it. Your Highliness."

She scowled. "So what put you in a bad mood at

work? Did one of your patients develop a secondary infection?"

"Hell no," he said frowning. "How did you know something happened at work?"

She rolled her eyes. "Because you're here and not here at the same time. You do everything the teachers say, but you're not really here. Some women would be insulted."

"It's probably best if I'm not completely here because looking at you in that bathing suit could make things embarrassing for me when I step out of the pool. But because you asked, there are some complications with the resident advisory position. I have to deal with the equivalent of the M.D. devil."

She winced. "That can't be enjoyable. Then again, would he be easier to deal with than you?"

He shot her a deadly look. "If you don't mind dealing with someone who will lie to your face."

She frowned. "Bloody hell for both of us," she muttered under her breath.

The teacher ended the class and Bridget and Ryder climbed out of the pool with the boys. Bridget changed Travis's drenched diaper while Ryder changed Tyler's. "You and your brother are the most brilliant, fabulous boys in the world. Never doubt it," she said and rubbed her nose against Travis's.

The baby laughed and grabbed at her. Her heart twisted in her chest. "So sweet."

"You're good with them," Ryder said.

"Shocking, isn't it?" she said.

"I think both of them have a crush on you," he said, leaning toward her. "Or maybe all three of us."

She smiled, feeling a surprising flood of warmth flow inside her. "You think they really like me? I've never thought of myself as good with babies."

Travis pressed a wet, open-mouth kiss against her cheek.

"Yeah, they clearly hate you," Ryder said.

She sighed. "I never thought I could adore babies this much."

"Me either," he said, drawing Tyler against him. The baby snuggled against him. "Not sure about this father-hood thing. I didn't have the best example."

"Neither did I," she said. "He couldn't ever remember my name."

"You're joking," he said, disturbed by the complacent expression on her face.

She shrugged. "My mother's job was to reproduce. There were a bonus of girls. She stopped after the second son which was after Phillipa and me."

"You weren't close to your mom either, were you?" he guessed.

"Hers wasn't a happy marriage. My mother had high hopes when she married my father, but she ended up terribly disappointed. So yes, I'm ill-prepared to be a loving mother. The only part of my background that gives me hope is my siblings. Stefan and Tina were more like parents to me."

"I guess that's another thing we have in common. We didn't have the best parents in the world. We were just on opposite ends of the spectrum. Yours were royal. Mine were dirt-poor," he said. "How did I get lucky enough to have a princess half-naked in a pool with me?"

"And your twin boys," she added, laughing. "I'm glad they like me. It's amazing how they get under your skin."

"Yeah," he said, looking down at Tyler. "I just hope I can figure out how to keep them safe, happy and feeling like they can conquer the world."

"I think you will," she said. "If anyone can, you can."

"The great thing about the swimming class is that it totally wears out the boys and they sleep like babies should," Ryder said, sitting on the couch beside Bridget with his hand wrapped around hers. "The bad thing is that it wears me out, too."

She gave a low, throaty chuckle that grabbed at his gut. "Times ten," she said.

"If you're as tired as I am, then you better stay the night," he said.

She slid him a sideways glance. "My driver could take me home. It would be no problem."

"Maybe not for him, but it would be for me," he said, drawing her head toward his and taking her mouth in a long kiss.

When he pulled away, Bridget sighed. The sound was magic to him. He couldn't get enough of her and he hated himself for it, yet he couldn't avoid it.

"Does that mean you'll stay the night?" he asked. "I can promise I'll wake you up in the middle of the night."

She lifted her hand to the back of his head and drew his lips to hers. "Just do your best," she said and he vowed he would.

The next morning, Bridget awakened to the sound of babies crying and the sight of an empty bed. She'd stayed the night with Ryder, and he had apparently left early this morning. Pulling one of his shirts around her and buttoning it, she walked toward the nursery.

Walking inside, she nearly bumped into Suzanne.

"Oh, please excuse me," Bridget said, covering a yawn.

Suzanne yawned in response. "No problem," she said. "I arrived a little late and Dr. McCall left right out the door."

"He has a lot on his mind," Bridget said.

Suzanne nodded. "I can tell. You can go back to bed. I can handle the boys."

"No, I'll carry him downstairs," Bridget said, changing Travis, then picking him up and holding him against her. "No need to cry. You're probably still tired from all that swimming."

"They can steal your heart pretty quickly, can't they?" Suzanne asked, smiling at Bridget as she cuddled the baby.

"Yes, I never dreamed I could feel this much affection for two little semi-humans who spit peas at you, scream bloody murder and can get downright stinky. Whenever anyone asked me how I felt about babies, I always thought they were fine if they belonged to someone else."

"I was just the opposite," Suzanne said. "I wanted to have children, but I couldn't. My husband felt the same way. That's a big part of the reason he left."

Saddened by Suzanne's confession, Bridget frowned as she followed the nanny downstairs. "But there are other ways, adoption, surrogacy…."

"He wanted children the natural way," Suzanne said.

"I'm sorry. It was clearly his loss. I have to believe there's a better man in your future," Bridget said.

Suzanne's cheeks turned pink. "Maybe, but I'll never marry again. The ending was just too painful. What about you? Is marriage in your future?" she asked as if she wanted the attention diverted away from her.

Bridget blinked, uncomfortable with the question, so she gave her automatic response as she put Travis into a high chair. "No time soon. Italy is calling me first, and then we'll see."

"What about Dr. McCall?"

"Oh, he's not interested in marriage. He has his hands full with the boys and his practice and the residents at the hospital. I'm certain it's not in his plans to marry anytime soon."

"Plans can change in an instant," Suzanne said. "I bet he didn't plan to be a daddy to twins either."

"So true," Bridget agreed, growing more uncomfortable with the conversation with each passing second. "It's definitely been a shock. That's enough of an adjustment without adding a wife into the mix."

"Hmm," Suzanne said as if she didn't quite agree but wouldn't say more.

Bridget felt a rush of relief. "Can you handle the feeding? I'd like to take a shower."

"No problem. Take your time," Suzanne said.

As Bridget stepped under the warm spray of water in Ryder's shower, she smelled the scent of his soap and felt surrounded by him again. She wondered if she and Ryder were making a mistake by becoming involved. She preferred the notion that her attraction to him was strong but temporary; however, between her surprising, growing feelings for the babies and her assignment to set up a program for doctors to Chantaine, their relationship was complicated at best.

Bridget dressed and allowed her hair to air-dry with the plan to perform her daily makeover at her hotel suite. She lingered at Ryder's house, playing with the twins until her phone rang and it was Stefan.

Her stomach sank with dread at the prospect of talking to her brother. So far, she'd successfully avoided speaking to him directly by keeping him apprised via email. Stefan was a wonderful, good-intentioned but interfering brother, and because he was crown prince, he could get more than a bit bossy. His new wife, Eve, had helped to rein him in, but the man had been born to rule. Some traits could never be eradicated.

"Hello, Stefan. My, you're up late. How are you?" she asked, moving away from the twins so he wouldn't hear them in the background.

"I'm fine. I need to discuss the progress with the doctor program—"

Tyler let out a loud scream as Bridget left his sight. Bridget winced, walking quickly toward one of the downstairs bathrooms and closing the door.

"What was that? It sounded like a wild animal," he said.

Close enough, she thought ruefully. "It was a baby. I guess it's naptime. Now, regarding the doctor program, I've hit a snag with—"

"Baby," he echoed. "What are you doing with a baby? You don't like children."

"I don't dislike children," she said. "I've just never spent much time with them. That was a twin infant I met by chance. I've gotten to know the family because they've had a bit of a crisis. Everything is headed in the right direction now, though. About the doctors for Chantaine—"

"This wouldn't be one of Dr. Ryder McCall's twin nephews, would it? Valentina told me you've been spending quite a bit of time with Dr. McCall and his children."

Valentina had snitched on her. She would have to be more careful what she said to her sister. "It turns out Dr. McCall is the resident adviser for the Texas Medical Center. I've been trying to persuade him to participate in our program, but he says that working on Chantaine isn't prestigious enough because we don't already have any specialized programs or research in place."

"Chantaine, not prestigious enough," he said, his tone dripping with fury.

Bridget had indicated that she'd not made as much progress as she wanted because the head adviser was ill and the hospital was undergoing transition, which was partly true. She'd hoped she wouldn't have to tell Stefan the full truth because she'd known he would be offended. "I reacted the same way. Told him he was the most insulting man I'd ever met. Now to accomplish my task, I'm stuck trying to get him to compromise," she said with sigh.

Silence followed. "Bridget, you're not trying to use seduction as a way of convincing the man, are you?"

Bridget laughed, partly from hilarity, partly from hysteria. If Stefan only knew. Heaven help her if he did. Then again, Raoul would talk if pressed. "If only it were that easy," she said. "The man is almost as stubborn as you are," she said.

Another silence passed, and Bridget could feel her brother's tension through the phone line. "That doesn't bode well for our plan. You've begun to approach other hospitals."

"Yes, I have, but I'm getting similar, though more politely worded, responses. Because of that, I've begun to invite various high-level doctors to Chantaine to conduct training and seminars. So far, three doctors have committed."

"Excellent," he said. "We may need to expand our search."

"I know. I'm hopeful that if I can recruit some additional specialists that we'll be able to overcome the objections of our top choices for hospitals," she said.

"Bridget," he said. "I know that part of the reason you feel strongly about this is because of what happened to Eve," he said.

"Of course I do. Thank goodness she received the care she needed in time."

"I feel the same way. Just keep your meetings businesslike," he said.

Bridget frowned. "What do you mean?"

"I mean, you can be charming and you're young and attractive. These men could become enamored with the idea of seducing a princess. I wouldn't want your reputation to suffer as a result of any misplaced determination."

"Now, I believe I'm insulted. Do you really believe I'm so easily swayed? And do you think this is the first time I haven't had to put up with unwanted advances?"

"There's no reason for you to be insulted. I'm just looking out for you. What do you mean, unwanted advances?" he demanded. "Raoul is supposed to stay on top of that."

"Unless you have something further to say that could be construed as helpful, I believe we've spoken long enough. I have things to do as I'm sure you do, too."

"Bridget, do not hang up on me. I'm not finished," her brother commanded.

She was tempted to push the button to disconnect. So tempted that her finger itched. "I'm waiting," she finally said.

"Phillipa is coming to Texas for a visit," he announced. "She's been acting depressed for the last few weeks and she's had a terrible time working on her dissertation. Eve thinks getting away from Chantaine and taking a break from her studies will help her."

Her stomach twisted in concern. "You don't think she's ill, do you?"

"No, she's been checked out by the royal doctors, but after Ericka's drug problems, I can't take any chances."

Alarm shot through Bridget. Her sister Ericka had become dependent on drugs and spent more than one stint in rehab. Thank goodness, she'd left her problems behind and she was now happily married to her French film-director husband. "I can't believe our Pippa would get involved with drugs. Not after how much all of us suffered when Ericka was having her problems."

"I don't think she is, but she's lost weight and seems miserable and distracted. A change of pace will refresh her."

"Between Valentina and me, we'll do our best," she promised.

"The initial plan is for her to spend most of her time at the ranch, but I'm sure she'll come into Dallas for a visit," he said.

"Yes," she said. "Thank you for letting me know. And how are Eve and Stephenia?"

"Eve is wonderful. Stephenia is a terror, but I swear I think she's already learning to read. Still quite demanding that I read to her every night if at all possible," he said, his tone a mixture of exasperation and tenderness.

"You're a lucky man, Stefan, to have a wife and daughter who love you," she said, then couldn't resist adding, "along with your loyal, subservient siblings."

He gave a short laugh. "Yes to both, although my siblings will never be subservient."

"It's not in our genes," she said. "Give my love to Eve and Stephenia."

"I will. And Bridget," he said, "if you can't work things out with this Dr. McCall soon, we'll move past him and onto someone more cooperative."

Bridget's stomach twisted at the thought. "I hear what you're saying."

"Good," he said. "All for now. We'll talk soon."

Bridget took a deep breath as the call was disconnected. Her mind raced with thoughts about Phillipa, Ryder and the twins, and her assignment to recruit new doctors to Chantaine. She grew dizzy under the opposing priorities and returned to the den with the idea of heading outside to clear her head.

On her way, however, Travis screeched at her.

"His version of hello?" she said to Suzanne.

"I think so," Suzanne said. "It's time for their morning nap and Tyler is almost there. Travis is next."

"I'll take him," Bridget said and went to the blanket on the floor to pick up the baby. "How are you doing, mister?"

He made an unintelligible sound and plastered his open mouth against her in a wet baby kiss.

Her heart turned over. "You're such a flirt," she accused in a voice she knew was far too affectionate.

He put an open-mouth kiss against her cheek again.

"Too much," she said and cuddled him.

Travis snuggled against her and sank his head against her throat. He sighed and seconds later, his breathing became more regular. Another half minute and she felt drool sliding down her neck.

It was the sweetest moment of her week. Or month. Or longer.

"You have a calming effect on him," Suzanne whispered. "He looks like he could sleep right there against you forever."

Travis sighed against her skin and she felt the terrible urge to tear up. Heaven help her, she needed to get her emotions under control.

Travis wiggled again and clung to her as if she were the most important person in the world. Her heart dipped at the way the baby made her feel. He was so vulnerable. She wanted to take care of him, make him feel safe…. Yet, he wasn't her baby.

Bridget savored his baby scent and the sensation of his healthy, chubby baby body in her arms. What an addictive combination. She wanted to hold him until nighttime…or later… Is this what happened to parents?

Perhaps this is why babies survived. They made you want to take care of them. Forever.

It took another few moments in the rocking chair, but Bridget finally decided Travis could hit the sack. She carried him upstairs to the nursery and gently placed him in his crib. Tyler was already asleep. Travis was the fussier baby. That should have made him less desirable, but Bridget considered it a challenge to comfort him and help him fall asleep.

"Very good for a princess," Suzanne said from the doorway. "Are you sure you don't have some magic you're hiding in your back pocket?"

Flattered, Bridget quietly stepped from the room and pulled the door shut behind her. "You should know better. The only magic with babies is if they feel safe."

"They both feel safe with you," Suzanne said.

Bridget's heart twisted. What did all of this mean? "I should go. I have appointments and phone conferences."

"Princess things to do," Suzanne said with a gentle smile.

Bridget nodded. "But if you have a problem with the twins, call me."

Suzanne sighed. "You hired me to take care of the twins. Yet you feel you need to help. Why is that?"

Bridget's stomach clenched again. "I'm not any kind of expert. It's like you said earlier. They sneak up on you and grab your heart."

Chapter Nine

After Bridget finally tore herself away from the babies, she threw herself into her task of soliciting visiting medical experts for Chantaine. It irritated her when the experts laughed off her proposal, but she persevered and won two maybes and one new definite yes for her efforts.

Between her schedule and Ryder's, they only managed text messages and a few phone calls. Although she was tired by bedtime, she was surprised at how much she missed Ryder and the boys. Just as she fell asleep, her cell phone rang. Her heart skipped at the caller ID.

"Hello," she said.

Before she could say another word, he said. "Dinner. Tomorrow night. 7:00 p.m. No excuses. It's been too long."

She laughed, crazy thrilled to hear his voice. "Oh my. Is it a doctor thing that you give orders like a royal?"

"Maybe," he said. "I can't talk. I've got to check on a patient," he said.

"This late?" she asked and heard the sound of voices in the background.

"He's diabetic and he's experiencing some complications from surgery. I'll stay another hour to make sure he's stable. Tomorrow night, I'm taking you out."

The next morning, soon after Bridget awakened, she received a call from her sister Tina. "We're coming to town for dinner tonight. You must join us."

"Oh no. I'm sorry, but I already have a commitment," Bridget said, immediately feeling edgy because she knew Tina had talked to Stefan.

"Is it business or pleasure? Because if it's pleasure, we can all go out together," Tina offered.

Bridget paused. Her dinner with Ryder promised pure pleasure, but if she discussed Chantaine's medical program, it could be construed as business.

"I can tell by your hesitation that it's pleasure," Tina said before Bridget could pull an excuse together. "We'll pick you up for a six-thirty dinner at the Longhorn Club."

"It'll have to be a 7:00 p.m. dinner," she automatically corrected. "Ryder has already set the time and I'm sure he'll be busy going from the hospital, home and back out again. In fact, this may not be such a good idea after all. He's extremely busy lately. I haven't seen him myself in three days."

"Three days," Tina repeated. "If that's such a long gap of time between your dates, then I would say the two of you are getting quite cozy. All the more reason for me to meet him."

Resenting her sister's interference, Bridget frowned. "And which member of the royal family gave your husband Zachary the stamp of approval while the two of you were seeing each other?"

"None, but my pregnancy put a different spin on the situation—" Tina gasped. "You're not pregnant, are you?"

"Of course not," Bridget said.

"But the two of you must be serious for you to get all snippy with me," Tina continued. "The only way you can disprove it is if you and your doctor meet Zach and me for dinner tonight. Ciao, darling," she said and hung up.

Bridget swore at the phone and tossed it on her bed. She didn't want to share Ryder with her sister or anyone else at the moment. She was appalled to admit, only to herself, that she'd missed Ryder and the twins terribly during the last few days. It had taken every bit of her self-control not to dash over to his house to hold the babies or to visit Ryder at the hospital. She knew, however, that she was growing entirely too attached to all three males. And now Ryder would have to face an inquisition from both her sister and her brother-in-law. She wouldn't blame Ryder if he ran screaming.

Deciding to give him the easy way out, she sent him a text message. *Change of plans. My sister and her husband insist we join them for dinner. I'll understand if you can't join us.*

When he didn't immediately answer, she suspected he was trying to word his response and took a shower, feeling glum, bordering pouty. Amazing how one phone call from her nosy sister could send her mood into the pits. When she got out of the shower, her cell phone dinged to indicate a message.

I'm in. Where?

Her heart turned cartwheels and she gave him the name of the restaurant along with a warning that her sister's interrogation could rival the American's CIA. Although she much preferred sharing an evening with Ryder without the company of her sister, she couldn't deny she was excited to get to see him, period.

That night, Bridget fought a surprising spate of nerves on the way to the restaurant. "Tell us more about your doctor," Tina said.

"You'll meet him soon enough," she said. "He's very work-oriented, but he's making adjustments now that he's the guardian for his twin infant nephews." She deliberately changed the subject. "Stefan told me Phillipa will be coming for a visit soon. He sounded worried. Have you had a chance to talk with her?"

"I've called, but she hasn't returned my call, which has me concerned. What about you?"

"I just left a message telling her I was looking forward to seeing her. She may need to relax a little before she's ready to talk. I didn't want to put any more pressure on her. I wondered if it was related to her studies, but Phillipa has always thrived under academic pressure."

"I think a little quiet time at our ranch will help her and we can come into town for a little fun. Of course, you could spend more time at the ranch, too," Tina said in a pointed voice.

"I have a task to complete and I can't do it from the

ranch," Bridget said, refusing to give in to her sister's dig. "Now I'm in the process of trying to lure medical specialists to come to Chantaine so we can attract more medical doctors to our program."

"And what about your Dr. McCall? How would he feel about visiting Chantaine?"

Bridget laughed at the thought, yet felt a twinge of sadness at the same time. "He's far too busy with his work at the hospital and with the twins. I can't imagine his even considering it."

"Oh, I don't know," Tina said. "Maybe because the two of you are so close—"

"Not that close," Bridget said flatly.

"If you're looking for doctors who would like to combine a vacation with teaching in Chantaine, I might know a few," Zachary offered.

"Oh, that would be fabulous. Please do let me know of any of your connections," Bridget said.

"Zachary recruited an obstetrician to the small town close to the ranch, so he might be able to give you some tips," Tina said.

"Part of it is finding the right person. Not every doctor wants to practice in a big city hospital. You may have your heart set on Texas Medical Center, but the truth is some highly qualified doctor in a backwater town might like the idea of spending some time on an exotic island with easy access to Europe."

"Thank you," she said, her mind already exploring possibilities. "I hadn't thought of that."

Tina squeezed her husband's arm. "What an intelligent, resourceful man."

"Well, I got you, didn't I?" he said and Bridget felt a

twinge of longing. How would it feel if Ryder acted the same way toward her? Biting her lip, she gave herself a hard mental shake. She had other plans. Italy beckoned.

She arrived at the exclusive restaurant and was seated with Tina and Zach. Ryder arrived fifteen minutes later, appearing distracted as he strode to the table. "Sorry," he said and leaned down to kiss her full on the mouth. "I've missed the hell out of you," he whispered.

He turned to Tina and Zach. "Your Highness," he said. "Your Highness's husband."

Both Tina and Zach chuckled. "Please call me Tina," she said.

"And I'm Zach," he said, rising to offer his hand.

"Excuse me if I'm checking my cell phone messages. I have a patient teetering on the edge tonight. He's diabetic and I would have preferred not to operate, but this wasn't an optional procedure."

"Is this the same patient you were watching last night?" Bridget asked.

"Yes," Ryder said. "He improved, but I'm concerned about circulation to his extremities."

Bridget automatically extended her hand toward his beneath the table. Ryder responding by clasping it against his knee. "If you need to leave," she began.

"I can stay for now. I just need to check my messages," he said.

"We're glad you could join us," Tina said. "You've certainly captured Bridget's attention and that's not easy to do."

Bridget fought a rise of heat to her cheeks. "Tina," she said.

"Really?" Ryder said. "That's encouraging news

because wherever she goes the men are chasing after her."

"I told you that's just because of my title," Bridget said.

"Not true," he said.

"Exactly," Tina said, and Bridget felt her sister study her intently.

Bridget picked up the menu. "I wonder what the specials are tonight."

The waiter took their orders, Ryder frequently checked his phone messages and even excused himself once to make a call.

"Is this what you want for your future?" Tina asked. "He's been half-focused on his phone throughout the entire meal."

"He could have cancelled, but he came. If someone important to you was in the hospital, wouldn't you want to know his doctor was this conscientious?"

Tina frowned. "I suppose. I just can't see you being happy with someone so intent on his career."

Bridget leaned forward. "Ryder and I haven't made any mention of commitment," she whispered. "We're just enjoying each other's company."

"As long as he's not enjoying the company too much," Zach said.

"I'm not pregnant, if that's what you're asking," she said.

"Low blow," Tina said.

"You deserve it," Bridget said, feeling pushed to the edge. "Stefan told me you tattled about me seeing Ryder. I would have expected better from you."

"It's my duty to look after you," Tina said.

"Isn't that the same thing Stefan said to you?" Bridget challenged.

Tina gasped in offense. "Well—"

Ryder reappeared at the table, relief written on his face. "Good news. My patient's condition is improving."

"Excellent news," Bridget said as the waiter cleared the plates from the table.

"Excellent," Tina agreed, though she shot Bridget a sharp look. "Bridget tells me you've recently taken over the guardianship of twin baby boys. That must have been traumatic for all of you. My sympathies on the loss of your brother and sister-in-law."

"Thanks," Ryder said. "Bridget has actually helped smooth the waters with the twins. She found a nanny who has been a perfect fit. Until she stepped in, I was scrambling. I had several quit on me. With my profession, I need dependable childcare."

"Well done, Bridget," Tina said, appearing impressed and vaguely surprised.

"Your friend Keely helped. She gave me the name of the top nanny agency in Dallas," Bridget said.

"But Bridget interviewed the candidates and selected the final choice," he said.

"Bridget isn't known for her affinity for babies," Tina said.

Thanks for nothing, Bridget thought.

"Neither am I," Ryder said bluntly. "But she stepped right in. She's been a lifesaver. The boys adore her."

"And what about you?" Tina asked. "What are your intentions?"

"Tina," Bridget scolded.

"It's a good question," Zach said, backing up his wife.

Bridget balled her fists in her lap. "You do not have to answer that question, Ryder."

Ryder placed his hand over hers underneath the table. "I don't mind answering. Bridget and I have just met. Neither of us know what the future holds. Based on the demands our lives place on us, I know our relationship is temporary."

Bridget's heart fell to her feet. Even though she agreed with Ryder's assessment, hearing the words wounded her to the quick. *She was temporary.*

The interminable meal finally ended fifteen minutes later. Ryder shook hands with her sister and brother-in-law, then brushed a kiss against the corner of her mouth. "Miss you," he murmured just for her ears. "Call me."

A few moments later, she sat in the back of her brother-in-law's SUV, still feeling shell-shocked.

"I can see why you like him," Tina said. "He's his own man and clearly isn't after you because you're royalty. Plus, it doesn't appear that he intends to keep you from going to Italy," she added with a low laugh.

Bridget couldn't muster the careless response she should have been able to toss back to her sister. Silence stretched inside the car.

"Bridget, are you okay? Why are you so quiet?" Tina asked, turning around to look at her.

Bridget thanked heaven for the darkness. "I'm just tired," she said.

"Are you sure? You were always such a night owl."

"I'm sure," she said, trying not to resent her sister for pressing Ryder. It had been so much easier for her when her relationship with Ryder had remained undefined. Some part of her must have craved the sense of possibility with him. He was so different from any man she'd ever known. Ryder and the babies almost made her rethink Italy.

Blessedly, Zach pulled in front of her hotel. Relief rushed through her. If she could just get upstairs without another inquisition. "It was so wonderful seeing both of you. Thank you for dinner," she said and stepped outside the car when the valet opened her door.

Tina rushed outside her door. "Bridget," she said, studying her face. "I know something is wrong."

"Nothing is wrong," Bridget said, pushing a strand of her hair behind her ear. "I told you I'm just tired."

"I don't believe you," Tina said. "I can sense you're upset."

Bridget lost her patience. "Why should I be upset? You just grilled my boyfriend and me. I had a perfectly wonderful evening planned with him, but instead we went to dinner with you and might as well have been sent to walk across coals."

She watched her sister's face fall in desolation. "I'm so sorry," Tina said. "Zach and I just wanted to make sure this man wasn't going to take advantage of you."

"Would you have wanted Zach to receive the same kind of grilling you gave me?"

"I didn't know you felt the same way about Ryder that I felt about Zach," Tina said.

"It doesn't matter how you judge my feelings. It matters how I judge my feelings. I'm an adult. I don't need my sister, brother, brother-in-law and everyone else legislating or judging who I see." She lifted her chin. "Have a little faith in me for a change."

Tina's eyes turned shiny with tears. "Oh, I'm so

sorry. I did the same thing to you that I didn't want done to me."

Bridget took a quick sharp breath. She hated to hurt her sister, but Bridget needed Tina to believe in her. Just a little. "Yes, you did. Do you really believe I'm so stupid that any man can get my attention?" she asked, then continued before her sister could continue. "I know I acted like a spoiled brat when I had to come back from Italy after two weeks to cover for you, but I still came back and I still covered. I'm not a total ditz."

"Oh, Bridget," Tina said, shaking her head and clasping Bridget's hands. "I never thought you were a ditz. I always knew you were underestimated. I owe you a huge debt for stepping in for me and also dealing with Stefan. I just don't want you to be hurt."

Bridget bit the inside of her lip. Too late for that, she thought. "I won't be," she reassured her sister and gave her a hug.

"Don't be mad at me," Tina whispered.

"I'm not," Bridget said.

"Promise?" Tina asked.

"Promise," Bridget said.

"You'll never bring another man around me, will you?" Tina asked.

"It'll be a while," Bridget said with a rough laugh. "I need to hit the sack. Long day tomorrow. I love you." She waved to Zach and gave her sister one more hug, then walked inside the hotel toward her suite. When she got inside, she collapsed on her bed and gave in to her tears.

Bridget soldiered through her appointments the next day. Just after four-thirty as she was headed back to her hotel to change for a dinner appearance, she received a call from Suzanne.

"Your Highness, I probably shouldn't call you, but I thought you should know," the nanny said in a tear-filled voice.

"What is it? What's wrong?" Bridget asked.

"It's Travis. His fever shot up to 105 degrees," she said. "We had to take him to the hospital because it was too late for the pediatrician."

Bridget's heart sank to her feet. "Where is Ryder?"

"He's at the hospital," she said. "In the emergency room with a pediatric specialist." She gave a muffled sob. "I'm at Ryder's with Tyler."

She fought the urge to hyperventilate. Nothing could happen to that baby. Nothing. "I'm going to the hospital."

"Ryder didn't tell me to call you," Suzanne said.

"Well, he bloody well should have," Bridget said and told her driver to head for the hospital.

Ryder had never felt so helpless in his life as he watched his nephew, now his son, suffer the tests necessary to make him well. Travis screamed at the top of his lungs. "I'm sorry, Dr. McCall, but I think we're going to need to do a spinal tap."

Sweating everything but blood, Ryder nodded. "Do what you have to do to make him well." Ryder was well aware that Travis's condition was deteriorating. He couldn't remember feeling this kind of terror ever before.

After the spinal, Ryder heard a ruckus outside the examination room. A nurse entered. "I'm sorry, but there's a woman outside. She says she's a princess. She insists to be allowed inside with you and your son."

The nurse may as well have hit him with both fists. *She's a princess.* It was Bridget. A crazy sliver of relief slid through him. *Your son.* The words echoed inside his brain over and over. "Let her in," he said.

Seconds later, Bridget burst into the room wearing a hospital gown. She glanced from him to Travis, who was curled up exhausted on the table. Ryder would have preferred his cranky cries to his silence. He touched the baby's arm.

Bridget touched Ryder's.

Struggling with a terrible sense of desperation, he covered her hand with his.

"Can I hold him?" she asked.

"Not yet." They'd been instructed to wait to hold Travis, who was hooked up to an IV.

"He's going to be all right," she said softly as she held Ryder's hand. "He's a strong baby."

"He's always the one to cry the loudest and the longest," Ryder said, surprised at the strength of the fear he was fighting. Medically, he understood everything that was being done, but some part of him felt it wasn't enough. There had to be more. There had to be a way.

A few more moments passed. Bridget squeezed his hand and took a deep breath. "Can we hold him now?" she asked the nurse when she entered the room.

"For just a few moments," she said. "Take care for his IV."

Bridget sat and held Travis. His vital signs showed less stress within a moment of her cuddling him. Ryder took his turn holding the baby a while later and he was surprised to see he had the same effect on him.

Sometime later, the pediatrician strode into the room. "Lab results are back. Strep," he said. "With antibiotics, he'll be better in no time."

"Are you sure?" Bridget asked. "He seems so listless."

The pediatrician smiled gently. "With the right treatment, these little guys recover so quickly they make me look like a miracle worker. You just need to make sure everyone who's been exposed to him receives preventative treatment, too."

"Tyler," Bridget said to Ryder.

"And Suzanne and the other sitters. Thanks, Carl," he said to the pediatrician. "I know you stayed late for this. I owe you."

"I'm glad it was so easy," he said and glanced at Bridget. "And I don't believe I've met your wife."

Ryder felt a twist of awkwardness, but rushed to correct his colleague for Bridget's sake. "She's not my wife, but we've been damn lucky to have her around. This is Bridget Devereaux."

Carl nodded. "You clearly have a calming effect on the baby. You must be a natural."

Bridget laughed wryly. "I'm not sure I'd call myself a natural, but I'm relieved Travis will be okay. Thank you so very much."

"No problem. We'll have him stay the rest of the night. I wouldn't be surprised if he'll be ready to be released by midday. I'll talk to you later," he said and headed out the door.

Ryder stared at Bridget tenderly holding his nephew, his child, as if Travis were her own child. Something

inside him shifted. Stone walls he'd long considered
closed cracked open and he felt a burst of sweet oxygen
in places that had felt dead. The expansion inside him
was almost painful. For a second, he looked away to
gather his defenses, to put himself back together the
way he needed to be.

When he looked at her again, he saw a tear drop
from her eye to Travis's gown. She gave a quick sound
of distress and swiped at her cheek.

The sight of her tears shocked him. Bridget was no
crybaby. "Are you okay?"

"I apologize," she said, not lifting her head. "I was
just so frightened for him. And I felt so helpless."

He couldn't not reach out to her. Pushing her hair
from her cheek, he felt the dampness of her tears against
the back of his fingers. "Yeah," he said. "Me, too."

She finally met his gaze. "They're so fragile. One
minute, he was screaming bloody murder and trying to
scoot to get a ball, and the next...this," she said, looking down at Travis as he slept, his energy clearly spent
fighting his infection.

Moved more than he'd thought possible, Ryder kissed
her cheek. "Thank you for coming."

"There was no other place more important for me to
be," she said and met his gaze again.

The powerful emotion he saw in her gaze resonated
inside him so strongly that it took his breath. What the
hell was going on? Later, he told himself. He would
figure it out later. For the moment, his priorities were
perfectly clear. Travis and Bridget.

Just as Carl predicted, within hours, Travis began to
make a miraculous recovery. He downed a bottle and

afterward seemed to be looking for the rest of the meal. "They told us to go slow on the solids," Bridget said as she fed the baby some applesauce.

"But he looks like he's wanting a steak dinner," Ryder said, pleased with Travis's improvement.

Bridget laughed. "I agree, but he won't be getting that from me."

"He won't be getting that from anyone, no matter how cranky he gets," Ryder said protectively.

Moments later, Carl dropped by, examined the baby and released him. Bridget wanted to ride home with him and the baby. As they walked out of the hospital in the hot summer sun, two men with cameras and microphones suddenly swarmed them.

"Princess Bridget, you've been spending a lot of time with Dr. Ryder McCall and his nephews. Are the two of you serious or is this just a fling?" the reporter asked.

Anger rushed through Ryder, and he stepped in front of her before she could respond. "It's none of your business. Leave her alone. Can't you see we're bringing a recovering baby home from the hospital?"

"But the people want to know," the reporter continued.

"The people don't need to know. It's none of their business," Ryder said.

"You obviously don't understand that royals belong to their people," the man said and tried to shove Ryder aside to get to Bridget.

"Leave her alone," Ryder said and knocked the man to the ground.

A half second later, Bridget's security guard swept her and the baby into a limo.

"But, Ryder," Bridget protested as her guard closed the door of the limo.

The reporter on the ground winced in pain at the same time he shouted to the cameraman, "Did you catch all that? It'll be worth a fortune."

Chapter Ten

"**Y**ou must leave Dr. McCall's house this instant," Stefan said to Bridget over the phone.

Bridget rolled her eyes. "I'm not going to do that. We just brought Travis home. He still needs comfort and Ryder can't do it all."

"Bridget, you're not the mother of these children. You have other duties, and now that the paparazzi has found you, Dr. McCall's house will be stalked day and night. For your safety, let alone your reputation, you can't stay there."

"Oh, to hell with my reputation. If I'm going to be crucified by the press, I can't think of a better reason."

"You're not thinking rationally," Stefan said. "Perhaps I should pull you from this assignment for your own good."

Bridget's heart froze. "You wouldn't dare," she said.

"Of course I would dare," he said. "I must make the calls for everyone's best interest."

"Give me two weeks," she said, determined to keep the desperation out of her voice. "You owe me that."

Silence followed. "It's true that Phillipa will be coming soon, but your doctor friend will need to be prepared for extra security at his house," Stefan said. "I get the impression he doesn't like a lot of intrusion in his private life. He may not like being told what to do."

"Of course he won't," she said. "Would you?"

"That's different," Stefan said.

"He won't what?" Ryder asked from the doorway, his shirt clinging to him in perspiration.

Her heart jumped and she covered the receiver. "It's my brother. He's being impossible."

"I'm not being impossible," Stefan said. "Let me talk to the doctor."

"Let me talk to your brother," Ryder said.

Bridget cringed. "I'd really rather the two of you meet in different circumstances."

"Sorry, sweetheart," Ryder said.

"Now is the time," Stefan said.

Bridget reluctantly handed the phone to Ryder. "Just start out with Your Highness," she whispered.

Ryder took the phone. "Good to meet you, Your Highness," Ryder said. "Your sister has been a godsend to my family."

Silence followed and Ryder tilted his head to one side.

"My position as adviser to the residents at my hospital can't be influenced by my feelings for your sister,"

Ryder said. "I can't send doctors to Chantaine if it's not in their best interest."

Bridget heard Stefan's raised voice and turned her head, wincing.

"I'm sure you understand my responsibility," Ryder said. "Just as you must make the best decisions for your country, I must make the best decisions in advising my residents."

Another quick silence followed, and Ryder met her gaze. "I have no objection to having additional security so that Bridget can come and go here as she pleases. I don't want what happened today to happen again."

A moment later, he said, "We agree on more than you think. Maybe we'll meet in person sometime. Bye for now, Your Highness."

He turned off the phone and handed it to her. "Your brother is a tough negotiator. Not as charming as you," he added with a low laugh. "And I'm sure he's not as hot."

She bit her lip, but couldn't keep from smiling. She closed her eyes for a second, then opened them. "I can be a lot of trouble. My family can be a lot of trouble."

He shrugged. "Everything can be trouble. Depends on whether it's worth it. Come back in the den. Travis is calling for you."

Bridget stayed the day and the day turned to evening. Ryder gave the okay for additional security around the house. He asked Raoul to keep it as invisible as possible. Raoul agreed. Ryder found he couldn't dislike Bridget's guard because he felt the same need to protect her. He was still trying to remember the time he'd punched someone in defense of a woman....

And he would damn well do it again and again for Bridget....

When those reporters had rushed him and Bridget, he'd acted instinctively, with a primitive response. They'd gotten way too close for comfort to Bridget and his baby. His head was still swimming with the reality.

Ryder hadn't realized how important Bridget and the babies had become to him. It was turning him inside out.

That night, against Raoul's advice, she stayed the night. Ryder took her to his bed and stripped off her clothes. He kissed every inch of her, then took her with every beat of his heart and every beat of hers.

His gaze wrapped around hers. At the same time that he took her, Ryder felt taken. In a way he'd never felt before.

Bridget clung to Ryder as he tried to rise from the bed in the morning. He gave a low chuckle that rippled through her.

"Don't want me to leave?"

"I don't," she said, sliding her hands over his muscular chest. "Pippa is coming to Dallas."

"Pippa?" he echoed, scouring her gaze.

"My sister Phillipa," she said. "She's having some problems. I'll have to entertain her a bit. You and I may not have as much time to be together."

"What kind of problems?" he asked, leaning down on his left forearm.

"I'm not sure, but she's stressed enough that my brother sent her here to visit Valentina and me."

He gave a slow nod. "You have a complicated family."

Her heart twisted. "I warned you."

He nodded. "So you did. When do I see you again?"

"I'll have to call you. I'm not sure when she arrives in the States."

"Call me today. I have surgery, but I'll check my messages in between."

Bridget scrambled to make her appointments for the day, then met Ryder at home that night. In between cuddling the twins, they ate sandwiches prepared by Suzanne and Ryder's friend Marshall.

"They seem to be growing very cozy," she said to Ryder as they leaned back against the sofa with the TV playing a ball game about which neither cared.

"Who?" Ryder asked, sliding his hand around hers.

"Suzanne and Marshall," she said.

Ryder groaned. "Don't tell me that. Marshall doesn't have a good history with women. His maximum time is weeks, not months. Days are more likely."

She shrugged. "You never know. Maybe she's the one. Maybe he's ready for the real thing and he's decided she's the real thing."

She felt him study her. "What do you think about the real thing?"

"I think the real thing starts on its own and then you have to keep it going," she said, but when she looked at him, she felt herself spin with emotion. "What about you?"

"I don't know. I always thought it was a figment of everyone's imagination," he said.

"And now?"

He shrugged his muscular shoulders. "Now, I'm not so sure."

Bridget hit the campaign trail for doctors for Chantaine hard. As one of her last resorts, she even met with the administrator of another medical hospital in Dallas. They were more open to her proposal of sending doctors to her country.

Bridget felt torn at the prospect. She wanted only the best for her country, but she couldn't automatically turn down the hospital's interest. It was more than Ryder could offer. The knowledge stabbed at her. She hated that he couldn't feel her passion for her country the same way she did.

In the meantime, she took deep breaths and decided not to make any impulsive decisions. That night, after rocking the babies, she joined Ryder in his bed. He made love to her with a passion that took her breath away.

Ryder drew her into his arms, flush against his body. She felt his heart beat against her chest. She had never felt closer to another human being in her life.

Travis recovered quickly. It seemed that one moment the baby had been listless and the next he was raring to go, trying to pull up and almost scooting, heaven help them all.

Phillipa arrived at DFW and Bridget greeted her sister with open arms. Bridget was concerned to see that Phillipa had indeed lost weight and there were circles beneath her eyes. "Hello, my darling," Bridget said. "I'm so glad to see you."

Phillipa slumped against her for a moment. "It's so good to see you, too," she murmured, squeezing Bridget tightly.

Bridget's concern deepened, but her instincts told her to mask it. At least for now. "I must prepare you for the Texas humidity," she said. "You can cut the air with a knife. We're headed to Tina's ranch. I'm sure she'll be calling any minute. She's dying to see you." Seconds later, her cell phone rang. "Just as I said." She picked up. "Yes, Tina, she's here and as soon as we get her luggage, we're headed straight for your house."

Bridget nodded and smiled. "Soon, soon. Ciao for now."

She hustled Pippa into the limo, plied her with a couple margaritas, and chattered during the drive to Tina's about Texas and the twins and Ryder. "Of course, Stefan is complaining," she said. "I swear he'd like to put us all in convents."

"So true," Phillipa said. "How did you deal with him?"

Bridget made a mental note of Phillipa's comment. Was Phillipa's problem romance? "Avoidance is the best policy," she said. "Emails. Text messages. Direct conversation is the worst because Stefan is disgustingly intuitive. If he would only get Eve pregnant, maybe he would be a bit distracted."

Phillipa chuckled. "Eve doesn't want to rush another child. She wants to give Stephenia plenty of time to adjust."

"Blast her practicality," Bridget said and took her second sip of her first margarita. "Well, you should know that Tina will arrange for massages and spa treatments.

Zach may take us out on his fabulous boat. We also have a social ball to attend in four days."

"Social ball," Phillipa echoed, clearly concerned.

"Oh, it's nothing to worry about," Bridget soothed. "It's a charity gala in Dallas. Tina and Zach will attend. If you like, we can make an appearance and bug out. You know I'm quick like that when it suits me. Stefan has fussed about it enough. Plus we can go shopping before and you can get a great dress out of it."

Pippa gave a mild smile. "So we don't have to stay all night?"

"Of course not," Bridget said, patting her sister on her knee. "Have the doctoral studies become a pain in the butt? You know, you work entirely too hard."

"My studies are fine, but Stefan insisted I take a break," she said.

"He means well," Bridget said. "But he still needs some work. I'm hopeful Eve can continue his needed transformation."

Phillipa sighed and took another sip of her margarita. "Bridget, you have no idea how much I've needed to see you."

Still concerned, Bridget managed a laugh. "Well, prepare yourself for an overdose."

Pippa smiled and Bridget felt as if she'd scored a small victory. Later, as they arrived at the ranch, Tina rushed down the steps. "Phillipa!" she called stretching out her arms.

Bridget watched her two sisters embrace and her heart squeezed tight with emotion. Tina pulled back. "Look at you. I love your hair. That dress is fabulous. What happened to my sister, the librarian?"

"I'm still here," Phillipa said. "A stylist put together some things for my visit to the States."

"Regardless, you look fabulous, but shorts and no shoes are the summertime uniform here. Come visit your niece. She can't wait to see Aunt Pippa," Tina said, and tossed Bridget a glance of concern before she led them inside the house.

Bridget and Phillipa played with their gorgeous niece until dinnertime when Hildie served a superb, filling meal. Between the margaritas, the food and the security of her sisters, Phillipa grew drowsy early in the evening. Tina ushered her to one of the bedrooms and returned to the den with Bridget and Zach.

"She's different than I expected," Tina said. "Stefan said she was stressed, but—" Tina frowned. "What do you think is behind all this?"

"A man," Bridget said as she sipped a glass of ice water.

Tina's eyebrows rose. "What makes you say that?"

"Something Pippa said on the way here."

"What? Who?" Tina demanded.

"I didn't pry. She just seemed too fragile," Bridget said.

Tina sighed. "How did you get that out of her?"

"It was a sideways comment. I was complaining about Stefan and how he doesn't want any of us to date."

"True," Tina said.

"Too true," Zach said from behind the newspaper he was reading.

Tina glanced at her husband and smiled.

"In this case, I was speaking of Ryder," Bridget said.

"Hmm," Tina said.

"So far, he seems like a good guy," Zach said. "If he was willing to punch out that reporter who was after you, he gets my vote."

"It's all about the violence," Tina said, rolling her eyes.

"Protecting a woman is a primitive response in a man. Protectiveness is an important trait."

"I'm sure Stefan will love hearing that opinion," Bridget said wryly.

"Stefan just needs to be reminded about what he would do to protect Eve," Zach said bluntly, then shook his newspaper and appeared to begin to read again.

"She needs a massage," Tina said. "A ride on the water. And perhaps Hildie's double-strength margaritas."

Three days later, the sisters went to Dallas and shopped for dresses. Bridget was distracted. She was late. Not for an appointment. She was late for her period, and she had been, well, exposed to the possibility of becoming pregnant. Although they had used contraception, Bridget wasn't sure if she had landed in the small percentile of women for whom it had failed.

"What do you think?" Tina asked as Phillipa tried on a gown. "I think the cocoa color is perfect on her."

Bridget blinked, looking at Pippa. "Yes, it's beautiful. It really accentuates all your positive attributes."

"Although, a pastel or dark navy would be fabulous, too, don't you think?" Tina said.

"I completely agree," she said and forced herself to pay attention to the rest of the shopping expedition. She rendered her positive opinion to Tina's choice for a dress, but nixed the idea of getting a new gown for herself.

Tina and Phillipa gasped at once. "Are you ill?" Phillipa asked.

"What is wrong?" Tina demanded. "You never turn down the opportunity to get a new designer gown."

Bridget brushed their concerns aside. "It's nothing," she said. "I have a ton of gowns I brought with me that I haven't yet worn. We've already spent enough time shopping. It's not necessary to find a gown for me."

"Enough time shopping," Pippa echoed. "You've often said there's no such thing as too much shopping."

Uncomfortable with her sisters' scrutiny, Bridget shrugged her shoulders. "Okay, I'll admit it. I'm hungry and we might end up with rubber chicken tonight."

Tina giggled and rolled her eyes. "Now we have the real answer. I could use a good meal, too. Crab sounds especially good."

The thought of crab turned Bridget's stomach. "Or even a nice sandwich. You know where we can find a good variety of food, Tina. Where should we go?"

Delighted to give the attention back to her sister, Bridget joined her sisters for a late lunch. Her phone rang during their meal and she excused herself to take the call. "Ryder, talk to me. I swear it feels as if it's been three months since I heard your voice."

He laughed. "Same here. Are you having fun with your sisters?"

"For the most part," she said. "We still haven't figured out what's wrong with Phillipa, but I think it's a man. I'm hoping she'll talk with us. It's always more miserable to suffer by yourself. And whatever your problems are, they seem ten times worse if you don't share. Speaking of worries, how are you and the twins?"

"The only way the twins and I could be better would be if you were around," he said.

Her heart went squishy at his words. "Oh, that's so sweet. They've probably already forgotten me."

"No chance."

"You know, the other day, I was wondering, did you ever think you were going to have children? I know becoming a doctor was important, but did you *ever* think you would start a family?"

"It wasn't a priority," he said. "My career was always number one…. Just a moment," he said and she heard him talking with someone else. Then he came back on the line. "Listen, I need to go soon. Are you okay? I'm hearing something in your voice."

"Oh, no," she said, lying because she knew she didn't have time to discuss her real feelings. "It's just family stuff."

He paused a few seconds. "But you mentioned starting a family. What's on your mind?"

"Nothing," she insisted. "I was just thinking about how you'd been thrust into the position of being a father so quickly. I wondered what your original plans were."

She heard him give a quick response to someone on the other end of the line. "Are you pregnant?"

Shocked at the accuracy of his question, she sucked in a quick breath. Something inside her insisted on denial. She would figure that out later. "Oh, my goodness. How could I be pregnant? You and I are so careful."

"Nothing provides perfect protection except abstinence," he said.

"Oh, that's ridiculous. We're fine. We're perfectly fine," she insisted, her heart racing.

"Thanks for the reassurance," he said. "You and I both have enough going on without adding a baby to the mix."

"So true," she said, but her stomach twisted viciously.

"I have to go. I'll call later."

"Ciao," she said and stared blindly at her cell phone. What if she *was* pregnant? It was clear that Ryder didn't want another baby. How would she handle this? Would she have to do it all alone? Panic raced through her. She broke into a cold sweat. She shuddered at the possibility of dealing with her family's disapproval and interference.

"Bridget," her sister Tina said, breaking her out of her reverie. "The food's been here for several minutes. What's wrong with you today? You seem totally distracted."

Bridget took a breath and pulled herself together, forcing a big smile. "Oh, Tina, you know how I am. If I've got more than one and a half things on my mind, I'm distracted. I'm still thinking about the babies and the medical program for Chantaine. I need that sandwich. Thank you for coming to get me," she said and marched back to the table, praying her sister wouldn't ask any more questions.

That night, Bridget and her sisters dressed at her suite at the hotel. She felt as if she were on automatic. A green dress. Green was a good color for her. Mineral powder, subtle eyes, bold, red lips. She didn't feel bold, but she needed to be confident. She needed to be someone bigger than her current self because her current self was feeling confused and vulnerable. Lord, she hoped it was late PMS.

She gave her sister Phillipa a hug. "You look fabulous."

"You overstate," Phillipa said. "You always have."

"Not this time. Look at how gorgeous you look," she said, pointing to the full-length mirror.

Tina stepped into the room from the bathroom. "What are you two arguing about?"

"I told Phillipa she looked fabulous and gorgeous and she said I'm exaggerating and I said I'm not," Bridget said.

Tina walked to Phillipa and put her hands tenderly on her cheeks. "For once, Bridget understated."

Phillipa closed her eyes and squeezed them tight as if she were fighting tears. "You two are being so kind. I know all of this is because you're worried about me."

"Well, it's true we're worried about you," Bridget said.

"Bridget," Tina said with a chiding expression.

"It's true. It's also true that I wouldn't include fabulous and gorgeous in the same sentence if I didn't truly believe it," Bridget said.

Phillipa's lips twitched. "You make a good point. The real you leaks out after a short time."

Bridget lifted her hand. "What did I say?"

Tina sighed. "We just want you to be okay. You're our baby," she said, stroking Phillipa's hair.

"I'm not a baby. I'm a grown-up. I can manage my life. I just need a little recalibration."

"And you can get that here," Tina said.

Phillipa smiled. Tina's cell phone rang and she picked up. "It's Zachary."

Moments later, Zachary arrived in a limo driven by security. The three princesses and Zach rode to the charity ball. As they stepped outside the limo, they were greeted by flashing cameras and reporters.

"Welcome to Dallas's premier Charity Ball, Your Highnesses. To what do we owe the honor of your presence tonight?" a reporter asked.

Just lucky, I guess, Bridget thought, but managed to swallow the comment.

"I live just outside of Fort Worth with my husband and daughter, and I've been so happy to receive visits from both my sisters, Bridget and Phillipa," Tina said.

"Your sister Bridget has been in town for over a month. There have been rumors about her and one of our doctors—"

"We're here tonight to celebrate the charity of the people of Texas, which is so much bigger than rumors, don't you agree?" Tina asked. "It was lovely to meet you."

They moved on to the next reporter, and Tina's responses reminded Bridget why her sister had done such a superlative job representing Chantaine.

"She's so good," Bridget muttered.

"Times two," Phillipa said.

"If only she could be in two places at once," Bridget said with a sigh.

"You're doing pretty well," Pippa said.

"My time is limited," Bridget said. "I don't have Tina's endurance."

"Maybe, this once, you underestimate yourself," her sister said.

"I think not, but I appreciate your kindness. On to our rubber chicken," she whispered and was thrilled she could make Phillipa laugh.

"What are you two talking about?" Tina demanded.

"You don't want to know," Bridget said.

Tina shot her a curt micro-look before she plastered a serene expression on her face. Zach escorted the group inside to their table at the front of the room. They made small talk with the others seated at their table. Soon enough, announcements and presentations began. Bridget was stunned when Nic LaFitte stepped forward to receive an award of recognition. The Devereaux had a long-standing grudge against the Lafittes. Nic's father had caused a humiliating scandal for the royal family.

"What is *he* doing here?" she whispered to Tina.

"Zach says he's a huge contributor here. Everyone loves him," Tina said distastefully.

"They clearly don't know him," she said and nudged Phillipa. "Why can't we escape him?" she whispered. "Maybe it's because he's the devil and that means he can be everywhere."

When Phillipa didn't respond, Bridget glanced at her face and saw that her sister had turned white as a sheet.

Chapter Eleven

"I'm not feeling well," Phillipa said. "Please excuse me."

"Do you want me to go with you?" Bridget asked, her stomach twisting in concern for her sister.

"No, no. I just need a little air," Phillipa said as she slowly rose and lifted her lips in a forced smile. "I'll be back in a little bit."

Bridget watched her sister move through the perimeter of the room as surreptitiously as possible and felt worried.

"Where is she going?" Tina asked in a whisper.

"The powder room," Bridget said. "She says she needs some air."

Tina frowned and glanced at Nic LaFitte as he left the stage. "Do you think this has anything to do with LaFitte?"

"I can't imagine that it would. I mean, none of us

would get involved with a LaFitte. Not even the most rebellious of us and Pippa is nowhere near the most rebellious."

Tina nodded and Bridget paid half attention to the speaker, more attention to her watch. "I'm going to check on Pippa," she whispered.

"I'll go with you," Tina said, and stood just after she did.

Bridget tried to be discreet just as Phillipa had been, but she noticed several heads turning in her direction. She immediately searched for the first ladies' room and didn't find Phillipa there. "Where is she?" she muttered to herself.

"I'm starting to get a bad feeling about LaFitte," Tina said as they left the room.

"I can't believe Pippa would be that foolish. She's extremely intelligent and quite practical," Bridget said as she scoured the lobby for her sister.

"I wonder if she went outside," Tina said.

"It's possible. She said she needed some air," Bridget said, then spotted a coat closet and pointed toward it. "You don't think she would be there, do you? It's the last place I would look in this hot, humid weather and the door is closed."

Tina glanced in the same direction and shrugged. "I don't think so, but we may as well check."

Bridget led the way to the door and stopped just outside, pressing her ear closer to listen. Hearing nothing, she cracked the door open.

"This is insanity," Phillipa said. "It will never work."

"Why not?" a male voice demanded. "If I want you and you want me, what is most important?"

"Want is a temporary emotion," Phillipa said. "There are more important things than temporary emotions."

"If that's true, then why are you here with me?" he asked.

Tina gasped and the sound traveled through the door like a thunderclap. Seconds later, Phillipa and Nic LaFitte appeared in the doorway.

"Get away from my sister," Bridget said.

"That's for her to say, not you," LaFitte said.

"You're just using her," Tina said. "You only want her because she can redeem your terrible family name."

"Not everyone finds my family name reprehensible. Some even respect it," he said.

"That's respect you've bought with money," Tina said. "Leave Phillipa alone. You can never be good enough for her. If you have any compassion, you'll at least protect her reputation by leaving now."

LaFitte tightened his jaw. "I'll leave, but Phillipa will make the ultimate decision about the future of our relationship." He glanced behind him and met Phillipa's shocked, pale face. "Ciao, darling. Call me when you get some courage. Some things are meant to be," he said and strode away.

"Oh, darling," Bridget said and immediately went to Phillipa and took her in her arms.

Tina soon followed. "Oh, you poor thing. The LaFittes are so evil. It's clear he intends to trick you."

Phillipa's face crumpled. "He was so kind to me," she whispered.

"Of course he was," Tina said. "He's a snake like the rest of his family. And you're too sweet to know the difference."

"Are you saying he couldn't possibly be attracted to me just because I'm me?" Phillipa asked, her voice filled with desperation.

Bridget felt her heart shatter at the pain in her sister's voice. "Of course not," she said. "You're an amazing, beautiful and wonderful girl. You're a precious gem and you must be protected from anyone who doesn't deserve you."

"And no LaFitte would *ever* deserve you," Tina said.

Moments later, out of consideration for Phillipa, they left the event. Bridget and Tina fought over where Phillipa should spend the night. Bridget eventually won. "She shouldn't have to ride an extra hour back to the ranch tonight," Bridget said. "I have plenty of room in my suite. Along with the makings of margaritas or any other toddy she may require tonight."

"But Zach and I could protect her from any unwanted advances from LaFitte," Tina said.

"His advances weren't unwanted," Phillipa whispered. "I was attracted to him and wished he would contact me. I finally gave in and sent a message to him. He met me and that was how it all started."

Tina sucked in a sharp breath, then silence fell in the limousine. Zach tipped back a glass of bourbon.

"Well, I'm glad you came to your senses," Tina said.

Bridget gave Phillipa a hug. "We don't need to talk or think about this anymore tonight. You've already had enough stress tonight. You're due some rest. You can come to my room and fall asleep all snug and safe in your bed. You can think about LaFitte tomorrow if necessary. Tonight it's not necessary."

"You sound like that Scarlett O'Hara in the American film *Gone with the Wind*," Tina said.

"In this case, she offered a nice bit of wisdom," Bridget countered.

"Please don't argue," Phillipa said.

"We're not," Bridget said, giving Tina a strong glance. "Tina and I agree, don't we?"

Tina took a quick breath. "Yes, we do. I think we all need some extra rest tonight. In fact, I think Zach and I will stay overnight at your hotel."

"What?" Zach asked.

"Yes," Tina said decisively. "We can stay overnight at Bridget's hotel in a separate suite, of course. I'm sure Hildie won't mind keeping the baby."

"Yes, but—"

"In the morning, we can wake up and all have brunch together," she said brightly.

"And if Phillipa sleeps in, then Mom and Dad can enjoy a night away from their little darling and Phillipa can visit you at the ranch later."

Tina frowned, but nodded.

Moments later, they exited the limo into the hotel and Bridget and Phillipa took the lift to the penthouse. "Thank you," Phillipa said after they entered the elevator.

Bridget took her sister's hand. "We all need a break every now and then. If your sister won't give it to you, then who *will* give it to you?"

"Yes, but Tina clearly hates Nic," Bridget said in a shaky voice.

"All of us hate the LaFitte family. Part of it is not

logical. After all, if Father had married the woman who married LaFitte, none of us would exist. Maybe we don't like to lose. Plus there's the matter of the LaFitte who killed one of our great-uncles." Bridget sighed. "And, after all the bad they did to us, they're so bloody wealthy and successful. That's enough of a reason to hate them."

"His mother is dying," Phillipa said.

Bridget glanced at her sister. "Really. How?"

"Cancer. It's been a terribly grueling experience. She's currently near the end."

Bridget took a deep breath. "I don't wish that on anyone."

"Neither do I," Phillipa said as the elevator dinged their arrival to the penthouse.

Bridget clasped her sister's hand. "You must promise me that you won't think about this anymore tonight. You need to take a break from it. It's hurting you. More important, you can't fix it tonight."

Phillipa squeezed her hand in return. "I may not agree with a lot of what you've said, but it's true that I can't fix all of this tonight. I should just go to bed and try to sleep."

Bridget nodded. "And get a massage in the morning. I'll keep Tina away."

"You're usually nagging me to take on more palace duties. When did you become my fairy protector?" Phillipa asked.

"Oh, well, I'll nag again soon enough. Enjoy the respite," Bridget said.

The next morning, Bridget did just as she'd promised and arranged for a soothing massage for her younger sister. Tina would only be put off so long before she was knocking on the door of Bridget's suite. Bridget opened the door. "We're sipping lime water and relaxing on the balcony. Would you like to join us?" she asked. "And whatever you do, don't hound her and don't bring up LaFitte. I've got her nice and relaxed after her massage."

Tina nodded in agreement. "We'll take her out on Zach's new boat."

"But don't try to matchmake," Bridget said.

Tina frowned. "You don't think a male distraction would help?" she whispered.

"No," Bridget said emphatically. "Pippa has fallen hard for LaFitte. She needs to get over him before she moves on to the next."

"You seem to have enormous insight on this matter. Surprising," Tina said, lifting her eyebrow in a suspicious manner.

Bridget feigned an airy sigh. "Underestimated again. When will it end?"

After her sisters left, Bridget returned several calls. As soon as she finished, though, the quiet settled over her like a heavy blanket. She still hadn't started her period yet. Tempted to wear a disguise and buy an early pregnancy test from a drugstore, she put it off. She never knew who was watching and who might discuss her purchase with the paparazzi. Perhaps by tomorrow…

Her cell phone rang and she saw Ryder's return number on her screen. He was the one person to whom she hadn't made a return call. Her heart hammered with nerves as she took the call. "Hello, Ryder," she said.

"Damn good to hear your voice. I was starting to

wonder if you'd disappeared or headed to Chantaine or Italy without letting me know," he said.

"I wouldn't do that," she said. "I've just been tied up with my sisters. How are my boys?"

"Your boys are screaming to see you. Even Suzanne says they miss you. Come over for the weekend," he said.

Her heart jumped again and she began to pace. On the one hand, she was desperate to see Ryder again. On the other hand, she was distracted by the possibility that she could be pregnant. Ryder had been much more intuitive about her worries than she would have ever expected.

He made a buzzing sound. "Time's up. Because you didn't say no, that must mean yes. I'll pick you up around five," he said.

"Wait," she said breathlessly. "Let Raoul bring me. That way he can go through his security protocol and I won't be hassled by him or my brother. Hopefully," she added in a low voice.

"Good," Ryder said. "The twins have a trick they want to show you. See you soon," he said.

"Trick?" she echoed, but he'd already disconnected the call.

Anticipation zinged through her and she giggled. Her mood felt as if it had lifted into the stratosphere. Amazing that he had that effect on her so quickly. Frightening, really, if she thought about it too deeply, so she wouldn't.

A few hours later, she tried to ignore the lecture Raoul was giving her about how she was taking risks and how she should stay away from windows.

"Your Highness, do you understand what I'm saying?" Raoul asked.

"Absolutely," she said.

"You haven't been listening to a word I've said," he said.

"That's not true. I've listened to at least every third word you've said. I'm not reckless, but I won't let my position steal my joy. You never know how long you'll have that opportunity. There's so much drudgery you have to grab the joy."

Silence followed. "That's remarkably deep, Your Highness," he said. "But after protecting you for five years, I'm not surprised. You hide your depth well," he said, glancing at her through the rearview mirror.

Bridget felt a twist in her chest at her guard's revelation. "Thank you, Raoul. You deserve sainthood for being my guard."

"You are not as bad as you profess," he said. "But stay away from windows and call me before you walk outside the house."

She laughed as he pulled the car to the curb of Ryder's home. "Way to slide in those instructions," she said and opened her door before he could. "Ciao."

Before she arrived on the porch, the door flung open and Ryder greeted her, sweeping her inside. "Your men are waiting for you," he said and pulled her into his arms.

He felt so strong and wonderful and alive. She felt as if she'd come home. She was safe and more whole than she'd ever dreamed possible. He picked her up and spun her around and she couldn't help laughing.

"You act like you haven't seen me in a year," she said, squeezing his strong shoulders.

"It has been a year," he said and searched her face. "Right?"

A shriek sounded just a few steps away.

Bridget glanced at the floor and saw the twins scooting toward her and Ryder. "Oh, bloody hell," she said, panicked. "They're moving! We have to stop them."

Ryder roared with laughter. "That was my first response, too," he said and squeezed her shoulders. "But crawling is next. After that, standing. Then walking."

Bridget stared, torn between exultation and cold fear, and shook her head. "What are you going to do?"

"Cope," he said. "Manage them, if such a thing is possible. The good news is they get worn out a lot faster," he said.

Tyler stopped at Bridget's feet and gurgled.

Her heart twisted so tightly that she could hardly breathe. "Oh, you darling," she said and bent down to pick up the baby. She groaned. "You've gained weight. Is that possible?"

Ryder picked up Travis and extended him toward Bridget. She gave the baby a kiss and cooed at him. He cooed at her in return and her chest expanded, filling her with an overwhelming sense of love and emotion. "Oh, you darlings. I've missed both of you."

"Both?" Ryder asked.

"All three. Especially you," she said and sank onto the sofa with the baby on her lap. "The last few days have been full of drama. Poor Phillipa has been seduced by one of our family enemies. She's such an innocent. I know he's taken advantage of her, but I'm hoping she'll regain her sense."

"Who's this enemy? I thought you Devereaux were peaceful and moderate," he said, joining her on the sofa.

"We are for the most part," she said. "But the LaFittes have been bad news for our family. One of them murdered my great-uncle. And one seduced my father's bride away from him," she said.

"I can understand the first, but the second, not so much. You wouldn't have been born if your father had married a different woman," he said.

"True," she said. "But the LaFittes are still on our don't list. No discussion," she said.

"What about me?" he asked in a rough voice. "Am I on your don't list?"

Her breath hitched in the back of her throat. "Probably, but that hasn't stopped me, has it?"

His lips lifted in a lazy half grin. "Guess not. I ordered Italian for dinner. Bought red wine on the way home."

"Sounds great, but I'm all about water these days. I'm on a new diet that favors lemon and lime water. It's supposed to cleanse the toxins. Do you have any limes?"

Ryder blinked. "Limes?"

"No problem. Filtered water is good."

"So, red wine is out?" he asked.

"Just during my lime phase," she said with a smile.

They watched the twins scoot around the den until they wore themselves out. Ryder rocked Tyler and she rocked Travis. It took only moments before Travis was drooling on her shoulder. She met Ryder's gaze and he gave a slight nod and they carried the babies up to their cribs.

Seconds later, they walked downstairs and shared a

late meal. Although Italian fare didn't appeal to her at the moment, Bridget pushed the food around her plate to make it look as if she'd eaten it. Later, she took her plate into the kitchen and pushed the contents into the trash can.

Did this mean she was pregnant? she wondered. She loved Italian food. If she hated it, now what did it mean? Her stomach twisted into a knot, but she took a deep breath and returned to the den. "Delicious dinner," she said and sat down beside him.

"You didn't eat everything. It must not have been that delicious," he said, sliding his arm over her shoulder.

"I had a late lunch and I'm watching my girlish figure," she said with a smile.

"I'll take care of that second job. I have no problem watching your girlish figure," he said, sliding his lips along her neck.

She laughed, exulting in his caress. Turning toward him, she lifted her mouth to his. "Kiss me," she said.

"Is that an order?"

"Kinda," she said.

He gave a low, dirty chuckle and did as she commanded.

The next morning, Ryder awakened early. Bridget's back was pressed against him. His hand was curled around her bare waist. Her skin was butter soft against his palm. It was a good morning. The best kind of morning. Bridget was with him.

He couldn't remember a time when he'd been more at peace. Something primitive inside him drove him to keep her with him. He started to understand why men kidnapped their women and kept them in luxurious captivity. Which was crazy. When had he ever felt this need for a woman? When had a woman ever filled up all his emptiness and need?

Bridget wiggled against him, then suddenly raced out of bed to the master bath. A couple moments later, she returned, carefully crawling into the bed and inching herself toward him.

Several things clicked through his brain. His gut twisted. "Bridget," he murmured against her ear.

"Yes," she whispered.

"Are you pregnant?"

Silence passed. Way too long. His heart sank. *Another baby?* He couldn't imagine it. How in the world—

"I don't know," she finally said. "I'm late."

A half dozen emotions sliced through him. He couldn't speak.

"How late?" he finally managed.

"A week and a half," she said, still not turning to look at him.

"We should do a test," he said.

"No," she said. "I can't take a test, and you can't do it for me. The press is watching me even more than usual now. I want to know as much as you do, but a few more days may give us the answer without any exposure to the press," she said and finally turned toward him.

"You're late. No red wine. Why didn't you tell me?"

Her eyes clouded with turmoil. "Our relationship is still new. We haven't made any sort of promises to each other."

His heart pounded against his chest. The thought of another baby scared the crap out of him. His brother's babies had become his own. The baby he shared with Bridget would be his to protect as well.

"If you're pregnant, you need to start taking prenatal vitamins as soon as possible. You need to get on a regimen—"

"And if I'm not, I can go back to my red wine-swilling, unhealthy ways," she said.

He bit the inside of his lip to keep from laughing. "I still think you should let me do a test."

She shook her head. "Three more days. I'll live healthy until then."

He searched her face. "I would protect you if you're pregnant with my child, Bridget. I would marry you. I would protect our child."

Her eyes still swam with emotion, some of which he couldn't read. "That's good to know," she said and tucked her head under his chin. "Can we talk about something else until then?"

Ryder spent the weekend secluded in happiness with Bridget. They shared the care of the twins, took the boys for a stroll in the neighborhood despite Raoul's protests and spent their nights together, his body wrapped around hers, her body wrapped around his.

He returned to work Monday wondering if she was pregnant, wishing he could keep her with him. He met with Dr. Hutt.

"Dr. Robinson is still having financial problems due to his family. It's distracting him from his duties," Dr. Hutt said.

Ryder immediately felt defensive. "We need to look

for a solution instead of immediately booting him out of the program."

"I agree," Hutt said, surprising Ryder with his response.

"What about your princess friend?" he asked, leaning back in his chair. "Wouldn't this be a perfect solution? She gives him a bonus scholarship, he takes a tour of her country. Win, win."

"Are you serious?" Ryder asked.

"Yes," he said. "You and I must manage residents from all eco-social backgrounds. Not everyone is from your background. Not everyone is from mine."

For the first time in months, he felt a measure of hope. Maybe, just maybe Hutt could see past his privileged upbringing. "Are you sure you shouldn't push him harder?" he asked. "Maybe he just needs to work more."

His colleague frowned. "He's already working hard. Harder than I ever did," he said.

Ryder was stunned. He'd never known Hutt was capable of such insight. "When did this change happen?"

"The last time you and I met, I went home and couldn't sleep. For several nights. Dr. Walters not only kicked my butt, he also *encouraged* you. He wasn't one man to the residents. He stepped into their shoes and gave them what they needed. As advisers, we have to do the same."

Ryder shook his head. "When in hell did you become a reasonable man?"

His colleague laughed. "It's amazing the kind of perspective a wife can offer when you choose to talk to her."

"Your wife did this?" Ryder asked.

Hutt shrugged. "Professionally speaking, of course, she didn't," he said.

Ryder felt a change click through him and extended his hand to Dr. Hutt. "Give my best to your wife," he said.

"And give my best to your princess," Hutt said.

One day later, Bridget called him. He was in surgery, so he checked his messages. "Meet me today. Name the time," she said. "I have good news."

His day was crazy, but he managed to meet her at a quiet cocktail bar after work.

"Rough day?" she asked as she sipped a martini.

He felt a crazy surge of disappointment. The last couple of days, he'd secretly begun to like the idea of having a baby with Bridget. "You're not pregnant."

"I'm not," she said and lifted her glass to his. She smiled in relief. "Cheers."

"Cheers," he said. "And damn."

She blinked. "Damn?"

"Maybe I could have forced you into a shotgun marriage if you were pregnant."

She laughed and took another sip of her martini. "I wouldn't want a shotgun wedding for you or me," she said.

"I don't know," he said. "I think we could have made the best of it."

She sucked in a deep breath and glanced away. "Perhaps, but now we don't have to," she said with a shaky smile. She bit her lip. "My other news is that another medical center has stepped forward to participate in our program."

Surprised, Ryder searched her gaze. "Really?"

"We finally have doctors willing to come to Chantaine," she said, relief crossing her face. "I followed your advice and found experts willing to visit Chantaine and give training. And this medical center is willing to offer our scholarship and package to their residents. So far, two have signed up for our program. They weren't our first choice, but Stefan is confident this arrangement will be in the best interest of the country."

"Wow," Ryder said. "What a coincidence. Today Dr. Hutt and I agreed to send one of our residents to Chantaine. He's a talented generalist, but he has financial issues you can solve. Still interested?"

"Of course," she said. "I shouldn't say we're desperate, but we're definitely open. We're also going to need a new director for Chantaine's Health Center, but that's clearly a work in progress."

"I guess this means you're headed for Chantaine… or Italy," he said, his gut tightening into a square knot.

"Not right away, but very soon," she said. "I'll go back with Phillipa."

Chapter Twelve

Ryder returned home well after 9:00 p.m. after meeting Bridget for cocktails and dinner. He had arranged for Suzanne to stay late to watch the twins, but Marshall greeted him.

Marshall handed him a beer. "Hey, big guy. Congratulate me. Suzanne and I got married this weekend in Vegas. I sent her home because she was tired out. I kept her pretty busy this weekend," he added with a wink.

Stunned for the third time today, Ryder stared at Marshall. "What?"

"Suzanne and I got married. Don't worry, she's determined to still be your nanny even though I told her she could be a lady of leisure."

Ryder accepted the beer and took a sip. "Oh, Lord help me."

"That's not quite a congrats, but I'll take it," Marshall

said, giving Ryder a fist bump. "You look kinda strange, big guy. What's up?"

Ryder shook his head and sank onto his couch. "Just a crazy day. Are you sure Suzanne is still going to take care of the twins?"

Marshall sat on the other side of the couch. "Yeah. She's determined. You know she can't have babies, right? That's why her husband left her. His stupidity, my good luck."

"Bridget mentioned something about it," Ryder said, his mind falling back a few days to when her pregnancy had still been a possibility. And now she would be leaving soon. He knew the twins would miss her.

"Yeah, I told her there's more than one way to crack that nut. Getting a baby. We'll check out the IVF stuff, then we'll look into our adoption options. She was surprised I would be open to that. She's an amazing woman. I would do anything for her," Marshall said.

"Why didn't you tell me you were going to do this?" Ryder demanded.

"You'd already warned me away from Suzanne, but I wanted to get to know her. It took some work to get her to go out with me, but I knew she was the one for me. She's the first really good woman I've met and I knew I didn't want to let her go."

Ryder felt a twist of envy that Marshall had been able to overcome the obstacles that might have kept him and Suzanne apart. "Congratulations," he said, extending his hand.

Marshall nodded and smiled. "Still can't believe I was able to talk her into eloping. Of course, now is the hard part, but with her, I don't think it's gonna be that hard."

"She's a strong woman. If anyone can keep you in line, she's the one," Ryder said.

"Yeah, speaking of women, what's up with your princess?"

Ryder's gut tightened again. "I think she's headed back to Chantaine soon."

Marshall's eyebrows lifted in surprise. "Whoa. I thought you two—"

"Temporary," Ryder said. "For Pete's sake, she's a princess, and I've got my hands full with the boys and my position at the hospital."

"Hmm," Marshall said. "I could have sworn you two had it going on. Shame you couldn't work it out. Sorry, bud," he said and thumped Ryder on the shoulder. "Hope you don't mind, but my *wife* is waiting for me at home."

"Okay, okay," Ryder said with a faint smile. "Just make sure she gets enough sleep to take care of the boys."

Marshall just gave a dirty laugh and walked out the door.

Ryder stared into the distance and felt more alone than ever. For the most part, he hadn't minded being alone. In the past, it had meant he had to take care of only himself. All that had changed when his brother had died and Ryder had taken on the twins. Now it was just him and the twins.

An image of Bridget floated through his mind and he got an itchy, unsettled feeling inside him. Trying to dismiss it, he went to the kitchen and glanced through the mail for the day, but that itchy feeling didn't go away.

Ryder rubbed at his gut, but it didn't do any good. A sense of dread that started in his stomach climbed to the back of his throat.

Ryder swore under his breath. He'd fallen for the woman. Worse yet, he'd begun to rely on her. He, who relied on no one but himself. Shaking his head, he called himself ten kinds of fools. A princess? Putting his trust in anyone was dangerous, but a princess. Talk about impossible situations.

He ground his teeth. She was leaving. He needed to get used to the idea immediately. He needed to cut every thought of her from his mind.

Bridget felt ripped apart at the prospect of leaving Ryder and the boys, but she couldn't stall any longer. She'd completed her assignment and it was time for her to return to Chantaine before she took her long-delayed gap year in Italy. Somehow, she couldn't work up the same kind of excitement she'd felt during the last two years about finally taking a break.

She didn't know which upset her most: leaving Ryder and the twins or the fact that Ryder had ignored all of her calls. Desperate to make arrangements to see him one last time, she took matters into her own hands, went to the hospital and parked herself in his office when his assistant was away from her desk. She wasn't going through any gatekeepers this time.

After forty-five minutes of waiting, she saw Ryder finally open his office door. He looked at her and his expression registered shock, then all emotion seemed to vanish from his face. "Hello, Bridget. Sorry, I don't have time to visit."

His remoteness stabbed her. "I understand. I just didn't want to leave without seeing you and the twins again."

"Why? We won't be a part of your life anymore. There's no need to pretend we were anything more than a phase."

She dropped her jaw, surprised at his evaluation of the time they'd shared. "A phase?" she repeated in disbelief. "Is that all I was to you? A phase?"

Ryder gave a bitter laugh. "There's no need for drama. Both of us knew this was coming. It just came a little sooner than expected. I appreciate everything you did to help the twins. You provided a needed diversion for all three of us."

"A diversion," she said, feeling herself begin to shake.

"Don't get so upset. We knew from the beginning that there was no future to our relationship. I sure as hell am not the right man to be a princess's husband and you're not the type of woman to put up with a doctor's demanding schedule."

She felt as if he'd slapped her. He made her sound like she was a selfish, high-maintenance shrew. She bit the inside of her lip. "I had no idea you thought so little of me." She swallowed over the lump in her throat. "You really had me fooled. I've spent the last few days searching for ways to continue to see you and be with you. I realize it would be the ultimate long-distance relationship, but I couldn't bear the idea of not being in your life. I fell for both you and the boys." Her voice broke and she looked away, shaking her head. "At least, I fell for who I thought you were. I thought you felt the same way, but clearly I was—"

"No," he said, gripping her shoulders. She looked up and saw in his eyes that he was as tortured as she was. "No, you weren't wrong. I fell for you, too, much more than I intended. I've spent the last days telling myself to forget you. I know that's impossible, but I have to try."

Her eyes filled with tears. "I don't want you to forget me. I don't want you to speak about us in the past tense. You—you've become so important to me."

He winced as if in pain. "But it can't work. Our lives are just too different. We need to make it easy for each other to get used to the facts. The fact is you have to return to your country. You have responsibilities there. I have mine here."

She tried hard to hang on to her composure, but she couldn't. It hurt too much. She dropped her forehead against his chest. "This is so hard," she said, feeling tears streak down her face.

"It is," he said, sliding his hand through her hair and holding her close.

"Promise me you won't forget me," she said and lifted her gaze to look at him. "Give me that much."

"Never," he promised. "Never," he said and lowered his mouth to hers for a kiss. Their last kiss.

Ryder couldn't remember a time when he had felt like his guts had been ripped out and put through a grinder. Every waking moment, he was aware of the breathtaking pain. He tried, but couldn't block the sight of Bridget's tears from his mind. The way she'd felt in his arms. He would never feel that again. He would never feel that sense of unexpected joy just by seeing her smile or hearing her tease him.

Swearing under his breath as he arrived home, he ripped open the top few buttons of his shirt. Not only was he in mental hell, but the hot Dallas weather seemed to be determined to put him in physical hell, too.

"Hey, big guy," Marshall said as he held one of the twins while Suzanne changed the diaper of the other. "You don't look too good. Did you lose someone on the table today?"

One of the babies squealed at the sight of him. The sound gave Ryder a slight lift. He walked over and gave each baby a hug.

"No, I didn't lose a patient. Just got some things on my mind. Sorry I'm late. Tomorrow should be better."

He saw Marshall lift his eyebrows. "Hey, Suzy Q, how about I help you take the boys upstairs for a while. Ryder and I can drink a beer and watch a couple innings of a ball game. Are you okay with that?"

"Sure," she said. "I'll play some music and read to them."

Marshall gave his wife a firm kiss, then carried both boys upstairs.

A moment later, his friend returned. Ryder had already gotten two beers out of the fridge. "I don't want to talk about it," he muttered as he sank onto the couch.

"Okay," Marshall said and used the remote to turn on the TV. The Dallas team was losing again. Marshall swore. "They just can't pull it together."

"They need a different pitcher," Ryder said.

"They need a different everything," Marshall said.

Silence passed. "Suzanne tells me your princess stopped by today to give the boys some gifts before she returns to Champagne or wherever the hell she lives."

His gut twisted. Tomorrow. "It's Chantaine," he said.

"Whatever," Marshall said. "Suzanne said she held it together with the babies but fell apart on the front porch."

Ryder narrowed his eyes against another stab of emotion and took a quick breath. "It sucks all around."

"Hmm. Seems like a lot of unnecessary torture to me," Marshall said.

Ryder shot his friend a hard glance. "Unnecessary?" he asked.

"Well, yeah, if y'all are that miserable without each other, then stay together."

Impatience rippled through him. "Okay, Mr. Relationship Expert, exactly how would we do that?"

"Ask her to marry you. Ask her to stay," he said and took a sip of his beer. "Nice play," he said, nodding toward the screen.

Ignoring Marshall's comment on the game, Ryder set down his beer. "How in hell can I do that? She's a princess from another country and she works for her country. I work eighteen hours a day and I have twin boys. No woman in her right mind would agree to that kind of life. She deserves better."

"I take it to mean you didn't have the guts to ask her what she would want," he said.

Anger roared through him. "Guts? Who are you talking to about guts? Guts is what it takes to let her go."

"Hmm," Marshall said. "You know, Suzanne and I are gonna have a baby."

"She's pregnant already?" Ryder asked.

"No. We don't know *how* we're going to have a baby. We just know we will. I told you about this the other day, but you probably weren't listening. There are lots of ways to have a baby these days. IVF, surrogacy, adoption in the States, overseas…" He nodded. "Yep, they're putting in the second-string pitcher. Let's see what happens now."

"What's your point?" Ryder demanded.

"There's more than one way to crack a nut," he said. "There's more than one solution to a problem. You could ask Bridget to move here. You could commute for a while. Just because you commute for a while doesn't mean you'll have to do it forever. Hell, didn't you say her country needed some doctors? If you really wanted to, you could move to Champagne and be a doctor there."

"Chantaine," Ryder corrected, mentally dismissing Marshall's suggestions in one fell swoop.

"Well, my man, you're going to have to make some career changes anyway," Marshall said. "Those babies are little now, but when they get older they're going to need to have their daddy around more than an hour or two every day. You're gonna have to figure out what kind of father you want to be, and I'm guessing it's nothing like the father you had."

Ryder mused over that for a long moment. He'd been fighting change ever since his brother had died. Although he'd done his best with the twins, he'd clung to what was most familiar to him, and that was his career. Outside of the hospital, he'd felt completely out of control. For a time, Bridget had made the new responsibility he'd faced feel a little lighter. She'd even made it fun.

He wondered how she would have responded if he'd asked her to stay. If he'd asked her to marry him. His heart hammered at the ridiculous possibility. The very idea of it was ludicrous. Even more ridiculous was the idea of his quitting his position, uprooting the twins and moving across the world for a completely different life with the woman who had made him fall in love with her. She hadn't asked for that because she hadn't wanted it. Ryder scowled at Marshall. The man was just stirring up a bunch of craziness because he'd found and married the woman of his dreams.

"At least, we can be miserable together," Bridget said to Phillipa, adjusting her dark, oversized sunglasses as she and her sister strode through the airport. She planned on keeping these sunglasses on her face night and day, inside and outside except when she was in her private quarters. No amount of cosmetics concealed the gutted agony in her eyes.

"It would have been nice to have the private jet," Phillipa said.

"So true, but Stefan always gets first rights to the jet. Plus, it's supposed to be much less expensive to travel commercial on the long-haul flights. At least we'll be together in first class. Hopefully they'll have a distracting movie. Although with my luck, it will be one of those dreadful tales with an unhappy ending from that American author. What's his name?"

"Robert James Waller," Phillipa said. "I've never liked sad movies. I know that some people say crying is cleansing, but I hate it."

"Me, too," Bridget said.

"I don't mean to upset you, but did you ever even ask Dr. McCall if he wanted you to stay?"

Bridget's stomach twisted. "He said our future was

impossible. He didn't even want to discuss the possibility of our seeing each other after this trip back to Chantaine." She felt her throat tighten with emotion and took a tiny breath. "No hope," she said.

Pippa reached over to take her hand. "I'm so sorry. You seemed so different once you met him. I'd thought he might be the one."

Her heart stretching and tightening, Bridget squeezed her sister's hand. "I'm lucky to have such a sweet sister."

"Your Highness," Raoul said, stepping to Bridget's side. "I apologize for the interruption, but Dr. McCall has arrived at the airport. He wishes to speak to you. I must warn you that you don't have much ti—"

Shocked, thrilled, afraid to hope, she felt her breath lodge somewhere between her lungs and throat. "I will speak to him," she managed in a whisper that sounded hoarse to her own ears.

Seconds that felt like eons later, Ryder stood in front of her.

"Hi," he said, meeting her gaze dead-on.

Her heart was hammering so fast that she could hardly breathe. "Hi. What brings you here?"

He took a deep breath and cocked his head to one side. "You mentioned that your country needs a new medical director. I wondered if you thought I could handle the job?"

Stunned and confused, she shook her head. "Excuse me? Are you asking for the position?"

He paused a half beat, then nodded. "Yeah, I guess I am."

Torn between throwing herself in his arms and trying to keep her head from spinning, she bit her lip. "Would you like me to talk to Stefan? I'm sure he would be thrilled."

"That's good. How would you feel about it?" he asked. "How would you feel about the twins and me coming to Chantaine?"

Bridget was so light-headed that she feared she might faint. She grabbed the back of a chair. "I would be beyond thrilled."

"Thrilled enough to marry me?"

She gasped, unable to register his question. "Excuse me?"

He moved toward her and took her hands in his. "I love you. I want my future with you. I want my children's future with you. I know it's fast, but will you—"

"Yes," she said, her eyes filling with tears of joy. Her heart was overflowing. "Yes, yes and yes."

Ryder took her into his arms and she hugged him tightly. The secret dream of having a man love her just for herself had just come true.

Five months later, Bridget stood in front of Ryder in the chapel of the oldest church in Chantaine and pinched herself. Her sisters dabbed at tears with handkerchiefs. Her brother Stefan beamed his approval. He was so thrilled one of his siblings had finally made a marriage that would benefit Chantaine. With Ryder as the newly appointed medical director of Chantaine, there was no shortage of residents clamoring to come to their country. Her sister-in-law Eve gave her an encouraging nod. The twins ran along the side aisle like the wild rascals they were. Her youngest brother and Raoul chased after them. Bridget had reached a new level of terror when the boys had started pulling up, and worse, walking. Not one day passed, however, when she didn't thank God for Ryder and the boys.

The priest led them in their vows. Ryder's voice was clear and strong. His gaze was resolute. She knew she could count on this man for the rest of her life. Surprisingly enough, she knew he could count on her, too. Ryder's love had triggered something hidden deep inside her, something she'd hoped she possessed, but it had never surfaced. With Ryder in her life, she didn't mind her royal duties, yet she could say no to Stefan when necessary.

Even with all the sacrifices and changes Ryder had made, he seemed happier and more relaxed. At the same time, he saw many opportunities for improvement and expansion in Chantaine's health program. She still couldn't believe how everything had worked out. Every day, she grew closer to Ryder and fell more deeply in love with him. She counted her blessings that she would spend the rest of her life with him and the twins. Despite her best efforts, though, he refused to reveal his honeymoon plans. As long as it didn't involve the desert, and it did involve just the two of them, she would be happy.

With the twins squealing in delight, the priest appeared to smother a chuckle. "I now pronounce you husband and wife. You may kiss your bride," he said.

Ryder took her face in his hands as if it were the most precious thing in the world and lowered his mouth to hers. She threw her hands around his neck and kissed him with all her heart.

Distantly, she heard the sound of laughter and

applause. She pulled back and turned to the many wit-
nesses seated in the chapel, glancing toward the twins.

Ryder's mind must have been moving in the same
direction. "Tyler," he called. "Travis. Come here right
now."

The twins turned suddenly solemn, but made their
way to the front of the church. Dressed in pale blue short
suits, both boys lifted their arms toward her and Ryder.
Heedless of her designer wedding dress, she scooped
up Tyler while Ryder picked up Travis.

"Ladies and gentlemen, may God bless this happy
union."

As the group in the church applauded again, Ryder
leaned toward her and kissed her again. "I'm taking you
to Italy, Your Highness. Tomorrow."

* * * * *

PREGNANT WITH
THE PRINCE'S
CHILD

BY
RAYE MORGAN

All the characters in this book have no existence outside the imagination of the author, and have no relation whatsoever to anyone bearing the same name or names. They are not even distantly inspired by any individual known or unknown to the author, and all the incidents are pure invention.

All Rights Reserved including the right of reproduction in whole or in part in any form. This edition is published by arrangement with Harlequin Enterprises II B.V./S.à.r.l. The text of this publication or any part thereof may not be reproduced or transmitted in any form or by any means, electronic or mechanical, including photocopying, recording, storage in an information retrieval system, or otherwise, without the written permission of the publisher.

This book is sold subject to the condition that it shall not, by way of trade or otherwise, be lent, resold, hired out or otherwise circulated without the prior consent of the publisher in any form of binding or cover other than that in which it is published and without a similar condition including this condition being imposed on the subsequent purchaser.

® and ™ are trademarks owned and used by the trademark owner and/or its licensee. Trademarks marked with ® are registered with the United Kingdom Patent Office and/or the Office for Harmonisation in the Internal Market and in other countries.

First published in Great Britain 2012
by Mills & Boon, an imprint of Harlequin (UK) Limited,
Eton House, 18-24 Paradise Road, Richmond, Surrey TW9 1SR

© Helen Conrad 2011

ISBN: 978 0 263 89416 5

23-0312

Harlequin (UK) policy is to use papers that are natural, renewable and recyclable products and made from wood grown in sustainable forests. The logging and manufacturing processes conform to the legal environmental regulations of the country of origin.

Printed and bound in Spain
by Blackprint CPI, Barcelona

Dear Reader,

As the song says, memories light the corners of our minds. Memory builds the structure of our lives, brick by brick, each representing happiness or regret or sadness or pride. It fills our thoughts with a rich background we wouldn't have without memory. But what if you lost yours?

Mykal Marten has lost his. He can't remember anything about Janis Davos, the woman he fell in love with two years before. That leaves Janis with a very big problem. How can you make up with a man who doesn't remember the terrible fight that tore you apart? How can you heal the wounds if one person doesn't know they're bleeding?

Her first impulse is to leave him behind and close off her memories. But one thing after another stops her, and soon she is trapped in a one-sided relationship. She loves him; he doesn't know who she is.

And that sets up an interesting experiment. Will he fall in love with her again? Was it just an accident of time and place, or is there something fundamental and important pulling them together? Were they made for each other? Was their love inevitable? Or would it crumble into ashes without those shared memories?

All this must play out against the excitement of Mykal being recognized as one of the Lost Princes of Ambria. But that only makes things worse for Janis. With her family's criminal past, she knows she can never fit in at the castle. She decides to fade out of his life before he finds out she belongs there—and before he knows about the baby.

Hope you enjoy reading about Mykal and Janis. All the best.

Raye Morgan

Raye Morgan has been a nursery school teacher, a travel agent, a clerk and a business editor, but her best job ever has been writing romances—and fostering romance in her own family at the same time. Current score: two boys married, two more to go. Raye has published over seventy romances, and claims to have many more waiting in the wings. She lives in Southern California, with her husband and whichever son happens to be staying at home at the moment.

This book is dedicated to CB—
which could stand for Clearly Beloved

CHAPTER ONE

"Look."

Mykal Marten held out his cupped hands and opened them slowly. Perched on his palm was the most stunning butterfly Janis Davos had ever seen. Its lacy wings sparkled pink and silver as they pulsed in the sunlight.

"Be careful," she cried without thinking. "Don't hurt it."

He gave her a quizzical look, as though wondering why her first thought might be that one. "I would never hurt it," he said, his voice low and rough with emotion. "I just wanted you to see it. It's so beautiful, so precious...." His voice went so soft she could barely hear his words. "It reminds me of you."

She turned to look up into his crystal blue eyes, her heart in her throat.

"Oh, Mykal," she whispered, tears threatening. She looked more deeply into his eyes, hoping for truth. Did he really mean it? About her? There had been so many lies in her life, she was almost afraid to believe. And then she laughed with happiness.

Her laugh must have startled the butterfly, because it

took off, circling above them, rising higher and higher in the offshore breeze, until it was just a sparkle against the blue sky.

They watched until it disappeared, and then she tucked herself into the crook of his arm and sighed.

"Here's the truth, Mykal. That butterfly was my heart. You set it free." She looked up, searching his eyes, hoping to see that he felt like she did, almost afraid that he wouldn't. "I never knew life could be like this," she said simply.

He pulled her in closer, wrapping her in his strong arms and smiling down into her face. "Neither did I," he said softly. "I never knew what love was until there was you."

He kissed her lips slowly, touching her tongue with his, savoring every nuance of her taste. "Promise me we'll never let it slip through our fingers, like other people do," he murmured. "Promise me we'll always remember this day and how we felt."

"I promise," she said, reaching up to get more of his kisses. "And what's more, I promise it will only get better."

Only get better. Only get better.

Her own words echoed mockingly in her head no matter how hard she tried to blot them out. That was then. This was now. How did you celebrate the death of a romance?

You didn't. You just tried to survive it.

And now, here she was in front of Mykal's family

home, ready to sign, seal and deliver an official end to all they had meant to each other only months ago. She shifted the satchel she was carrying and wrapped her fingers around the beautifully twisted bars of the wrought-iron fence that topped the limestone wall that held back those who didn't belong inside.

Of course that meant her. Especially her.

Blame it on the war. Everybody else did. She'd used that excuse herself when she'd married Mykal, a man she'd known at the time for less than two months. Their marriage had been passionate, intense, and only lasted for a few weeks before their separation. All in all, it hadn't quite been half a year since they'd first met, though it seemed a lifetime. Blame it on the war. A whole generation of young Ambrians had given in to impulses they never would have thought of before the war drums had begun to beat a rhythm to their lives.

She and Mykal had both volunteered for military intelligence work, both taken some very tough training, and when they met later on as the war was ending, they'd seemed to be so well matched, she found it hard to believe that the man she'd married could have possibly grown up in this…well, it was a mansion, wasn't it? There was no way to put a more modest face on it. Rich people lived here. Very rich people.

She and Mykal had never talked much about their backgrounds. She hadn't realized he was hiding his just as surely as she had been hiding hers. She'd been pretty sure he didn't secretly have a family in organized crime like she did. But then, she didn't talk to anyone but her brother Rolo about that.

And here she was, standing outside of the address where she'd been told he now lived, trying to get up the nerve to go to the door and ask to see him. She didn't belong here. Her heart was beating a wild salsa in her soul and her knees felt like water. She was scared stiff.

But what she was most afraid of was her own traitorous heart. Would she let him walk all over her emotions again? Would she be able to keep the cold, sharp edge of her bitterness alive once she looked into his mesmerizing blue eyes?

She had to. She wasn't just building a life for one any longer. She couldn't afford to follow her heart. Two months in a prison camp had taught her to stop dreaming and start facing reality. That tended to happen when the man you thought was the love of your life turned you over to the secret police.

She looked at the brass bell meant for visitors to announce their business. What was she going to say to the butler? She had to get in to see Mykal one last time.

Mykal. It still took her breath away to think of him, and she had to control that. He didn't love her anymore. That much was perfectly clear. But she needed his signature on a couple of official documents. And then they could cut the last ties between them and walk away and never look back.

Her hands were trembling. Could she hold it together long enough to get all that done? She had to.

The street was empty. Clumps of grey snow lingered

in the shadows. It was almost twilight. It had been a long, hard journey to get here and she'd hurried to make it before dark.

"So, what now?" she murmured to herself. "Shall I ring? And if they say, 'No visitors', then what? Do I make a scene? What do I do?"

Suddenly, a medical van turned onto the street, siren blaring. Janis jumped back, stepping behind a bush. She knew it was coming right for this house. Somehow, she knew. And as it turned in, the iron gates began to open.

Despite everything, she was still quick and resourceful. She didn't know if the van was bringing someone in or taking someone away, but she did know this might be her only chance to get onto the property without anyone challenging her. Trying to stay inconspicuous, she held the satchel with her papers close and slipped in through the gates alongside the van, staying well away from where the big side mirrors could pick her up. She was still wearing the dark blue jumpsuit they'd made her wear in the prison camp and now she was glad for it. Anyone looking out and seeing her would assume she was in uniform and working with the medical van. This way she would have a chance of finding Mykal before someone kicked her out.

The van turned and pulled slowly into place, backing toward the wide stairway. A serving person had opened the double doors to the house and was on his way down the stairs toward the van. She went the opposite direction and seemed to escape notice, as all attention was on the van as the door opened and a paramedic jumped out, shouting orders forward to the driver.

She was almost in when a voice stopped her.

"Hey."

She gasped and looked up. A medic was looking down out of the ambulance at her.

"Hey, miss," he said. "Can you make sure they're ready for him inside?"

"Oh." She almost laughed with relief. "Sure. No problem."

"Thanks."

That answered that question. This was a delivery, not a pickup. There had to be a lot of people living in a house this big.

A few more steps and she was inside, giving only a quick glance at the beautifully appointed foyer and the sweeping stairway to the second floor. She had to figure out how to find Mykal and in a house this size, that wasn't going to be easy.

"Yes? Can I help you?"

"Oh!"

She whirled and faced an imposing-looking gentleman in formal wear. She was caught. She had to think fast. She wasn't sure just exactly what was going on, so it was difficult to make adjustments. She needed a story that would fit in. Luckily, her military intelligence training had been thorough and it kicked in now.

"I came in with the medevac van," she said, careful not to do any actual lying. She glanced out at where the van had backed up to the front stairway. The double doors were open and someone was being unloaded on a gurney. She looked again, gaze sharpening. There was a man...and he looked familiar.

Her heart stopped and she reeled.

The man on the gurney was Mykal.

Mykal! her mind screamed, and for a split second, everything went black. Mykal was hurt. All the love, all the feeling came pouring back. The anger, the pain, the betrayal—all that disappeared in a puff of smoke. Mykal was hurt. Everything in her demanded she go to him.

But she couldn't. She saw his head move. He even nodded in answer to something one of the paramedics said to him. Relief filled her heart. At least he wasn't unconscious.

But what was he? Wounded? Ill? She couldn't tell. But she knew what her plan had to be. It came to her very clearly in a lightning-quick flash. To people in the house, she had to appear to be with the medevac team. To the medevac team, she had to appear to belong at the house. Mykal was hurt and she knew she had to pretend she didn't know him for now. Until she had a chance to see him alone, she couldn't let anyone know who she was or why she was here. For all she knew, there might be standing orders to keep her away.

It would be more than tricky, because she needed to stay out of Mykal's line of sight at the same time. If he looked up and saw her...

All of that thought process transpired in a fraction of a second. As she knew from her training, acting like you belong there and you know what you're doing is half the battle. She turned back to the butler and managed to put on a professional smile.

"If you could direct me to the room he'll be using, I'd like to check it out and make sure the accommodations will suit his needs."

The man hesitated a moment and she thought she could detect just a hint of suspicion in his eyes. But he didn't say anything. Instead, he stood back and gave her a gracious bow of welcome, then turned and led her past the sweeping curve of the huge staircase to a room at the back of the house.

"We decided to prepare the extra bedroom here on the first floor rather than his usual suite so that the stairs could be avoided for now," he told her, and she nodded her approval of that decision after a quick look inside. But his words also made her wonder—was he in a wheelchair? Was he paralyzed? Each thought made her quiver inside.

"It looks fine," she said, noting there was a bathroom attached. All in all, it was larger and nicer than any apartment she'd ever had in her life and it was just a spare room. "I'm sure we will be able to make him comfortable here."

There was a shout from one of the technicians escorting Mykal in and she noted it with a gesture. "Please don't feel you have to stay with me," she said. "I think the medical team might need some guidance right now."

"Of course." He gave her a quizzical look, but he did as she suggested, and she sighed, sinking like a sack of rocks onto the bed, her head in her hands. This was outrageous, as complex as any undercover assignment she'd ever had. She should be laughing—at herself for doing this, at anyone who took her seriously.

Mykal was hurt in some way but she couldn't think about that. All she needed right now was a measure of time to talk to him before someone ordered her off the premises. And she knew very well that someone might end up being Mykal himself.

She closed her eyes for a moment, trying to center herself. This had seemed so simple. Her anger at Mykal had been simmering for a long time and she had planned to find him, glare right into his face and let him have it. She'd been all primed and ready, so filled with pain and resentment that she'd been sure she could pull it off. But she hadn't counted on him being hurt.

Mykal didn't get hurt. She'd shared enough espionage adventures with him to know that. He was like a golden child, unique and untouchable. Magic happened when he went undercover. Safes opened to reveal their bounty at his touch. Women swooned and gave away their deepest secrets. He smiled and doors opened. But he didn't get caught and he didn't get hurt. Others did, but not Mykal. Those were the rules. It left her shaken to know someone had breached them.

She heard the paramedics coming down the hall and she stood back as they brought him into the room, skimming the shadows, trying to stay out of his line of vision as long as she could. Luckily, the butler didn't come in with them so she only had to play one part of this multiple-sided game. So far, the paramedics were focused on their job and hadn't seemed to notice her beyond an original nod as they entered.

She didn't let herself really look at Mykal. She was afraid of what she might see and of the emotional response she might have. All of that had to be saved for later…if there was a later.

And then he spoke to her.

"Hey. Could you get me some water?"

The voice was rough, strained. He was obviously in a lot of pain. She looked up, meeting his eyes for just a second before they closed.

"Sure," she said, her heart thudding against the walls of her chest so hard she was sure everyone could hear it. "I'll get some right away."

He hadn't realized who she was. But she couldn't keep herself from staring at that face she'd loved so deeply. Despite the obvious ravages of his injuries, he was still as gorgeous as ever. She had to rip her gaze away, afraid she would be hypnotized by his beauty if she didn't take care.

She drew in a sharp breath, set her satchel down in a corner and slipped out of the room before he looked again, feeling very, very lucky. He wasn't totally himself and she hated to see him in this condition. But at least he hadn't realized who she was. She could breathe easy for a few more minutes.

Actually, being sent on this errand was a good thing. She needed to reinforce the impression she belonged here. She walked toward where she assumed the kitchen and butler pantry must be. Sure enough, the man himself was taking a sip from a suspicious-looking bottle as she came through the door. He put it away hurriedly and cleared his throat, trying to put the best face on it.

She smiled. More good luck like this definitely made her feel more secure and she waved away his apologetic look.

"We're getting him settled," she told him, attempting an air of professional courtesy. "But we'd like to have a tray with a pitcher of water and a glass available for him at bedside. We've got something in the truck I can use, but I thought something he was familiar with using here at home would feel more comfortable for him."

"Of course, miss." He began to set one up for her right away. "My name is Griswold, by the way. I'm in service until nine tonight. After that, it's just the night watchman, but you can dial the nine on the phone and you'll get him." He handed her the tray. "Here you are. Would you like me to…?"

"No, I'll take it myself. Thank you so much."

She started off but he called to her.

"Miss…"

She turned back, her heart in her throat. Had he noticed something?

"Yes?"

He frowned at her for a moment and she held her breath. Then he shrugged and asked, "What kind of food shall I tell cook he will be needing?"

She bit her lower lip, trying to look thoughtful but

panicking just a little bit. How the heck did she know? She didn't even know exactly what was wrong with him.

"I'll have to look at my instructions," she said quickly, "and get back to you on that. But I would assume it would be the usual light, bland sort of things."

Ouch, that sounded lame, didn't it?

"To start, I would prepare some chicken soup if I were you," she added quickly.

You could never go wrong with chicken soup. At least, she hoped not.

"Ah, yes. Thank you, miss."

"Of course." She nodded and left the room.

Once she was far enough from the kitchen, she paused and leaned against the wall, closing her eyes and catching her breath. What the heck was she doing, anyway? This had started out as a ploy to get close to Mykal without gatekeepers barring her way. But it was fast becoming something much more serious.

Funny. She'd spent the last few weeks in the prison camp going over everything she was going to say to him when she got out, again and again. It was how she'd kept herself sane. But now, the words were fading. Things weren't quite what she'd thought they would be.

Her emotions had run the gamut while she was imprisoned. She'd gone through sorrow, raging anger and finally, a deep, painful bitterness when she realized he really wasn't going to come and save her. No one was. She was lucky the camp had been liberated by the royal forces a few days before, or she would have been there still.

And Mykal—had he been here all that time, living like royalty, while she endured the horrors of the camp? Anger began to bubble up inside her again and she had to tamp it back. Anger got in the way of clear thinking and she would need her wits about her.

She was about to go back into his room. If he were dozing, she would have a chance of staying until the paramedics left. She wished she knew what had laid him low like this. An illness? A wound of some sort? She ached to know so that she could do something to help him.

But if he were wide awake, he would take one look, stare for a second, hardly believing she would have the nerve to show up here, and then probably order her out of his house and out of his life, just as he had the last time they'd been together.

She took a deep breath and steadied herself. In a moment, she would be alone with Mykal. That was what she'd come for, but when she came right down to it, that was really the scariest part of this.

CHAPTER TWO

"READY, set, go," Janis muttered to herself, her own private little pep talk.

She was about to face Mykal and make demands. She would be cool, calm and collected. She would remember her talking points. And she would be tough.

She'd never been very good at holding him to account. Their life together had been full of excitement, danger and fun. Neither one of them had ever insisted on guidelines. Neither of them had ever set out principles. Maybe that was what had doomed them from the start. When problems rose up between them, they had nothing to fall back on.

She hesitated outside the bedroom door, listening. They seemed to be finishing up, and in another moment, they were filing out the door.

The one with the curly red hair saw her first. "Oh, good. You've brought him water. I was going to go find some, but that will be better."

"We've settled him in," the dark-haired paramedic added, nodding as though he thought she was in charge here and he was making his report. "Have you been updated on his condition?"

She shook her head, maintaining a professional reserve. "No, I haven't. I'm hoping you can fill me in."

"Sure. Well, here's the deal. You probably know he was badly wounded when his motorcycle hit an IED a few weeks ago."

She didn't know. Emotions choked her throat, hitting her hard. She managed to hide it pretty well, but inside, she felt the trauma. The horror of picturing him in a motorcycle accident was almost too much to bear. But she couldn't show it. If she could control the trembling, she would be all right.

"He ended up with some broken bones, damage to a few internal organs, including possible brain damage, and shrapnel in his back. Most of the shrapnel was removed, but a few slivers are very close to his spinal cord. They haven't decided yet if they can risk going for them."

"Oh." Reaching out, she used the chair rail to keep herself upright, but he didn't seem to notice.

"We've got him braced pretty tightly. He won't like it when he fully wakes up. But you've got to keep him in it."

"Can he..." Her voice was choked and she had to clear her throat. "Can he walk? Is there paralysis?"

The paramedic hesitated. "So far, so good. But he has to be kept quiet. No physical activity. No major emotional upheaval." He shrugged. "I'm sure you know the drill."

"Do I?"

A wave of panic crashed over her. She couldn't help it. This was making her very nervous. She wasn't qualified for this. These people had the idea that she would take care of him. She wouldn't. She couldn't. What if she did something that injured him?

"I...I'm not experienced with spinal injuries," she stammered out. "Maybe you should call in someone who..."

He shook his head. "No need for that. Just keep him down as long as possible, that's my advice. That's why we've given him something to make him sleep. I left a couple of bottles of the medications prescribed for him and some other supplies on the shelf in the bathroom. The doctor will be coming in to see him tomorrow, about ten, so be ready for that."

"About ten," she repeated robotically, still stunned by what she was hearing.

"I left a list of the numbers to call if he needs anything." He shrugged. "But you seem to be pretty well staffed here. I don't suppose there will be any problems."

He gave her a half smile, as though he'd suddenly realized she was pretty. He shrugged. "He may be a little hard to handle. And he's got a wicked temper." He grinned. "But I guess that's understandable after all he's been through."

She blinked. That didn't sound much like the man she'd been married to. But she supposed things were different now. Then she remembered what he'd been like that last day, once he'd found out what she'd done. Yes, his temper had come out, cold and biting. *Wicked* hadn't been the word for it.

"Of course," she said weakly.

"And I guess that's it."

She nodded, not sure anymore if she was glad the medics were leaving. She'd wanted them to go before the butler came back, but now she wasn't so certain. Maybe he should have been here to hear all this. She bit her lip, not sure what to do, but they were leaving and what could she use as an excuse to stop them?

"Thank you so much for all your help," she said instead, feeling breathless. "Shall I show you the way out?"

"Don't bother, miss. We know the way." He gave her a grin. "See you again soon, I suppose. We'll be the ones to transport him to the castle when that comes up."

"Oh. Of course." She knew her smile was shaky but that couldn't be helped. "Goodbye." Then she watched as they made their way out. What could she say? She was completely bewildered.

It sounded as though his injuries had been life-threatening—and maybe still were. She felt as though she were taking a dive on a roller coaster every time she thought of that. Obviously, he might have died. Despite everything, she couldn't bear to think of it.

And the castle? Why on earth would he be going to the castle?

But that didn't matter. She had to get out of here.

Time to face facts: she'd been kidding herself. All

this talk of tying up loose ends and coming to closure was a bunch of baloney. Deep in her heart, she'd been hoping for a confrontation, a knock-down drag-out that would curl Mykal's hair and set him back on his heels. She'd wanted him to know how he'd misjudged and hurt her. She'd wanted him to admit he'd been wrong to betray her. She wanted to throw his legendary self-confidence into disarray.

He wasn't always right. He'd been wrong. Very, very wrong.

But all that was impossible now. She couldn't confront him. He was in a precarious condition and had to be handled with kid gloves. It made her cringe to think of hurting him further. That confrontation she'd been so ready for would have to wait for another time.

She would have to go. There was no choice. She would go back to the kitchen and repeat everything the paramedics had told her, then tell the butler to take over Mykal's care himself.

How strange this all was. How frustrating.

With a deep, heart-felt sigh, she looked at the bedroom door. He was probably asleep by now. She might as well take in the water. It would give her a chance for one real look at him before she went.

She stopped, unsure. Should she risk it? She shrugged. What else could she do? Softly, she opened the doorway and slipped through it, her heart beating hard. Taking a deep breath, she entered the room and set the pitcher of water down before she looked at the bed.

Mykal's eyes were closed. It looked as if he were

sound asleep. She swayed with relief, then took the opportunity to look at him more closely. Even though his face looked pale and drawn and there were dark circles under his eyes, he was as gorgeous as ever. Despite everything, her heart yearned for him. Was there any way to stop it?

No. She was just going to have to shove her feelings aside and learn to move on. She'd been tough before. Her whole life had been filled with hard choices, unpleasant consequences. She had to be totally tough now, and she knew she could do it. It wouldn't be easy. But she could do it.

But she was stalling and had to get away soon. Being this close to him again was hard. All the old feelings were still there, waiting to be released. And she had to make sure that didn't happen. He hadn't trusted her when she'd needed his support. He hadn't done anything to save her from the Granvilli secret police. Anyone with this sort of wealthy background surely should have had the influence to make things easier on her at least. But no help had come. That was something she would find hard to ever forgive.

Quickly, she went over in her mind exactly what she needed to get done. He had to sign the divorce papers she'd had drawn up. But most important—he had to sign away his parental rights to the child she was carrying. That, she knew, might be the sticking point. That was the one she would really have to fight for.

Sighing, she turned and looked around the room. It was plain but elegant, decorated in white and gold. A flat-screen television sat on a table in one corner. A tall bookcase filled one wall. She walked over and began to study the titles, one by one.

She ought to go.

Now.

Well, in a minute.

Something deep inside was telling her that once she walked out the door, she might never be able to get this close to him again. Did she still love him? Her eyes filled with tears and she couldn't read the titles any longer.

"Hold it together," she told herself softly. "Just keep it calm."

But the sudden sound of a male voice made her jump and gasp at the same time.

"Looking for something?" he said.

She froze in sudden horror. The voice was Mykal's. There was no doubting it. She'd missed her chance to avoid this. Slowly, she turned, heart beating in her throat.

"Hello," she said, attempting a bright tone but achieving only a shaky rasp. Her version of a smile felt awkward. But she met his stunning blue-eyed gaze steadily. Like Anne Boleyn, she was ready to face the guillotine. "How've you been?"

"I've been better," he said, and grimaced.

She waited, hardly breathing, watching his eyes. The hair was standing up at the back of her neck. She expected fireworks. She expected he would call out her name, yell, shout, order her out.

Something. Some harsh emotion. But as she waited another second, and then another, her surprise began to grow. It wasn't happening. There was nothing.

The longer the silence lasted, the more breathless she became. Was he having trouble seeing in this dim light? Recognition should flash across his face any second now.

But his attention seemed to have drifted. Maybe it was the drug they'd given him. Maybe she could still slip out and…

Suddenly, he turned his gaze and looked at her penetratingly.

"Did my brother hire you?" he asked.

She stared at him, completely at sea. What was he talking about?

Mykal, she wanted to say. *It's me. Janis.*

But she couldn't say a thing. All she could do was stare at him. His eyes were just as blue as ever, just as beautiful, but nothing in there seemed to recognize her.

Was he playing a game with her? Torturing her in some creative new way? But no, he wasn't the type to do that, and anyway, he looked completely sincere. And what would be the point?

"Or did the castle send you over?" he went on, stretching back and closing his eyes. "I'll bet that's it."

What? The castle again. What was going on here?

"I…no, uh…" What could she say? She knew very well what she *should* say. She should tell him who she was and remind him of their past together. That was why she was here, wasn't it? But did she dare? Wouldn't that be inviting the very thing she had to avoid in order to keep him calm?

"I guess they thought I could use a day nurse," he muttered, sounding more irritable than friendly. "If they would just stop with the medication, I have a feeling I would do just fine without anybody's help."

She stood on the spot, paralyzed. He didn't seem to know who she was. But that was crazy. How could he forget? They were married, for heaven's sake. It might not have been a traditional sort of marriage, but it had been intense and wonderful while it lasted. Disappointing him had been a big mistake, and it had been ugly when he realized what she'd done. He'd lost all trust in her, and his response had broken her heart.

She looked at him, at the pale complexion, the short dark hair that curled about his head like a laurel wreath. He seemed very tired and as she gazed into the depths of his eyes, she could see that his injuries had done deep psychic damage along with the physical wounds. Soon, whatever the paramedic had given him would kick in and he would fall asleep. She had to leave.

But she hesitated. This was the man she had loved with all her heart and all her passion. This was the father of her coming child. How could he not see who she was?

Deliberately, she stepped into the light right in front of him. He looked surprised.

"Don't you know who I am?" she said, hating that her voice trembled as she spoke. "Don't you know why I'm here?"

He stared at her as though he were trying to see through a fog. "Sorry. Have we met before?"

She stared at him, frozen in wonder. Was she dreaming this? Searching his face, looking for answers, she had to conclude it was real. He was disgruntled, but there was no lurking animosity. And there was definitely no lurking recognition. He really didn't know who she was.

"If you were a nurse at the hospital, I really am sorry." He managed a crooked grin of boyish-looking apology. "I wasn't exactly a model patient at all times." He winced as though something hurt. "I guess I was pretty much out of it a lot of the time. I just might not have ever noticed you."

She half laughed, nervous and unsure. "I'm not a real nurse, you know," she said quickly. "I'm actually more of a…a…"

"A guard?" He nodded as though her puzzling behavior was finally becoming clear to him. "I understand. With these negotiations going on endlessly, I guess someone decided I might need extra protection. Especially considering the condition I'm in."

"Protection." She felt like a fool, parroting his words. But she needed something to give her a clue as to how she should act. She had no idea what negotiations he was talking about and the casual way he brought them up made her think they were somehow common knowledge—at least to anyone who had paid attention to the news and hadn't been wasting away in prison camp for weeks.

"Uh…what is your condition exactly?" she asked, knowing she might be opening a can of worms she wasn't going to be able to control, once opened. She wanted to hear from him just what he felt was damaging and dangerous—and why he didn't seem to remember things he should know by heart.

He grimaced, looking annoyed at the question. "Shrapnel from an IED. Most of it removed, but some slivers still close to the spine. Broken collarbone that's already mostly healed. Traumatic brain injury that doesn't seem to be as bad as they first thought." His voice took a bitter tone. "But either that, or the induced coma they put me in, seems to have wiped out a chunk of my life. Like, the last two years. Hope to get them back at some point." He looked at her wearily.

"You…you don't remember anything?"

"Nope. All gone."

She stared at him, speechless. He had amnesia? Their love, their marriage, the things he'd caught her doing—everything gone, like wiping a slate clean? She could hardly breathe. And she could hardly believe it was true.

His face darkened as he watched her reaction. "You're a funny sort of medical guard," he said, almost angry. "Where's your hard, Nurse Ratched attitude?"

Still stunned, she was having trouble working up anything coherent to say. She shook her head, blinking rapidly.

He made a gesture of disgust. "Listen, just go and leave me alone," he said, shifting against the pillows. "I really don't need anybody here. I'm okay. Just get out, why don't you…."

His voice broke and he gasped, turning to find relief from whatever was torturing him. She bit her lip. Obviously, the pain medication hadn't kicked in, or wasn't working. His eyes were closed and he was breathing unevenly.

She stared at him, still so beautiful, but with a line of bitterness around his mouth and a slow, smoldering sorrow that she'd noticed in his blue eyes. He looked like a man who'd had too much suffering and didn't want to have any more.

What had happened to him? What had made him lose his memory? And why didn't he respond to her the way she still responded to him? Had it all been a sham from the beginning? That thought made a bitter taste rise in her throat and she pushed it away.

He began to look better again. Whatever had been torturing him seemed to have weakened and she decided to attribute his bad attitude to pain and leave it at that. In another moment, he took a deep breath and straightened, looking almost normal.

"What shall I call you?" she asked as he blinked toward her in the light.

"Are you still here?" he asked, looking surprised. "I gave you every opportunity to go."

"I don't scare all that easily," she told him with a twisted smile. "What shall I call you?" she asked again.

"Mykal will do." He didn't smile back but he didn't look angry anymore. "If you really think you can handle it here, we might as well operate as though we were friends." A shadow passed over his eyes. "God knows it's going to be hard to find a friend soon. I'm afraid I'm being drawn into a world where such things can't last."

She had no idea what he was talking about, but she didn't ask.

"So what is the deal with your memory loss?" she said instead.

He gave her a mock wounded expression. "Do you know how hard it is to talk about something you can't remember?" He shifted his position carefully. "I lost over two years of my life. But it doesn't really bother me unless someone brings it up."

"Oh." She made a grimace of apology. "Sorry."

He grinned as though happy to be able to set her back a bit. "No problem," he said. "Troublemaker," he muttered, just to tease her.

It warmed her, this back and forth. It was very like what they'd done together all the time in the old days.

"You don't wonder what you did?" she asked him. "All that time."

"I've been told what I did. At least, I've had a rough outline."

Sure, they'd probably told him about his military service, about working in intelligence. But had they told him about her? Had they told him he'd been married? Probably not. After all, very few people even knew. They'd kept it secret. If their commanding officers had found out, they would both have been expelled from the corps. Not even their friends had known about it. If she hadn't found the marriage license and her wedding ring in among her important things when they'd let her out of the prison camp, she might have begun to believe it was a fantasy herself.

"And?" she prodded.

"I guess I was in the military, but so far they haven't been able to confirm that with the right agency. It seems I was doing some sort of undercover work or something. Very hush-hush. No one will admit anything. But I'm sure they will get paperwork squared away eventually. In the meantime, I'm a man without a past."

That was a pity. She had a big chunk of his past right here in her heart, but she couldn't hand it over. Not yet.

The pain came back in waves. She could see it as it came, read it in his eyes. He groaned softly and she could see that he was in real agony. Everything in her wanted to go to him, to help. But what could she do? She had no medical training. She was afraid anything she tried to do might only make him worse.

He groaned again, writhing, and she couldn't hold back any longer. She slipped into the bathroom, grabbed a washcloth and ran cold water over it, then hurried back and sat on the edge of his bed. For all she knew, this might be exactly the wrong thing to do, but she had to do something. Moving smoothly, she pressed the cool cloth to his forehead and began to murmur soft, soothing nonsense as she held it there. At any moment, she expected him to lash out at her, kick her away, yell something awful.

But to her surprise, he did none of that. Something in her touch seemed to calm him almost immediately. Little by little, his body began to relax.

"Do me a favor," he said suddenly, his voice choked. He was looking up at her with a strange expression on his face, as though he weren't sure how she was going to react to what he asked of her. "Could you hold my hand?"

She stared down at him, hardly breathing.

"I...I'm spinning," he explained gruffly as he reached out, closing his eyes again. "The medication. I just need... I don't know. To feel like I'm anchored to something."

She took his hand in hers and held it tightly, then pressed it to her heart. There was something so real, so vulnerable about the way he'd asked her, tears filled her eyes again and her throat choked with emotion.

This was so strange, a complete reversal of roles. Mykal was always the tough guy, the one whose arms she'd run to, the man who knew all the answers. And now here he was, asking her for reassurance. Asking for trust. For a solid center to cling to.

But she wasn't the one who could do that for him. Not now, not after all that had happened between them. Didn't he sense that?

"Mykal," she whispered, tears spilling over. "I...I can't..."

But he didn't hear her. He was already asleep.

She looked at the long, strong hand she was holding in both of hers. His beautiful hands had always been

one of the things she'd loved best about him. She ached
inside for what they'd had, what they'd lost. Bringing
his hand up, she put it against her cheek and sighed.
Then she kissed the center of his palm and laid it back
down on his covers, letting her gaze run over every vis-
ible part of him. The light from the lamp made his skin
glow and seemed to put every muscle in relief, like a
beautiful landscape. Everything in her yearned to touch
him. She'd missed him so much and hungered for this
for far too long.

For just a moment she remembered the first time
she'd met him.

She'd been sent to check out rumors of a commotion in a pub in the seaside town near where she'd been
working. Walking into the room, she'd seen him and
he'd filled her gaze like a star, brilliant and shining, the
center of everything.

At first, she'd thought she'd caught him in the middle
of a giant con. She knew he wasn't who he said he was
and he knew she knew it. But it hadn't fazed him one
bit. He'd given her a great big grin that told her everything she needed to know about him.

The war was already over at the time. The phony
truce had begun, making things even more dangerous
than they had been before. They were working in a
border town filled with people who changed sides as
easily as they changed their toothbrushes. Or maybe it
just seemed that way as most people were busy playing
both sides against the middle.

The little pub was filled with local officials scared

to death their money-laundering scheme had been discovered by the Granvilli authorities. They were looking for a way out. Mykal had convinced them they were
about to get caught and that they should let him hold
the money for safekeeping. They were grateful as they
turned the cash over to him. They even bought him
drinks and made him the center of a general toast.

He loved what he was doing. He loved pulling the
wool over their eyes and getting away with—well, not
with murder exactly. But something pretty wrong at any
rate. He took their money and left them feeling good
about it. Sort of a modern day Robin Hood—if Robin
Hood had been a spy for France.

And when she caught up with him outside the little
pub and challenged him on it, he laughed. And then he
picked her up out of sheer exuberance and twirled her
around as though to the music still pumping out through
the double doors of the place.

"You're right," he said. "And what are you going to
do about it?"

She'd stared at him for a moment, then her lips
twitched. He was completely adorable and impossibly
mischievous at the same time. She was smitten. And she
also knew she would never, ever forget him. So pretty
quickly, she was laughing right back at him.

"Tell you what," she'd said. "I'll buy you a drink.
But not here."

She wasn't all that surprised to find out they were
both working for Granvilli Military Intelligence. Well,

not exactly both. She was doing that, but he was doing something else as well.

He was a spy for the royal side. But she didn't learn about that until later. Still, she couldn't hold that against him. After all, she had some secrets of her own. And that was pretty much the heart and soul of the problem between them. Even when she'd thought he was deliciously devious, she hadn't understood just how convoluted his motives really were. And he still didn't know a lot about her.

The man she'd loved so passionately was still in there, somewhere. He needed her, even if he didn't realize what all that implied. There was no way she could leave until she knew he was safe.

With a sigh, she slumped down on the small couch that was set next to the bed. In another moment, she was curled into a ball and thinking protective thoughts. And then she was asleep herself.

Mykal woke carefully. He was doing everything carefully now. Even his dreams were tentative. Something was always warning him not to move. The excessive caution created a growing rage inside him, pure frustration. He wanted to shout and throw something. He wanted to punch something. He couldn't live the rest of his life this way.

Still, for now, he would be careful. The world around him seemed to be so full of changes, so many things happening to him and his future, so many things lost in his past, that he didn't want to risk making a wrong move. For now.

Lifting his head slightly, his gaze fell on a young woman curled up and sleeping on the couch next to his bed. It gave him a start but then he remembered who she was—someone the powers that be at the castle had sent over.

He didn't need her here. In fact, he resented it. He could take care of himself. Once this medication wore off, he would be okay. He would tell her to go back where she came from and leave him alone.

Still, he had to admit, he'd felt a tug of attraction from the first. It was stronger now. She was young and pretty with evidence of a lean, agile look to her nicely shaped body—though he couldn't see much of it under that shapeless jumpsuit of a uniform. Her sleek ash-blond hair fell over her cheek, shining like corn silk in the summer sunlight with a beauty that almost choked him for a moment. He hadn't had much beauty in his life lately. Suddenly, he had an overwhelming urge to reach out and touch it.

But he couldn't, he thought to himself sarcastically. He had to be careful. His groan was heartfelt and he shook his head. No, he wasn't going to be able to keep this up for long. There came a tipping point when life just wasn't worth living without a few common human activities. Touching a beautiful woman was one of them.

Currently he was clinging to optimism. Surely this would pass. He'd seen the X-rays. The pieces of shrapnel were mere slivers. How could such tiny things be so dangerous to his life? Maybe they would begin to move away or melt or…or something. And maybe his memory would come back and things would get back to normal.

He was blaming the amnesia on the fact that they had kept him in a drug-induced coma for weeks while they worried about a possible traumatic brain injury and debated what to do with the shrapnel. That ought to be enough to knock anybody's mind for a loop. He had no doubt the fog would clear away soon. But as for the shrapnel…

If he just could remember what exactly had happened. What had he been doing, what had he been thinking when he'd hit that IED? But it was gone— along with a few years of his life. He'd just lost it all. How did you do that? How did it happen? Whatever— it didn't make a lot of sense, but it seemed to be true that it had happened to him. And there was a deep, dark hole in his soul because of it.

The woman moved and murmured something in her sleep. It sounded like "get away from me," but it might have been something totally different. Still, it made him frown and wonder what was bothering her. He wanted to reach out and comfort her. And then he remembered. He couldn't do things like that anymore.

He grimaced.

Think about something else.

He looked around the room. His usual bedroom was upstairs, but he'd stayed in this one a time or two in his childhood—mostly when all the Swiss cousins had come to fill the house for the holidays. The furnishings had a nice heirloom look to them, although he knew his mother had worked hard to make bargains into antiques during their poverty-stricken period in his late teens. It was nice to be in a familiar place after all that time in the sterile rooms at the hospital.

He hadn't actually lived here since he'd gone away to university, more than ten years before. But he had a lot of childhood memories. It had been here on his eighteenth birthday that his parents had told him he was adopted. An admission like that was supposed to be a big shock in a young man's life, but as he remembered it, he had nodded thoughtfully, taking it in as something less than surprising.

He'd always known he was sort of an ugly duckling in the wrong nest—though most would have disputed the "ugly" appellation. His parents were nothing like him. All through his childhood they had watched him in a sort of state of awe, their mouths slightly open, as though they couldn't believe a child of theirs could act like that.

Not that they didn't adore him. If anything, they'd loved him a bit too much, to the point where his brother, Kylos, their natural-born son, felt as though he had to do ever more outrageous things in order to get noticed himself.

So once they had told him the truth, he felt vindicated in a way. That small, illusive memory sense deep inside that only came out in dreams to tell him something was deeply, horribly flawed inside him had it right after all. He was in the wrong family.

And now someone at the royal castle had decided he might be one of the lost princes who had scattered into hiding at the time of the original rebellion that overthrew the monarchy almost thirty years before. He had no idea if there was any truth to it. If there was, he wasn't so sure he wanted to participate. But his mind was too fuzzy right now to try to think it through.

The way he saw it, only two items were blemishing an otherwise charmed life for him. First, this damn injury that kept him drugged at the edge of disaster. And second, his loss of memory regarding the last few years of his life. Other than that, things were coming up roses.

He sighed and went back to sleep.

CHAPTER THREE

JANIS woke to a cooler, darkened room. Someone had come in and turned on a side lamp, but the light it shed was minimal. They had also left a tray with a covered bowl. She rose and went over to take a peek. Chicken soup. She smiled. At least the butler took her seriously.

But the soup had cooled. How long had she been sleeping? She looked around for a clock and didn't find one.

And finally, she looked at Mykal.

Her heart was in her throat again. Just looking at him sent her over the moon. She was in big trouble. How was she going to convince her traitorous heart not to love him? She began to pace the room, hands clenched into fists, thinking furiously, trying to get a handle on her situation.

Obviously, she couldn't stay here. What had she been thinking? The need to make sure Mykal was safe had overwhelmed her good sense. See how he contorted her emotions? She didn't dare stay and let that happen time after time, as it surely would.

She'd come with three objectives and not one of them

was in the bag. That was a pretty poor performance. But how could she fight a man who was in such a precarious position? No way. She would just have to leave and hope she could get this close to him again later.

"Or else, send him a sternly worded letter," she muttered to herself ruefully. "Arrgghh."

All right, that was settled. She was leaving. She glanced at him again and winced. He was so darn beautiful. But he made her heart ache with a longing she didn't need right now. She was going. Just exactly where, she didn't know. These last few weeks in the prison camp, all she'd thought about was finding him and confronting him for all the misery she'd been through. It still hurt so badly to know he could have spared her all that if he'd cared enough to lift a finger.

But he hadn't. And now he was the one in trouble. Why should she bother with him?

She shouldn't. It was over.

She was deep in thought but suddenly her senses tingled. Someone was coming into the room behind her. The butler? Another servant? Before she could turn to see who it was, a male voice shot across the room like the flash from a flamethrower.

"Who the hell are you?"

The words hit her from behind but the man's hand was on her neck before the words even registered. She didn't have to think. She reacted on instinct and training, setting her foot and shifting her weight and grabbing the man by the neck. It was all a matter of balance and leverage. She'd done it so often it came naturally, and she slung him over her head, onto the floor. He landed with a grunt and lay very still. She gasped, wondering if she'd killed him.

But then a string of obscenities came pouring out of his mouth and she sighed with relief. Anyone who could swear like that still had a lot of life in him.

"Hey, I'm really sorry," she said, sounding less than sincere. "But you shouldn't touch a woman without warning like that."

The obscenities didn't stop, and suddenly she realized there was a background sense of chuckling going on. Turning, she found Mykal sitting upright and grinning from ear to ear.

"I see you've met my brother, Kylos," he said, half-laughing. "Wow, as a guard, I'd say you fill the bill. I hope you stay forever."

She flushed. The tiniest hint of praise from him and here she was, blushing. This was crazy and exactly why she couldn't stay.

"Why the hell do you need a guard?" Kylos was grumbling as he clumsily pulled himself to his feet. "A nurse I could understand, but a guard?" He glared at her. "And why did you pick one who shoots first and asks questions later?"

She tried to smile, but it wasn't easy. She'd never even known Mykal had a brother, and this man seemed so unlike him, it was eerie. His face was long and his skin was sallow and he tended to twitch as though he had an itch he was chasing. Where Mykal had been

open and welcoming and warm—at least in the past—
this man seemed cold and sly and calculating.

And if Mykal had this brother, what else did he have?
He'd never told her anything about his family. Looking
back now, she realized that their short relationship had
been built on some pretty shaky ground. They'd existed
in a fantasy bubble of their own. They'd kept their marriage a secret from most of the world, knowing they
could lose their jobs if the intelligence service found
out. It had seemed daring and exciting at the time. And
it had only lasted a few weeks—barely time for them
to get to know each other, much less discover anything
about their respective families.

Crazy days—but as she remembered them, she
couldn't help but smile to herself. If it hadn't ended so
badly, just think where they might be now.

"The castle sent her over," Mykal responded, sounding cool and cynical. "She's probably supposed to keep
me from killing myself by doing something normal."

She was dying to ask what the castle had to do with
this, but if they thought that was who had sent her, any
questions on the subject might seem odd. So she decided
to fulfill her role instead, raising her hand in warning
as he seemed to be leaning forward with a bit too much
vigor.

"Careful," she said. "I'm sure the physicians have
warned you against any sudden movements."

He sent her an icy look before settling back against
the pillows. "I heard their advice. I accept it—for now.
They seem to think my life, as I've known it, is fully

over with." He looked at her in a way that implied an intimacy he couldn't possibly think they shared, and then his gaze took on a challenging look. "Little do they know. This human hulk will rise again. And that's a promise."

"Not on my watch," she said firmly, chin in the air as she looked back into his frosty eyes. "I haven't lost a patient yet."

"Well, that's encouraging." But his attention was fading and he winced. It was obvious he was still in pain.

Her heart lurched and she had to stop herself from moving toward him. She looked toward the doorway instead. Once she was out again, she wasn't coming back. But then her gaze fell on the bowl of soup.

"You should be hungry by now," she said, reaching for it. "I'll go get this soup heated up for you. You probably want to talk to your brother anyway."

He appeared surprised. "No, not really," he murmured, but she was out the door.

There was no one in the kitchen, but the microwave worked fine and she was back in a flash, more determined than ever to wrap this thing up and take her leave.

"Can you handle this on your own?" she asked Mykal as she set the soup up for him on a bed tray.

He gave her a look but didn't say anything. Taking the bowl from her, he proceeded to drink from it as though it were a large cup. She stood back and tried not to smile. Everything he did, every move he made, caused her to resonate like a tuning fork. The only problem was, each response was paired with a touch of fear at the same time.

His brother was hanging around grimly. He'd turned on the television, seemingly more for background noise than for any programming content. He made a face and gestured at Janis, making it clear he wanted to talk to her alone. She was tempted to go ahead and leave without letting him get his way, but she reluctantly hung back as he drew her aside in order to speak without Mykal overhearing.

"Listen, did they leave any medication for him?" he asked her urgently, leaning close. "I've looked all over and I can't find anything. I was told they would leave something to help keep him quiet."

She nodded, surprised at his intensity. "In the bathroom," she said, pointing it out. "On a shelf in the medicine cabinet, I think."

"Oh. Of course." He looked as though he was starting off in that direction, then he hesitated, grimacing. "I guess that's supposed to be *your* job, right?" He gestured toward Mykal. "Don't you think you ought to give him something? He seems awfully wide-awake to me."

"I think he's allowed a little awake time," she said, feeling slightly annoyed, then realizing she was talking through her hat. For all she knew, Kylos had talked to the doctors himself and knew much more than she did.

But actually, he didn't act like it.

"Oh. Of course," he said, fidgeting. He gave her an arch look. "But we wouldn't want him to hurt himself."

She frowned. "Don't worry. I think he understands the possible consequences."

She moved a little away from him. There was something definitely unpleasant about the man. Funny. Mykal had always been the sort of man who drew people to him. His brother seemed to be just the opposite.

"I think he can probably monitor his own need for the drugs, don't you think?" she added.

He didn't look convinced, but Mykal was holding out his empty bowl and she turned to take it from him and put it down on the top of the dresser.

"That ought to help make you feel a little more alive," she told him.

He nodded, looking at her with a spark of interest in his eyes. "What's your name, guard lady? What shall I call you?"

She took a deep breath. "Janis," she said. And she didn't give her last name.

"Janis?"

He was still frowning, thinking it over as though it might ring a bell. She held her breath.

And then he showed the hint of a smile. "Nice name," he said. His eyes drifted shut again. "Will you still be here when I wake up, Janis?" he asked her softly.

She couldn't answer that. After all, he'd told her to leave earlier. But he didn't seem to remember that.

"I hope you will," he said groggily. "I have some things I want to talk to you about. Later."

"I…I'll try," she said faintly.

He held out his hand and she knew what he wanted.

Quickly, she moved closer and took his hand in hers. He smiled and held on tightly, as though he really did need her to anchor his existence. Then his smile faded as he fell quickly into another deep sleep.

She stared at the hand she was holding, then pressed it to her heart and gazed down at him. He looked like a wounded warrior. Her heart filled with love for him. She couldn't help it. No matter what he did, she couldn't seem to shake it. And in truth, she didn't really want to.

Their marriage had been short, barely two months, but oh, so sweet. They had been friends as well as lovers, but the love had been the best. She remembered the night he'd aroused such passion in her, she'd clawed his back with her fingernails. He'd laughed and teased her that he was going to go around without a shirt for the day so everyone could see what a hot woman he had. She'd been mortified, and so apologetic. But he'd just kissed her and before she knew it, they were making love again.

If they could go back to what they had created between them in the short time they were married, before it all fell apart…

But that was dreaming and in her experience, dreams very seldom came true. She'd grown up hard and tough, learning how to defend herself early. Her mother died when she was young and her father was a mobster. He'd been killed in a police raid when she was ten. Her brother, Rolo, had been the only real family she had left, though they had both gone to live with her uncle, Max Gorgonio. Rolo had been the only person who'd ever been close enough to gain her trust, until she'd met Mykal.

Trust. The word tasted bitter on her lips. What good had all that trust done when the rubber hit the road? It melted away like a springtime snowfall and left cold comfort behind.

"Hey, what's the deal?"

She dropped Mykal's hand with a start. She'd forgotten his brother was still here.

"Nothing," she said quickly. "I was just…thinking."

"Oh, yeah?" He gave her a doubtful look. "Well, I've got to go meet…uh…my lawyer. I've got to get going now. Are you going to be here for the night?"

Was she? No. She had to go. Staying wouldn't accomplish anything. She looked back down and sighed. She hated to leave him, but what else could she do?

Kylos twitched, blinking rapidly. "If you are, you can keep an eye on him. But I want to be perfectly clear. I want to make sure he stays quiet, and in order to do that, I think we ought to keep him pretty drugged up."

The way he'd phrased that gave her a bad feeling and she looked at him, curious. "Drugged up?" she repeated doubtfully.

"Sure. That's what they did in the hospital, didn't they? No one wants to take any chances with that shrapnel thing in his back."

"Oh, I agree. But he doesn't have to be out cold in order to stay quiet, does he?"

He shrugged and looked bored with it all. "Whatever

it takes, honey. I'd just as soon you kept him groggy. He's easier to handle that way."

Her mouth dropped. What on earth was this man talking about?

"Hey." He pinched her cheek and grinned at her. "Just play along for now and I'll make sure you get a bonus when this job is over. I just need a couple more days and then…" He twitched nervously and looked as though he was afraid he might have said too much. "What I mean is, I'm really worried about my brother's chances. He's got big things in the works and we have to keep him calm. Get it?"

No, she didn't get it at all, but she nodded. And at the same time, she had a sinking feeling. She wasn't going to leave, was she? Not while this vulture was strutting around asking her to drug Mykal. She couldn't allow that. Someone had to monitor the situation. She sighed. Maybe she would be here for the long haul after all.

Or at least until Mykal's last few years came back to him and he realized that she was his wife—and that he hated her.

She woke up feeling odd. For a moment, she looked around, disoriented. Where in the world was she? And then it flooded back to her and she jerked upright. The bed was empty. Where was Mykal?

She heard water. A shower. The bathroom.

Leaping to her feet, she raced to the bathroom door and flung it open without thinking twice.

"What the heck do you think you're doing?" she demanded into the steamy room.

"Well, hello to you, too." He leaned around the shower curtain, amusement dancing in his eyes. "Care to join me?"

She drew in a sharp breath, realizing this must seem odd to him. At the same time, the sight of his naked body, which was clear at the edge of the shower curtain, did nothing but bring back delicious memories. It was a body she knew only too well—but he didn't know that.

"You're not supposed to do anything without support," she said crisply, making it up as she went along, but pretty sure she had the melody right, if not the exact words. "I'm here to help you. Any sudden moves could kill you!"

He made a face. "Okay, take it easy. I'm not suicidal. But I can make some decisions for myself."

"Not until you clear them with me." She might have gone over the top, but she was genuinely worried. He was being reckless. She had to find a way to make him think things through before he acted.

"Clear them with you?" He looked at her as though she were a slightly annoying insect he could bat away at will. "Sorry. I don't mean to be rude, but you're nothing to me. You're an employee."

Something choked in her throat. He was right, of course. She was nothing to him. Not anymore. She started to turn away, but he seemed to regret his harsh words.

"Wait a minute," he said, calling her back.

She stopped and glanced back at him, hoping he couldn't see how much he'd hurt her. She had no right to be hurt. She was nothing to him. But there was one problem. He was still everything to her. She just needed time to train herself not to care. Slowly, reluctantly, she turned back toward him and waited for his explanation.

"I apologize," he said. "That was uncalled for." He smiled at her, then turned off the water and leaned out. "And anyway, I need you here to hand me a towel."

She made a face, but did as he asked, handing him a nice thick one. He dried himself behind the shower curtain, then wrapped it around his waist and stepped out onto the bath mat, being careful and a bit tentative, but able to manage it on his own. And looking proud of himself for it.

About then she told herself she really ought to be backing out of the bathroom. Ordinarily, with a stranger, she would have been long gone. But being here like this with Mykal felt natural and familiar. And so here she was.

She should have gone. But her body didn't seem to be obeying orders from the top right now. Every piece of her attention was being soaked up by the sense of the beautiful man standing before her. A few weeks in a coma didn't seem to have sapped away any of that long, lean muscle mass that worked together to form a hard, sleek classic statue of a man, and the memory of what his strong arms had felt like as they tightened around her took her breath away. Her gaze trailed from his wide shoulders down across his gorgeous chest with its fine mat of dark hair.

This was the man she had loved with a crazy passion such a short time ago. Something inside, some insane impulse, told her to throw herself into his arms. That he would remember if she only held him and kissed him like she used to. That all would be forgiven and they would laugh together and make love together and blot out all the bad times as though they had never happened. It was worth a try. Wasn't it?

Everything in her yearned to take the chance.

But then she looked up into his eyes and what she saw there stopped her cold. There was no love. There was no memory. There was only a faintly amused look of surprise. He thought she was being overwhelmed by his manly presence, and he was right. Only, he thought she was an employee who could be flirted with, to a point, but needed to be kept at arm's length. And she wasn't.

Taking a deep breath, she tried to get her bearings and get back to the job at hand.

"Uh…" She swallowed hard and lifted her chin, blinking in the light. "Listen, playing Russian roulette is not just a fun option. It's risking your life. And I'm supposed to make sure you don't do that."

His frown was stubborn. "But that's just it. It's *my* life. It belongs to me. Not you. Not the doctors. Not the wise guys at the castle. Just me."

He was right, but it made her want to cry. She

couldn't explain to him why she felt she had a stake in this situation. She couldn't tell him much.

He hitched up the towel and gave her a look of pure skepticism. She drew in her breath, startled by his distrust. Still, he was so beautiful, she was tempted to start letting her gaze travel over him again, a simple, guilty pleasure. But his look suddenly hardened, as though he'd remembered she was an interloper and wasn't sure why she was still hanging around.

"So let's get this straight," he was saying. "I'll do things at my own pace. You can give advice. But you're not going to set any agendas. I'll do that." He gave her a challenging look. "No rules."

She nodded reluctantly. "Okay." She drew in a deep breath. "But…"

"Uh-uh." He shook his head. "This is my game. I'll play it my way. If you can't handle that, it's time for you to go."

CHAPTER FOUR

JANIS'S pivot wasn't graceful but at least she didn't fall on her face, shaky as she was. He couldn't have been clearer. He wanted her gone. She headed back into the room and reached for her satchel. This time she really would go. If he wanted to risk ruining his life, she wasn't going to try to stop him.

She stopped and looked around the room, making sure she wasn't leaving anything. She was angry and feeling wounded. She'd only been trying to help. She'd had enough.

Where would she go? She wasn't sure. It was getting pretty late. This was a nice neighborhood. Maybe there was a hotel nearby. Maybe. If not, she would wander around until she got her bearings. She only hoped she wouldn't have to end up sleeping under a bridge in the cold.

One last glance back over her shoulder and she was stepping out the door. And that was the moment she heard his gasp of pain.

She was back in the room in a flash. He was leaning against the doorjamb, his eyes closed.

"Oh, no, oh, no," she whispered like a prayer as she rushed to help him. He'd managed to put on pajama bottoms, but his chest was still bare. She quickly slipped under his shoulder and became a crutch for him.

"What happened?" she asked.

His mouth twisted into something resembling a sort of grin, but he shook his head. "I'm just too damn weak to support myself once the pain starts shooting through me," he muttered, sounding resentful.

"Lean on me," she told him firmly. "Come on. I'll get you back into bed."

He felt like heaven, even this way—all hard muscle and slick skin. She turned her face toward him and took in his familiar smell and then wished she hadn't. Emotion came surging up her throat. She'd missed him so.

She hardened her heart and forced herself to hold him steady as they made their way across the floor. And then she had him at the edge of the bed and he groaned as he slid down onto the covers.

For just a moment, she caught a glimpse of his back, at the horrible red scarring, and her heart lurched. Horror shivered through her and then she steadied herself and thought of basics instead of pain.

Where was his brace? He should be in it. And surely he'd had bandages on the wounds when he'd been brought in here. He must have taken them off when he went into the shower. Should he have done that? She highly doubted it. But there wasn't much she could do about it right now. He'd been very clear. This was his game. Carefully, she pulled the sheets from under him and then pulled them over and tucked him in, looking down at him anxiously.

He was looking up at her. He didn't smile, but there was something going on behind his crystal gaze.

"Okay," he said roughly. "Just let me rest a minute."

She nodded, thankful he seemed to be tired but largely okay. She resisted the impulse to tell him to wiggle his toes and prove nothing had touched his spinal cord at this point. Making a quick trip back into the bathroom, she saw where he'd thrown away the old bandaging. She opened the cabinet and grabbed a round of tape and a package of fresh gauze pads, snagged the brace and took it all back out into the bedroom.

His eyes were open and he looked alert, but he shook his head when he saw what she had.

"I want to let air get to it," he told her.

She hesitated, not sure that was a good idea, but she couldn't argue with him, could she? With a sigh, she put her supplies down and sank onto the couch.

"You always have to do it your way, don't you?" she grumbled.

He was feeling better by the minute and he managed a lopsided smile. "Is it that obvious?" he asked. "I'd almost think you knew me well."

That was putting it mildly. It was very strange to realize that he didn't remember anything about the last two years, and especially that he didn't have any of the past they'd shared in his system. They hadn't been together long, but it had certainly changed her life. To

think any changes he'd gone through were lost, or re-
versed, or whatever had happened to them, was unset-
tling to say the least. She didn't like it. It just might be
that when he remembered, he would hate her again. But
that would be better than not remembering and being
untouched by all they had gone through together.

The way he was watching her, his head back, his
eyes half-closed, she wasn't sure what he was thinking. The seconds stretched out longer and longer. He
didn't speak, but he kept looking at her. She bit her lip,
nervous but ready to deal with whatever he was getting
ready to throw at her. Somehow she knew it was coming.

But when he finally spoke, his question was awkward for her, but rather ordinary in its way.

"Are you married?" he asked at last.

Her heart lurched, but she managed to hide it. "Yes,"
she said quickly. "Yes, I am. But we're pretty much sep-
arated right now."

"I see." He nodded slowly. "The war."

"Yes. The war." She almost laughed aloud. "Blame it
on the war." Why not? The war had been the supposed
reason behind everything in their relationship so far.

He frowned. "I was in the war. So they tell me. I
don't remember." He twitched as though he wasn't really comfortable. "They say I did some good things, but
I guess I'll never know for sure."

"Well, of course," she said with a smile that quickly
turned bittersweet.

Something told her that he knew, without having to

be told, that he'd been brave and honorable. It was the essence of who he was. And it was also why they were so badly matched. The ache in the bottom of her heart seemed to throb more painfully than ever. You could change your mind, you could change your behavior, but you couldn't change your bloodline.

"When do you go home?" he asked.

"I was just leaving when you collapsed," she said defensively. "I'll go. Don't worry."

He frowned at her, seeming furious all of a sudden. "Why would you go?" he demanded. "Isn't it your job to stay here with me?"

"Not when you kick me out like you did."

"Kick you out?" He obviously thought she was making things up. "I would never kick you out. I need you. Has anyone made up a room for you?"

"No." She looked at him, exasperated and confused. "Actually, I haven't told anyone I need one yet. I thought…"

He moved impatiently. "Get Boswell in here. He'll make sure you have good accommodations. I'm surprised he didn't take it upon himself to do it already."

She stared at him blankly. "Boswell?"

"Our butler."

She wrinkled her nose. "I thought his name was Griswold."

"Oh." He grimaced as though he'd just remembered something best left to the shadows. "That's right. Kylos replaced the entire staff for some ungodly reason." He frowned fiercely at her. "Do you know why he did that?"

"Uh…no."

"Neither do I." He sighed, looking restless. "Poor old Boswell. I wonder what's happened to him? He was here from the time I was a toddler. Practically part of the family."

"Well, now you've got Griswold. But he went home at nine o'clock."

He stared at her, nonplussed. "Went home! What the hell's a butler doing going home? Doesn't he live here, in the house?"

She threw up her hands and laughed at him. "I don't know. He's your butler."

The situation seemed to bother him. "Boswell wouldn't have left his post," he muttered to himself.

She nodded, sure that was true. But then, she'd never had a butler. The thought made her want to giggle. She only hoped it wasn't plain old hysteria threatening.

Because this entire situation was strangely weird and getting weirder. She certainly felt tugged in two directions. She had a deep underlying feeling she ought to have kept going once she was on her way out a few minutes before. And at the same time, she wanted to stay. She wanted to make sure he was okay. Not only was she worried about his condition, but there was also something about his brother that didn't sit well with her.

Or was she rationalizing again?

"Hey," she said as she noticed he was sitting up and

beginning to swing his legs over the side of the bed. "What are you doing now?"

He stopped, eyeing her with a certain cool moodiness. "I'm doing whatever I feel like doing. And right now, I've got a yen to see my old house."

"You mean, this one?"

He nodded. "If I've got another, I don't remember it." He gazed at her levelly. "I'm counting on you to be my crutches. To catch me when I fall. Okay?"

She was tempted to argue with him but she knew it would do no good. "Sure," she said wryly. "I'm adjustable. That's why they pay me the big bucks."

"Don't go expecting diamonds and pearls from me," he said, teasing. His grin was lopsided. "But play your cards right and if this royal thing comes through, I might be able to buy you an iced latte one of these days."

"I'm excited," she said, a trace of sarcasm showing. But she was smiling as she rose to help him up. He leaned on her lightly with one hand on her shoulder and they walked slowly out onto the beautifully finished maple floors on into the foyer with its marble inlays. She took the time to look around and appreciate how much care someone had taken in making this home a beautiful showplace. The fact that the décor was about fifty years out-of-date didn't matter. The warmth and character of the home shone through.

He took her through the study and into the library, where the walls were filled with floor-to-ceiling, glass-enclosed bookcases full of books. They strolled through the kitchen and she realized it had only been the butler's pantry she'd visited before. The central kitchen was huge with large ovens of all kinds and a refrigerator that took up one wall.

"We used to have huge parties," he told her. "And people staying for the weekend. There was always something going on. But that was before…" His voice seemed to trail off.

"Before?" she asked, but he ignored her and went on, pointing out the herb garden from the kitchen window.

"Let's go upstairs," he said. "You can see almost the whole estate laid out in front of you from my old room."

She thought she'd caught signs already that he was flagging a bit. "Mykal, do you think you should?"

"Sure I should." He grinned at her. "We'll take the elevator."

"You have an elevator in your house?"

"Sure. My father got very weak after…after some financial reverses and this house has three levels."

The elevator swayed a bit, but it got them there.

"Here's my bedroom," he said, leading her in and pointing out the bay window. "I used to sit on this window seat and stare out for hours."

She could see why. Night had fallen but the place was littered with solar lamps that flickered from the trees and from the side of walkways. It seemed to be an enchanted garden. But she was more interested in looking at the artifacts of his boyhood that filled the shelves, books and trains and bats and soccer balls.

"Your parents left a lot of your things here, almost

on display. You know what that means, don't you?" She looked at him teasingly.

He shrugged. "That they were too lazy to throw it all out?"

"No. That they loved you so much they wanted to hang on to everything that reminded them of you."

He smiled as though what she'd said had touched him, just a little. "Yeah. My mom likes me."

She looked at him and thought, *Who wouldn't?* He was such a charmer. Her eyes met his and she realized he was still thinking about what she'd said. Was he missing his parents? How sad. Funny that he'd never told her about them at all.

"How could they have left this beautiful house?" she asked him.

"You should have seen it when I was a kid. The estate was twice this big and the condition was ten times better. Financial reverses did my father in about fifteen years ago."

That made her curious. "Where did they go?" she asked. "To the continent?"

"No." He flashed her a quick look. "Believe it or not, they went to Florida and bought a condominium and have been quite happy ever since. I don't think they'll ever come back." His eyebrows knit together and he looked at her as though he found that hard to believe.

She nodded, suppressing the trace of a grin. "Some people like sunshine on the water."

"As opposed to fog and rain clouds?" His smile was

quick and humorless as he described the usual weather in Ambria to a T. "I suppose."

They were standing very close and he turned, putting his hand on her shoulder for a moment, as though to balance himself. Then his face changed and he moved closer, leaning in, spreading his fingers over the small of her back.

"You did say you were married, right?" he asked, his voice low and musical.

"Yes." She looked away. "Technically, I'm married."

He touched her chin with his finger. "No hope of getting back together?"

She met his crystal gaze and shook her head. "No."

He raised an eyebrow. "You're sure?"

"Positive."

"Good." He pushed her hair back behind her ear. "Because I want to kiss your neck."

"What?" She reacted, but she didn't really pull away. How could she when every nerve in her body was reacting as though violins were playing?

"Don't move, now," he said in a soft, half-teasing voice. "I'm a sick man, you know. I must be humored."

"That's outrageous." But she was laughing low in her throat. "And it's cheating, too."

"I'll have to plead guilty to that." His breath was warm on her skin. "But something about you makes me crazy. I can't stay away."

His face was nuzzling her neck by now, and then she felt his tongue, sending shivers all through her system.

"Mykal," she said, and her voice almost sounded

like a whimper. She turned her face and he brushed his cheek against hers. And then he'd pulled back, as though nothing had ever happened.

The look in his eyes as he cupped her cheek with the palm of his hand was heavy with a sensual vibe that made her blood feel like maple syrup. "You're pregnant, aren't you?" he said simply.

Shock slashed through her like a lightning bolt and her eyes went very wide. How could he tell? No one knew. She hadn't told a soul and she was still so thin from the prison camp ordeal.

"I…uh…no…" she stammered.

"Don't worry. I can keep a secret." His wide mouth twisted in a half smile. "But I thought I could tell when you were helping me to the bed. I could sense it." He looked at her with a sense of regret. "I hope it's true. You should be very happy."

She glanced away, but her throat was choked and there was no way she could force out any words. How on earth could he tell? She'd been sure it would be weeks before anyone would see it. Did he remember…? But no, there was nothing to remember. He'd never known. She hadn't even known until she was in the prison camp.

Was it because he was the father? Did he have some special, magical sense of his own child? It seemed impossible. And yet…

He led her to a guest room and showed her the view along the other side, one that was partly lit with electric lights. She followed him willingly. It was almost as though he'd hypnotized her now.

"Take a look out here. There's the duck pond. Too bad it doesn't look like anyone's maintained it for a long time."

She loved the quaint setting. "What's that burned-out house behind it?"

He didn't answer for a moment and she realized that he was too emotional to speak at first. Then he cleared his throat and said, "That was my mother's Victorian tea house. She loved having her friends over for high tea. They would sit on the little porch and watch the ducks and eat their watercress sandwiches and sip their Darjeeling. Nothing made her happier."

She hesitated to ask when he was so affected by it, but her curiosity was running wild. "What happened to it?"

He took a deep breath. "Long story. Bottom line, enemies of my father burned it down."

How awful. "What? Why would anyone do such a thing?"

"There are bad people in this world, Janis." He touched her cheek again, but playfully this time. "Stay away from them if you can."

"I try to. Were your parents hurt?"

He looked at her in surprise, then smiled. "This happened years ago. My father left it that way as a reminder."

"I see." Though she didn't, not really.

He stood brooding over the view for a few more minutes, and she waited, not wanting to break into his reverie.

"Okay, here's what happened," he said at last, as though he just couldn't hold it in any longer. He reached out to use her shoulder, leaning on her as though his legs were getting tired. "Well, my father made some bad decisions. Kylos got into some trouble. He was always getting into trouble, but this time it was really bad. My father needed money fast, but times were tight, and he couldn't find anyone who could lend him that much. So in the end, he had to turn to the mob."

At the sound of that three-letter word, disbelief filled her. This couldn't be happening. She'd never heard a whisper of it. Her heart turned to stone and something deep inside her began to pray. *Please, please, please, don't let it be the Gorgonios.*

"It was a lot of money and he couldn't pay it back. He went into hiding for a long time. My poor, tiny little mother had to fend for herself." Anger began to boil up in him. "The police could keep the mob from hurting her, but they couldn't keep them from ruining her financially. She was just barely able to hold on to the house. But in the meantime, they did burn down my mother's tea house, just to make sure we knew they were serious."

She murmured something, hoping it sounded sympathetic, but there was a loud buzzing in her ears. Was she going to faint?

"Everyone knows what happens when you don't pay off your loan in time to a member of the mob. They ruin your life or they break your legs." His laugh was humorless. "My father was lucky. He still has his legs.

He finally pulled together the resources from some old friends and came back, paid off the loan and eventually all was well. But it took him years to get back into shape as far as money went and it broke their health in the meantime. And so they finally gave up and went overseas to live."

"Oh." It sounded to her as if she were drowning, but he didn't seem to notice. He was caught up in his story.

He looked at her and suddenly his hand slipped around her shoulders, pulling her in close. "I guess you know that in Ambria, the mob means the Gorgonios. Luckily, I recently heard that most of the family is in prison. Especially Max Gorgonio, the lousy bastard. I say don't rest until you get them all behind bars."

She could hardly breathe. Would he still want her if he knew she was one of them? She flailed about fruitlessly, trying to find a way to change the subject. Turning toward him, she was horrified and confused, and he took her emotion to be something very different. Softly, slowly, he kissed her lips, and she found herself curling in against his warm body, hungering for more, yearning for the strength and protection he could provide.

"Oh, Mykal," she whispered so softly he couldn't hear. "If you only knew…"

"Sorry," he murmured as he pulled back. "There's something about you that just calls to me."

She searched his eyes. There was still no depth in his feeling for her. Still no memories. But his warm and wonderful kiss was a start.

She winced, remembering his family's encounter with her notorious uncle. How she wished she could blot that out forever. The most hated crime family in Ambria, and it had to be hers.

It was tragic, really. The more she tried to distance herself from her background, the more it seemed to crop up all around her. She wasn't a crook and she hated being associated with some really terrible people, people she was tied to by blood. But not by choice. Never that.

Suddenly she noticed that Mykal was getting more tired than she'd realized.

"I've got to sit down for a few minutes," he told her, grimacing as he moved his leg. "Just give me a minute here."

She helped him sit on the bed, then sat beside him. He took her hand in his and laced fingers.

"Kylos says he's contacted our parents about my accident and they may be coming soon," he told her, trying to take deep, cleansing breaths. "I told him to let them know I'd rather they stay put. They're a little old to go rampaging around the world." He shrugged. "And it's probably just as well they aren't here, considering what's happening."

She looked up, wary. "Do you mean…?"

He nodded. "This whole royal thing. I suppose you've heard about it. Everyone seems to know." But he was frowning, searching her face.

She hesitated, wondering if she should pretend to know what the heck he was referring to. But she didn't have a clue. Pretending would only give her more to trip over.

"I don't have any idea what you're talking about," she admitted at last.

He looked incredulous. "You really don't know?"

She shook her head. In for a penny, in for a pound. "I've been out of town on a field assignment," she said carefully, trying not to put it in terms he would recognize from their undercover work. "I haven't had time to pick up a paper or listen to the news for weeks." She gave him a quick smile. "I'm as innocent as a newborn child. So tell me. Why are you so popular at the castle these days?"

"Interesting." He raised an eyebrow and gave her a teasing smile. "I'm the one with amnesia, but I have to fill you in on what's happening. You're in worse shape than I am."

"Oh, just tell me," she said impatiently.

He shrugged. "It's simple, really." He gave her a teasing smile. "Do I look like a royal prince to you?"

She frowned. That was something she'd never thought of. "No."

"Me neither. But people at the castle seem to think I do."

"Ignore them," she said. It was her instant reaction.

He laughed. "It's tempting to do that. But someone at the castle has gotten it into their head that I'm one of the long-lost princes we always used to hear legends about. You know, the ones who disappeared the night the castle burned, during the rebellion that brought the Granvillis into power."

She stared at him, stunned. "But…wait…"

He gave a short laugh. "Yes, that's exactly what I said when they first told me."

She shook her head. This was incredible. "That would mean…"

"That I was adopted by the parents who raised me." He shrugged. "Yes, but I've known that for years."

Her eyes widened. "So it is possible."

"Yes. Possible. Not necessarily probable."

Her head was spinning. Mykal, royal? That was just so crazy on so many levels. "And so…?"

"Blood samples have been taken. Physicians have been poring over my painfully crumpled body. Psychologists have been analyzing my poor puzzled brain." His tone was world-weary and cynical. "Analysts have tried to trip me up and prove I'm lying."

"About what?"

He shrugged. "Anything, mostly about when I was eight years old. What I called my mother. Where I hid when I was afraid my father was mad at me. The name of my first toy horse."

She sat back, almost dazed. "Wow."

He nodded. "Believe me, it's been no bed of roses. This royalty gig is not for the faint of heart. They put you through the wringer."

She stared at him. Royal. Could it really be true? An ache started deep in her heart. She knew what this was—a death knell for her marriage. Sure, she'd told herself it was all over many times in the last few weeks, but there had always been a small, pitiful hope in the furthest reaches of her soul. Now that hope was dying.

Royalty. That was a bridge too far for her to go. He had no idea, had never had a clue, just how far from royalty her family was. Neither one of them had thought twice about what sort of families they came from. They hadn't given a thought to where they planned to go in life. There was a war on and they both had dangerous jobs. Love and passion were all they cared about. Nothing else mattered. They had to be together every possible moment, and when they weren't, all their energy went into keeping their relationship a secret from their respective commanding officers. Any hint of a marriage would have had them both out on their ears.

Under normal circumstances they would have begun to ask each other questions in time. But they never got the chance. It was all over much too soon. When he'd walked in to their bedroom and found her going through his hidden papers...

She drew in a shuddering breath, pushing that awful memory away, and tried to keep calm. "And what are the results?"

He shook his head, wondering why she seemed so emotional about something that was only happening to him. He appreciated the concern, but it seemed a bit extreme. "Tests are ongoing."

A lost Ambrian prince. Incredible. That changed everything.

CHAPTER FIVE

"Why does this house seem so empty?"

Janis and Mykal were downstairs again, walking arm-in-arm through the kitchen into the foyer.

"Because the people have gone," Mykal answered her. "All we've got left are the ghosts of lives gone by."

As if on cue, the sound of provocative feminine laughter came at them from down the hallway and they both came to a shocked standstill.

"Ghosts?" she whispered, glancing at him sideways.

He frowned. "I'm putting my money on flesh and blood in this case," he muttered, starting for where the sound came from.

The evidence of someone having a good time seemed to be coming from the library. The feminine simpering had been joined by a deeper male voice, seemingly egging her on. As they reached the door, Mykal held out his arm.

"Stand back. You might not want to see this," he warned.

She half laughed. "But you do?"

"It's my duty," he said with a wink. The door came

open and the giggling came to an abrupt halt. All Janis could see over his shoulder was a flash of frilly skirt and Mykal's brother's angry face as he jumped up off the couch.

"Okay, Kylos," Mykal said in his best authoritative voice. "You want to explain this?"

"What the hell, Mykal? You could knock on the door, you know."

"And you could lock it if you plan some really heavy lovemaking here."

"I…I…no, I…"

"Who is this lovely young lady?"

She was giggling again and now Janis could see her plainly. A little too blond and a little too old for Kylos, she was still pretty, but didn't look too bright.

"This is our cook," Kylos said angrily. "I hired her yesterday. I was just conferring with her. I have to do that, you know."

Mykal was obviously holding back a hoot of laughter. "I suppose you do. I'd suggest she could probably understand your instruction better if you left her clothes on, though."

The "cook" was giggling again. Mykal shook his head and gave up. "I hope she knows how to make a good lasagna," he noted as he turned away. Janis hid her smile and followed him to the bedroom he was using. There were no more festive sounds coming from the library.

"I think you ruined their party spirit," she said.

"I hope so," he replied. Turning, he captured her for

a moment, looking deep into her eyes. "Just wait. When I'm healthy, I'll be chasing you around the place."

"In your dreams." But she was smiling. Despite everything, she loved him more than life itself.

She helped him get back into bed and she could see by the strain in his face that he'd probably overdone it. She wished he would listen and take it easy. She could see he was in pain again. If only he would listen.

Mykal tried to avoid wincing as his back cramped up. This was what the pain medication was for, but when he took it, he paid too high a price. He was going to try to tough it out. He needed his head clear so that he could think about what was about to happen to him. He wasn't sure, at this stage, that he liked it.

He'd always considered himself a free spirit. Some had even called him untameable at one point in his life. And now he had a chance to be one of the royals? One of those people who drank tea with their pinkies sticking out? One of those miserable bastards who stood around in dress uniforms at boring luncheons? One of those sad sacks who followed daily schedules drawn up for them by weaselly assistants who insisted on rules being followed? That wasn't the life for him. He would smother in that thick pea-soup sort of atmosphere. If that was what it was all about, better that he turn it down right away and save everybody a lot of time.

But he wasn't sure yet. He needed some time, some space. He needed to think. Looking at Janis, he knew he needed something else, too, but as far as he could tell, he didn't have a woman of his own. Once the pain faded a bit, maybe he could find one—maybe one who looked as good as this one sitting across from him. He grimaced, fighting back the thought. Messing around with employees was never a good idea.

Still, he enjoyed her sinuous movements and the way the two ribbons of her silvery-blond hair linked around her collarbone. Surely she had a man in her life. Some guy was lucky to have her.

That was what he needed, someone just like Janis. A woman who captivated the imagination as well as the libido. Someone with a soft, provocative touch and a sensual smolder. He had vague stirrings just thinking about it. He looked into her eyes.

"Ready for some medication?" she asked hopefully.

He smiled. "Why would I need medication when I have you?"

"Oh, brother." She loved that he flirted with her, but she hated it, too—and that was a reaction she didn't even want to begin analyzing.

She wished she could help him. If he knew she was his wife, would he let her do more? If she told him who she really was, could he stay calm? Should she go ahead and do it? That was the question that was torturing her.

He wouldn't remember what had happened anyway. But if he knew they were married, that they had once been in love, then he might be able to accept her in the role of his wife and she could make these decisions for him, give him better support. But until she assumed that place in his life, how could she dare to even try?

She examined his bandages and brace and then looked back at him. He seemed so unprotected. And he was moving too much. Maybe he should take the medication. It had been a long time since the medics had given him that last dose. Yes. She made up her mind. She'd hesitated, mostly because of his brother being so strangely insistent. But now she knew it was necessary.

"I think it's time you took something," she said, trying to sound brisk and professional, rising from the couch. "It's been over four hours. I'll just go into the bathroom and…"

"No." He said it with a finality that quite put an end to the matter. "I'm not going to take any more of that stuff. I want to clear my head and begin to live again."

She drew her breath in, tottering between decisions. "But, if it was prescribed for you… It keeps you still and that is what we want."

"If the pain gets too bad, I'll let you know. I'm not a masochist. But for the first time in weeks my mind is clearing and I can think things through again. I no longer feel as though demons were flying around in my head."

She sighed. "Sober is always better." She admitted.

"Anything that's an antibiotic or something I need directly in order to heal, I will gladly take. Medication just to keep me drowsy, or even just to deal with pain, I'd rather hold off on that until I really need it. I've been under heavy sedation too much lately. I don't want to go there again."

He was firm on this. She could tell he wasn't going to budge an inch. Sighing, she sat down again.

"Then please, please just stay quiet," she told him earnestly. "At least until you see the doctor tomorrow."

He nodded, but he wasn't all that convincing. She was having a hard time herself. The way they had been on their little expedition around the house had brought up memories of how they'd been when they were in love. And then to think that her family had caused his family such pain—that alone should make a relationship between the two of them a no-go at this point. It would never, never work again.

"Are you hungry?" she asked, needing to leave the room and looking for an excuse.

"A little."

"You should eat something." She frowned, thinking it was important even as a hedge against the very drugs he wanted to avoid. If Kylos came back and talked him into taking more medication, it would help if he had some food in his stomach. "Do you want me to warm up some more of that chicken soup?"

He shook his head, making a face.

"I know." She brightened as she remembered. "I'll go make you a cheese omelet. Your favorite."

He looked at her in surprise. "How did you know that was my favorite?"

She stopped, stunned that she'd made a mistake like that. For just a moment, she couldn't think of a thing to say and she stared at him, deer in the headlights.

"I...I didn't," she finally improvised. "But I assume

eggs and cheese are bound to be in the refrigerator, even if nothing else is. So I thought I'd go with that."

He was still frowning at her. She gave him a bright smile and left the room, leaning against the wall in the hallway once she was clear and trying to catch her breath. That had been a clumsy move. She was going to have to do better than that if she was going to survive this little adventure.

But wait. Just how long did she plan to let this masquerade go? She knew she couldn't leave until someone else came to watch over him, but once that happened, was she going to leave at last? Shaking her head, she headed to the kitchen. She had no answer for her own questions.

She walked into the kitchen and looked around, hoping she wasn't going to run into the so-called cook. She was lucky. There was no sign of anyone. But she was cooking the omelet when Kylos came in through the outer door. He immediately threw out his hands like a gunfighter showing he wasn't near his guns.

"Hey, babe, I'm not going to scare you this time. So no fair trying to take me down, okay?"

"No problem," she said as she flipped the perfectly cooked omelet onto a porcelain plate. "As long as you come in peace, I'll be peaceful."

"I just got back from taking the cook home." He looked at the food appreciatively and sniffed the air. "Hey, can you make me one of those?"

She gave him a look. "Do you have shrapnel wounds all over your back?" she asked.

He looked pained. "You know the answer to that."

"Then you know my answer as well." But she said it loud and clear, just to be sure. "No."

He took it calmly and sighed as she walked past with the plate in her hand. "Pity," he muttered. "Hey, we need to talk."

But she just kept going. Now that Mykal had told her about being adopted, she could see why the two of them were so different. Brothers in nurture, not in nature. But was Mykal really royal? Yikes.

"Your brother is back," she told Mykal as she pushed open the door and made her way into the room. "Do you trust him?"

His eyes widened in surprise. "Kylos? Why, did he make a pass at you?"

"I can handle passes from men like Kylos," she said scornfully as she set up his eating situation. "What I want to know is, do you have reason to suspect him of ulterior motives?"

He shook his head, not sure what she was getting at. "For what?"

She shrugged. "I don't know. He just seems a little devious."

"Devious." He grinned and picked up a fork. "Kylos always has ulterior motives. And he's very often devious. So you're right on both counts. Watch your step around him." And he began to eat the omelet. Very quickly, his time was taken up by sounds of epicurean pleasure.

She watched him for a moment, glad he seemed to

enjoy the food. But she was worried about Kylos. She didn't trust him. Still, she really didn't have any evidence of anything substantive, did she? If she tried to tell him her intelligence work training had developed antennae that had always proven uncannily accurate, he would begin asking questions she didn't want to answer.

"So do you have anything you can pin on him right now?" Mykal asked her.

"No," she said at last. "If feelings don't count, I've got nothing."

"Feelings, huh?" He pushed away his half-eaten meal and hummed a few bars of a song, looking off into the distance as though trying to remember something.

She felt herself flushing. She remembered it all only too well. She remembered what a great tenor voice he had and how he loved to sing. He'd sung love songs to her. He'd sung comic songs to make her laugh. All at once, she was dying to hear that beautiful voice again, hear it in full voice. She turned her face away so he wouldn't see that her eyes were misting over.

He began to drift off to sleep. This time he didn't seem to need her hand to hold. She assumed that meant whatever he was taking that made him artificially drowsy had mostly worn off.

She'd pulled a comforter out of the closet and she used it now, curling up on the little couch again after turning down the lights. Just as she was falling asleep, she heard a sound and looked up quickly, just catching a glimpse of Kylos in the doorway before he disappeared. That startled her, but she was too tired to worry about it.

"Tomorrow," she promised herself. "Tomorrow I'll have it out with him." And her eyes closed two seconds later.

Mykal was on his own, walking in the garden. He felt as if he'd escaped from some sort of tender trap, a silken-threads sort of imprisonment, where they tortured you with kindness. He'd slipped out at dawn without waking Janis, found his father's old walking stick in the hall closet and now he was free.

Not that he was going anywhere. In fact, now that the adrenaline of sneaking out had died down, he was beginning to feel the pain again. Also the weakness. Not to mention the cold wind. He wouldn't be able to go much farther. He stopped beside what had once been his favorite pond. It was empty now and he lowered himself carefully to sit on the bench that sat close by. He felt sad to see the bare concrete form without water, and without the colorful koi that had splashed about here when he'd been younger. He frowned, wondering why Kylos was letting the place go this way. He would have to speak to him about it.

But right now, he didn't want to dwell on that. He'd come out here to try and get his head straight. He had to think and decide what he wanted to do with his life, before others made that decision for him. The way things were going, it looked like he just might be the lost prince. Wow. Wonderful. What was that going to do for him? He took a deep breath and frowned. That and a half-crown coin might get him a pint at the local pub.

Hey. He smiled wryly to himself. Maybe it actually would. Maybe people did give princes free food and drink just for showing up at their place. If so, it might actually be worth something.

But he had to get serious and be practical. Did he really want to become a prince and go to live in the castle with the rest of the royal family? Offhand, he didn't think he was suited for the job. It seemed superfluous. He had half a mind to tell them to take their royal crown and… Well, if he did turn it down, he probably wouldn't be quite that rude about it. But he was tempted just to say no.

And yet, he didn't want to be too impulsive. What if there were more to it? What if he could step in and find an important job to do? What if being royal could really put him into a position where he could make a difference?

Probably a pipe dream. Still, this was all sort of interesting, being tapped as a possible lost prince and all. It wasn't quite as good as being a war hero, of course, but it was something. He'd been told he'd done some pretty good things in the war, and he hoped that was true. But what good did it do if you couldn't remember it?

When you got right down to it, it all seemed so pointless. He'd never wanted to be a prince. Most of his childhood had been spent wanting desperately to be a football star. As that dream died, others took its place. He wanted to be a fireman. Then an astronaut. And finally he'd settled on architecture. He'd had a thriving business, but the war had loomed and he remembered thinking being a spy would be great fun. They told him that was exactly what he'd become, though he didn't remember it at all.

But a prince? No, that had never been on his horizon and he wasn't really sure what royalty did beside stand around and look important. Was it really a full-time job? Or were you allowed to follow other pursuits on the side? Someone would have to explain all these little details to him at some point, and then he would make the final determination whether he would submit to the royal rigmarole or not.

Still, it wasn't really filling his mind with eager thoughts. In some ways, it seemed almost irrelevant. His own two lost years were more of an obsession. That was what he couldn't stop thinking about. Where had he been? What had he done? Whom had he offended? Whom had he made love to?

Two years. A lot could happen in that amount of time. He could remember how excited he'd been to begin his military career. He'd prepared himself in every way he could think of. He'd worked out and read books and agonized over his own belief system. He'd filled out the paperwork.

And then—nothing. It was as though he'd walked through a door into another world and stayed there for two years. Now he was back and he wanted to retrieve what he'd lost.

Loss. The word resonated with him. Yes, that was what he was feeling, why he was so restless and dissatisfied. He felt loss—and not just of time and experience. He felt a deep, dark, aching loss in his soul. He needed someone. Something was missing.

He started to stand and the pain hit him like a knife in the back. Gasping, he fell back down onto the bench. For the moment, pain was all there was.

Janis was muttering to herself as she hurried through the house toward the backyard. She'd overslept and then she'd had to deal with a little bit of morning sickness, something she hadn't had until recently. Now she didn't know where Mykal was and she was furious with herself.

"If I'm going to make a fool of myself hanging around here, I might at least do a good job of keeping tabs on the man," she muttered aloud. "What is the point if I'm not even vigilant?"

She'd woken up, pulled together her clothes and dashed through the house finding absolutely nobody. He had to be outside. She was out the door and into a garden that must have been beautiful once, but had gone a bit too much to seed lately. And then she saw Kylos and Griswold on either side of Mykal, bringing him back to the house.

She gasped. He looked terrible, drawn and pale. The two men were holding all his weight and practically carrying him along. Her heart was in her throat as she ran out to meet them.

"What happened?" she cried.

Kylos gave her a murderous look. "I guess his pain medication wore off and he decided to go gallivanting around," he said coldly. "Too bad you can't be bothered to make sure he's medicated."

"No," Mykal murmured, shaking his head. "I don't want any pain medication."

"What you want and what you need are two different things," Kylos told him sternly.

The house phone began to ring, adding to the sense of frenzy.

"Oh," Janis said, reluctant to leave them but knowing there was no one else to answer the phone in the house. These three were definitely occupied. "Shall I...?"

"If you please, miss," Griswold said, staggering under Mykal's weight. "I'm afraid I'm tied up at the moment."

"If you wouldn't mind," Kylos added through clenched teeth, his eyes shooting daggers.

"Of course." She threw a pained glance at Mykal and a glare back at Kylos and ran into the house and then headed for the study, picking it up in the nick of time.

"Hello," she said breathlessly, looking back to see where they were taking Mykal. "This is the Marten residence."

"This is Queen Pellea," the musical voice on the other end announced in a friendly manner. "I'd like to speak to Mykal, please."

"Oh." Janis stood as though struck dumb. It was the queen. She'd never spoken to a queen before. "Oh, my goodness."

"Is he available?" Her voice rose as she began to intuit that something might be amiss. "What's wrong? Has something happened to him? Please, fill me in right away."

Janis could hear the emotional connection in her voice and for some reason, it touched her heart and caused all her own emotions to come pouring out. Suddenly, she found herself talking to the queen as though she'd known her all her life.

"Oh, Your Royal Highness," she said, not sure if she had the right address but too upset to care. Looking around again, she could see that the men were taking him back into the bedroom. She needed to get to him. She needed to help.

"I've been trying to keep him quiet," she said quickly, "but you can't believe how hard it is. I just woke up to find he's been out running around in the yard and of course now he's collapsed and…and…"

"Okay," Pellea said briskly. "We're moving up the timetable. I'm sending someone over as soon as possible with an ambulance. I want him here at the castle where we can keep an eye on him."

"Oh." She swallowed. She supposed that was probably for the best, but it seemed sudden.

"What is your name, dear?"

She drew in her breath sharply. She had so many names to sift through before deciding what name to give. There was her natural name, Janis Gorgonio, a name that would send up red flags anywhere it was mentioned. Then there was Marten, her married name. And Davos, her mother's name, the one she had mostly gone by all her life in order to avoid people knowing she was born a part of the Gorgonio mob family.

"Uh…Janis. Janis Davos."

"And you are…?"

"I'm helping. I'm sort of an assistant. Trying to keep him calm. I know any sort of movement can be so dangerous for him." Her voice was shaking with her fear for his safety and she stopped for a moment, embarrassed. "He doesn't want to take anything that will make him drowsy, so I'm just trying to keep him from hurting himself."

"Really?" The queen's voice was all sympathy. "How long have you known him?"

"Uh… Actually…"

Janis drew in a shuddering breath. She couldn't lie to the queen! "It's sort of a strange situation. You see, he has this amnesia thing and so he doesn't remember me. But we knew each other quite well and…"

"Say no more," Pellea said as though she understood everything that was still unspoken. "I get the picture and I trust you. I can hear your honesty in your voice. I want you to come to the castle with him."

"Oh, Your Highness…" That was something she hadn't expected.

"And call me Pellea. I know we're going to be good friends."

Call me Pellea. This was the Queen of Ambria talking to her like this. She was touched and grateful. "Oh, I hope so."

"I'll get the medics ready to roll. Someone will call when they are on their way."

"Thank you so much."

She rang off and turned to go to Mykal, but Kylos was standing just a few feet away, glaring at her and her heart jumped.

"So you knew him before, did you? I knew there was something fishy about you. Why keep it a secret? What's your angle?"

Mentally, she shook herself. It wasn't easy making the transition from the queen's kind generosity to Kylos's feral animosity.

She looked toward the bedroom. She really wanted to go in and see about Mykal. "It's a long story and I..."

He grabbed her arm, fingers digging in. "You're a lying little thief, aren't you?"

She looked up into his face. She had the urge to send him sprawling again, but she resisted it. "No. No, I swear, I didn't really lie, I just let you think things that weren't true."

"Oh, really! I'm afraid the subtlety of that distinction is somewhat lost on me, darling." He squeezed her flesh painfully. "I want an explanation and I want it now."

Giving him back as fierce a glare as he was giving her, she began to peel his fingers off her arm, one at a time. "I have to check on your brother first. Then I'll fill you in on the background to this. I swear."

He grabbed her chin in his other hand, holding it roughly. "You'd better keep that promise. I'll give you exactly ten minutes and if you don't meet me back here, I'll tell Mykal what a lying little rat you are."

And then, to her surprise, he let her go. As she hurried back to the bedroom, she couldn't help but wonder at his motives. He must want to know her story awfully badly to bargain with her like this. And the way he'd said it implied he wasn't planning to kick her out—at least not yet.

But was he going to tell Mykal? Maybe yes, maybe no.

Mykal looked drained but recovering his strength. He gave her a crooked smile as she came in and began fussing around him. "Who was on the phone?" he asked as she poured him a glass of water.

She flashed him a brilliant smile. "The queen. She wants you there at the castle as soon as possible."

"Oh." He grimaced, looking unhappy. "And what if I decide not to go?"

"What?" She stared at him, aghast. "Why wouldn't you want to go?"

He met her gaze for a long moment and finally he confessed. "I'm not sure I want to be a prince," he said.

CHAPTER SIX

JANIS caught herself and held back the cry of dismay that came quickly to her lips. "But…" She swallowed hard. "Mykal, if you are one of the royal DeAngelis family, you can't pretend you're not. The DNA doesn't lie. If the final judgment says you're a prince, you're a prince. You don't get to pick and choose, do you?"

"Imprisoned by my bloodline. Is that the way it goes?"

She bit her lip, thinking how that statement could apply to her as well as to him. She'd been trapped by her family's past and she'd worked hard to put it behind her, only to have it crop up again and again.

But that background was criminal and she'd known it could ruin her chances of a decent life. This was so different. His true ancestry could transform his life into something so wonderful. But obviously, that wasn't the way he was looking at it.

"I'll make the decision on what I want to do with my future," he said simply. "I don't have to accept a life I don't want."

"But here in Ambria…"

"That's just it. I don't have to stay here in Ambria. The rest of the world doesn't give a damn about princes from Ambria. I can go somewhere else."

He was right, of course. This was his decision and if he didn't want to be a prince, what right did anyone have to make him do it anyway? None.

In some ways, she was torn. If he accepted the royal position, she knew he would be lost to her forever. Even if he didn't she didn't have much hope with him. But everything in her yearned for his success and happiness, and she had a feeling he shouldn't pass up this chance.

"Fair enough," she said at last. "But I would just say one thing. They have wonderful medical care at the castle and that is what you need right now. It wouldn't hurt to get opinions from the best physicians in the country." She sighed. "And Queen Pellea seemed so nice." She gave him a halfhearted grin. "And anyway, since they want you, why not at least give them a shot at convincing you? It can't hurt. If it's not meant to be, you'll find a way to turn it down gracefully, I'm sure of it."

He stared at her and she couldn't tell if he'd really been listening. She bent down to fluff his pillows and he reached up and sank his fingers into her hair, letting go easily as she straightened again, watching her hair pour out of his grasp as though it were liquid gold. She looked at him, wide-eyed. He'd loved playing with her hair in the past. Did he remember, even a little bit? The feel of his touch made her shiver.

"I cannot begin to express to you how much I hate

this," he said absently, as though half his attention was still on her hair.

"Hate what?" she asked quickly.

"Not being able to get around by myself." His gaze met hers. "Depending on other people just to walk in the yard."

"Have some patience," she said, shaking her head. "You came in here on a gurney not even fifteen hours ago. You can't get up and dance. Not yet."

His eyes were hard as they looked into hers. "Will you dance with me, Janis?" he asked softly. "When I can dance again, I want you for my partner."

Her pulse began to race. He was half-teasing, playing with her for his own amusement. Little did he know how she wished he really was serious about it.

"I will," she told him earnestly. "If you still want me."

She loved him so. Might as well admit it. That hadn't changed and she didn't think it ever would.

She'd loved him from the moment she first saw him. She knew very well that the whole concept of love at first sight was ridiculous. She didn't believe in it. You couldn't really love someone you didn't know. So she wasn't sure just what that was that had grabbed her the first time her eyes had met Mykal Marten's.

There was no doubt she'd been blown away. After all, he was incredibly good-looking. His dark hair was cut short but it still managed to curl around his head, reminding her of a statue of an ancient Greek Warrior. His body was warriorlike, too—hard and muscular and broad in all the best places. His eyes were pale, pale blue, like spring flowers, but burning with a hard, fearless light that seemed to blaze out from those gorgeous thick eyelashes.

All in all, her heart had stopped in her throat and for a moment, she thought she'd never breathe again. Maybe that wasn't love, but it was something. It had almost seemed like some sort of force field had sprung between them, electric and throbbing, like a beat at a really hot dance club.

One look and she knew—he was the one.

Had he felt the same? Maybe. Maybe a little. But she didn't think it had happened to him in quite the same full-throttle way. Still, she'd let him know how she felt from the first. She had no choice. It was as though she needed the breath from his lips to survive.

Now was no different. She would do anything to bring their relationship back to the way it had been. Anything.

And that was her misfortune, because she knew nothing would work. The longer she stayed near him, the more she realized that. Roadblocks were piling up, one after another. It was no use. She'd made up her own mind. She couldn't go to the castle with him. This would be a final goodbye. She turned away, afraid he would see the tears shimmering in her eyes.

"I'll just go refill this with water," she said, blinking rapidly as she took the porcelain pitcher and turned toward the door. "And I think I'll see if Griswold has made some breakfast for you. I'll be right back."

"Janis, wait a minute," he said, stopping her. "Could you do me a favor?"

She turned back slowly, keeping her face averted. "Of course."

"There's something I've got to do. If you look in the desk in the study, I think you'll find some writing paper and a fountain pen. I'd like to send a note to my parents. I know they'll be affected by all this royal speculation when they hear about it and I want to reassure them that I'm still their son."

She smiled, loving him, loving his decency. "Of course," she said, turning to look at him and barely able to resist the urge to throw her arms around him and give him a hug. "Just give me a few minutes."

He nodded, closing his eyes, and she left quickly, hoping to make quick work of her meeting with Kylos and do the chores for Mykal at the same time.

The study was empty. She found the desk quickly and pulled open one drawer after another until she found the paper Mykal had asked for. She drew the whole packet out and chose two sheets, then looked down, about to put it back. But an official-looking form on the bottom of the drawer caught her attention and she stopped to glance at it, feeling slightly nosy, but interested.

It was a death certificate. That gave her a start, but once she'd read the name on it, as well as the date and place of death, she was even more shocked. This had to be Mykal's adoptive father. She couldn't ignore that and she reached down to bring it up, immediately noticing another death certificate, this one for his mother, right under it. She read them over quickly, noting they both seemed to have died in a traffic accident, then heard Kylos coming down the hallway.

Moving as fast as she could, she put back the two documents and placed the packet of paper back where it had been, then closed the drawer just as Kylos entered the room. Turning, she stared at him. His parents had passed away and he hadn't told Mykal. At least, that was certainly what this looked like. What on earth could be his motive? Should she challenge him on it? Or just add it to the list of things she didn't trust about him?

But Kylos had his mind on other things.

"Okay, let's hear it," he said, facing off in front of her like a prizefighter. "Give it to me straight or you're going out on your ear."

She looked at him and wondered why he gave off such bad vibes. She really didn't like him much. Why did he want to know all this and what did he plan to do with the information? There was no doubt she had better be careful in what she told him.

"Mykal and I met a good six months ago. We were both in the military, still wrapping up war business in a way, and we worked together on a couple of assignments."

"The war is over," he said caustically, as though that somehow invalidated her story.

She rolled her eyes. "The war is not over. Sure, there's a truce of sorts between the royals and the Granvilli side. The Granvillis think they run one small, mountainous part of the island. But things there are falling apart and the royals are just biding their time. They'll take over soon."

"'They'?" He smirked. "So you fought on the side of the Granvilli murdering traitors?"

She winced. Just whose side had she been on when the Granvilli secret police had thrown her into the prison camp? "What does it matter anymore?" she said softly.

"It matters a lot to those of us who are loyal." But he said it in a pro forma way that let her know he really didn't care all that much. He'd gone on to something else and he frowned, thinking it over. "But that means Mykal was there, too, on the wrong side. Is that right?" He stared at her. The light of something eager gleaming in his eyes. "Was my brother a traitor?"

She shook her head, but before she could say anything, he went on, frowning. "So that's why I'm having so much trouble getting any records of his service out of our military bureaucracy. The royals asked me to get together all his history and papers and I've been having a hard time. But I'm asking the wrong side for info." He shook his head as though thoroughly confused. "And that's why no one could find him for the last two years. He was with the enemy. Who knew?"

She sighed. "It's more complicated than that and you're going to have to ask Mykal to explain it. I can't."

Kylos stared at her for a moment, then snapped his fingers. "Double agent. Am I right?"

"Ask him."

He scowled. "You know I can't do that right now.

We can't do anything that might upset him. And anyway, he claims he can't remember anything." His gaze sharpened. "Are you buying that?"

"You mean, do I think he's telling the truth?" she asked, incredulous. "One thing about Mykal," she added coldly, "he's not like the rest of us. He never lies."

"Wow, you really have been brainwashed, haven't you?"

She shrugged and threw her hands out, starting to turn away, but he stopped her.

"Okay, you haven't finished. Tell me more."

She couldn't hold back the long-suffering look. "About what?"

"You and my brother. Come on. Lay it on the line. What's the story?"

She hesitated, but she knew she would have to comply, at least with some sort of sketchy outline of the truth. He'd overheard what she'd told the queen and she couldn't go back on that. "Well, we became quite close."

"Really." He gazed at her levelly. "Was the word *love* bandied about?" he asked with some sarcasm.

She drew in breath through her nose while she considered what to say to that. He didn't have to know they had actually married. No one had to know about that. At least, not until she and her baby were long gone.

"Sure," she said at last. "A time or two."

Something flared in his eyes and then they narrowed. "Sounds just peachy. There's nothing like a good love story to touch the heart." He snorted his derision at the concept. "But then there was trouble in paradise, wasn't there? What happened?"

"We...we had a pretty bad fight a little over two months ago. We broke up and I hadn't seen him since. I came by yesterday to...to..."

He grunted. "You were hoping to patch things up, weren't you?"

"Yes. No." She grimaced in frustration. "Actually I just wanted to tie up some loose ends. I didn't know about the accident. I had no idea about the injuries. So I was shocked when the ambulance arrived and when everyone assumed I was here to take care of him, I let them believe it."

"Sure," he said, sounding as though he didn't buy a word of it. "And hearing about the royal thing didn't have anything to do with it. Right?"

"It didn't."

His mouth twisted cynically. "But it sure must have pricked up your ears once you heard about it, huh?"

She despised the man. How dare he impugn her motives like this? She had enough to be ashamed of, she didn't need to regret things she hadn't even done. "No, honestly, I didn't know a thing about it."

"Be serious," he said scornfully. "It's been all over the news."

"I hadn't heard any news. I've been...away."

His gaze narrowed. "What's your game, Janis Davos? What is it that you really want here?"

Her chin rose and she looked him in the eye. "I want Mykal to be safe and healthy and happy."

"That's it?"

"Yes."

"Bull."

"It's true. When I got here, I was all set to meet with him. I didn't know he had amnesia until I was talking to him and realized…" Janis shivered, remembering, and suddenly most of the fight went out of her. "It's just so crazy," she said weakly.

"So he doesn't remember you at all?"

She shook her head. "No."

Kylos nodded, thinking that over. "Why haven't you told him who you really are?"

She shrugged. "I expected him to know the minute he saw me. But when that didn't happen, I'd already been told he wasn't supposed to get too physical or too emotional. And after the fight we had…well, I had to hold off. I couldn't tell him."

He gave her a completely skeptical look. "You're lying."

"No, I…"

"You heard about him maybe being the lost prince and you came running back to cash in on some of that glory. Am I right?"

She glared at him. "No, you are not right."

"Then why haven't you told him who you are?"

In order to explain that, she would have to tell him about the marriage and how she'd destroyed it with her own foolish actions. She couldn't do that. Instead, she went on the offensive herself.

"I've already gone over all that. And you have a thing

or two to explain, yourself." She used an index finger to poke at his chest as she made her points. "Why haven't *you* told him the truth about your parents? Why haven't you told him that your parents have passed away?"

Kylos's dark face registered shock at that. He looked visibly shaken and he took a step backward, away from where Janis stood. "What? What are you talking about?"

"I saw the death certificates." She gestured toward the drawer in the desk. "Mykal just told me a few minutes ago that he wants to write a letter to them. So he obviously doesn't know. Why haven't you told him the truth?"

He was backing away now. "You know why. He can't take the shock. It could kill him."

"That's your story and you're sticking to it, huh?" She glared at him. "That excuse sounds a lot like mine, doesn't it? Funny how you didn't buy it when it was coming from me."

He muttered something but she wasn't listening.

"It looks to me like we have a standoff," she announced, hands on her hips. "You keep your secret and I'll keep mine. Okay?"

He appeared defiant, then grudgingly agreeable. "Okay. For now. We'll see." Then his eyes narrowed and his confidence seemed to return. "In the meantime, I'm going to look into your background, Janis Davos. Why do I have a sneaky little suspicion that you have things to hide?" His dark eyes glittered maliciously. "Who can I talk to about you? Anyone at the castle?"

Hoping he was just trying to shake her, she fought back with sarcasm. "I don't know. Why not try Queen Pellea? She seems to be my best friend there."

Moving forward, he grabbed her arm, twisting it painfully. "Listen, you little tramp," he began, but the sound of someone clearing his throat in the doorway stopped him cold and he pulled away from her.

They both turned to see Griswold trying to look as though he hadn't seen a thing out of order.

"Your visitors are here, Mr. Marten," he said formally. "Perhaps you had better come and see to them."

"Oh." He headed for the door, leaving her behind, and she breathed a sigh of relief, rubbing her arm and watching as Griswold turned away with barely a glance at her.

Kylos was a real problem. She knew she shouldn't be goading him. She was probably going to regret it. But he was so obnoxious, she couldn't help herself. Turning on her heel, she made her way back to the room where Mykal was.

She'd forgotten all about the water pitcher and breakfast, but luckily, Griswold had already brought him a plate of eggs and fried potatoes and he was eating with gusto.

That made her feel better instantly. He would get healthy again, she was sure of it. She settled back to watch him eat and listen to him talk about simple things that needed little or no response. He seemed to have forgotten about writing a letter to his adoptive parents, and she didn't want to remind him. How sad and awkward that would be. But he seemed so free and easy, she could almost fool herself into thinking this was like the old days as she laughed at some silly joke he'd made. And then something would remind her that her heart was broken and she would lose the glow for a moment or two. But all in all, she just loved being with him.

She took the used plates to the kitchen and was surprised to see Kylos ushering a nice-looking older couple down the stairway. But she was hardly shocked when he treated her like a servant in front of them, leading them away quickly to another side of the house. What a strange one he was.

The castle called. An ambulance had been scheduled and would soon be on its way. A castle physician called and suggested that Mykal take his pain medication before making the trip to guard against jostling that was bound to happen. He made a face but accepted the pills with good grace once she'd explained the reasoning behind it.

"Okay," he said. "Just one more time. After this, it's going to take a stake through my heart to get me to take any more."

She counted out a dose and gave it to him. He washed it down with water and looked at her with sad eyes.

"I'm ready for this to be over and done with," he told her. "I'm going to give my permission to go ahead and operate. Let the surgery begin."

That startled her. "No," she said anxiously. "Wait until you get a proper evaluation before you make up your mind. Don't make any rash decisions now."

"Why not?" he said cynically. "What have I got to lose?"

"Everything!"

Looking at her, he grinned and before she realized what he was doing, he'd reached out and taken her hand, pulling her closer. "Okay, my beautiful guardian. I'll take your word for it." Bringing her hand to his lips, he kissed her in a courtly fashion, then looked up earnestly. "And anyway, you'll be there to help me make the right choice."

Slowly, she shook her head. "I don't think I should go to the castle with you," she said breathlessly.

"But I thought you worked for the castle."

"Not really. I'm…" What was she exactly? What could she say? Suddenly, she wanted to tell him the truth.

"Hey, how's this?" He pulled her hand to his chest. His eyes sparkled with something close to his old charm. "I command you to come with me."

She looked into those eyes for a moment, then rolled her own, half-laughing. "Oh, brother."

"You can't defy me."

"Oh, yeah? Watch me."

He pretended to frown fiercely. "We have dungeons for people like you."

"Only at the castle. Where I'm not going."

"Of course you're going." He thought that over for a moment, then gave her a disgruntled look. "What good is it going to be being royal if I can't throw my new power around?"

She smiled, loving him. "Maybe being royal isn't all its cracked up to be these days," she teased. "Maybe you're going to have to get used to some limits." And just to show him that she had some of her own, she slipped her hand back out of his and moved a little farther from the edge of the bed.

It wouldn't be long before the ambulance arrived. And then she would have to make good on her decision not to go to the castle with him. It was really the only choice. They couldn't go on like this. She couldn't live this lie any longer. She only hoped she could stay strong and determined enough to follow through with it. In the meantime, she began to look at him for evidence the pain medication was working. He wasn't acting as though anything was bothering him much, but she didn't notice him getting sleepy, either.

"How are you feeling?" she asked him.

"Stiff. My back is aching, but not as badly as it was earlier."

"Are you getting drowsy?"

He grimaced. "A bit. It's coming on. Don't worry."

"I just want you to be comfortable on the trip," she reminded him.

He nodded, but his mind was obviously on something else. He searched her face. "So how did you become a guard, Janis?"

She hesitated, but decided to try to get closer to the truth if that was possible. "I'm not really a guard. This assignment just kind of fell into my lap."

He nodded. "I have a feeling you did some military work during the war. Am I right?"

Her breath caught in her throat. Could he be beginning to remember? "Yes."

"Special forces? Or intelligence?"

She laughed, shaking her head. "Why would you think that?"

"Instinct. The kind of things you say. The way you handled Kylos. The way you look at me, as though you know what I'm thinking before I think it."

She smiled. "So you think I can read minds?"

He shrugged. "I wouldn't put it past you." He raised an eyebrow. "So am I right?"

She nodded slowly.

"Good. Then you are just the woman I need."

"Really? In what way?"

"Talent and training. I have something I'd like you to do for me."

"What is that?"

He met her gaze with his own and stared hard. "I want you to find my wife for me."

Her heart stood still, then raced so hard she thought she would keel over. "Uh...did you remember getting married?" she asked breathlessly.

He shook his head. "No. But it seems I did." He gestured toward a wooden box sitting on the dresser. "They gave me all the effects I was carrying with me when I was brought in, after the accident. I finally took a look at it a few minutes ago. You look, too—you'll see what I mean."

Rising, she went to the box and opened it. Inside she saw his wallet, his keys and his wedding ring. Their wedding ring. Her heart began to pound. She turned to look at him.

"You were wearing this ring in the accident?" she asked. That didn't seem reasonable. They had exchanged rings in their wedding, but they only wore them at home, when they were alone. Their wedding had been a secret that could have resulted in them both being fired from their jobs if they'd been found out. And after the fight they'd had, after what he'd said, why would he have been wearing the ring? She stared at him, completely at sea.

He shrugged. "So it seems."

"But…" She pressed her lips together to keep from saying something she would regret.

"Kylos doesn't know anything?" She only asked in order to see what he would say.

"No. We didn't have much contact over the last couple of years." He shrugged. "At least, not that I remember." He looked into her eyes. "You're wondering where my wife is, aren't you?" he said sensibly. "I don't know. I feel like something must have happened. That's why I want you to find her."

She was numb. What on earth could she say to that? "What if she doesn't want to be found?" she murmured, then wished she hadn't.

"You've got a point," he said, looking sleepy. "If she still wanted me, she would have shown up by now, wouldn't she?"

"Oh! Not necessarily. Maybe she doesn't know what happened."

"Maybe." He flexed his back and grimaced at the pain. "There are a lot of screwy things going on with this whole issue. For instance—look at the ID in the wallet."

She pulled the wallet out and opened it, but she already knew what it would say. There it was, a picture of Mykal, and the name John Blunt on the card. John Blunt. It was a name she knew well. It was the name he'd been going by as he infiltrated a local shipbuilder's union in the small seaside city of Pierria where they had both been working undercover.

So Mykal had been racing down a road on that old rattletrap motorcycle he loved with his John Blunt identity card in his pocket and the wedding ring he owned as Mykal Marten on his finger. It didn't make any sense.

"When was your accident?" she asked him, her mind working a mile a minute. "Where was it? Do you know?"

He shook his head. "About two months ago. And somewhere in Granvilli territory, from what I've been told. But I don't know where exactly."

She stared at him. Certain things were beginning to put up little red flags in her thinking. "How did they find your real identity?"

"It took a while. I was in a Granvilli hospital for a few weeks, I guess, and then I got transferred to the royal side in a prisoner trade. It seems they figured out I was a spy for the royals." His smile was endearingly crooked, but getting more and more sleepy. "I only wish I could remember. It sounds like I was living quite the life over there."

"Yes," she said softly, holding the memories close. "You were." She stared at him for a long, trembling moment. This had gone on long enough. Her resistance was melting. He had to know the truth.

But he didn't seem to notice what she'd said. He shook his head as though to clear it and looked at her through squinted eyes. "So will you help me?" he asked, his voice getting slurred. "I just have this aching void inside, and I feel like, if I could find her, if I knew who she was, I could fill this emptiness. And maybe find a reason to care whether I survive these operations or not."

"Oh, Mykal."

She went to him. She couldn't help it. She slipped right onto the bed beside him, being careful not to put any pressure on him in any way, but taking his face between her hands and kissing him firmly on the lips.

He kissed her back and she clung to him, so hungry for his affection, so thirsty for his taste. It was heaven to hold him.

But she had to pull away so that she could tell him the truth.

"Mykal," she said softly, touching his beloved face with the palm of her hand and looking into his eyes. "I know where your wife is. I'm so sorry I didn't tell you right away." She took a deep breath and plunged in. "I'm…I'm the one. It's me. You and I were married about four months ago."

He was staring at her but his eyes were blank. She bit her lip, disturbed by his lack of reaction. Frustrated, she leaned her head back on the pillow and stared at the ceiling as she talked. She couldn't look at him. She didn't want to see growing awareness in his eyes as he listened to her.

"We met in Pierria. We both worked there. I was with the Granvilli intelligence, and you were…well, I never understood exactly who you worked for or why. But we fell in love. Crazy in love. And we got married on a wing and a prayer, hardly knowing what we were doing. And then…"

She took a deep breath and closed her eyes. "And then we had a terrible fight. I ran from our little house to my brother's apartment. And I never saw you again." She opened her eyes and turned to look at him. "Until yesterday, when I…"

Her voice faded away as she realized he was asleep.

"Mykal!" she cried, but he didn't budge. She stared at him and then she began to laugh until tears filled her eyes. Here she'd painfully revealed it all to him, and he wasn't even listening. "Oh, Mykal."

She rose from the bed and looked down at him, shaking her head. She heard voices out in the foyer. The ambulance had arrived. They'd come to take him to the castle.

Well, things had changed. She'd said she was leaving, but now she was going to stay with him. This was her husband and he needed her. There was no way she was going to stay behind.

She picked up her satchel and turned, looking at the wooden box. Should she take it along? She didn't like leaving it here. But did she have the right?

"Nuts," she said to herself. She was married to the man. Of course she had the right. Moving quickly, she opened her satchel and put the box inside it. She'd barely completed the move before Kylos came rushing in the room and stopped abruptly as he saw her fastening her satchel.

"What are you doing?" he asked suspiciously.

"Getting ready to go to the castle," she said, trying hard not to look guilty. For a second, she thought he was going to ask her to empty out her bag so he could take a look at what she had in there. But the moment passed and he turned to look at Mykal.

"Where's the medication?" he asked her. "How much is left?"

"It's in the bathroom," she said, frowning. "I don't think he'll need it. They'll surely prescribe their own preferences once they examine him."

"Hmm." He looked at her sideways, then disappeared into the bathroom at the same time the paramedics appeared in the doorway.

She turned to look at Mykal. This was it. Who knew what would happen once they got to the castle? She took a deep breath and said a little prayer. It was time to go.

CHAPTER SEVEN

"The first thing you're going to do," Queen Pellea said as she swept into the personal royal library where she'd told Janis to meet her, "is tell me all about my brother-in-law, the new prince." She took Janis's hands in hers and beamed at her. "Tell me everything you know."

Janis held on as though she were a life raft. She was overwhelmed by it all—the gorgeous castle, the sumptuous décor, the beautiful queen who looked like she'd stepped right out of a Renaissance painting. She'd helped bring Mykal in and she'd even had a chance to talk to one of the doctors about his symptoms over the last few hours. And then she'd received the message from the queen and had hurried here for a meeting.

"So you're sure of it?" she asked, wide-eyed. "He is the lost prince?"

Pellea shrugged. "The wise men won't say as yet, but I'm sure of it." She smiled impishly. "I just peeked in at him in the examining room. There's no doubt in my mind."

Janis smiled back, but the mood that filled her heart was melancholy, because she knew what that meant.

"You may have to talk him into it," she told the queen. "He's grumbling about loss of freedom and that sort of thing."

"Oh, don't you worry. We'll have him singing a different tune soon enough. I'll have Monte deal with him," she added, referring to her husband, King Monte, oldest brother of the new prince. "Come, let's sit down and talk."

Janis followed her to a pair of comfortable chairs situated in front of a wide stone fireplace.

"And I'll tell you the second thing we're going to do," Pellea went on, eyeing her askance. "We're going to get some decent clothes for you and get you out of that blue jumpsuit." She shuddered. "Is that a uniform for something?"

"Sort of." Janis drew in a shaky breath. She hadn't expected this question to come up so quickly. It threw her off balance. She couldn't lie to the queen—especially after looking into her calm, kind eyes.

"Where did you get it?"

Wishing she could disappear, she whispered, "Prison camp."

"What?" Pellea said, leaning toward her and frowning as though she hadn't heard.

"Prison camp," she said aloud. Might as well own it. "I've been in a Granvilli prison camp for the last two months. I just got out."

"Oh!" Pellea sank back into the chair and stared at her. "Oh, my."

Janis drew in a sharp breath. She'd known this would

make all the difference. The queen had been anxious to meet with her, but now they would throw her out. And who could blame them? You couldn't let a recently released prisoner hang around in the castle. True, at least she'd been in a Granvilli camp, not one run by the royals. But still. Her heart sank. She should never have come here.

Even if the queen were ready to hear her side of things, what could she say? There was no easy excuse. She could still hear her brother Rolo's voice hissing in her ear, "You really screwed this one up, Janny. You botched things so badly, your own husband turned you in." But she couldn't tell Pellea about that.

If she got up and walked out right now, could she avoid the humiliation of being escorted out by an armed guard? She eyed the doorway nervously.

But, though shocked, Pellea wasn't through with her yet. "What on earth did you do to end up there?" she asked sternly.

Janis shrugged. Was there really any point in going on with this? Why didn't the queen just call for the guard and get it over with? She took a deep breath and decided to give it a try. It was the least she could do, she supposed.

"You have to understand what it's like in the Granvilli territory right now. Society is falling apart. Everything is in chaos. People are reacting out of fear and anger. I don't really know why I was arrested. And I don't know why they let me go when they did."

That much was true. She knew what had angered

Mykal, but she didn't think that had anything directly to do with the reason she was held. If he really had been the one to turn her in, what reason had he given them? She didn't have a clue.

Pellea frowned, searching her eyes. "You were never charged with anything?"

Janis made a face. "That would require a functioning court system. They don't have that over there at present." She hesitated, ready to get up and go. "I know this is a shock to you." She began to rise. "I should have told you before."

"No." Pellea's voice had the unmistakable tone of command. "Sit down right now and tell me all about it."

"But why would you believe anything I say?" she protested, trying to be realistic about it.

Pellea tossed her head. "Talk," she ordered firmly. "Start with what happened once you were arrested. Where did they take you and what did they tell you?"

That wasn't as easy to do as it might seem. Janis licked her lips, remembering her conversation with the warden and trying to think what she could tell the queen about it.

"What is my crime?" she'd cried desperately.

The warden had stared coldly. "Espionage."

Espionage. That was what they paid her to do. How could they arrest her for it? "What kind of espionage?"

The warden's gaze didn't waver. "Illegal espionage."

That was all she was ever told. She was taken to the makeshift camp near the border, stripped of all her clothing and possessions, along with her dignity, and

given her blue jumpsuit to wear. The next two months
had been a nightmare. The food was terrible but not
plentiful, so hunger was more important than quality.
She lost twelve pounds, but she wouldn't have recommended it as a diet experience. The work assignments
were uniformly disgusting. And every night she had to
fight off the prison guards. Luckily the army had given
her some good basic self-defense moves and she held
her ground, leaving the guards to go after easier pick-
ings. But just the fact that she'd had to maintain that
struggle night after night was enough to make her bitter.

What of all that could she tell the queen? But she
had to tell her something and she tried. And she managed, haltingly, leaving out a few things, like the marriage, and her brother, and some of the seamier aspects
of prison camp life. But all in all, she stayed pretty true
to the real story line.

The queen listened impassively. "What was this espionage they arrested you for? You must have some idea
of the catalyst."

She took a deep breath. Maybe she was ready to give
a fuller picture of what she was involved with now that
she'd told her this much. Maybe she could outline a hint
of what Mykal had caught her doing that had led to his
outrage.

"It was a surveillance report on things another agent
had done," she said. "I…I made some copies and gave
them to someone I thought I could trust." Why she'd
done that for her brother was a story she couldn't get

into. "But…" She stopped, fighting back tears as she remembered Mykal's face when he found out what she'd done. Shaking her head, she couldn't go on.

Pellea watched her for a long moment, making no move to comfort her in any way. "Well, that all sounds very spy-versus-spy, doesn't it?" she said in a cool voice at last.

"Something like that," Janis admitted, her voice choked.

"Janis, nothing personal, but you do realize I have a responsibility here. I must be the guardian of my people, the protector of all who are in this castle."

"Of course. I understand."

Pellea paused, then added, "I'm afraid I'm going to have to ask you to leave."

Janis nodded. That was what she expected, once her imprisonment was known. It would be even worse if they knew about her family background. She was ready to go. She only wished she could see Mykal once more before she left, though. She had a feeling that, once she left, she might never see him again.

They rose together and Janis turned away. She wanted to get this over with as quickly as possible. But she stopped, realizing she couldn't leave the room before the queen did.

Pellea came toward her, hand outstretched, looking ready to say goodbye, but a courtier was suddenly in the doorway.

"Your Majesty," he said, bowing deeply. "You are

wanted in the hospital wing. Dr. Pheasar asks that you come to him immediately."

Pellea turned to Janis. "This must be about Mykal," she said. She stared at Janis for a moment, then reached out for her again. "You'd better come, too," she said, then turned without another word and hurried for the elevator.

Janis was right behind her. Had something happened to Mykal? Her heart was thumping and she was hurrying as they exited the elevator on the hospital floor, but she could hardly keep up with the queen. In a moment they were in the medical unit.

"No entry, please," the nurse said, jumping up to stop them, but then shrinking back when she saw who it was. "Oh, excuse me Your Majesty."

They rushed right through the barriers and finally they were in the examining room where the doctor was looking at X-rays in a computer screen. Mykal was still unconscious, covered in a sheet and lying on a table on the other side of the room. Janis looked from him to the doctor to the X-rays and back to Mykal again, hardly knowing what to think, but terrified of what they might hear.

"Take a look at this," the surgeon was saying, pointing to where tiny lines that looked like needles were scattered so very close to a section of Mykal's spinal column. "This is not good. I've conferred with a number of my colleagues and we have mixed opinions. But most of us think it's too dangerous to attempt any removal of the closest ones at this time. I'll be sending copies of their reports along with my own and you can read them for yourself. But I wanted you to see this." He turned and looked at them both. "He can still live a full and active life. But I'm afraid he will need to be confined to a wheelchair most of the time."

Janis drew her breath in with a gasp and Pellea frowned.

"I thought you told me initially that you felt the shards were too close to leave them," she said. "That they might move in and compromise his mobility on their own if left alone."

"Yes, that was what I thought before I got a look on my own. But examining this more closely makes me think we just can't risk it."

Pellea looked at Janis. "What do you think?" she asked her. "How will he take this news?"

Janis was startled to be asked for an opinion. But she had one. "If it were up to me," she said, head high and voice clear, "I would keep him as safe as possible. I wouldn't operate. I would wait and see." She looked at them both and shook her head. "But I know what he wants. And he couldn't stand a cosseted life. He'll choose surgery. You can count on it."

Pellea frowned, looked at the doctor and shrugged. "We'll talk again once he's awake and lucid," she said. Looking at Janis, she gestured for her to follow. "Come with me," she said.

Janis tried to do just that, but she couldn't. She had to turn and look at Mykal again, then go close and touch him, just for a quick second. This might be the last time she would see him. The second stretched out, and she leaned down to kiss his forehead. "I love you," she whispered, then straightened and turned to find Pellea watching her.

"I'm sorry," she said awkwardly. "I just couldn't leave."

Pellea didn't say a word, but turned and started down the hall, with Janis hurrying after her.

"I'd like you to come to my room for a moment," she told her as they boarded the elevator again. "We need to finish our talk."

Janis nodded and quickly found herself in a beautiful courtyard, with a greenhouse roof, open to the sky, that served as a sitting room. Exotic plants had turned the space into a barely controlled jungle. Brightly colored birds flew from plant to plant, and frogs croaked in a little stream that wound through the area.

"Sit," Pellea told her. "And tell me the rest of the story."

She sat. "What is it that you want to know?"

"I want to know who Mykal is. What sort of man. I understand I am going to have to learn these things on my own, but you can start the process by telling me how you met and why you were together."

Janis frowned, curious. "I'm sure you've researched him."

"Of course. We have a complete record of his activity up until a little over two years ago. Then the trail goes cold. And that is exactly the time he can't remember. So you see, it does become a bit of a problem."

"Oh. And you want me to fill you in."

"If you will, please."

But should she? Was the queen just going to use her for all the information she could gather, then throw her out into the street? Probably. But she realized she didn't have a lot of choice—unless she wanted to be a jerk. And she really didn't want that at all. So she nodded. "You know he was in the military."

"Yes. We've found the paperwork on his recruitment in the royal army two and a half years ago. But after that…nothing. We can't find anyone by that name in the service at all. And no one seems to be able to tell us anything."

Janis nodded. "That's because we were… I mean, he was recommended for intelligence work from the beginning. On the black side."

"The black side."

"That means he had volunteered to take training to do extreme espionage work. Only the most dangerous missions. And so they probably blotted out his identity right away. That way, if he was caught, no one would be able to trace him back to the command group."

Pellea nodded. "I see." She sighed. "And did he see much action?"

"During the war, yes. Once the truce was declared, the hot war turned cold and our assignments got a bit more ordinary." She smiled, remembering. "For a while I was actually going up and down streets, pretending to be a meter maid, but really checking who lived there. We did a lot of that sort of thing."

A tiny smile appeared in the queen's eyes. "Someone's got to do it."

"Unfortunately, that someone was me."

Pellea frowned. "But wait a minute. You were in the Granvilli military. Is that right?"

Here came the sticky part. "Yes. My family was based in Granvilli territory. It just seemed natural."

She waved the explanation away. "Of course. But what about Mykal?"

"When we met, he was in Granvilli intelligence, just as I was. And I assumed…"

"But he was actually working for us?"

She nodded. "Yes."

Pellea's smile was full this time. "That's a relief."

"But I didn't know that until later."

"So he was a double agent?"

She nodded, then shook her head, troubled. "You know, I don't feel right telling you things about Mykal. He should tell you himself."

Pellea looked frustrated. "But he can't. It's possible that he will never be able to remember what happened during the war. In the meantime, we have to be prepared for everything. And the only way that can happen, is if you tell us."

Janis thought for a moment, then looked up. "I have to ask him first. I'm sorry, but I just don't feel free to explain his life for him without his permission."

Pellea looked as though she were about to say something, then stopped herself. "Of course," she said instead. Then her gaze sharpened. "Tell me this. Who recruited you into intelligence service?"

She hesitated. Just how much of herself did she owe them?

"My brother," she admitted at last. "He wasn't in the service but he did contract work for them. And he thought I was a perfect match."

"Was he right?"

She bit her lip, considering. "Sort of. I enjoyed the work. But I wasn't particularly proud of it. Do you know what I mean?"

"You were good at it, but you weren't sure it was honorable."

She nodded. Pellea had hit the nail on the head. It was such a joy to talk to someone who understood so quickly. "Exactly."

"And Mykal?"

She couldn't help but smile. "He enjoyed it thoroughly. He loved putting things over on the bad guys, so to speak. He loved being smarter and more aware than other people."

"So playing a double game was right up his alley."

"Yes. So it seemed."

Pellea stared at her for a moment, then said, "I can see that you love him. But tell me this. Do you like him?"

Janis laughed. "I adore him," she said with passion. "I love and admire everything about him. I would do anything for him."

Pellea thought for a moment, then said, "Janis, can

you think of any reason why it would be dangerous for me or my family if you stayed here with us for a few days?"

Janis took the question seriously. She thought for a moment, then shook her head. "No."

"I don't have any documents you might want to copy," she said, half-teasing. "At least, not that I know of." She smiled. "In fact, I don't have any secrets at the moment. My life is an open book."

"Oh, Your Highness, that was such an anomaly. I would never…"

"Yes, yes, I'm sure of it. And I can tell you care deeply for Mykal. How he feels about you is a mystery, even to him." She smiled, touching Janis's cheek. "So I think you should stick around. He needs all the friends he can get right now."

Janis was overwhelmed. She hadn't expected this. "Your Royal Highness," she said, her voice cracking, "you're too kind."

"I'll have someone show you to a room you can use for the short term. And I'll make sure they let you know as soon as he is awake enough to see people."

CHAPTER EIGHT

MYKAL looked gaunt, like a Halloween version of himself. Janis leaned over the bed and put a hand on his chest to make sure he was breathing. He was. When he didn't react, she glanced around to make sure no one was lurking in the hallway, then leaned down and kissed his lips.

His eyes shot open and he smiled at her.

"Wow," he said faintly. "That wasn't a dream?"

She kissed him again, just to prove it, and he kissed her back.

"Did you find my wife?" he asked as she drew back.

She hesitated, looking down at him. He didn't remember. Or maybe he'd never heard a word she said. Should she say it again? She frowned. No. Not now. Once things were settled and secure, that would be the time.

"I've got a good strong lead on it," she said instead. "I'll tell you about it later."

He nodded, not taking his eyes off her. "Okay. I'll trust you."

That took away her smile and made her anxious

again. He couldn't trust her. That was just the problem they had between them. What she wanted more than anything was to make things so that he could trust her again.

The surgeon came in and turned on the computer monitor to show Mykal the X-rays and Janis melted into the background, leaving them alone. She knew what they were discussing and she also knew she would have no say in the outcome. Pellea came by, gave her a hug and went on into the room. Janis watched through the window as she talked animatedly to the other two.

Suddenly a man appeared in the doorway, the sort of man who had a presence about him, the sort of man who made you step back a bit and stare in awe.

"Your Majesty," the nurse said, jumping up and dipping her head.

"Good evening," he replied in a friendly but distracted manner. He gave a faint smile to Janis as well as he walked on into the recovery room. She stared after him, sure this must be King Monte, Mykal's oldest brother. Now that she'd seen the king, she knew why Pellea had been so sure Mykal was a prince. They looked very much alike.

The king joined in the discussion. Mykal sat propped up with pillows and looking very determined.

Finally, she caught a sentence or two.

"We can operate first thing in the morning, if you're sure," the surgeon said.

Monte said something to Mykal, and then reached down take his brother's hand. It was an emotional moment. Janis had tears in her eyes as the king swept through again, avoiding her gaze as he left the area. She looked at Mykal and saw that he was blinking himself.

Pellea came out and smiled at her. "Go in and talk to him," she said. "They will try to remove the shrapnel first thing in the morning. That's his decision. I only pray that they are successful."

Janis went in and looked at him.

"So I guess it's true. You are royal."

"Ya think?"

They grinned at each other, and then his eyes sharpened as he looked her over.

"Hey. You look really pretty."

"Queen Pellea rustled up some clothes for me." She twirled in front of him, showing off the cute short skirt and the gauzy top. He smiled approvingly, but then a strange expression came over him. His gaze seemed to cloud over, as though he were remembering something. She waited, holding her breath, but he smiled again. Still, she could have sworn there was a hint of recognition, even for just a moment.

And then Kylos came barging into the room. "What the hell is this about operating on your back?" he demanded. "I don't think you should do it. Not yet."

"What are you doing here?" Mykal asked him.

"Talking to you. Trying to talk sense into you."

"No, I mean here at the castle."

"Oh. I asked to come. I thought you could use the moral support."

"No kidding?" Mykal met Janis's gaze and grinned.

She grinned back. Kylos went on talking, trying to convince Mykal to hold off on the operation but never making any real sense. And Janis and Mykal ignored him.

"What do you think?" he asked her. "Have you changed your mind?"

"I guess we'll follow your instincts and hope for the best," she told him. "I just want what will leave you safe. That's the most important thing to me."

His eyes darkened. "Why do you care so much?" he asked her. "You hardly know me."

She tried to smile. "I know you better than you think."

He nodded slowly. "We knew each other during my lost period, right?"

She nodded, trembling slightly and waiting for the hard questions. He studied her for a long moment, then smiled, and the hard questions didn't come.

"Have you got a date?" he asked her instead.

"A date?" She laughed. "Not yet."

"I mean, do you have something to do tonight?"

She shook her head, looking as him questioningly.

"Then how about staying with me for a while?" he asked simply. "I'm really feeling dopy and I'm probably going to fall asleep soon. But if you could stay with me until that happens…"

"It would be my pleasure." She sat down in the chair, feeling a rosy glow of happiness like she hadn't felt in a long time. "Anything you want."

He stretched back and began to talk, telling her about

his childhood, about the parents who'd raised him with
so much love and kindness, about his vacations at the
beach. She listened and enjoyed finding out things about
him she'd never known. She only wished she could have
told him about their life together. Short as it was, it had
been a joy. And it had resulted in a baby. She cupped
her hands around her child and wondered if he would
ever know about him or her. Too many unknowns littered their future. It was hard to tell which way the wind
would blow from this vantage point. But whatever happened, she knew she would always love Mykal. If only
she could count on him feeling the same.

The day seemed hectic. There was so much going on in
the castle, it seemed like a small city, set up vertically
instead of on the horizontal. Everyone she passed in the
halls seemed to be bustling with a sense of urgency, on
their way to do important tasks in interesting places.
There was a certain electric excitement in the air. She
liked it. She wandered about and gazed at everything
as though she were at Disneyland.

But it was hard to immerse herself into any one thing.
She couldn't erase the worry and push what was happening in that operating room out of her mind.

She'd been there when Mykal had woken in the
morning. She'd kissed him again before she left, knowing it must be a bit confusing to him to have the woman
he thought he'd tasked with finding his wife seeming
so affectionate. But she couldn't help it. As soon as she

could, she would tell him the truth, and this time she would make sure he was awake when she did it.

Still, that wasn't going to make the difference where the future of their relationship was concerned. Their marriage was doomed. She hoped and prayed that his operation would be successful, that he wouldn't be damaged, that he would be free to take his position in the royal family and enjoy it to the fullest. Everything should be perfect for him. He so deserved it.

She'd forgiven him in her heart for not coming to rescue her from the prison camp. It was her fault, after all. That day when he'd told her he could never trust her again had been the worst of her life. When the secret police had shown up to take her away, she'd almost felt she deserved whatever they might do to her.

But later, she began to wonder how it had come to that. After all, Mykal wasn't a die-hard Granvilli supporter. He was actually a secret royalist. So why would he have turned her in to the Granvilli authorities? It didn't make any sense.

But that hardly mattered anymore. Mykal was a part of the royal family and that was something she could never be. It wasn't as though the family she came from was just some run-of-the-mill crime family. The Gorgonios defined organized crime in Ambria and had for over a hundred years. They were part of a dynasty, a sort of royalty of its own milieu. Her grandfather, her father and her uncle had been the rulers of the organization, each in turn. And each had been the most hated and wanted criminal in his time. There was no getting around it. She came from people who were scum.

She had tried to distance herself from her family in every way she could and she'd tried to get Rolo to join her. When he was younger, it had seemed to be working. Lately, she was afraid she was losing that struggle. She constantly tried to pull him away, and he just as stubbornly pulled back. He didn't seem to be able to make the commitment to leave organized crime forever.

She went into the library and picked out a couple of magazines, but she couldn't concentrate on the stories. And then she had a thought. Libraries kept old newspapers. Maybe some paper they'd collected might have the news of Mykal's accident when the IED exploded. It was worth a try. So she spent a good hour looking through everything she would find that covered the first month after their separation. Nothing. She couldn't find a single item, and she was so disappointed, she had to get up and walk around the entire floor of the building to get her equilibrium back.

She visited the recreation center and considered playing a little table tennis, something she once had been good at. But she couldn't keep her mind on that, either. Her heart and her mind were in that operating room and there was no way to get around it.

At one point, she stopped into the royal breakfast room. Pellea had given her a pass. The tables were covered with a sumptuous feast of a breakfast spread. Everything looked delicious. But she knew she wouldn't be able to get anything down, so she made a short tour of the room, smiled at a couple of people who eyed her curiously and left again.

Outside, she went to a railing and looked down at the crowd in the halls on the floor below. And then she caught sight of something that chilled her blood, and she stepped back quickly so as not to be seen. Down below she saw her brother, Rolo, with her cousin Jasper. From what she knew of both those men, no one should have ever let them inside these castle walls. She began to walk, getting as far from them as she could. She could hardly breathe. What were they doing here? And what was she going to do about it?

Nightmare scenarios as to what they might be up to went swimming through her head, one after another. She knew she should tell Pellea about these two inter-lopers, but if she did, Pellea would find out quickly what sort of family she came from. She'd been gracious with her, but that would be a step too far for her to go. Rolo and Jasper would be sent packing—but so would she herself! And she couldn't go until she knew that Mykal was all right.

But not much longer than that. She had to leave be-fore anyone knew she was pregnant. Of course, Mykal thought he knew already, but he wasn't going to tie it to her unless he got his memory back. And that was the abyss that yawned before her. They wouldn't want her once they found out about her ancestry. But they would want her baby.

A frantic wave of panic swept through her. No one must know. She would leave as soon as she could, go to the continent, maybe immigrate to Australia or Canada and take her baby as far from Ambria as she could get. She would get a false ID. She'd done that often enough in the past. She knew people who could help her. She had to go. No one must know.

She looked at her watch. Suddenly it was time to go back to the medical unit. She had to be as close to Mykal as she could get. It would be another hour or more before the surgeon would come out and give them the verdict, but she couldn't stay away any longer. Turning, she hurried to the elevators.

The waiting room was brightly painted and well-lit, but it seemed like the gloomiest place on earth to Janis. She sat in the plastic chair and flipped through a magazine, not even seeing the articles. Inside, she repeated a prayer over and over.

Please let him be safe. Please let him be safe.

It was impossible to sit still. She got up to pace, but as she passed the window to the nurse's station, she noticed the chair was empty. No one was manning the entryway. And that meant there was no one guarding the information.

Information—like files with background on a patient's health—or the details of the accident that had put him in the hospital in the first place. Should she? She stopped, thinking. Why not just ask to see them? But no. That never worked with people in charge of information. She would be told she had no standing. Better to try to do it on her own.

Gliding quickly, she went to the file cabinet and pulled open the drawer she thought should have Mykal's records. The folders were filed alphabetically and she began to search through them. She heard footsteps in the hall. She only needed another second or two.

The door opened and she was back pacing, but her heart was beating a mile a minute.

"Hello," the nurse said before dropping down into her seat behind the desk again.

"Hello," Janis said back. "I don't suppose you've heard anything?"

The nurse shook her head. "Sorry. I'll let you know as soon as I do."

"Thanks."

She went back to her chair and slumped into it, calming her heart rate and picking up her magazine. Mykal's folder hadn't been in the file drawer. She supposed it might be in the room where he was staying. At some point, she had to get hold of that file. It had become an obsession with her. She had to know.

She hadn't been there long before Kylos came sauntering into the room, dressed in black, as usual. She looked up and gave him a slight smile. She assumed his twitch was his answering salute. She went back to the magazine and he slipped into a chair beside her, looking just as tense as she felt.

"Have you heard anything?" he asked.

"No. Nothing." For a moment she thought they were going to have a bonding moment over the fate of his brother. He really seemed to care. A small wave that was almost affectionate went through her.

"I guess it was pretty much a surprise to you when he was told he was one of the lost princes," she commented.

"Not really," he replied, a pinch of bitterness in his tone. "Mykal always gets the gold ring. It seems to be his birthright."

"Yes," she said faintly. "I know what you mean."

"And what about you?" He leered at her. "How do you think someone like you is going to hang on to him?"

She blinked at him. "What do you mean?"

"I told you I was going to look into your background. I've already found out a few things."

Icy fingers traveled up and down her spine. "Like what?"

"Never mind." He leered again, acting as though he liked making her wait. "I'll talk to you about this later."

She shrugged, reminded of how annoying he was. But she couldn't think about her own problems right now. She had to worry about Mykal.

He moved restlessly. "What do you think? Is he going to die?"

She looked up, shocked. "No, he's not going to die! Where did you get such a ludicrous idea?"

He shrugged, looking uncomfortable. "I thought the shrapnel was pretty deep and pretty bad, and since they kept saying—"

"He's not going to die." She said it with passion, but she shivered deep inside. "What we're hoping for now is that he has no impaired motion. That his legs will work. That the operation won't leave him damaged in any other way."

Kylos frowned. "He probably won't be needing the pain medication anymore, huh?"

She stared at him, wondering at such a strange question. But then, Kylos was a strange man. "I have no idea."

He growled. "He shouldn't have done it."

"I'll tell you this. If this operation is successful and he comes out in good health and spirits, we're both going to tell him our secrets. Aren't we? I'm going to tell him who I really am and you're going to tell him about your parents. Right?"

"Are you crazy? He won't be ready to hear about that. Not for days." He shook his head and muttered, "Not for at least a few more days," but she had a feeling that wasn't really meant for her to hear.

"Kylos, do you have a job?"

"Of course I have a job. Well, I do contract work."

"What sort?"

He took a deep breath and let it out. "Okay, here's the deal. I went to law school. But the dean had it in for me so I never finished. But I got enough so that I can do some kinds of paralegal work. And that's what I do."

"Freelance?"

"Sort of. I've got a good friend, Leland Lake. He's an attorney and he hires me for various things."

She went back to her magazine. He moved nervously

for a while, then got up to visit the restroom. Looking over at the seat, she noticed he'd left his mobile behind. And almost immediately, it rang.

She had to make a decision. His ring tone was awful, shrill and demanding. It seemed to echo off the waiting-room walls. It was way too loud. It had to be stopped.

Ordinarily she wouldn't answer someone else's phone like this, but the noise was unbearable. Snatching it up, she flipped it on and said, "Yes?"

"Kylos Marten, please."

She recognized the voice. It was Griswold, the daily butler.

"He's not here right now, but this is Janis Davos. Hi, Griswold."

"Oh. Hello, miss."

"Can I give him a message?"

"Uh… Oh, well, why not? Please tell him that the party in question has arrived."

"Okay, Griswold, you're going to have to be a bit more specific. What party in question?"

He paused, then said, "The people interested in the house. He'll know what I mean. Tell him I will escort them about the grounds until he gets here, unless he calls and tells me differently."

"I see."

"Just tell him that. Thank you, miss."

Janis sat very still with her lips pressed together, thinking that over as she waited for Kylos to come back. And when he did, she waited until he had picked up his phone and began to take his seat.

"You had a call."

He reacted badly. "What! You answered it?"

"I had to stop the noise."

"That's not noise." He seemed quite offended. "That's my favorite band."

Rolling her eyes, she told him, "Griswold says the people interested in the house have arrived and he will go ahead and escort them about while waiting for you to show up." She frowned, gazing at him sharply. "What are you doing, selling the house?"

He didn't answer, but he gave her a furious scowl and bolted for the door. "I'll be back," he muttered as he disappeared.

Janis frowned after him. The little bugger was selling the house, and without talking to Mykal first. She had a very bad feeling about that. She didn't think Mykal was going to be happy when he found out. But of course, Mykal didn't know their parents had died. And here was Kylos, selling the house out from under him. That just wasn't right.

She went back to her magazine but she couldn't even see the pictures anymore. *Please, please,* she kept chanting silently. *Make him be okay.*

It was already half an hour later than she'd been told it would be. Time seemed to be going in slow motion. Pellea looked in.

"Have you heard anything?" she asked.

Janis shook her head, feeling lost.

"I'll find out what's going on," the queen said,

marching in through the double doors. And marching right back out again.

"No one's talking," she told Janis. "I'll be back a little later and see if I can get anything out of any of them."

Another half hour dragged by. Then another. She was up and pacing now, fear and panic chasing each other throughout her system. What could be wrong? Why wouldn't anyone tell her anything?

She'd tried going in to the operating room but a nurse had sent her back out. She was going crazy with worry.

Pellea came back to sit with her. She made a few calls on her mobile, trying to scare up some information, and finally she did get a scrap.

"They've sent for more experts from Vienna," she told Janis. "They sent for them quite some time ago and they are coming in as fast as they can get here."

"What does that mean?" Janis was as shaken as she'd ever been.

"I assume it means they've hit a problem. But don't worry. These guys are the best in the world."

Don't worry! She was nothing but worry. Any more and she would be lying in the corner in a fetal position, whimpering like a baby lamb.

But before she had time to really panic, they arrived, three of them, sweeping in through the waiting room and on into the operating theater like gods down from Olympus. Janis and Pellea stood holding each other, each whispering their own prayer. At one point, they heard shouting and Janis's eyes filled with tears.

"Oh, no!" she cried. "Something's happened to him."

"Hush," Pellea told her. "He'll be okay." But somehow her voice didn't have the conviction it had held earlier.

Another half hour passed. Kylos was back. When Janis introduced him to the queen, he was like a different man, all smiles and good manners. Janis could hardly believe the transformation, but she had no time to mull it over. She had to worry. If she didn't worry enough—superstition being what it was, she didn't know what would happen, but she knew she had to keep worrying. It was all she had left to do.

And then it was over. Dr. Pheasar came out, taking Pellea by the hands and shaking his head. Janis began to sob, but he looked up, surprised.

"No, my dear, don't cry. I think the prognosis is fairly good. Not perfect, but much better than I expected."

"Oh, doctor." Janis grabbed his arm. "Are you sure? Do you mean it?"

"Yes, I mean it. I think you'd better leave him alone tonight, but you should be able to go in and see him first thing in the morning."

Now she was really sobbing, and so was Pellea. But they were both laughing through their tears as well, looking at each other.

The doctor shook his head. "Women," he muttered.

But Janis didn't care. One hurdle had been crossed. Now all that was left was for Mykal to heal from the surgery—and get his memory back.

CHAPTER NINE

CLOSE to dawn, Janis slipped into Mykal's room and went right to his bed. Leaning over him, she kissed his lips and then she took his hand in hers. Slowly, he opened his eyes and looked at her. She waited nervously to see what her reception would be.

It was all that she could have hoped for. His smile was slow but it grew until his mouth was wide and his happiness reached his eyes. His gaze alone seemed to reach out and wrap her up for the keeping. Instinctively, he loved her. She could feel it. His head hadn't gotten the word yet, but his heart knew it.

"Hey," he said to her. "You're back. I've been waiting to see you."

"Me, too," she said simply. "We've got a lot to catch up on."

His smile wavered. "We did know each other before, didn't we?"

"Yes."

"I knew it. Funny how I can feel it, even though I can't remember it." He looked at her expectantly. "And...?"

She tried to smile was her nerves were getting the better of her. "First tell me how you feel."

"I feel great. I could practically get up and dance right now if I didn't have this damn IV stuck in my arm."

"None of that. You need to stay still and heal."

"Sure." He smiled at her, reassuring her again. "But, Janis, I'm going to be okay. I'm not going to have to spend my life walking around wondering if any slight little jostle will render me paralyzed." He shook his head. "You don't know what a relief that is."

"Oh, don't I?"

She smiled back at him and he searched her face, then reached out with his free hand and touched her cheek. She wanted to bury her face in his palm and kiss it, but she didn't dare do that. Not yet.

"Okay," he said, pulling back. "I've told you my news. You tell me yours." His eyes darkened slightly. "Did you find my wife?"

She nodded and she could tell her eyes were sparkling. Too bad she couldn't hold back the excitement she felt. It might just be her undoing. And yet she was about to tell him the truth. That had to be a good thing, no matter how he reacted. "Yes, I did."

He watched her, just barely holding back a smile. "Is it you?"

She nodded again.

His grin widened. "I had a feeling." Reaching out, he pulled her to him. "I knew it was going to be you." He hugged her a bit gingerly, using only one arm, but he breathed in the scent of her hair and shivered. "You couldn't have told me anything that would make me happier."

Janis laughed, full of joy. She ran the flat of her hand inside the opening of his hospital pajamas, caressing the chest she knew so well. This was almost the old Mykal. This was almost the old feeling. If only this moment could last forever.

Lifting her face, he kissed her lips and she kissed him back.

"Why didn't you tell me from the beginning?" he asked huskily.

"I couldn't." This was going to be the hard part. "We had to be so careful not to upset you in any way."

"But finding out I've got a wife like you wasn't going to upset me," he began. Then he saw the look in her eyes and his face changed. "Or would it?"

She closed her eyes, took a deep breath and sat up on the bed beside him. "It would," she said sadly, "if you knew the whole story."

He looked away for a moment and she wondered what he was thinking. When he looked back, his eyes were troubled. "Maybe we should just leave it alone, Janis," he said quietly. "Maybe it would be better to pretend it never happened—whatever it was."

She shook her head. "We can't do that, Mykal. Even if we wanted to. In fact, now that you are going to be royal, every single fact of your life is going to be common knowledge. You're not going to be able to hide from it."

He groaned and leaned his head back. "Okay. Lay it on me. What was so horrible that you've felt you had to hide it from me?"

"Okay." She looked at him, all her love in her eyes. This might be the last chance she had to look at him without seeing anger and resentment coming back her way. "When you got blown up on your bike," she began, "we weren't together."

"What happened?"

"Let me start from the beginning."

She filled him in quickly, telling him how they'd met, how they had both been working for military intelligence, both experts at undercover work. "As you used to say, we lived in a world of lies and spies. We had to work hard to keep our own reality apart from that."

His gaze never left her face as she went through their time together, how they had lived and loved, how they had secretly married.

"We were so happy together," she told him earnestly. "We really were so well-matched. It was like a miracle. We could hardly stay away from each other all day."

"Now that I can believe," he said with the hint of a grin.

"But there were a couple of clouds on our horizon. Things you didn't even know about. And it was my fault." Her voice broke.

Reaching out, he took her hand in his, but he didn't say a word.

"Okay, now you know most of the background. But I haven't told you about my brother, Rolo."

"Your brother Rolo." He said it slowly, as though running the name through his memory banks, trying to find the right folder.

"You knew him. He wasn't military but he did some contract work for us and you worked with him a couple of times. He's my baby brother. I basically raised him, as our parents weren't around much." She took a deep breath. How to explain this? "When he was young, I adored him. He was the cutest little boy. He didn't turn out to be what I would have wanted, but I tried." Her voice was shaking, but she couldn't stop now. "And I kept hoping, always hoping, if I could give him just one more chance, maybe this time he would catch on and do well at something. He always needed a break, always had everyone working against him. At least in his mind. You get the picture?"

He nodded, and she noted he was beginning to look a bit distant. That chilled her. But what did she expect?

"We'd been married about two months when he came to me in distress. He was about to be fired once again. He needed evidence to prove he could do the work they were expecting him to do. He had to have something to show them, just one bit of good information. And he wanted me to get it for him."

Mykal winced. "I don't like where this is going," he murmured, eyes hooded.

Her heart sank. He was ready to condemn her without even hearing the whole story. Oh, well. She knew she deserved it.

"I wanted to help him. I wanted to believe him. He's

all I have left of my family." She steeled herself, but
her words were coming too fast now. She just wanted
to get it over with. "In trying to help him, I did something very bad and very stupid. I...I went into your papers and looked for something, anything, something
innocuous and simple, something I could give him to
use. Something that you wouldn't even notice."

He was no longer holding her hand. She clenched it
into a fist.

"I found the study you had done on the Grieg harbor
patterns. You'd said they were useless. So I picked that.
I made a copy and I gave it to him."

He was staring at her. "Wow."

She nodded. She knew how bad this was. "I gave him
what I'd found, but he called me and said he needed the
second page. When I went in to make a copy of that,
you walked in and saw me."

"Janis..." His voice was strangled and his eyes were
filled with horror and he seemed to be moving as far
away from her as he could go.

She closed her eyes for a moment. She didn't want
to see that look on his face. She remembered what he
had said at the time. "Janis. My God, what have you
done? You were my one island of safety and sanity in
this crummy world. And now that's gone."

That probably hurt her more than anything else. To
think that she had let him down cut like a knife into her
heart.

"I told you this was bad. And it is the reason we
aren't together anymore." She took a shaky breath and

as she went on, her voice began to sound mechanical. "You could hardly believe what you saw at first. And you told me in no uncertain terms that you could never forgive it. That you could never trust me again. I tried to explain, but of course, it was a stupid explanation anyway and you had every right not to listen to it."

She shook her head, wincing as she remembered that scene. "You were so angry. You felt completely betrayed. You said…" Her voice broke. "You said you never wanted to see me again. I…I ran out of the apartment and I ran and ran. I ran for miles. I finally ended up at Rolo's new apartment, a place you didn't know about. And I stayed with him until the next day." She swallowed hard and went on. "The next day when the secret police came and dragged me away."

He was staring at her. "I don't get it. Why did they do that?"

She shrugged. "Rolo said you'd called them and given information about me, and I…"

"Me?"

"Yes. And I figured he was right. Who else would have done it?"

He shook his head as though he couldn't believe she'd thought that of him. "I thought you said I didn't know where you were."

She shook her head. "Someone must have told you."

He stared at her for a long moment, obviously frustrated that he couldn't remember the facts for himself, and then he said, "I don't believe it."

She shrugged. At this point, she really didn't know

what to believe. But she'd been arrested. That much was real. "At any rate, they came. And they took me to the Granvilli prison camp in Swanson, near the border."

He shook his head as though his mind and his heart were too full to say anything.

"I spent two months in that camp. I just got out a few days ago. And I went hunting for you. I heard you'd gone over the border and were living in the city. Someone gave me your address. And I went to your house, still in my prison jumpsuit."

He was staring at her. "Oh, my God, Janis…"

"And there you were, all shot up with shrapnel. And about to be named a prince. So you see, I didn't want to add to your stress level at that moment in time. That's why I didn't tell you."

He closed his eyes and shook his head. Then he looked at her again. "So that wedding ring is ours?"

She half smiled, liking the way he put that, despite everything. "Yes. We only wore them when we were home. We weren't supposed to be married. It was against the military rules." She frowned. "So I don't understand why you were wearing it when your bike hit that IED. Do you?"

He shrugged. "Obviously not."

"And you don't remember what date that was?"

"No."

She glanced at the end of the bed where his chart and other papers were usually posted. There was nothing there.

She looked at him. He looked tired, confused. She

reached out and touched his hand, but he made no move to reciprocate. Her throat threatened to swell closed if she didn't get out of here.

"Listen, I've given you a lot to think about," she said, holding back tears. "I'm going to go for now. I'll be back around noon. Okay?"

She looked at him again, wondering if he would tell her not to bother. But he didn't answer. He just stared at her as though he'd never seen her before. She turned and quickly left the room. And once she was in the hall, the tears began to flow. Their marriage was so over.

She walked through the halls, trying to calm herself. There was more to be done. She had to remain competent or things would get even worse. Slowly, bit by bit, she got control again.

A few minutes later she realized she hadn't said anything to him about Kylos showing the house. But that was just as well. She would leave it to Kylos to tell him. He didn't need to hear all the bad news at once.

She hated to leave Mykal all alone like this. She felt as though she was leaving him in the middle of a pack of wolves and expecting him to fend them off all by himself. But she couldn't let herself use that as an excuse to stay longer. She had to leave before it became impossible to go.

And then, as she was passing a group of offices, she saw someone she'd known years before and it occurred to her he might be useful.

"Mr. Dreyfer," she said, approaching the distin-

guished looking older man. "I don't know if you remember me?"

He smiled and held out his hand. "Of course. You're
the Gorgonio girl, aren't you?"

She smiled at him as well, remembering years before
when her uncle had tried to engage Mr. Dreyfer as his
defense attorney when he'd first been charged with organized crime activities. Mr. Dreyfer had come to the
house for extended meetings, but in the end, he'd recommended another attorney.

"Everyone has a right to decent representation," he'd
said at the time. "But I can't justify taking a case that
won't let me sleep at night. I have a family to consider."

His words had stuck with her and helped her to make
her decision, years later, to try to cut her ties to the
Gorgonios.

"Actually, I go by my mother's maiden name, Davos,"
she told him now.

"Ah. Perhaps that's just as well."

"Yes." She took a deep breath and launched into an
explanation of why she was at the castle and what had
happened to Mykal. "It's wonderful that he is being
given this opportunity," she told him. "But I was thinking he really ought to have representation. It's all so new
and unexpected. Would you be interested in talking to
him?"

"Yes, of course. It all sounds very exciting and sometimes people get swept away by that. They can often use
a bit of wise counsel, which is just what I pride myself
in supplying."

"Yes. I trust the people here at the castle and all they're doing, but I think it would be best if he had someone looking after his interests, just to be sure. And since I won't be with him after today…"

"I have some things to wrap up, but I'm at your service. Will tomorrow morning do?"

"I would so appreciate that." She explained where Mykal was and then left the attorney, feeling satisfied.

She knew what she was doing. She was tying up loose ends after all, just not the ones she'd come seeking to tie up. She'd wanted Mykal to sign their divorce papers. He would probably do that on his own. And she'd wanted him to sign away parental rights. He would never do that. She would have to go and hide where he couldn't find her. But since she wasn't going to be here to help him through all this, she was glad she'd found someone who could do a lot of it for her. One more item off her list.

She still had one of the hardest ones to go. Before she left, he had to know about her family. That might make all this easier for him. Once he wove all that into the background of their relationship tapestry, he would know why she had to go. He would understand.

After all, he was starting on a journey, going somewhere that was beyond her reach. How could she even contemplate going with him when she knew the sort of people she came from? Her uncle—her father's brother—was Max Gorgonio, Ambria's most notorious mobster and the man who had almost ruined Mykal's parents all those years ago. A man who was right now sitting in the royal prison, sentenced to life. His was a name known, feared and despised, all through the country. It was a name she'd been born with. And that was something she could avoid for short periods of time, but ultimately she couldn't run away from.

She stopped into the coffee shop to get an iced mocha drink, and there was Rolo, sitting with her cousin Jasper, both looking glum.

"Janis!" Rolo cried when he saw her. "Thank God. I heard you were here. I've been looking all over for you. We need help."

Her shoulders sagged. Rolo always needed help. This was the first time she'd seen him since the secret police had marched her out of his apartment, and all he could do was ask for help.

She shook her head. "Rolo, I just can't deal with it right now. I need a rest." She saw the shocked expression on his face. He wasn't used to big sister not being there for him. She relented, feeling like a fool. "Oh, why don't you come to my room around three this afternoon. I'll see what I can do." She told him where she was staying and hurried away with her drink. She was going to lie down and think about Mykal. She wouldn't waste one thought on her brother until she had to.

But that only worked for a short time. Eventually she had to think about what Mykal had said about Rolo, and how adamant he'd been that he wouldn't have called out the secret police. She wanted to believe him.

* * *

She met Pellea coming out of Mykal's room as she was going in.

"How is he?"

Pellea was beaming. "Tired, but great."

That startled Janis. "Tired? How tired? You don't mean groggy, do you?"

"No, not at all." The queen shrugged. "I assume it's still from the operation."

"Oh. Of course."

Pellea seemed concerned, but she was in a hurry. "I've got a meeting with the ball committee," she said. "You do know there's a royal ball next week?"

"Oh." Too bad she was going to have to miss it.

"Yes. We need to work on a ball gown for you." Pellea laughed. "Originally we thought we were going to be parading a lot of young beauties for Mykal to pick from for his bride. But now I understand that is not an issue."

"Oh." That surprised her. "What did Mykal tell you?"

"Nothing, darling," she said, giving her a hug. "But I can tell by the look on his face when your name is mentioned. We're going to have to have a long talk before we start doing any matchmaking."

Janis pretended she didn't know what the queen was talking about. "As long as he's healthy," she said vaguely, not sure what that meant, but it filled an awkward pause and that was what she used it for. Young beauties? It made her gag to think of it. Still, it was probably good that he begin to think of other women. She was sure the handpicked ladies the crown would bring in for the ball would be perfect in every way. Unlike her.

Pellea went off and Janis went in to see Mykal, steeling herself for the visit. This time, she was going to tell him about her family.

The nurse waved her on through and she went into the room he'd been assigned to.

"Hi," she said, smiling at him lovingly, but not sure what her reception would be.

"Hey." He turned to look at her. For a moment, he didn't smile, as though he was compiling all the new things he knew about her and deciding how to respond. Finally, he smiled back but he seemed sleepy. "You look prettier every time I see you," he said. "I would think just the sight of you should jog my memory back. How could I forget loving you?"

"Amnesia is a tricky thing."

He took her hand in his. "There are so many things I don't know. Where did we live? How long were we married? Did we have a cat?"

She laughed. "No cat. But we did have a lizard that we named Ferdinand. He lived in the courtyard."

He pulled her onto the bed beside him. "Did we live by the ocean? Did we go for long walks in the sand? Did we make love on rainy afternoons?"

"All those things," she said with a sigh, curling into his embrace. "We were so very happy."

"Until…"

"Yes. Until that awful day."

He held her close, his face buried in her hair. "Forget

that day," he murmured. "Leave it behind. Let's go on without it."

She turned and kissed him. "We can't forget it. You heard what I did. You know you'll never feel the same way about me."

He looked pained. "How can I know if I don't feel the same about you when I don't remember how I felt in the first place?"

"When you get your memory back, I think you'll realize..." She took another breath. This was hard to get out. "I think you'll realize that you hate me."

"I hate you?" He shook his head in derision. "Janis, I've felt a lot of things about you since you showed up on my doorstep, but hatred is not one of them."

She sat up, frowning at him. "I don't think you fully understand what I did."

"Yes, I do."

"I betrayed you. It was unforgiveable."

"Yes. And I can't forgive it. But I can understand it. You weren't thinking about me. You were trying desperately to help your younger brother. I'll bet you'd been trying desperately to help him most of your life. You followed a known pattern. It's a pattern you're going to have to work on breaking. But I can understand it."

"Mykal..."

"Enough." He put a finger to her lips to stop her. "Let's put it behind us and go forward."

"We can't. Don't be happy yet. There's more." She steeled herself, ready to begin the tell him about the Gorgonios.

"I don't care," he said. "Come here."

His blue-eyed gaze was mesmerizing. It always had been. She was in his arms and kissing him again, and she knew she wasn't going to tell him about her family. Not yet. This was just too wonderful to forfeit at the moment.

By the time Rolo arrived at her door, she was angry.

"Okay, Rolo. I want the truth," she said as she let him in. "Why did the secret police come for me? Mykal has told me he didn't call them and I believe him."

Rolo looked pained. She could almost see the thoughts going through his head as he tried to decide what part of the truth he should give her.

"Yeah, you're right. See, it was a trap. When I turned over those papers you gave me, they wanted to know where I'd gotten them. I wouldn't tell them."

"And?" she asked coldly.

He threw out his hands as though beseeching pity. "They tortured me, Janis. What could I do?"

"You told them it was me."

"I...yeah, sort of. I couldn't help it. They were torturing me."

"Yeah, I'll bet." She didn't see any marks on him. They'd probably threatened to withhold his video-game-playing time.

"And you told them I was at your apartment."

"No." On this he was adamant. "I wouldn't tell them where you were. Honest."

"Even though they tortured you?" she said sarcastically.

"No, see, what happened was, they followed me back to the apartment. I should have been more careful, I guess."

She remembered that sick, horrible feeling of looking out and seeing that the secret police had surrounded the building.

"Rolo, why didn't you tell Mykal? Why didn't you let him know where I was?"

"Mykal?" He looked surprised. "I thought he was the one you were running from. I didn't think you would want him to know."

She closed her eyes and smiled bitterly. It was a trap, all right. But she was the one who fell into it.

"And anyway, I actually did tell him a couple of days later."

"You did?"

"Yeah. He found out where I lived and he came over and…" He glanced at her furtively. "Well, he sort of made me tell him. He can be a real jerk sometimes."

"And then what did he do?"

He shrugged. "And then he went off to find you and blew up on that motorcycle of his."

Janis closed her eyes and folded her arms over her chest and rocked herself for a moment. He'd been looking for her. All that time she'd been so angry that he hadn't lifted a finger to help her, he'd been looking for her, and then he'd been injured. It wasn't that he hated her. He couldn't help it. She was amazed at how much this changed things. A certain happiness that had died two months before had just sprouted new leaves. He tried to find her. Hallelujah.

She wanted to be alone, wanted to hold this new information to her and revel in it, but her brother was still here and he wouldn't stop talking. She frowned at him, wishing he would go.

"So anyway," he was saying, "all I need is for you to vouch for me. The guard is beginning to ask questions and I know what's coming next. They're going to want to kick me out of here. So if you could just tell the queen I'm okay."

Tell the queen he was okay? Tell her he was her criminally inclined brother, a great example of what could come out of the Gorgonio family. Tell her just to trust him anyway. Yeah, the way she did.

It was hard. She turned and looked at him. He wasn't a baby anymore but she could see those baby features hidden by the mustache and the unpleasant expression on his face. She was crying inside, crying for the loss of the sweet little boy he'd once been. It was painful.

"No," she said sadly. "Sorry, Rolo. Not this time. The only thing I'll tell the queen is that you're untrustworthy."

He didn't believe her at first. "You…you can't do that to me. We're family."

"We all make choices. You've chosen badly."

"But…"

"I'm choosing to look ahead to a bright and honest future. You would rather look back at a disreputable past and copy it. We're going to have to have a parting of the ways, I'm afraid. You'd better go."

He pleaded for another few minutes, then got angry, but she was adamant. Mykal was a prince here now. She was just as protective of what happened inside these castle walls as anyone.

"Goodbye, Rolo. Maybe we'll meet again some day, but I don't think it will be soon."

He cursed her as he left, but she hardly heard him. She needed to get back to Mykal. She needed to tell him about what he'd done. She also had to tell him about the Gorgonio family before someone else did. Although, if Kylos had been there, she might already be too late.

Mykal lay on his hospital bed, feeling frustrated and impatient. He knew it was going to take some time for recuperation, but he wanted it over with. It was time to get on with his life. He wanted to move.

But right now was not the time. He was exhausted. The physical therapist had arrived about an hour ago and had him up and walking laps in the hallways, no matter how hard he protested. And that was a good thing. He might complain, but he knew getting up and getting back to normal was the best thing he could be doing right now. He didn't want to be babied. He wanted to heal so he could face his future.

But most of all, he wanted to understand his relationship with Janis. Waves of warmth swept through him when he thought of her. His mind might not remember

her, but his heart and soul responded as though nothing was wrong.

He knew as strongly as he knew anything that he
wanted her. He wanted her in his life, he wanted her in
his bed, he wanted her in his corner. The past was over
and gone. No matter what ugliness had come between
them, all he had to do was look into her face to know
they could overcome anything.

Looking at the IV pumping fluid into his arm, he
contemplated yanking the needle out and getting up and
going after Janis right now. But that was probably a bad
idea. He'd been warned again and again that doing anything of the sort would only make his recuperation last
longer, and probably do other damage as well. Besides,
a half hour with the physical therapist had totally wiped
him out. Trying to go off on his own would probably
kill him. He grunted and lay back, angry all over again.
He wanted to get out.

But right now, he needed some sleep. Surprisingly,
despite his anger, he began to drift off quickly.

He heard a sound at the door and looked up, hoping
to see Janis. But it was Kylos. Disappointment flared,
but he nodded a welcome to his brother.

"Hey," he said coolly. "What's happening?"

"Not much." Kylos looked nervous, his gaze jerking
about from one part of the room to another as though he
were looking for something. "You still don't remember
the last two years, right?"

Mykal frowned. "Right. So what?"

"Nothing." He came all the way into the room. "So, how are you feeling?"

"Okay. Hey, I meant to write to Mom and Dad, but I didn't get to it. Can you contact them for me? Can you tell them I love them and want to see them, but that they should stay in Florida until I tell them otherwise? Okay?"

Kylos stared at him for a minute, then jumped as though he'd just realized he was supposed to answer. "Oh. Sure. Listen, I'll take care of that. No problem."

"Good. I wouldn't want them to worry."

"No. Of course not." He grimaced. "Okay, sorry to do this to you, Mykal, but I've got some bad news."

Mykal groaned, not sure he could take any more right now. "You, too?"

"Yeah. I'm afraid you're not going to like it."

He shrugged. "Fire away."

Kylos started, then stopped and fumbled in the pocket of his jacket. "Hey, listen. I forgot." He pulled a little white pill cup out and handed it to his brother, then turned to pour him some water. "The nurse asked me to have you take these. Some kind of vitamins, supposed to make you heal faster."

Distracted by all the confusion, Mykal downed the pills without a second thought. "And the bad news is?" he reminded him.

Kylos grinned, as though he'd suddenly heard good news himself. "Oh, yeah. Your little friend, Janis Davos? That's not her real last name."

Mykal looked at his brother and almost smiled. "No

kidding?" he said, expecting to find out Kylos had heard that she was his wife.

"No. I know what her real last name is."

"Marten?"

Kylos looked at him blankly. "Huh? No." He made a face. "It's Gorgonio. Max Gorgonio is her uncle. She's a Gorgonio. What are the odds, huh? A name our family has hated for fifteen years."

Mykal stared at him. "What?" he said, not really believing it. "Kylos, if you're just trying to pull my chain…"

"No, I swear. Leland, my lawyer, got the goods on her. Andre Gorgonio, Max's brother, was her father. He died when she was a little girl and she was raised in Max's house."

"No."

"I'm just telling you for your own good. I could tell you liked her a lot. So I thought you ought to know. I had my suspicions about her so I had Leland look into it. I'm surprised they didn't pick up on it here at the castle. If they had, they never would have let her in the door."

"No." Mykal was shaking his head, feeling stunned. He couldn't believe it. He didn't want to believe it.

"Funny thing is, Leland knew the family. So when he was here to give me the info this morning, we met in the coffee shop and he identified her right away. She was meeting with her brother Rolo, who I guess is a well-known crook himself." He shrugged. "You never know, do you?"

Mykal didn't respond, and Kylos glanced at his watch. "Hey, gotta go. I'll catch you later." He started off and turned at the door. "Don't feel bad, Mykal. You can see why she's a lying little cheat. She was born to it." And he was gone before Mykal could muster up his sluggish outrage.

And he was outraged. He was enraged at his weakness, enraged at his brother, enraged at Janis. He didn't want to believe it and if it were true he was enraged that it was so. This was just too much. It was as though Janis had purposefully come into his amnesia-damaged life to ruin it further. What the hell!

CHAPTER TEN

JANIS had cleared out her room. Everything she owned was back in her satchel. She was wearing slacks and a jacket that Pellea had given her, but she had no choice. Her blue jumpsuit had disappeared. That was a good thing, she supposed. But she was leaving as lightly as she possibly could.

She had a plan. She put her hand over the slight bulge in her belly and smiled.

"Don't worry, sweet thing," she told her baby silently. "By the time they know we're gone, we'll be on a ferry to the continent. They'll never find us."

No one was manning the nurses' station and she was glad. At some point soon, they would begin denying her entry to places like this. But she had one more lucky chance to see Mykal without interference. She slipped into his room. He was sound asleep, his free arm thrown over his eyes. She stood very still and watched him breathe, loving him so that her throat choked and tears swam into her eyes. It was hard to have to lose him again.

"Mykal." She put a hand on his arm. She needed to

tell him goodbye without actually saying it. "Mykal."
Bending down, she kissed his lips, then drew back, puzzled. He was sleeping very heavily. She'd never seen
him so out of it before. "Mykal." She shook him, beginning to feel a touch of panic, and he moved his arm.
His eyes opened slightly.

"What?" he said, slurring the word. He didn't look
as though he'd recognized her.

She looked down, stunned. He was drugged.

"Mykal, are you okay?"

"What? Oh, sure. I'm okay." He fought to keep his
eyes open, his face contorted in the effort. "Why are
you still giving me pain medication?" he asked.

"I'm not."

"Someone is. I can barely keep my eyes open."

"How long have you been like this?"

"I don't know. Come back in about an hour. I should
be okay by then." He yawned widely and was back to
sleep in no time at all.

She stared down at him for a moment, furious.
Turning on her heel, she rushed out to the nurses' station. It was still empty, but the log book was there and
she turned it to see who had been in to see him most
recently. Her own name was jotted down twice, and
Queen Pellea's. King Monte had come by earlier. And
the only other name was that of Kylos. He'd been there
almost two hours ago.

"Kylos," she breathed, shaking her head as anger
surged through her body. It had to be him. But why?

The nurse came in and didn't smile. Janis tried to get

her interested in checking Mykal, and she reluctantly
agreed to go over his vitals, but at the same time she
had a warning for Janis.

"A man from the palace guard came by just a little
while ago," she said. "He told me to let him know when
you showed up. So I'm going to have to call him."

"Oh." So it had begun. Someone had told the authorities about her and suspicions were beginning to swirl.
Her heart sank, but she had expected it. "I wish you
wouldn't. I want to come back and check on him in an
hour or so to make sure whatever someone gave him
is working its way out of his system." Her gaze sharpened. "Did you give him the medication?"

"Me?" She looked horrified. "No. It wasn't me."

"Has any physician been by to see him today?"

"Only the surgeon, but that was early this morning.
Oh, and the physical therapist."

"But none of them gave him anything?"

"There's nothing in the notations."

She sighed and glanced at the young woman sideways. Would she call the guard? Maybe yes, maybe
no. It would probably be wise not to be here if she did.
"Fine," she said at last. "I'll just go then."

She had to leave so as not to be kicked out, but she
didn't plan to go far. She found the most inconspicuous
seat she could in the waiting area, situated right behind
a large fig-leafed plant, where she could keep an eye on
both entrances. And there she planned to stay, boiling
with anger, until she caught Kylos going in again.

Kylos had been intent on keeping Mykal drugged

from the first. She hadn't been able to figure out why exactly, but she was pretty sure it had something to do with his trying to sell the Marten estate without Mykal knowing it was happening. Mykal couldn't defend himself, so she was going to have to do it for him. And so, she sat.

Mykal was moving slow motion in a dream. He could see Janis and hear her, but he couldn't seem to get through to her. It was as though a misty barrier stood between them and no matter how much he waved at her and called to her, she didn't know he was there. She began walking and he ran after her, trying to make his way through the fog to get closer. Every now and then he could reach through and touch her silky hair or catch the hem of her shirt, but that was as close as he could get, and even then, things slipped away. Frustration was building in him. He wanted her to look over and see him but she just kept walking, her head in the clouds.

And then he saw the cliff ahead. She was walking right toward it. She wasn't looking. He ran, he yelled, he threw himself against the misty barrier, but she just kept walking toward the abyss. Closer and closer. His breath burned in his throat from trying so hard to reach her. She was going to go over. One more step…

"No!" he screamed.

But she went over the edge of the cliff. Certain death!

But then he remembered—he could fly! He could still save her. All he had to do was jump after her and use his flying powers. He ran as hard as he could for

the edge and leaped over. He could see her plummet-
ing toward the rocks below. He spread out his arms and
arched his back to fly. But it didn't happen. He'd forgotten how to do it. Below, she hit the rocks. In a moment, he would, too. It was the end. No more happiness.
Just…nothing.

It was after ten when Kylos finally showed up. Only a
few stragglers were left in the halls. The coffee shop
had closed. Most people on this floor had gone to their
rooms. Janis heard him coming down the hall and
shrank back even farther behind the plant that hid her
from view. And there he was, looking furtively to right
and left before ducking into the medical center. The
moment he vanished into the offices, she jumped up
and followed him.

Anger at Mykal's brother threatened to surge in her
but she forced it back. She didn't want anything to shake
her concentration from the job at hand. She was certain he was the one drugging Mykal, and she was determined to catch him in the act and stop him cold.

Once again there was no one manning the nurses'
station and she made a mental note to file a complaint
against the lax security situation. But she couldn't think
about that now. Kylos had just disappeared into Mykal's
room and she had to stay focused. Stepping quietly up
to the door, she stopped and listened to what was going
on inside.

"Hey, buddy," Kylos was saying. "How are you feeling?"

"What's going on?" Mykal's voice was bleary, startled. It was obvious he was mostly still asleep.

"Not a thing. Take it easy. I'm glad you're still groggy. That'll keep you quiet for a while."

"What? I don't get it."

"No problem. Just stay cool."

"Where's Janis?"

"Janis? She's gone. No one knows where she is."

"What?"

"Listen, the nurse gave me a couple more of those vitamins she wants you to take. Let me get you a cup of water. Okay, here you go...."

Janis thrust the door open, rage consuming her. "Drop the pills, Kylos. And get your hands off my husband."

"Your what?" He stared at her, thunderstruck.

"Do what I say. Now." She'd trained for months to give her voice this sort of authority and it was coming in handy now. Kylos looked downright terrified. "And give me those pills." She grabbed them out of his hand while he was still off balance, glaring at him. "How could you do this?"

She leaned over Mykal and pressed the nurse's call button. Glancing at him, she saw that his eyes were closed. Could he possibly be asleep again with all this going on?

"You don't know what you're talking about," Kylos said, but he was backing toward the door. Then he stopped and a crafty look came over his face. "You may think Mykal is your husband," he said. "But that

won't last long. I told him about your background, that
you were a Gorgonio. He pretty much came right out
and said that was the last straw as far as he was concerned."

She looked down at Mykal, telling herself to ignore
what Kylos was saying. He was obviously using any
weapon he could think of to shake her. But at the same
time, she knew Mykal's reaction to her background
would not be good. And that was why she was leaving.

"Come on, Janis. You know the royal family will
never accept a Gorgonio." He shook his head. "Game
over, baby." He gave her an evil grin. For some strange
reason he didn't seem to be anxious to get out of the
room any longer.

The nurse came in and looked at them all, wide-eyed.
"What is going on in here?" she demanded.

"Hey," Kylos said quickly. "I just caught her trying
to give my brother those pills she's got in her hand. I
think she should be arrested."

Janis turned to the nurse, never dreaming she might
believe him. "Actually, it's the other way around," she
said calmly. "I caught him trying to drug Mykal. Please
call the castle guard."

The nurse looked from one to the other, put her mobile to her ear and called the guard.

"Someone's lying and I don't know which one of
you it is," she said testily. "But you," she said, pointing
to Janis, "are the one the guard was looking for earlier,
aren't you? And the patient is his brother. So I guess
I'm going to have to take his word for it."

"What?" Janis realized, to her horror, that Kylos might just get away with drugging Mykal. And not just that, he was going to have free rein to do it again. "No, you can't believe him."

"You're the one with a record, babe," Kylos said with a grin. "We know all about you now. Did a little time in prison camp, didn't you?"

"On the Granvilli side."

He shrugged. "Once a con, always a con, that's what they say, don't they?"

"Please listen to me," she said to the nurse, desperate now. "I was not the one doing this. You may not believe me. Okay. But please, please, make sure there is better security so he can't do this again. You've got to put a guard on Mykal. Please."

The castle guard had arrived, eyes beaming as he saw Janis. "We've been looking for you, lady. You've got some questions to answer."

"I'll answer anything you want. I'll go anywhere you want and do anything you want. But please, please, just put a guard on Mykal. And don't let his brother get anywhere near him."

No one gave her any promises. She could only hope for common sense to rule. Two guards marched her through the halls to the little old-fashioned jail cell they kept for situations like this. She was thinking that this couldn't be happening, that it was a nightmare scenario, and yet, she'd been through it before. So it could happen. And it was.

There they were again—the bars. The clang of metal

on metal. The scrape of the key in the lock. She was back, but for how long?

She sighed as she settled in. At least she'd alerted them to Kylos. That was the most she could do at this point. If she could just talk to Pellea…

"Can you ask the queen to call me?" she asked her young, gum-chewing jailer.

"Are you kidding? At this time of night?" But he relented a bit. "Listen, here's a pen and paper. Write her a note. I'll make sure her maid gets it in the morning."

And that was the most she could do. Her first goal was to make sure that Mykal was safe. And her second was to get out of the castle before Pellea realized she was pregnant. Once the royal family knew that, and knew she and Mykal were married, they would never let her go. Even if they would scorn to make her royal, they would certainly want her baby to be one of them.

Royal—hah! Here she was with a cot for a bed, one thin blanket and nothing much else. She'd left her satchel with all her worldly possessions in Mykal's hospital room. So she had nothing with her. It would be a long night.

Janis got a plate of soggy scrambled eggs in the morning, and then Pellea arrived.

"What on earth is going on?" she asked sharply.

Janis looked up and the first thing she noticed was the queen's demeanor. Her eyes were lacking the usual warmth and affection she was known for. She was holding back a bit, staying well out of reach beyond the bars.

"Please explain this to me."

Janis rose and faced her resolutely, trying to explain. She told her about her suspicions of Kylos and his motives. She described finding Mykal's parents' death certificates though Kylos refused to tell the truth about them while he seemingly tried to sell the house, about how he'd been pushing to keep Mykal drugged from the first, so that he couldn't ask any questions or really get his mind around what his brother might be doing.

"When I realized that he was drugging Mykal again, I had to do something. I watched him go in and I caught him at it."

Pellea's gaze hadn't warmed a bit. "Only he says he caught you."

"Yes. That's not true." She looked at Pellea, wishing she knew a way to convince her. "Your Majesty, I know you are caught in the middle."

"Tell me this." Now her eyes were cold as winter ice. "Is it true that Max Gorgonio is your uncle?"

Her heart sank. This was the coup de grâce, wasn't it? This was the one thing she couldn't explain away. "Yes," she said in the soft voice of a lost one.

"Is it true that you were raised in his house along with his family?"

"Yes." Gathering all her nerve, she raised her gaze to meet Pellea's and try to get her to understand. "But that has nothing to do with this."

Pellea raised a hand to stop her. "I'm sorry, Janis. I can't just take your word for it. I should never have let you stay in the first place. It's my fault."

Janis choked and her eyes stung. "I…I'm sorry."

Pellea didn't smile. "I'll have to look into this further," she said. "Take care. I'll send you word on how things are going."

Janis watched as she left through the heavy steel door. Once it clanged into place, leaving her all alone again, her tears began to flow.

The next stop for Pellea was Mykal's room. He was still asleep when she entered, but she got a washcloth dripping with cold water and applied it to his face. That did the trick and he was soon sitting up, squinting at her.

"Arrgghh," he said.

"And well you might," Pellea said. "You look like hell."

He groaned again and tried to widen his eyes. "I feel like I have a very bad hangover. Either that or someone used me for shark bait during the night. What happened?"

"That's what I'm here to find out."

He closed his eyes, letting his head fall back. "Okay. Let me know when you come up with an answer," he muttered.

"Mykal, listen to me. Someone drugged you yesterday. The nurse has run some tests and it seems to be true. Who could have done it?"

He tried to think but his brain wasn't really ready for that yet. "I don't know. The doctor?"

"No." She looked at him impatiently. "You had a number of visitors, including Janis and your brother.

Would either one of them have wanted you out cold for any reason?"

He tried harder, but all he got was static. "No. I don't get it."

Pellea sighed. "All right. I'll come back later when you're feeling a bit more alert. But remember. We're trying to pull all the threads together on a few different stories of what might have happened. I'll let you know as soon as we have all the facts." She patted him and turned to go. "You just get some sleep and rest up."

He groaned. Getting sleep and resting up were all he ever did anymore. He was sick of it. But he closed his eyes and the next thing he knew, it was two hours later and an attorney was sitting in the chair beside his bed, going through papers and telling him things he didn't really understand.

Mykal stared at the attorney, Mr. Dreyfer, who had just said Janis had sent him.

"Why? Are you sure it was Janis?"

"Yes, I'm sure. She thought you needed representation. Someone to be on your side."

Mykal stared at the wall, trying to figure this out. "She's leaving, isn't she?" he said softly.

"I believe she said she had business to take care of."

"No." His voice was rough and adamant. "She should be here taking care of my business. But she sent you to do it instead." He frowned. "Not a good sign."

"Janis is a wonderful young woman, but I don't believe she has the legal background to understand."

"Of course not. But she understands us and what we

need better than you could ever do." He shook his head and stared at the wall again. "No offense. But Janis is my wife and I'm afraid she just walked out in order to make things easier for me."

The attorney left, saying he would be back again tomorrow when Mykal's life had calmed down a bit. Mykal stared at the wall until the nurse came in to check his bandages.

"Hello, nurse," he said, looking at her in a friendly manner. "Is the sun shining outside?"

"I'm sorry, sir, I have no way of knowing. We're in a castle, you know. We don't see the outside all that well most of the time."

"Oh. Sorry. I didn't know."

She worked on him for a few more minutes and then pulled back as though finished with the job. He frowned at her thoughtfully. Just beyond her, he saw Janis's satchel shoved into the corner. She must have left it here. But when?

That meant that she was still here in the castle, didn't it? She hadn't gone off and left him. Not yet. Maybe, if he could gather his strength, he could find a way to go after her. He would have to think about it.

"Nurse, could you tell me if Janis has been by today?"

The nurse's face changed dramatically. "Uh…no, sir. I thought you knew. She was caught last night."

That hit him like a thunderbolt. He stared at her, appalled. "Caught? Doing what?"

The nurse's eyes got very big. "From what I heard, she was trying to drug you with pills, sir."

"What?" How absurd. Utterly ridiculous. She had to be joking. "What?"

"Your brother caught her doing it." She looked very satisfied. "But don't you worry, she's in the castle jail, waiting for justice to be served." She smiled at him. "In the meantime, we're on orders to make sure no one comes in this room without a witness."

Janis, drugging him? No. Someone was making that up. Janis would never do anything like that. She had her moments. Like when he caught her stealing his work to give to her brother. But other than that, what had she ever done to make him angry? Nothing.

He closed his eyes and remembered things—Janis in a bikini, jumping off the side of the pool into the silver water. Janis cooking pizza and catching the ancient old stove in their apartment on fire. Janis, in his arms, making him think an angel was making love to him, a very sexy angel with breasts just made for his hands and skin like buttered honey....

His eyes shot open. He had his memory back.

"Nurse!" he called as he ripped out the needle to his IV. "I've got to get out of here."

He looked down, glad to see he had on pajama bottoms and not some diminutive hospital gown. No pajama top, but that hardly mattered. No shoes. No time to find some.

"Sir!" The nurse had come in and was trying to stop him. "What are you doing? You can't go out like that."

"Oh, yeah? Watch me."

A doctor came into the hall, trying to stop him as well.

"Sir, think of your position. You're about to be named a prince. You can't do this."

"I have to do this." As gently as he could, he moved the physician out of his way. "Now tell me how to get to the castle jail."

A moment for directions and he was off. He wanted to run but he was pretty sure things were still too newly patched together to take the jostling. But he walked very fast and could tell by the reaction coming from everyone he passed that he made quite a spectacle with his bare, muscular chest glistening in the artificial light of the castle halls. But he didn't care. He had to get to Janis before she spent another minute in that place.

He burst through the jail doors and looked into a pair of startled faces as the jailors realized who he was.

"I've come to get my wife," he told them. "Give me the key."

"Uh, I'm afraid we can't."

"Now," he roared, and then he followed the inevitable glance they each made toward where the key was hung and got it for himself. Next, he was marching down the hall to the cell where she was standing at the bars, wondering what all the commotion was about.

"Mykal!" she cried when she saw him. "What are you doing? You're going to hurt yourself." But she was half laughing as she took in his casual attire.

"I'm coming to get my woman," he told her.

"You can't do this," she protested happily. He stood there before her in all his glory, the pajama bottoms riding low on his beautiful hips, the muscles rippling in his arms and chest, and she nearly swooned.

"Really?" he said as he turned the key in the lock. "What the hell good is it being royal if I can't even rescue my own wife from the castle jail?" He opened his arms to her. "Come on," he said. "Let's go."

She flew into his arms and held him close. "You don't think I was drugging you, do you?" she asked as he buried his face in her hair.

"Of course not," he said. "And even if you were, I'd know it was for a good reason."

That made her laugh again. He swept her out of the jail and out into the halls again. She was vaguely aware that Pellea was there, calling out directions to them, but she was too busy holding on to Mykal to pay attention. And then she found herself in Pellea's garden and Mykal was kissing her just the way he used to. Birds were chirping. The waterfalls were sending music through the area. The scent of roses filled the air.

"Isn't this Pellea's room?" she asked.

"Yes. You wait here. I've got to make a few phone calls."

She sighed and closed her eyes, settling into the sumptuous couch. Just moments before, she'd been lying on a thin cot in a jail cell, and now she was in the queen's private suite. Mykal had ridden to the rescue this time. The winds of fate blew erratically, didn't they? As long as they blew true in the end, it didn't matter.

Mykal was back, still looking gorgeous in his pajama bottoms. He sank into the couch beside her.

"Pellea said for us to make ourselves at home," he told her as he took her into his arms. "She knows we need some time to talk and she won't be back for hours."

"Hours," she breathed, rubbing her face against his chest. "Hours to hold on to each other. Heaven." She peeked up at his face. "So you know it was Kylos who was drugging you?"

"Yes. And I think I might know why. My memory seems to be back."

"Oh!" She looked up into his face and laughed. "Now do you see? Do you remember what is was like when we were together?"

He nodded, smiling at her.

Her own smile faded. "Do you remember what I did?"

"You already told me all about that." He pulled her close again. "I remember everything," he told her, his voice low and husky. "I've got you back, now and in the past, and this time, I'll never let you go."

He kissed her and she melted into him, all heat and tenderness.

"Wait," she said, struggling to come back to the surface and get a few things settled before they gave themselves up to pure passion and pleasure. "You said you thought you knew why Kylos was drugging you?"

"Janis, I've got my memory back. I knew about my

parents dying in the accident before I even met you. I also knew their will gave everything to me to handle as I saw fit. But when I showed up injured, with no memory, Kylos and his lawyer friend, Leland, thought they saw their chance. They tampered with the will and were trying to sell the estate before I came back to normal and could stop them. The longer I was under sedation, the better chance they had of getting it done and taking off with the money."

"Your own brother!"

"Yes. I guess we all get saddled with family members we'd rather not have to deal with," he said significantly.

She looked into his eyes. He must know about her ties to the Gorgonios, even though she hadn't had the nerve to tell him. And he understood. How had she gotten so lucky? She sighed and nodded. "What's going to happen to them?" she asked.

"I'm afraid they will both be prosecuted for their crimes. I only hope that Kylos finally learns his lesson." He kissed her nose. "But enough about him. I have something I have to explain to you. I'm sure you wondered, all that time you were in the camp, why I didn't do something about getting you out."

She drew in a shaky breath. "Actually, I did wonder at the time."

"Of course. That was an awful day. I was so angry with you and I said some awful things. And regretted them almost immediately. But you were gone. I couldn't find you anywhere. I nearly went crazy. I looked for you everywhere and no one knew where you'd gone. For days I searched and searched. I couldn't find your brother, I couldn't find any of your coworkers. Finally someone told me where Rolo's new apartment was and I went over right away. He told me that he'd seen you being carted off by the secret police. It looked like you were going in the direction of the prison camp. So I put on my wedding ring and fired up my trusty old motorcycle and raced out there."

Janis reveled in happiness. This was exactly what she would have expected him to do. But she had a question. "Why the wedding ring?" she asked.

He smiled and hugged her close. "I wanted to show you that my commitment to you was stronger than my work, my patriotism, than anything else in the world. It was just you. You are all that matters to me. And we're going to be together through all this royalty nonsense. Nothing is going to tear us apart again."

She shook her head, still worried. She just didn't see how it could work. "Mykal, don't you understand? There are just too many things against us."

He pulled her up where he could look into her face. "Like what?"

"My betrayal, which is something you can say you'll push aside, but you know it will always be there. Then there's my time in prison camp. How many royals have been there? There's the problem of my birth into the most notorious crime family in the nation. There's the fact that my family almost ruined your adoptive parents. How could anyone accept that you might want me after all that?"

He shook his head, mocking her. "And then there's the baby."

She made a worried face. "Oh, yeah. The baby."

He smiled down at her, covering her tiny belly with his big, wide hand. "I can't give up my baby."

"But, if the royal family won't accept me, I'm afraid they'll still want the baby and I can't leave the baby with you."

"No, Janis." He smiled at her. "You're getting all confused. You won't leave the baby with me, because I won't be here, either. If you can't stay, I can't stay. I go where you go."

He was ready to give up a place in the castle for her. She could see it in his face. She loved him more than anything and she was beginning to believe they just might be able to do this thing.

"Oh, Mykal. Are you sure?"

"If this royal family can't accept me with a wife like you, they can't have me. It's simple as that."

She threw her arms around his neck and clung to him. "I love you so."

He winced. He still had those wounds on his back. But he didn't let her see it. Right now, he wanted her happiness more than anything else.

"That goes double for me," he said huskily and he drew her closer. "Because I've got two of you to love."

* * * * *